LOSER

A dead lawyer ... a stolen Rembrandt ... a bloodied 3 iron...

When a lawyer is found bludgeoned to death in his own home and Jim Ormerod is fingered as the killer, his wife, an ex-girlfriend of Sam Carew's, has nowhere else to turn. Sam believes Jim to be innocent, but his investigation becomes increasingly complicated as he gets involved in a dispute with troublesome local travellers. To make matters even more interesting, his skills are called upon to escort a valuable painting from Amsterdam to Unsworth. It should be a simple operation, but somehow nothing ever is where Sam is concerned. Then there is another gruesome murder...

Dedication

To my son, Dean.

LOSER

by

Ken McCoy

Magna Large Print Books
Long Preston, North Yorkshire,
BD23 4ND, England.

British Library Cataloguing in Publication Data.

McCoy, Ken
    Loser.

    A catalogue record of this book is
    available from the British Library

    ISBN   978-0-7505-3062-0

First published in Great Britain in 2008 by Allison & Busby Limited

Copyright © 2008 by Ken Myers

Cover illustration © Brighton Studios.com

The moral right of the author has been asserted

Published in Large Print 2009 by arrangement with
Allison & Busby Limited

Magna Large Print is an imprint of Library Magna Books Ltd.

Printed and bound in Great Britain by
T.J. (International) Ltd., Cornwall, PL28 8RW

*All characters and events in this publication,
other than those clearly in the public domain,
are fictitious and any resemblance to actual persons,
living or dead, is purely coincidental.*

He wrote to ask what present she would like
from Mad Carew;
They met next day as he dismissed a squad;
And jestingly she told him then that
nothing else would do
But the green eye of the little Yellow God.

J MILTON HAYES
The Green Eye of the Little Yellow God

CHAPTER ONE

'You're a complete and utter bastard!'

'True, but I'm a solicitor, which means I'm a legally qualified complete and utter bastard. In fact, the very worst kind of bastard.'

There was a bit too much of a sneer in Alistair Waring's voice. His arrogance showed him to be a poor judge of human emotions. Had his degree been in psychology and not law he might not have died that Sunday morning. He was denying this man the life he'd dreamt of and he was assuming he would take it lying down.

'You knew the rules right from the start. I did warn you, but did you take any notice? I think not.'

The man standing in Alistair Waring's living room didn't want to hear this. He was being treated like a piece of dog shit, just like Private Shooey, back in the bad times. It was actually twenty years since anyone had called him by that name – the one given to him by his so-called army pals.

He didn't mind the nickname – it reminded him of the woman he had thought was his mother. His mam. It reminded him of when he was seven and she showed him how to polish his black shoes until he could almost see his face in them. They had laughed together, he and his mam. Good times. It was why he was so enthusiastic about shining his army boots. He shined his army mates' boots as well, hence his nickname – The Shoe Shine Boy – which they eventually abbreviated to Shooey. It reminded him of his mam and of his good times. These had stopped when he was seven.

The army was good for a while but his soldier mates had stopped being his mates when he killed that youth in Londonderry. 'Jesus! There was no fuckin' need for that, Shooey!' Out of loyalty they stood by him at the enquiry, but blew him out after that. Bad times. He hadn't been right since. The bullet from his Lea Enfield SLR hadn't even knocked the kid down. It had gone straight through him, clean as a whistle, leaving the kid standing there, first looking down at the blood spouting out of his chest, then up at Shooey, with a look of indignation on his face. Then shock and fear and silent tears – the sort of tears which come to an injured child's eyes just before it begins to howl. Only there had been no time for howling. What little time the youth had left was taken up by dying. Those tears had haunted Shooey all these years. He had dropped his rifle in shock. That might have got him into even more trouble than shooting the youth had his fellow soldiers not closed ranks behind him. For twenty years he had harboured anger and guilt; at first in equal proportions, then the anger had begun to outweigh the guilt. It was their fault. They'd given him a gun and they'd sent him out on patrol in an area where Republicans take pot-shots at soldiers just for the hell of it. What the fuck did they expect? He hadn't been much more than a kid himself. It hadn't been his fault, so why had he let people take advantage of him? It was still happening. People taking advantage. People taking liberties. People such as Waring.

And just who the hell did Waring think he was? Pompous dickhead! There was a bag of golf clubs leaning against the wall. He took out an iron and wrapped his fingers around the grip, as much to calm his nerves as anything.

'Come on.' He made a short, practice swing. 'This is obviously a wind-up. Can't you do better than this, Waring?'

Alistair shrugged, nonchalantly and said, 'No wind-up. You know me, there are certain things I don't joke about.'

The one-time soldier didn't look up. He pretended to concentrate on the club, swinging it like a pendulum, thus emphasising how unconcerned he was at Alistair's attempt at winding him up.

'What? You actually mean it?'

'I actually mean it.'

Shooey went quiet for a few seconds as he considered the implications of Alistair's decision. 'You're costing me more money than I've ever dreamt of, you know that, don't you? Destroying my life just to prove you can.'

Alistair sneered again. 'Don't talk rubbish. What you never had you never miss. How come I'm destroying your life?'

'Do the others know what you're doing?'

'They don't know anything yet.'

'They will,' said Shooey. He felt his temper rising. 'I'll make bloody sure they find out!'

'Of course they'll find out, and when they do they'll have to go along with my decision,' said

13

Alistair. 'We have an agreement and it is binding.'

'What – like a blood oath or something?' muttered Shooey, scathingly.

'Oh, much more binding than that. Look, face the facts, in this life there are winners and losers, and you're one of life's losers. Live with it.'

Alistair turned away – a serious lapse of judgement. It meant he didn't see the look in Shooey's eyes change from ill temper to rage. It meant he didn't see the golf club arcing through the air, hitting him in the temple, the thinnest part of the skull. It didn't render him completely unconscious, it simply numbed his senses and caused him to collapse. More blows rained down. Shooey wept with fury as he swung the club. He continued his frenzied assault until his strength left him and he sank to his knees, dragging in noisy lungfuls of air. The solicitor was alive, just, but Shooey had neither the strength nor the inclination to deliver any more blows. Waring would have to die of his own accord. It was the least the inconsiderate bastard could do.

Shooey got to his feet and viewed the carnage with amazement and revulsion, as if it had been caused by someone else. His rage was now exhausted. Blood was all around, much of it on him. He remembered the sickness he'd felt in his stomach when he realised he'd killed the kid in Londonderry. It was a sickness that wouldn't go away. Not for years. He had been invalided out, his army career in tatters, abandoned on to Civvy Street, a world he didn't know, without help or advice. The army had been the only job he'd had since leaving the Barnado's Home. He was thoroughly institutionalised and not equipped to cope with the outside world. He discarded his nickname when he made a new life for himself, just as the army had discarded him. But it was a name which, in his mind, he would revert to from time to time, as and when he slipped into his alter ego. Like now.

So, after all these years, Private Shooey had killed again. But this was different. Waring had asked for it. The kid hadn't. The carnage was revolting but he was able to view it as he would a nasty traffic accident – revolting to look at, but hardly his fault. There was no sickness in his stomach this time. No guilt.

Then it slowly dawned on him that there was an excellent advantage to be had. *No one else knew.* Maybe that's what had spurred him on in the first place; subconsciously given him the stomach to kill this man who was about to do him harm. The youth had done him no harm and yet the youth had died. This was very different.

He grinned. Then he looked in a mirror and grinned again. God you are such an ugly bastard! He would need a wash before he went out of here. Clean off the blood. Things to do. Things to find – one thing in particular. Can't be far away. Waring probably had it on him. Yes. Got it. Brilliant. Clean as a whistle, which was good. Oh, yes! This will unlock the door to a fabulous future. Got to get the timing right though. Don't rush into anything. Think, man. What now? Bathroom. Good shower. Then what? Change of clothes to go home in. Nick some of Waring's. Put yours in a plastic bag and dump them far

15

away. Far, far away. Council rubbish tip would be good – it's open on a Sunday. Dump the ones you nick off Waring as well. Good thinking, boy wonder. After that, what's the best way to act? Come on. Think. Choose the way the police would least expect a guilty man to act.

There was a moan. Blood was bubbling from Alistair Waring's mouth. It would be the humane thing to do to finish him off. But Shooey was suddenly squeamish. For God's sake die, you stupid bastard! He went over and knelt beside the prostrate man. Surely you can't last much longer.

'Fuck you, Waring, and your principles! Things to do. Stop making things harder for me. Be sure you're dead when I get back.'

CHAPTER TWO

'Oh, Alistair rang, by the way.'

'What're you tellin' me for? He's your boyfriend, Trace, not mine. Personally I'd have gone for someone a bit taller.'

'Jim, that never happened. It's all in your mind. If I was going to have it off with someone it wouldn't be Alistair.'

Tracey Ormerod was thirty-eight which made her six years younger than her husband. She was sprawled on the leather settee, listening to *The Archers* and painting her nails in readiness for Sunday lunch at the Red Lion. She always favoured Sunday lunch out – on account of her hating cooking. She pretty much hated everything to do with the running of a home. A cleaner came three days a week and there were three take-aways within delivery distance. Chinese, Indian and Italian. It all helped to make her life as stress-free as possible. If Jim could be a bit more enthusiastic in the bedroom it would ease even more of her stress.

Ten years ago she had brought a ready-made son into their marriage. Matthew was now fifteen and spent his sabbaths playing Sunday League Football, which suited Tracey down to the ground. There had been no more children. One was enough, she'd told Jim, despite him fancying a child of his own.

'He was a bit mysterious,' she said. 'He wanted you to go round there straight away. I told him you were out getting your *News of the World*.'

'Oh yeah – scornful, was he? Maybe he wants me to help him with his *Sunday Times* crossword.'

'He just said to go straight round.'

Tracey spread the fingers of her left hand and examined the finished product before putting an extra dab on her thumbnail. She was still very pretty and she didn't like to waste her assets on just one man, especially one such as Jim, who really didn't appreciate her rare talent to please a man. Her hair was short and blonde and very expensively cut and her figure was only slightly fuller than the one the boys used to ogle when she was a teenager. She'd married Jim because he had his own house and earned plenty of money, whereas she had been skint and had a son to take care of. On top of which he was quite a likeable bloke and there weren't too many of them around. Although he did have his bad habits – like sitting with his feet on her glasstopped coffee table. It was supported by four brass elephants and was designed to display slim, leather bound classic volumes, silver photograph frames and the occasional coffee cup, but not Jim's unsavoury feet. He put down his paper and addressed himself to a hole in the big toe of his left sock.

'Straight round? Right now? Drop every bloody thing and go straight round? His tap's probably leaking and he hasn't got the brains to fit a new washer.'

'I think it's something to do with golf. He said he was ringing the other lads from the club. It actually sounded important.'

Jim's eyes were still fixed on his sock. 'How come socks wear out so quick? Socks never used to wear out as quick as this.'

'They wouldn't if you cut your toenails more than once a year – and will you take your feet off the coffee table?'

'And he didn't say what it was?'

'No.'

Jim took out his mobile and stabbed in Alistair's number. He listened for a few seconds then mimicked the woman's voice that came on the line.

'The person you are dialling is engaged. Please try later.'

He scowled at his uncovered toenail and swung his legs off the table. 'He'll be ringing the others and he'll not be able to get hold of 'em. They'll be out on the course 'til about two.' He folded his paper and slipped on his shoes, still grumbling. 'Everything's so bloody important to him. Why

18

does everything have to be done right this second? For a flash bastard he's a right old woman.'

'He's a solicitor. Solicitors like to do things right.'

'Oh, as opposed to a jobbing builder like me, is that what yer tellin' me? I like to do things wrong, do I – unlike darlin' bloody Alistair?'

'For God's sake, Jim, don't start! It doesn't bother me if you don't go round at all. I'm just passing a message on. I'll know better next time. If you do go round, don't make it an all day job. We've a table booked at the Red Lion for half twelve.'

'You mean *you've* got a table booked, I've nev–'

'Shut up, Jim, I'm trying to listen to *The Archers*'.

CHAPTER THREE

Rudolph Mace was the type of nightclub doorman who, because of his intimidating, steroid-assisted size, rarely got much trouble from punters. Rudolph was six feet three inches tall, two hundred and sixty pounds, twenty nine years old, originally from Jamaica and the worst golfer of the six who played every Sunday at Bostrop Park Pay and Play Golf Club. He had been married for eight years to an Unsworth girl who thought he had a nice face. They had two daughters. Today was Sunday and he was out in a three-ball with Dave McLeish and Shane Outhwaite.

Shane was an unemployed, 23-year-old graduate, who had yet to find a career to suit his talents. He was good-looking in an impudent sort of way and was the sort of young man who would do well if only he could channel his considerable energy in one direction. He supplemented his Job-Seekers Allowance by working as a DJ whose popularity was growing, not so much from his flair for music or his skill at the turntable – more to do with his amusing patter.

Dave McLeish struck a superb 270-yard drive, straight down the middle at the third. At 8 handicap he was the best golfer, despite being the oldest of the six. He was a 46-year-old art dealer, twice married, twice divorced and father of five children. Dave was a diabetic who battled with his ailment by spending hours at the gym each week. Given the chance he would play golf every day. Unfortunately he had to earn a crust to keep the CSA at bay.

Alistair Waring was a junior partner in Compton, Croft and Co. He was 38 and had never married, nor had he ever felt the need to. He had lived with several women, who had either tired of him or vice versa. The only reason he played golf at Bostrop Pay and Play was because his applications to join three private clubs in the area had all been blackballed by the secretary of the Unsworth and District Golf Union. He was a man with much influence with the Unsworth and District golf clubs and had once been cuckolded by Alistair.

Alistair's other vice was gambling. He was a 16 handicap golfer but no better than 24 handicap at poker. Over the past few months he'd been involved in a highstake Texas Hold 'em game at a private club with men who didn't like being owed money for too long by such a big time loser. Alistair's gambling debts were currently over seventy thousand pounds and his creditors were pressing very hard for their money. To pay off such a sum would have meant him re-mortgaging his house, which he was reluctant to do, especially when he felt a winning streak was just around the corner.

He could be quite charming at times, and ruthless and unpleasant at other times. His five golf companions only put up with him because he had helped each one of them with legal problems, at a reduced fee – or so he told them. They were the type of men who often had legal problems. Alistair was also very good at organising golf trips. Unfortunately he regularly got up people's noses, which caused much ill feeling.

Right now he dearly wished he'd made more of an effort to be popular. If only he could have his time over again he'd treat people differently. He didn't deserve this, though. No one deserved this. Christ! Why did this have to happen just when his fortunes had taken such a dramatic and beautiful turn? His eyes flooded with tears of terror and self pity as he stared upwards at the splashes of his own blood on the ceiling.

CHAPTER FOUR

Jim rang Alistair's doorbell twice, but got no reply. He tried the door. It was open, which presumably meant that Alistair was in but not deigning to answer the bell. Typical bloody Alistair.

'Ally? I hope yer in, you annoyin' tosser. I've come over special. The wife made it sound like a royal bloody command.' He walked into the hall and shouted again. 'Ally?' No answer. Jim let out a loud sigh of exasperation and walked into the living room.

'Aw, bloody hell fire!'

Alistair was lying face up on the carpet. His head was a pulpous mess. Blood was splattered all over the carpet, furniture, walls and ceiling. On reflection Jim's next words seemed stupid.

'Ally, are you all right?'

A gurgling sound came from deep within Alistair's throat. Jim knelt beside him. His friend's frightened eyes stared up at him through the shattered mess of his face. They were glazed in near death. Blood was bubbling from his mouth. Jim ran his hand across his own mouth in readiness to apply the kiss of life. He'd never done it before and he knew it was a pretty useless thing to attempt right now, but he knew he had to try something. He leant close to Alistair, wiped his sleeve across his friend's mouth, and gave him what he hoped was the kiss of life. Then he depressed the dying man's chest, but this only made blood spurt from his mouth. Jim was covered in Ally's blood. He took out his mobile to dial 999. Before he'd entered the first number he heard a police siren approach, then die to a halt outside. Sound of running footsteps. He turned to see two uniformed police come into the room.

'I just found him like this,' said Jim, standing up. 'I tried to revive him, but er...' He shrugged to indicate how useless this had been. 'I were er, I were just about ter dial 999.'

He showed them the phone in his hand as though they might want proof. It was the sort of thing that aroused suspicion. One of the police-men was already radioing for an ambulance, the other was kneeling down beside Alistair. He shook his head and concluded, 'I'm afraid he's beyond needing an ambulance, sir.'

'Aw, bloody hell!' said Jim.

His colleague was speaking into his radio. '...Yes, I'll tell him that, sir.' He spoke to Jim. 'We'd like you to stay here, sir. CID are on their way, they may need you to answer a few questions.'

During the course of the next three hours the other four members of the golfing group turned up at Alistair's house, responding to a call from him to go there. Emmanuel Green arrived first, just as the police were taking Jim down to the station for further questioning. Manny was the sixth member of the group. He was 42, un-married, scruffy, balding, with a wispy beard and sallow face. A used car dealer of dubious reputation, he didn't live far away from Alistair.

'What's happening?' he enquired of a policeman standing at the end of Alistair's drive. 'Where are you taking Jim?'

'He's kindly agreed to help us with our enquiries – and you are, sir?'

'Er, what? Manny Green – I'm a pal of Alistair's. What's happened?'

'I'm afraid Mr Waring's met with an accident, sir – a suspicious death to be precise.'

'Dead? Jesus Christ – Ally's dead?'

'Would you mind telling me the reason for your visit?'

'What? My visi–? Erm, sorry, er, he rang me and asked me to come round. Bloody hell! He only rang me about an hour ago. When did it happen?'

'Did he say why he wanted you to come round, sir?'

'Well, no. He just said it was important.'

'Did he sound agitated?'

Manny got his cigarettes out and lit one without answering. His hands were shaking.

'Agitated, sir – did he sound agitated?'

'What? No – I don't think so. He just sounded, you know – normal.'

'I'll need your address and telephone number, sir. We may need to speak to you further.'

A worried look spread over Manny's face. 'What? Why?'

'It's not as ominous as it sounds, sir. We may genuinely need you to help us.'

'Oh, yes, course I will – anything at all.'

'Right – would you mind if I ask you if there was any bad blood between Mr Waring and Mr Ormerod?'

Manny gave the constable a nervous glance.

24

'Bad blood?'

'Yes, sir, bad blood. Obviously if there was we'll find out in due time.'

'Will you?' said Manny, uncomfortably.

'You can be assured of it, sir.'

'Right – well there was a daft rumour about Alistair and Jim's wife.'

The policeman wrote this down. 'Presumably this rumour was about them having an affair?'

'Well, yeah, but you know what rumours are. I took no notice, personally.'

Two hours later Dave, Shane and Rudolph turned up together and were confronted by the same policeman. All of them had messages on their mobiles to go round to Alistair's house straight away.

'Could I have your names please, gentlemen?' said the constable, taking a notebook from his pocket.

'David McLeish.'

'Shane Outhwaite.'

'Rudolph Mace.'

'So, if Mr Waring rang this morning why did you all leave it so late to come round?' enquired the constable.

'We've been playing golf,' David explained, 'and we didn't get the messages until we finished the round. Mobiles aren't allowed on the course. Jesus! How did he die?'

'The details will be made known in due course, sir. Did Mr Waring indicate why he wanted you to call and see him?'

Dave and Rudolph shrugged and shook their heads. Shane said, 'I was hoping we might have had a touch on the Lottery. To me it sounded as if Ally had some good news for us.'

'He likes … liked, to squeeze the last bit of drama out of everything,' Dave said.

'And have you won anything on the Lottery, sir?'

'No,' Dave went on. 'I checked the numbers when Shane mentioned it – not a sausage. I keep telling 'em, we'd be better off giving the money to Joe Coral and sticking it on a fifty-to-one donkey.'

'Is it true that you've taken Jim Ormerod in for questioning?' asked Rudolph.

'Mr Ormerod is helping us with our enquiries, sir.'

'You mean you think Jim did it?' said Rudolph. 'Bloody hell!'

'Would that surprise you, sir?'

'What? Oh, course it would. He wouldn't do owt like that wouldn't Jim…' Dave said it in such a way that the constable half expected him to add, *would he?*

'You don't sound very surprised, sir.'

'Well,' chipped in Shane, 'he's a bit of a hothead but he wouldn't go round killing anybody.'

'Not even if the other man was having an affair with his wife?' said the constable, who had applied for CID and figured his findings would do his application no harm at all.

'Oh,' said Dave, 'is that what it was about?'

'I knew it'd end in trouble,' said Rudolph.

'Never shit on yer own doorstep,' said Shane. 'Bloody hell! I never thought it'd end up like this. Poor old Ally. How did he die?'

The constable saw no reason not to tell them. 'At the moment it looks as if he was hit several times with a golf club.'

'Was it his 5 iron?' Rudolph asked curiously. 'He were good with his 5 iron.'

'Bloody hell, Rudy!' admonished Dave. 'What a stupid thing ter say.'

'I believe it was a 3 iron,' said the policeman. 'Favoured the 5 iron, did he? Maybe he felt he needed a bit more club.'

Dave and Rudolph said nothing, Shane found himself nodding. The three of them watched as the constable scribbled in his notebook. He looked up and said, 'I'll need all your addresses if you don't mind, gentlemen.'

CHAPTER FIVE

Detective Inspector Janet Seager switched on the tape recorder. 'Interview with James Ormerod started at 17.40 on Sunday June 5th. Also present are duty solicitor, Steven Peat, Detective Inspector Seager and Detective Constable Price.'

Jim was dressed in a white paper coverall, his clothes having been taken away for forensic testing. Owen was chewing the last bite of a bacon sandwich he'd stuck in his mouth just before entering the room. He had assumed that his superior officer would be opening the interview but she indicated that he should start. It was her way of telling him not to eat bacon sandwiches at such a time. Owen surreptitiously covered his mouth with a hand as he swallowed the remnants. He looked down at his copy of the notes.

'Mr Ormerod,' he began, 'your wife tells us you left home at 11.15 this morning.'

'About that time, yes. Look I had nothing ter do with this. I've told yer what happened.'

'Your wife was very precise about the time,' said Owen, 'because she had been listening to *The Archers* on the radio, which was finishing just as you were leaving.'

'That's right, she was. Never misses *The Archers* doesn't my Trace.'

'So, how long had you been at Mr Waring's house when the police arrived?'

'No more than a minute. I'd just walked in.'

Janet Seager took up the questioning. 'Let me see,' she looked at her notes. 'That was at 11.37. Which means it took you twenty two minutes to drive two miles. That's very careful driving.'

Jim stared at her, he squeezed his eyes together as if he'd just remembered something he should never have forgotten in the first place. 'Shit! I'm sorry. I'm not used to all this business. Me mind's all over the place. I had a puncture. It took me ages ter change the wheel – the wheel nuts were jammed tight. I couldn't budge the buggers.'

'But you never thought to mention this to the officer at the scene?'

'What? Why should I? There were more important things ter worry about than a bloody puncture.'

Owen nodded. 'Puncture? Hmm.' He looked at Jim's hands. 'Whenever I change a wheel I get my hands filthy from handling the tyres. Your hands look remarkably clean, Mr Ormerod.'

28

Jim looked at his hands and then back up at Owen. 'Well, I washed 'em at Alistair's. They were covered in blood.'

Janet looked taken aback. 'Did the officer at the scene give you permission to wash your hands?'

'Permission? He gave me permission to go for a pee, which is when I washed me hands.'

Janet sighed and wished uniform would think before allowing anyone to destroy evidence. Still, they had enough on Ormerod to nail him. She picked up a long, polythene bag containing a golf club, and placed it on the table. The head of the club was covered in blood.

'Do you recognise this golf club, Mr Ormerod?'

Jim looked at it in some surprise. 'Well, it's a Ping 3 iron. I've got one exactly like it, but so have thousands of other people.'

'Not exactly like this one. This one was found in Mr Waring's dustbin. It's covered in blood matching Mr Waring's blood type and we're currently checking for a DNA match.'

'So?' said Jim. 'It's not my club. My club's in me bag, in the boot of me car.'

'Then why has this club got your fingerprints all over it?' asked DC Owen Price.

'What?'

'Mr Ormerod,' said DI Seager, 'the club's got far too many of your prints on it for it to be anyone else's. If the blood on it, as we suspect, proves to be Mr Waring's blood, we couldn't ask for clearer evidence of your involvement in his death.'

'But I didn't do it, honestly, I didn't do it.'

Jim looked at his solicitor for help. The solicitor shook his head, as if to say, *Just own up, you*

29

obviously did it.

Jim spent the night in a cell, wondering just what the hell was going to happen to him. At eleven o'clock the following morning he was taken to be interviewed again. This time he was shown his bag of golf clubs.

'Is this your golf bag, Mr Ormerod?' enquired Janet Seager.

There was a club membership tag hanging from it. 'Yes,' he said, 'that's definitely my bag. And if yer look inside, yer'll find me 3 iron.'

'We found this bag in the locker room at Bostrop Park Golf Club.'

'What? Oh – yeah, maybe I did leave it there. It won't be the first time. I don't make habit of it. There's some right bloody thieves up at that place.'

'Apparently one of your friends brought it back from the golf club yesterday morning, with that same thought in mind. He gave it to us about half an hour ago.'

'That'll have been Dave.'

Owen checked his notes. 'It was Shane Outwaite.'

'Shane, oh, right.'

Janet leant towards him with her chin resting on her fists. 'There's no 3 iron in your bag, Jim. I'm willing to bet that the 3 iron missing from your bag is the one which was found in Alistair Waring's dustbin.' She paused for a long time before saying, 'I think you killed Alistair, Jim. And I also think the murder was premeditated, otherwise why would you go to his house armed with a golf club that should have been in your golf bag?'

Jim was shaking his head all the time she spoke, as if he was trying to obliterate from his mind every word she said. 'No, no, no, yer wrong.'

Janet took the bull by the horns. 'He was having an affair with your wife, wasn't he, Jim? Come on – all your friends know about it. It's only natural you should blow your top at some time.'

Jim shook his head. 'I heard the rumour, never believed it.'

'Well, I've spoken to your wife and I'm afraid she's confirmed the rumour, Jim.'

'What?' He looked at Janet through narrowed eyes, trying to detect a lie. 'Oh yeah, and why would she suddenly confirm a rumour that puts me in the frame? I think yer lyin' ter try and get a confession out of me. Well there'll be no confession because I've nothing to confess.'

'It's the truth, Jim. I wouldn't dare lie during a taped interview.'

Jim looked at his solicitor, who nodded to confirm that Janet would be telling the truth.

'I'm sorry, Jim,' Janet went on, 'but she's admitted the affair to us and she's bereft that she's driven you to this. She's blaming herself, Jim. Come on, tell me what happened. Was Alistair taunting you about it? Maybe I'm wrong about it being premeditated. Maybe you went round with the golf club just to put the frighteners on him and he taunted you into doing something you now regret. I would understand that, Jim.'

Owen nodded his agreement. They were following a tried and trusted interview tactic. Telling the accused that they fully understood, even sympathised with his reason for committing the crime

31

– anything to elicit a confession. As she spoke, Janet watched his eyes for that sign of defeat which comes when the accused finally realises the game is up. She waited for the truth to come tumbling out; for him to unburden the awful guilt he could conceal no longer. But all she saw was confusion and tears.

'It wasn't me, miss,' he said. 'I don't know what to say.' He buried his head in his hands and muttered to himself. 'Bloody hell, Tracey, how could yer do this ter me? If yer can't keep yer knickers on, the least yer can do is keep yer mouth shut about it.'

Janet looked from Jim to his solicitor. 'We'll be applying to keep Mr Ormerod in custody until the DNA results come through which, hopefully, will be within 48 hours.'

DNA confirmed the blood was Alistair's and Jim was remanded in custody in Armley prison, Leeds.

CHAPTER SIX

When she was in her teens Tracey Ormerod had gone out with Sam Carew a few times, and she still held something of a torch for him, apparently. This was more likely down to Sam's notoriety than his sex appeal – at least it was according to DC Owen Price.

'Tells me she knew you when she was younger, boyo. Reckons you and her had a thing going on – to quote her, look you.'

Owen always exaggerated his Welshness when he was trying to be funny. They were in the Clog and Shovel tap room, waiting for their turn on the dartboard.

'I knew her,' admitted Sam. 'I don't remember us having a *thing* going on. Took her out a few times. She was a bit much for me, actually.'

'And...?'

'And what?'

'And did you give her one, boyo?'

'Detective Constable Owen Glendower Price, you have a really seedy mind, has anyone ever told you that?'

'I'm only asking because I wouldn't mind giving her one myself. She's very well preserved for her age.'

'For her age? She's the same age as me – which is many years younger than you, by the way.'

'Anyway she's asked me to ask you to call round and see her. I do believe she wants to engage your professional services – at least that's how she put it to me.'

'You mean she wants a bit of building work dong? Maybe it's a job her old man never got finished and she needs the money.'

'I think it's more likely she wants you to wear your Sherlock Holmes hat rather than a hard hat.'

'Did you tell her I prefer to do my sleuthing in winter? Spring and summer are for building. I like to lead a balanced life.'

Carew and Son (Builders) Ltd were working flat out on a retail park development for a Manchester company called Plessington Holdings PLC. It was a contract that could lead to bigger and better things.

'Could mean anything,' said Owen. 'Woman in her prime; lover bumped off by jealous husband; husband banged up for murder. Doesn't take much working out, boyo. You're not renting out your body on the side are you?' He laughed at his own joke. 'Sam Carew, the universal man: bricklayer, private eye, gigolo.'

'You may laugh,' said Sam. 'I'm still the object of many a sexual fantasy.'

'Only from the sexual deviant brigade – necrophilia, bestiality, flagellation, Sam Carew...'

Out of habit Sam didn't react to DC Owen Price's lame attempt at humour. Sam had been a cop himself up to three years previously, but had been obliged to resign as a detective sergeant due to a revenge prank he'd played on Inspector Bowman, with whom he had never got along, due to Bowman being, in the eyes of most of his colleagues, a prat. Sam cleaned a speck of dirt from behind his fingernails with the point of one of his darts. 'Jim Ormerod worked for us on and off,' he said. 'Seemed a decent enough bloke. You never can tell, can you?'

'Actually,' said Owen, 'I don't think he did it.'

'You don't? How's that? I thought you were the arresting officer.'

'Given all the circumstantial we had against him I had no option.' Owen took a huge gulp of his pint and looked at Sam. 'But ... you know how you get hunches?'

'Yeah?'

'Well so do I – I sat in on the interview.'

'Right ... and?'

'And I don't think he did it. I think DI Seager has her doubts as well.'

'I gather it was called in fairly quickly,' Sam said. 'Have you spoken to the caller?'

'Man on a pay-as-you-go mobile, apparently. Didn't give his name. Said he was passing the house and he could hear screams. Then he rang off.'

'Didn't want to get involved,' Sam said. 'Bloody typical. What about Tracey, does *she* think Jim did it?'

'She's not sure. She certainly gave him good cause to do it.'

'So I gather.'

'Did she put it about when you knew her?'

'She was very uninhibited,' remembered Sam. 'Very free spirited in many ways. Not what you'd call a one-man woman.'

Before Owen could ask for explanation of this the dartboard became free and, for a while, all doubts about Jim Ormerod's guilt were forgotten.

CHAPTER SEVEN

Sam knocked on Tracey Ormerod's door with one eye on the street where a couple of mean-eyed kids were walking around his car. Tracey opened the door and looked, nervously, beyond Sam at the two boys, one of whom spat on the car bonnet.

'Hello, Tracey,' said Sam, 'friends of yours, are they?'

'Travellers' kids,' she said. 'They're making my life a misery. As if I haven't got enough to cope with.'

'Give me a second, will you?'

He strolled, casually, towards the two boys who were probably about fifteen but looked physically a lot older. Not for the first time Sam wished he looked a bit more threatening. He had his work clothes on but that didn't help much.

The smaller of the boys smirked at his pal and spat on the driver's window. They both had grey faces under their baseball caps. They had earrings, nose rings, eyebrow rings and poor quality tattoos on their necks and hands. A couple of feral street kids who didn't look as if they belonged to anyone. As Sam approached they folded their arms. The bigger boy set his face into an ugly scowl and said, belligerently, 'We've gobbed on yer motor. What her gonna fuckin' do about it, mister?'

Sam gave them a wild-eyed grin. It was a grin he'd perfected over the years. He often used feigned madness as a weapon. People can't cope with madness. He fixed his manic grin on the smaller of the two boys and pushed his face up close into the boy's face as he suddenly reached out with his right hand and grabbed the bigger boy by the scruff of his neck and twisted his hand so that he was choking, whilst all the time Sam's eyes were intently fixed on the smaller boy.

'Ye spat on me car winder.' His voice was whiny and crazed. 'Why did yer spit on me car winder, youth?'

The bigger boy was trying to say something. Sam pulled him close to him and spoke into his ear with his gaze still fixed on the small boy. 'Did I say yer pal could speak? DID I?'

'No, mister.'

'What's he speaking for then? Why's he speakin' when I didn't say he could?'

The smaller boy began to back away. Sam went after him, dragging the choking boy along. 'Come back here, youth,' he said. 'I haven't finished with yer. D'yer know what happened to the last person what spat on me car winder? D'YER KNOW!'

'No mister.'

'I cut his tongue out with me best knife – cut his tongue out and I pickled it in a picklin' jar and I ate it with some nice chips.' He licked his lips.

Such was the quality of Sam's acting that even Tracey thought he'd gone mad. He turned his attention on the bigger boy, to whom he said, 'You, wipe it off.'

The boy was still trying to catch his breath after being half-choked. The madness in Sam's eyes terrified him. He was far stronger than the boy had imagined. Madmen were strong, the boy knew that much. Sam thrust his face right into the boy's.

'WIPE IT OFF!! Make it nice and clean or I'll have you, lad.'

The boy wiped the spit off Sam's bonnet with his sleeve.

'Properly!' ordered Sam. The boy set to work again. Sam turned to the smaller boy. 'You as well. Do me winder. Do it good.'

The boy obeyed. Sam stood back with his arms folded, his head twitching and his eyes rolling. 'I'll tell yer when yer've finished,' he said, 'which is not fer a while. WHAT'S YER NAMES?'

He screamed his question right into their faces as they polished away at his car.

'Brendan Smith.'

'Marlon Wilson.'

'Who said yer could come round here, spitting on people's cars? Who said that? Brendan Smith an' Marlon Wilson. I'll remember them names. Brendan Smith an' Marlon Wilson. If I ever see yer around here again I shall have ter try some of me voodoo on you boys. If yer wake up in the night,' he cackled, 'an' yer think yer've been stabbed, it means you have. It'll be me what's doin' the stabbing.'

Brendan and Marlon backed away with Sam following them, making a stabbing motion. They turned and galloped off, with Sam in pursuit for a few yards until he let them go. Tracey stood on her doorstep in bewilderment as Sam examined the job they'd done on his car. He looked up at her.

'You've just got to know how to talk to kids,' he said.

'Really? Is that why they call you Mad Carew?'

'One of them,' he conceded. 'It's a game I play with awkward customers – rarely fails.'

'I'm not surprised. You had me scared and I knew you were putting it on.'

'Did you?'

'Actually, no – I wasn't sure what was happening.' She led him through into the house and motioned him to sit on the settee. He took out his cigarettes and offered her one. 'Smoke?'

She considered his offer then shook her head. 'I shouldn't,' she said. 'I'm supposed to have given up.'

Sam put the cigarettes away.

'No, no,' she said, 'you go ahead.'

'Wouldn't dream of it. Besides, I'm trying to give it up myself. Trouble is, now that smoking's practically illegal makes a fag taste all the more sweet.'

'You never were one for sticking to the rules, were you, Sam? Oh, sod it,' she said, 'let's have one.'

They enjoyed their cigarettes and went over past times for a while, then Sam asked her why she wanted to see him.

'You've just seen part of the reason.'

'What – those boys?'

'It's not just the two of them, there's about half a dozen – some a lot bigger and nastier. They've all started going to the same school as our Matthew. I'm keeping him off because he's terrified of them.'

'I'm guessing they're travellers' kids,' said Sam. 'I've noticed they've taken over a field at the bottom of Cenotaph Hill.'

'Taken it over? – they've bought it and put a road in. I've complained to the school but the headmaster's too worried what they might do if he excludes the troublemakers. He's had threats, so have I.'

'What sort of threats?'

'Two women and a man stopped me in the street and told me they'd torch my house with me in it if I gave their kids trouble. I'm telling you, Sam, it's got me scared stiff.'

'Have you told the police?'

'I have – that's mainly why I was threatened, I reckon. Matthew daren't go out. He's not going to school – he's in his bedroom now. The last time he went out he got beaten up and told they were coming round to rape me. The ringleader's a girl – about sixteen. Apparently she tells them who she wants beating up and rewards them with sex.'

'She sounds like a well brought up young lady.'

'It's not a joke, Sam. Matthew isn't the only one who's suffering.'

'So, what did the police say?'

'Pretty much the same as the headmaster. They reckon if they go round there arresting people just on hearsay there could be a riot. I was told by a sergeant to go back with proper evidence which could be taken to court.'

'That sounds like Sergeant Bassey,' Sam guessed.

'That was his name, all right,' confirmed Tracey. 'I didn't like him.'

'Not many people do,' said Sam. 'Hates getting his hands dirty, Sergeant Bassey.' He looked at Tracey and remembered what he'd seen in her all those years ago. 'I'm not actually sure what I can do to help,' he said. 'What did you have in mind?'

She shrugged. 'I don't know really – it's just that I've heard that with you not being a copper any more you sometimes have an er … unconventional way of getting things done.'

'Well, I have a private detective agency but it seems there's not much to detect. We already know who the villains are. It's a question of persuading them to mend their ways.' He thought about it for a while then shook his head. 'I don't have any sway with uniform. I can have a word with DI Seager, but it's not really a CID matter.

I assume you've mentioned it to DC Price.'

'Yes, he came round asking questions about Jim. It was him who suggested I come to you.'

'Was it now?' said Sam. 'Well, he didn't mention that to me.'

'I have some money,' Tracey said, 'if that's what it'll take. Jim owns a few houses which we rent out. I'm nicely placed financially.'

'Glad to hear it. How's Jim coping?'

'Badly – he didn't do it.'

'I've heard there's doubt.'

'I wasn't sure at first – which made me feel lousy. Thinking that Jim had killed Ally because of me. I didn't sleep for a good month after he got arrested.'

'But you're sure now?'

'I'm positive, Sam. I went to see him yesterday. If there's one thing I know about Jim it's when he's lying.' She took Sam's arm. 'Jim and me got on OK, but it was never 'til death us do part. If you don't believe me, go round and talk to Cassie Blake.'

'Who's Cassie Blake?'

'Jim's bit on the side. We were both at it, Sam. It wouldn't have been the end of the world to Jim that I was having a thing with Alistair. He already had suspicions.'

'How long have you known about her?'

'Three days. She came round to see me – to tell me there was no way Jim would kill for me – she reckoned he loved her. I booted her out of the door, but then I got to thinking. Jim and me had never been really close. We get on, but that's about as far as it goes – he's not much cop in bed, to be honest. Once a month – wham, bang, thank you, ma'am and all that. So, I very much doubt if he was up to committing a crime of passion because of me. He just wasn't all that passionate about me wasn't Jim.'

Sam nodded his agreement. 'Cassie could be a valuable witness,' he said. 'I shouldn't antagonise her too much – that's if you want Jim back. Do you want him back?'

'Well, of course I want him back. Like I said, we get on OK. The thing is, as long as Cassie thinks he'll be going back to her – that's if he gets off – she might try to help him. Mind you, I doubt if Jim's the only feller she's got in tow. Anyway, as far as I'm concerned, he's all mine. She won't stand a chance.'

Sam smiled as he remembered Tracey's irresistible charms. 'The way things stand,' he cautioned, 'she might not be in with a chance, nor you for that matter.'

'The evidence against him's all circumstantial,' Tracey pointed out, 'and, at the moment, Cassie Blake's a circumstance he's got in his favour.'

'You always did have a devious mind, Tracey.'

'Sam, if you can't help me with the travellers, can I hire you to help Jim? His case comes up in September, which is only two months away. The police aren't looking for anyone else. As far as they're concerned it's cut and dried.'

Sam held her in his gaze. She returned it, steadily. 'How sure are you that he's innocent?'

'I'm willing to bet twenty grand on it – if that's what it costs to hire your exclusive services for the next two months. I'm hardly going to throw good money down the drain for something I'm not sure of.'

'That's very generous.' Sam thought about it. If she was so sure Jim was innocent it meant there was a killer on the loose. And a killer on the loose would get careless in the knowledge that he wasn't being sought. The more he thought about it the more it intrigued him.

'OK, you've hired yourself a detective.'

She smiled and raised her eyebrows, suggestively. 'Just how exclusive will your services be, Mr Carew?'

Sam remembered Owen's remark about him doing gigolo work on the side. 'I have a fiancée, Mrs Ormerod,' he said. Sally always became his fiancée when he needed to protect himself from such advances.

'I assume that's Sally Grover.' Tracey had known Sally at school. 'Why you ever married that stuck up Susan Jenkinson I'll never know. Everybody thought you were mad.'

'It's called stupidity,' said Sam. 'Anyway, you're talking about the mother of my boys, so it wasn't entirely a bad move.'

'You've made a few bad moves, Sam. Electrocuting your inspector and getting the sack wasn't your finest hour.'

'I didn't get the sack. I made a strategic withdrawal. My dad needed help with the business.'

'Yeah, sorry to hear about your dad. He was a good man – produced a good son.'

Tracey smiled at him and he sensed he was being invited to step into the late Alistair's shoes. He got to his feet and paused as he thought. 'I want you to write down everything you know about Alistair.'

'Such as?'

'Everyone he's ever spoken to you about. His work, his hobbies. Did he gamble? Did he have any enemies? Are there any other cuckolded husbands or boyfriends about? Anything at all that might give me a lead. Even if it sounds daft or insignificant. Let me be the judge.'

'Well,' she said, 'I doubt if it's got anything to do with the murder but Jim and Ally were both members of the Syndicate.'

'The what?'

'It's a golf society. It was Ally's idea – most golf societies have daft names, Ally didn't do daft.'

'Ah, these golfers, they like their comedy names, don't they? My dad played a bit. He was a member of a society called the Toffs. He told me it was The Over Fifty Fives Society, then I found out it really meant Too Old For Frequent Sex.' He paused in anticipation of a smile from Tracey. It wasn't forthcoming. 'Er, right,' he said, 'so we're not talking scratch golfers then. How many are in this er, this society?'

'Six – well five, now that Ally's gone.'

'I'd like you to write down everything you know about them.'

'OK.'

She went to a drawer, took out an address book and note pad and began writing. Sam looked at her and remembered their brief time together. It had only lasted about four weeks but she'd given him a lifetime's sex education, which is handy when you're only seventeen.

44

'What's happening with Alistair's house?'

'How do you mean?'

'Is it being sold? Do we know who his executors are?'

Tracey shrugged. 'No idea. As far as I know the house is still just as it was. His dad died a few years ago and I think his mother lives in Derbyshire – that's pretty much all I know about his family.' She went across to a drawer. 'If it's any help, I er, I actually have a key.'

Sam grinned and took the key from her. 'Do you have anything else that might be of help?'

'Such as?'

'Anything connected with the case.'

She thought for a while. 'I've got the rest of Jim's clubs here – the ones he didn't murder anyone with. Whoever killed Alistair with Jim's 3 iron must have taken it out of the bag and left the bag at the golf club.'

'What? – and the police didn't need to hold on to them for evidence?'

'Why would they? They've got the murder weapon. If he'd been killed with a kitchen knife they wouldn't have confiscated the whole knife drawer, surely.'

She probably had a point but it didn't wash with Sam. 'I'd sure have held on to it,' he said.

'Why?'

'Not sure why.'

He occasionally got fleeting ideas, which were so fleeting that they came and went before he had time to retain them in his memory. One came and went right then. Sometimes they came back. He hoped this one would – it had been a very

45

handy thought. All he knew was that it was something to do with the clubs.

'Do you mind if I take them? I'll let you have them back.'

CHAPTER EIGHT

Sam was putting the golf bag into the boot of his car when he heard a noise behind him. He turned to see three hard-looking men getting out of a pick-up truck. Sitting in the back were the two boys he'd scared off earlier. The men were probably what the boys would grow into. Hard, shaven-headed, tattooed, bad teeth, mean-faced, and intent on doing harm.

'Is this the mad bastard what threatened yer?'

The boys confirmed that it was. Behind him, Sam's hand closed around the head of one of the clubs protruding from the bag. Without them seeing, he pulled it out. The three men advanced with menace. This situation wasn't open to discussion. Sam swung the club round in an arc. The men stepped back, out of range, before suddenly rushing him. He swung the club again, and this time caught one of them on the side of his head, knocking him to the ground. The other two were swinging vicious punches, urged on by the howling boys, practically knocking Sam into the boot of his car. He held on to the golf club, knowing it might well be his only hope of surviving this onslaught. He turned his back to them and pushed, with one foot, against the back of the car, forcing them back, giving him room to swing. He caught one of them with a decent blow, eliciting a grunt of pain and a foul curse as his attackers stepped back out of range once again. Sam slammed the car boot shut, locking away the bag of potential weapons.

A fist slammed into his face, another into his body. One of them aimed a kick between his legs but he managed to dodge a direct hit and take it on his thigh. He kept his back to the car, limiting their field of attack – so he thought.

The first man he'd hit was still down. Blood was pouring down Sam's face. Someone was screaming in the background, Tracey probably. The two men charged again. Sam just had enough strength to dart to one side and swing the club, with all his might, in a scything action about a foot from the ground. It caught one of the men on his shin, cracking a bone and sending him to the ground, roaring in agony. Sam knew he'd be shown no mercy were they to get the better of him.

The first man down was now staggering to his feet with blood pouring from his ear where Sam's club had struck him. His face was contorted with rage as he jabbed a fat finger in Sam's direction. 'You are seriously dead! You are a fuckin' dead man!' He staggered towards Sam with arms outstretched, like Frankenstein's monster. Sam swung the club and knocked him down again, then he looked around for the third man who had disappeared. A shout of encouragement from the boys had Sam spinning round to see the man had climbed on top of his car and was about to leap on him. He had a long-bladed knife in his hand. Sam managed to take a step back. He held the club, horizontally, with one hand at either end of the shaft, to ward off the knife blow. His attacker jumped and, as he stabbed downwards, his wrist slammed into the steel shaft, breaking a bone and causing the man agony. He fell to the ground awkwardly. Sam gave him a kick in the stomach to keep him there. The man's screams were drowned by the scream of a siren as a police car skidded to a halt beside them. Two uniformed constables got out. Sam was doubled up, trying to catch his breath. He managed to look up and say, 'Morning Steve,' to one of them.

'What the hell is going on, Sam?'

'I was giving them … a golf lesson,' said Sam, between breaths. 'Wasn't I, gents?'

All of the travellers were on the ground and making lots of noise. One of them was clutching at his shin and cursing obscenely. The one with the damaged wrist had blood pouring from his ear and was also cursing. The third was just regaining consciousness for the second time. Not only had they been humiliated but it had happened in front of two of their boys. The only thought in their minds was to regroup so they could come back and kill Sam.

Sam's face was dripping blood, one of his eyes was closing, his ribs were hurting and he wasn't sure if his jaw was broken. But, on balance he'd come off best. He looked at the golf club in his hand and marvelled at its versatility and effectiveness. In open combat it was more effective than the police ASP. He made up his mind to buy one and keep it in his car.

'Bloody hell, Sam!' muttered Steve into his ear. 'There's a whole bloody tribe o' these buggers back on Cenotaph Hill. What the hell are you thinkin' about?'

'I was thinking about defending myself.'

But Sam could see Steve's point. The way most police forces dealt with travellers was to ignore their crimes and get them to move on to someone else's patch. They might look rough but they had a lot of savvy. Even if they didn't come back to kill him, in Sam's experience they might well hire some wise guy lawyer to sue him for damages. He needed an edge. He needed them to be charged with something, no matter how trivial.

'I think they want to kill me, Steve,' he said, breathing heavily. 'So it might be an idea to charge them with breach of the peace and maybe take a DNA sample. Then, if they do manage to kill me, you know where to look.'

'I'm trying to think of a reason why we shouldn't charge you with breach of the peace.'

Sam looked across to where Tracey was standing, horrified, in her doorway. 'I have an independent witness,' he said, nodding in her direction. 'I'm the injured party here.'

'And will you be pressing charges, Sam?'

'Not sure yet. Just get their DNA while I think about it. You never know what a DNA sample will turn up nowadays. If it was up to me I'd get DNA off the whole bloody camp, including the women and kids. I reckon you'd get a real result from that lot.'

'Would that we could,' sighed Steve, reluctantly

49

turning his attention to the cursing travellers.

As Sam looked at Tracey he knew she wasn't going to be a witness to anything, and he could hardly blame her. The police themselves had seen enough of the incident to make a breach of the peace charge stick.

The thug with all his limbs still intact, Lemuel Wilson, commonly known as Lemmy, was cuffed and put into the back of the police car. An ambulance had been sent for, to take the other two to Unsworth General. Sam wouldn't have minded a bit of free NHS treatment but he decided it would be more expedient to call in to see the private doctor who patched him up from time to time for an exorbitant fee.

The two boys were still sitting in the back of the pick-up, not knowing what to do. Still breathing heavily, Sam walked over to them and resumed his mad act. This time he really did look scary, with his face covered in blood, one eye half closed, and hoarse with exhaustion.

'Been tellin' people that I'm mad have yer? Bad boys, very bad boys. Yer'll find out how mad I am when the voodoo man comes ter stab yer in the middle of the night. It might not be ternight. It might not be termorrer night. But it'll come. Mark my words, boys. If you carry on with yer wicked, wicked ways, one night, when yer least expectin' it – it'll come.'

The boys climbed out of the truck and ran away. Steve had been listening to it all. 'Jesus, Sam! What was all that about?'

'Just giving the boys a bit of a pep talk, Constable.'

50

CHAPTER NINE

Sam was wearing surgical gloves. He picked each club up by the end of its grip, examined it, then laid it, side by side with the others, on the office carpet. Sally got up from her desk and stood beside him.

'You've played a bit of golf, haven't you, Sal? Do you notice anything unusual?'

'Well, he obviously doesn't use his 5 iron much.'

'Because it's so clean, you mean?'

Sally nodded. 'Mind you he's got a 7 wood, which does much the same job.'

'Does it? ... right. So that would be the reason why the 5 iron's the only spotless club in his bag, then?'

'Possibly – it doesn't look as if he used it on the last round he played which, from the state of the other clubs, was in muddy conditions. As a matter of interest which club did you use yesterday?'

Sam pointed at the club he'd used. 'That one.'

Sally nodded her approval. 'It's a fairly new type of club. It's called a rescue club – good for getting out of tight situations.'

'So I've found out, in fact I think I might get one,' Sam said. 'Right, we have what?' He counted the clubs. 'Twelve clubs, excluding the 3 iron the police are holding as evidence. Every club in this bag had dirt on it except the 5 iron, which we assume is spotless because he hasn't

51

used it since they were last cleaned.'

'They might *all* have been spotless before he played his last round of golf,' Sally pointed out.

'What you're saying is that these golf clubs are of no help whatsoever,' Sam concluded. 'So, why do I get the feeling that I'm missing something?'

'Because,' Sally said, 'knowing you, you probably are.'

'OK, what is it?'

'I've no idea. You and Owen do the Sherlock and Dr Watson bit – I'm more your Mrs Hudson.'

'Right, pass me that list of Syndicate members, Mrs Hudson. I've got to start somewhere, might as well have a chat with them.'

There were many places that gave Sam bad memories and the Queen of Clubs was one of them. Rudolph was working the door when Sam arrived at ten o'clock. He gave Sam a cursory glance then stepped to one side to allow him through, saying, 'Good evening, sir.'

'Are you Rudolph Mace?'

The defensive look in Rudolph's eyes told him the answer was 'Yes', so before the black man could ask him who the hell he was, Sam held out his hand and added, 'Sam Carew, I'm working for Tracey Ormerod.'

'Sam Carew, I've heard the name.'

Rudolph enveloped Sam's hand in his and gave him a crushing squeeze, which told Sam who was boss around here. Sam fought off a wince and withdrew his hand. 'It's just a name like any other name,' he said. He found that having people know of him was a definite drawback in the private-eye line of work. 'Do you have a break due? I wouldn't mind a quick word.'

Rudolph glanced at a big Rolex Oyster on his wrist, which Sam figured had to be either hot or a very nice fake, probably the latter. The door-man spoke into a slender microphone clipped around his head.

'I need ta take ten, can someone come to the door?'

The answers sounded to be in the affirmative. He gave Sam a broad smile. 'I got ya now, man. Youse the buildin' detective. Half Inspector Frost, half Bob the Builder.' His whole body shook as he laughed. 'Man, we have some good laughs over you an' yo' stuff. Didn't you once get involved with old Milo, what used to own dis place?'

'If you mean did he try to kill me? Yes I got involved.'

'Jeez, man! Ya must be some piece o' work, man. Milo Morrell was a bad, bad boy. How come ya still alive?'

'More by good luck than good judgement.'

'I imagine dat mus' be so.'

Another doorman arrived. Rudolph beckoned Sam inside. He walked up stairs which were fami-liar enough to produce a shiver as he remembered the last time he'd done this. At the top of the stairs was a small bar, occupying a room which Sam remembered as Milo's old office. No amount of alteration and refurbishment would ever sweep away the evil exuding from its walls. Sam was surprised that the customers couldn't feel it. Rudolph ordered himself a vodka and Diet Coke and turned to Sam.

'What can I get ya, Mr Sam Carew?'

Behind the bar was a sign saying Milo's Bar and beneath it a quotation:

The evil that men do lives after them, the good is oft interred with their bones.

Sam thought there wouldn't be too much good interred with Milo's bones. Rudolph saw him reading it. 'It's a quotation from a famous writer – Charles Dickens or someone like dat.'

'I think it's Shakespeare,' said Sam, '–Julius Caesar.' He told Rudolph he only wanted an orange juice. His drink arrived and Rudolph grinned. 'They ought ta call some of dis place after you – the feller what done for ole Milo.'

'If I thought they'd do that I'd be tempted to burn the place down.'

Rudolph let out a guffaw. 'An' I guess ya would as well. I heard about the way ya dealt with the pikies.'

'What?' Sam exclaimed. 'What the hell have you heard?'

'Mr Carew, I work in a business where a man hears everything there is ta hear. Word is that the pikies offended you and ya dealt with them good an' proper. If I wuz you I'd be watchin' my ass.'

'I seem to spend my life watching my arse,' Sam sighed. 'Anyway, I'm here to find out the truth about Jim Ormerod.'

'I thought the truth about Jim Ormerod was that he killed Alistair.'

'You tell me,' said Sam. 'You knew Jim a lot better than I did. There's only a few people in this world capable of committing such a violent murder, especially in cold blood. Do you think Jim

54

Ormerod's such a man? According to the police he was sitting at home, reading the Sunday paper, when his wife gives him a message to go and see Alistair. Jim goes along, armed with one of his own golf clubs, and bludgeons Alistair to death – apparently because Alistair was having it off with his wife. Does this sound like the Jim you know?'

'No, it don't, but who knows what goes on in a man's mind when his missis is sleepin' around?'

'Were they close – Tracey and Jim?'

Rudolph shrugged. 'Not so's you'd notice. I never heard him talk about her with any great affection.'

'Did he know she was sleeping with Alistair Waring?'

'Well, it was pretty obvious to us, man. Jim, he never said nuthin' about it.'

'Do you think he cared enough to kill Alistair over it?'

Rudolph finished his drink and set the glass back on the bar. It was immediately refilled by the barman. 'To be honest, I don't tink Jim gave a rat's ass who she went with, so long as she didn't bother him.'

'So,' summed up Sam, 'does it make any sense to you that Jim murdered Alistair and ruined the rest of his own life because his wife was being unfaithful?'

'No, man. That don't make no sense ter me.'

'It doesn't make any sense to Tracey either, nor to me. I think Jim walked in on a murder scene. I think his version of events is true.'

'Well, it wouldn't be the first time the pigs have fingered the wrong man just ter get a result.'

'So, you don't think he did it?'

Rudolph gave a shrug and screwed his face. 'No, man. Now I come ter tink of it, I guess I don't.'

'Have you any idea who might want to kill Alistair?'

Rudolph raised his eyebrows and screwed his face again. 'Ally was a pain in the ass, but he was never a violent man.'

'No vices, then?'

'Apart from screwing other men's wives, ya mean?'

'Are you saying Tracey wasn't the only one?'

'She was the only one I knew about – he liked his poker, did ya know that?'

'No, was he a big gambler?'

'I got the impression he played for higher stakes than I ever played for. Fancied himself, did Ally.'

'Do you know any of the people he played with?'

'Now that I don't know. He kep' the different parts of his life separate. We wuz the golfing part – then he had his work, his women an' his gambling. He never liked ter let one ting interfere with another.'

'Except when it came to screwing one of his golfing buddies' wives,' Sam remarked.

Rudolph let out a roar of laughter. 'Jeez man! Ya got dat damn right! Just show what happens when ya let tings overlap.'

'Only if it *was* Jim who killed him,' Sam pointed out, 'and we've decided it wasn't.'

Rudolph furrowed his brow, then nodded.

'How can I find out who his card playing partners were?' Sam asked him.

Rudolph turned the nod into a shake. 'No idea

– maybe Tracey knows.'

'I don't even think she knew he gambled. What about the rest of the, er … his other golfing buddies?'

'You mean the Syndicate?'

'I believe so.'

'You can ask dem – I doubt if they know any more than I do.'

Sam finished his drink and fished a business card from his pocket. He handed it to the doorman.

'If you think of anything that might help – anything at all.'

'Sure ting, man.'

'Everything OK, Rudolph?'

They both turned round. A tall man in his mid-forties had entered the bar. 'Am I to take it that you're the famous Sam Carew?'

'I don't know about famous,' said Sam.

'Dis is my boss, Mr White,' said Rudolph.

White held out a hand for Sam to shake. 'Stuart Kenneth White, people have always called me Stuke. I can't stop them doing it so you might as well do the same.'

Sam nodded. 'White's Security, yes I've seen your vans.' Stuke's handshake was firm and such was his bearing that Sam guessed him to have a military background.

'Have you finished your conversation with Rudolph? I believe he's supposed to be working.'

'I was on a break boss,' protested Rudolph.

'Yeah, I'm just about finished,' said Sam. 'I'm investigating the murder of a friend of his.'

'Ah, Alistair Waring,' said Stuke. 'He came in

57

here from time to time.' Before Sam could ask he put up his hands as if to ward off the question. 'Which doesn't mean to say I can help you. I didn't know the man.'

'Fair enough.'

'I'd like a word with you on another matter,' said Stuke. 'If you'd like to come through to the office, I might have some work for you.'

Rudolph watched Sam and Stuke go, then he took out his mobile and spoke into it in a low voice that couldn't be heard by any of the customers.

'Tracey's put a guy called Sam Carew on the case … yeah, *that* Sam Carew. She told him she don't tink Jim killed Ally, an' Carew thinks she's right. He's gonna be sniffin' around big time, which is just what we need, man. I'm due back on the door. He'll be comin' ter talk to youse all. Better warn Shane.'

He clicked off the phone and shook his head. Worried. They were too close to pulling it off for some part-time gumshoe to screw things up for them.

The office wasn't exactly salubrious, just a small room with a table, four chairs and a cupboard with a tea urn and some dirty cups on top.

'It's not exactly my office,' explained Stuke, 'Just a room the club lets us use.' He sat down, as did Sam. 'Are you aware that this is the bicentennial year of the Unsworth Museum of Art?'

Sam said he'd heard something about it. Two hundred and one years ago a local philanthropist, Sir Rodney Bickersdike, had died, leaving a massive bequest for the funding of an art gallery in Unsworth, a town which was otherwise a cultural desert. People came from all over the country to visit the gallery. Few of them lingered long enough to sample the other tourist attractions of Unsworth, which were a bit thin on the ground. Stuke lit a cigar.

'Galleries from all over the world,' he said, 'are lending paintings to the exhibition which will run for three months. We've got the security contract.'

'Good for you,' said Sam, who wasn't interested in security work.

'Which includes,' Stuke went on, 'bringing a valuable Rembrandt from Amsterdam. It's worth quite a lot of money so I don't want to give the job to just anyone.'

'Why don't you go yourself?'

'Oh, I fully intend going, but hearing that you were in the club gave me an idea. I need a man who can anticipate trouble before it happens. A man who has a nose that tells him something's wrong. This painting's worth a fortune and when fortunes go on the move I have to suspect that someone might want a piece of it.'

'Where do I fit in?'

Stuke shrugged and examined the end of his cigar. 'I just want you to accompany it. Be with it from the second it's taken off the wall in the Rijksmuseum to the second it's hung on the wall in Unsworth Gallery. Couldn't be easier. The whole job'll take less than 24 hours. You'll be put up in a nice hotel and flown there and back in an executive jet.'

'Really? The security business must be good business.'

'Not that good. I'll make a loss. It's the publicity I'm after. I'll be paying a PR firm as much as I'm paying you.'

'And how much will you be paying me?'

Stuke gave this some thought. 'Two grand to bring it, two grand to take it back in three months' time.'

Sam was impressed but it wouldn't do to show it, so he didn't. Stuke added a sweetener.

'Plus a grand bonus on successful completion.'

Sam saw no reason to turn it down. It would hardly interfere with his work for Tracey. 'When do I go?' he asked.

'Next Monday.'

The following morning Sam looked across the desk at Sally who was filing her nails. 'Nothing to do, Miss Grover?'

She gave his question due consideration then shook her head. 'Nope, nothing of any interest.'

'Do you fancy a day and night in Amsterdam? Private jet, nice hotel?'

'I thought you'd never ask. You were thinking of going on your own, weren't you, Carew?'

'What? How the bloody hell do you know these things? I only got the job last night.'

'Mr White rang this morning, before you got here. He asked me if I minded organising the hotel for you because his own secretary's rung in sick and he's got a busy day ahead of him. I booked us an Executive Suite in the Amstel Hotel.'

'Us? How much?'

'Does it matter? He's paying.'

'Not for the two of us.'

'He said he would, because I asked him. He seems a very nice man. Anyway it's only an extra 150 euros for the two of us and that includes dinner.'

'What includes dinner?'

'The 750 euros Mr White is paying.'

'Does he know how much?'

'Well, I assume he will when he gets his bill.'

'If he takes that out of my wages I'll take it out of yours.'

'Don't be such an old skinflint, Carew.'

CHAPTER TEN

Sam standing up to the travellers had given Tracey Ormerod a certain misguided confidence. Some of the neighbours had seen the fight through their windows and had expressed their support for both her and Jim. Matthew had gone to school for the first time in a fortnight; he was due home for lunch. Lemmy Wilson came in the back way. One kick at the back door and he was in. Tracey rushed into the kitchen, wondering what the hell had happened. She thought maybe a pan had boiled over and somehow fallen off the hob. Lemmy took one step towards her and grabbed her by the throat.

'Ye were warned, bitch!'

His eyes were wild with drink, his face un-shaven for many days and his breath foul.

'I want the bastard's name.'

61

He released his grip enough for her to talk. 'I don't know what you're talking about,' she whimpered.

He slapped her hard enough to send her staggering backwards into the hall. 'Don't give me that shite! Who's the bastard what was here the other day? Ye know full well who I'm talkin' about.' He grabbed her top in both hands and tore it, viciously, off her body. She tried to cover herself with crossed arms. He spun her round, ripped off her brassiere and knocked her to the floor.

'Strip,' he ordered. 'Strip, or I'll fuckin' kill ye!' Tracey could hardly hear him through her own sobbing. He bent over her until his nose was touching hers. 'An' while yer strippin' ye can tell me the bastard's name.'

Matthew ran up the path. He'd been chased by Brendan and Marlon. Luckily he could run faster than either of them. They were just rounding the corner into his street when he ran in through the door. He almost tripped over his mother who was lying naked in the hall, sobbing uncontrollably. Her face was savagely bruised and there was blood all over her thighs. Her son just didn't want to see her like this. He took a coat off the hallstand and threw it over her.

'Mum,' he said, 'Mum, it's Matthew.'

Tracey sobbed on, deep in shock.

'Shall I call an ambulance or the police?' He picked up the phone. His mother reached out a hand to stop him. 'No, love – you mustn't do that.'

Slowly he put the phone down. His face was drip white as realisation dawned. 'Was it them, Mum?'

Her eyes were swimming in tears as she nodded her head. 'We can't tell the police, my darling. Please don't ring the police.'

Matthew began crying. 'I don't know what to do, Mum.'

'Bring me my dressing gown, darling. I need a shower.'

'Mum I hate these people.'

'So do I, Matthew. Just bring me my dressing gown.'

She watched her son go slowly up the stairs. It wouldn't do to tell him about the threat Lemmy Wilson had made on Matthew's life. Wilson would make that threat come true just as surely as he'd made the threat of rape come true. She picked up the phone herself and dialled Sam.

She was showered and dressed by the time Sam called. Matthew hadn't gone back to school. Sam didn't mean to be over-critical, but he had to say it:

'You shouldn't have showered. He'll have left enough evidence on you for the police to bang him away for ten years.'

'I know that, Sam, but there's not only him. He said Matthew would die if I told the police – and I believe him.'

'Ah.'

'He was a totally inhuman bastard, they all are.'

'Not all of them. There are some decent ones.'

'I've never heard of a decent one. If the police lock him up I'm sure there'll be plenty left who are willing to carry out his threat. They don't seem the type to make idle threats.'

'Had you seen him before?'

She hesitated before saying, 'He was one of the ones who attacked you.'

Sam walked over to the window and looked out, shaking his head. Why was it that he couldn't do anything without someone getting hurt? 'I see – that makes this my fault. I'm sorry.' He remained there for a while, leaving her to wonder what was going through his mind. Eventually he turned to face her. 'You should go to the police. They'll tell him they're doing a DNA match. He won't know you've washed off the evidence. DI Bowman's a prat but he's good at tricking confessions out of people.'

'Sorry, I can't risk Matthew's life.'

'No,' sighed Sam. 'That's what he was banking on.' He took out his cigarettes and remarked, 'Do you know, Sam Carew the brickie doesn't smoke half as much as Sam Carew the detective.' He offered her one and she took it.

'The only way out of this,' she said, 'is for us to move out of Unsworth.'

'Which you don't want to do.'

'Well, no – Matthew likes his school, I like where we live. I'm like you – I've always lived in Unsworth.'

Sam smiled at her words. 'Always lived in Unsworth eh? I wonder how many people say that?'

'Probably everyone who lives here,' Tracey said. 'It's a very close knit community.'

'United in our collective squalor,' said Sam, gloomily.

'Excuse me. It's not squalid round here,' protested Tracey. 'Anyway, you've got every chance to move away. What keeps you here?'

'Ah, now that's the great mystery of Unsworth,' said Sam. 'What keeps us here? Even the ones who escape always seem to come back. But that doesn't solve your problem.' He looked at her, keenly. 'Even if you're not pressing charges you should see a rape counsellor.'

'I'll be OK – honest. All I want is for Matthew to be safe. I can handle all the other stuff. I'll get Jim back because I know he didn't do it – and it's not as if I've just been savagely de-flowered. A man's had sex with me against my will. Bad men do this to women. I'm not the first, I won't be the last.'

'Rape isn't sex,' Sam pointed out.

'Yeah, I know all about that,' she said. 'I've read the books. Rape's all about power. Trying to make a woman feel worthless.'

'Whereas in reality it's the rapist who's the worthless one,' Sam added.

She took his hand. 'I really do need help.'

He exhaled a long breath. 'Well, short of buying an AK 47 and shooting the camp up I'm a bit stuck for ideas.'

'But you'll help me?'

'I'll do what I can. Is there anything else I should know that might help.'

'Well, there is something, but I doubt if it'll help.'

'Oh?'

'He made me tell him your name. He said you were a dead man.'

'Right.'

Sam paused and gave this some thought. This wasn't something he wanted to hear. An idea came to him. He'd already had an offer of help

65

but he'd turned it down as being a bit drastic. But these were now drastic times.

'OK, I'll er, I'll deal with it, Tracey. Don't worry.'

As Jimmy O'Connor drove slowly past the travellers' site a scowl creased his wizened face and he cursed to himself in his harsh, Ulster accent. One of the caravans, the nearest one to the road, was flying an Irish tricolour. This was OK by Jimmy, his mother had come from the south but she, as much as anyone, would have condemned what was written on the side of the caravan: *Up The Provos. Fuck The Brits.*

It amazed him that the police allowed such a thing, here on British soil and, not for the first time, he thought the British public were far too tolerant for their own good. He parked his car just a short distance beyond the site and strolled back, knowing that to drive his car past once again might arouse suspicion.

The encampment was pretty much as he expected. A roughly made tarmac road with a couple of dozen assorted caravans parked in staked-out plots. The state of the vans ranged from tatty and propped up on bricks, to a couple of top-of-the-range mobile homes. He reckoned the IRA van was worth maybe ten grand. He also figured that none of them would be insured.

There was the usual travellers detritus scattered around the site. General rubbish, piled or blowing around the site in the strong breeze, oil drums, builders' materials, three wrecked cars that would never move under their own steam again, horse boxes, a ten-ton wagon, two pick-ups, a couple of motorbikes, two small vans, several cars – some of them quite expensive looking, and various barking dogs. A cacophony of loud music came from several caravans and some scruffy-looking young kids played on a black and white horse which had seen better days. A group of older women were gathered at the far side of the site and three men seemed to be working on the tipping mechanism of one of the pick-up trucks. Jimmy paused to light his pipe. Pipes often took some lighting, so it wouldn't be unusual for a man to pause for a while as he lit up. Although it would in Jimmy's case as he didn't smoke a pipe. It gave him an excuse to pause long enough to count the caravans and memorise the whole scene in one long look between puffs of disagreeable smoke. A plan came immediately to mind. It would require the site to be uninhabited for a few hours but, from what he'd heard, that requirement would take care of itself very shortly.

He'd been asked by Sam to give them no more than a kick up the backside that might persuade them to be more civic-minded, but the writing on the caravan was like a red rag to a bull.

His father had been murdered by the Provisional IRA back in 1977. Jimmy had been in the British army, thus making the O'Connor family a legitimate IRA target. His mother had been told to move out of Belfast or she'd be next. She had the choice of moving to England where she knew no one, or back to County Cork where she had grown up. She chose Cork.

An embittered Jimmy had applied for SAS training and eventually joined a covert active service unit working under the indirect control of MI6. His expertise was in explosives and his targets were known Republican terrorists and arms caches. As the legality of this was highly questionable the responsibility for his work was always laid on the shoulders of different Loyalist factions, who happily accepted the blame. Jimmy lived in the community and worked as an electrician – a trade for which he'd served an apprenticeship as a youth. With the rank of sergeant he operated as unit leader in a unit of four, all of whom were Ulstermen, and he took his orders from a controller known as Michael Witney. In 1986 he'd been ordered to assassinate a man for whom he'd done electrical work and knew well. Jimmy refused the order, as was his right – no military court would dare court-martial him for disobeying such an order. Instead he was arrested by the RUC for another crime he'd been ordered to commit – blowing up a Catholic presbytery which housed a priest sympathetic to the Republican movement. The priest had been given sufficient warning and no one had been hurt. But it was a crime which had greatly offended the Catholic community, so much so that it would do the Brits no harm at all to find and punish the culprit. Michael Witney handed the RUC all the evidence it needed and Jimmy was sentenced to 8 years imprisonment – all of it in Wakefield Prison in Yorkshire.

After five years he became eligible for parole, a condition of which was that he found suitable work on the outside. He had answered an ad in the *Yorkshire Evening Post,* placed by Ernest Carew, Sam's late dad. Ernest was the only person who offered him employment.

Jimmy worked for Ernest for four years before moving back to Belfast to get married. His marriage broke up after a year, as happens to many men with such troubled backgrounds, and Jimmy came back to Yorkshire where he worked as a jobbing electrician. He'd been working on Carew and Son's site when Sam got chatting to him about the problems the travellers were causing. He offered to help and Sam had eventually taken him up on his offer.

The blaze in Cenotaph Hill encampment was quite spectacular and drew a large, admiring crowd. It made both the *Yorkshire Television News* and *BBC Look North*. Every single one of the travellers had gone off to Appleby Horse Fair in Cumbria leaving the encampment in the care of three vicious dogs of indeterminate breed, which were now on the loose and causing mayhem in and around Unsworth. DC Owen Price had been put in charge of the investigation. He was on the site with a uniformed constable when the travellers began arriving back. They came in a convoy of four-wheel drives, pick-up trucks, vans, ten-ton wagons, a Mercedes and three motorbikes. Although word had got through to them about what had happened they got out of their vehicles and stared at the carnage in a stunned silence which was eventually broken by one of the women.

It was a piercing, feral screech, which had Owen placing a hand over the ear nearest to her. She had arrived on the back of a Harley Davidson. She took off her crash helmet and shook loose a mass of her greying hair. Then she threw the helmet at the smoking embers of what once had been her home, sank to her knees and screamed a string of chilling and obscene threats to the heavens. Owen dearly hoped that none of her threats were meant for him as she was a very scary woman.

There had been twenty-three caravans and mobile homes on the encampment. Whoever the arsonist was had done his job with military precision and expertise. Every one of them was completely gutted. Owen knew of only one man capable of this, and the last time he had seen him was on Carew's site. Under normal circumstances he would have put wheels in motion to have the man interviewed. But in this instance he thought it might be advisable to question Sam Carew first. He knew that Sam had had an altercation with the travellers not too long ago and had been the subject of serious threats.

The travellers had a leader called Elias John Higgins, better known as Eli John. He was a small, wiry man with a west of Ireland accent and a cunning face that could have been made out of old boot leather. He stepped out of the Mercedes and approached Owen.

'Dis is a fine kettle o' fuckin' fish, mister polis.' He spoke without taking his hands from his pockets or a hand-rolled cigarette from out of his mouth. It was of the slender variety, much favoured by Her Majesty's prisoners who could eke as many as 200 cigarettes from a single ounce of *Old Holborn*.

'DC Owen Price,' said Owen, 'and this is PC Wade.'

70

'An' d'ye have any bright ideas, DC Owen Price?'

'I've only just arrived. Forensics should be here shortly.'

'Forensics eh? And what are forensics gonna make out of all dis fuckin' mess? Can they get finger prints from ashes, mister?'

The other travellers had shuffled after him like a flock of sheep and now stood behind him in a group of around fifty or more.

'I'm not sure,' Owen said, 'for the time being we can give you a crime number so that you can contact your insurance companies.'

Eli John let out a howl of humourless laughter. 'We're Irish fuckin' pikies. Do we look like anyone the insurance companies might be interested in, mister? Do we look insurable?'

'Well, I hope your road vehicles are insured.' Owen spoke loud enough for it to carry to all the travellers, some of whom looked uncomfortable at this. Eli John said nothing. Owen glanced around the site. 'Well, there's a fair amount of damage.'

'Well over half a million euros,' said the gypsy leader. 'My van alone was worth sixty-five grand. We'll be lookin' ter the police for criminal compensation.'

'In which case may I wish you the very best of luck,' said Owen, keeping his face straight. 'I've been trying to get a bit of compensation out of them myself with regards to a couple of bullet holes I acquired on their behalf. Very frugal with their money, the police. I've often thought of taking up plumbing. More money in plumbing, see.'

Eli John was trying to work out how the con-

71

versation had switched to plumbing when Owen walked away from him to greet the arriving forensics team.

The travellers dispersed to survey their individual, burnt-out homes and somehow Owen knew this was a result of the death threat they'd issued to Sam and Matthew Ormerod, plus what had happened to Tracey Ormerod.

People issuing death threats need to be side-tracked with something more important. Those had been Sam's actual words. *Bloody hell, Carew! What have you been up to?*

The general feeling down at the station was that whoever had done this had done the police a favour. Since the arrival of the travellers, crime in Unsworth had gone up by a third and much pressure was being put on the police to get rid of them.

Owen turned to look, as they were now grouping at the far end of the field to listen to the words of their leader. He edged closer so that he could hear.

'They've done for us big time, this time,' Eli John was saying. 'If ye have fathers or brothers or sons or mates anywhere in the country, ye go to them. They'll take ye, the same as ye've taken people in the past.' He stabbed a finger downwards. 'But dis is our piece of God's earth – bought an' paid for. We'll come back when we can.'

Owen noticed a wooden sign leaning against a fence post. He signalled for Eli John's attention and pointed it out to him. The whole group shuffled across. Those who could read, read it to those who couldn't.

THIS IS WHAT HAPPENS TO PROVO

72

RAPIST SCUM.
COME BACK AND IT GETS WORSE.
One of the men ran at the sign and kicked at it in helpless rage. The crowd watched in silence as he vented his impotent fury on a piece of innocent wood.

'If I have ter leave this bastard place it will know I've been here, by God!' He turned around, with legs spread wide and fists clenched in a gesture of general rage and defiance. 'What d'ye say, lads? Let's rip this fuckin' town apart!'

No one seemed ready to join him. Some of the women began to weep. Most of the men didn't look as if they knew where to turn. This one action had ripped the spirit out of them. It was a sobering thought that a whole town hated them so much. Their lives had been clinically destroyed. Everything they had, had been taken away from them. Homes, possessions, everything. They were hard, often ruthless people, who lived by their own laws, but they were up against a faceless enemy who was at least as ruthless as they were. They were pariahs whom no one wanted to help, not even the police. Owen couldn't help but feel sympathy towards them. Not all of them were villains. As in all walks of life there were saints and villains. Unfortunately the travelling community had more than its fair share of the latter.

They had moved into Unsworth and tried to stamp their authority on it. Unsworthians had enough to put up with without outsiders coming in and adding to their troubles. The travellers' desperate plight would arouse no sympathy from the locals. Owen could have told the travellers that it wasn't the whole town which had done this to them, but it did no harm for them to think it *was* the whole town.

'There are no rapists in this camp,' said Eli John to Owen. 'We don't hold with harmin' women.'

The three men who had attacked Sam were standing together. One on crutches, one with his arm in a sling. The rapist, Lemmy Wilson, stood a little apart from them – or were they standing apart from him?

'Oh, I think you'll find there's at least one,' said Owen, without looking in Wilson's direction. 'He's safe enough for the time being. The poor woman he raped is too scared of reprisal against her son to press charges. The trouble is, word got round and this is the result. Very singular people, Unsworthians, they look after their own – a bit like yourselves – only there's a lot more of them.'

'We live and we let live,' said Eli.

'Really?' Owen commented. 'I couldn't help but notice what was written on the caravan. I don't suppose that helped.'

'Eejit kids,' grumbled the gypsy leader.

The two troublesome boys were standing near them, ashen-faced. One of them walked, hesitantly, towards Owen.

'Was this voodoo, mister?'

'No, boy, this isn't voodoo. This is the work of a pyromaniac. For all I know he might set fire to the town next.' He was trying to deflect suspicion from his number one suspect – a certain bricklayer of his acquaintance.

Neither the boys nor the men seemed to know what a pyromaniac was, but the thought of the

74

whole town burning down seemed to lighten the general mood.

'Well I hope the bastard does burn the whole town down,' called out one man, 'and himself with it.' He earned murmurs of approval from some. Others, especially the women, were mulling over the thought of them harbouring a rapist.

'This is the work of more than one bastard,' said Eli, surveying the damage all around him. 'There's a whole bunch o' people want us outa this town.'

'Can we fuckin' blame 'em if we have a rapist among us?' muttered a woman. Other women murmured their agreement. One of them called out, 'An' what's all this shite about us all bein' Provos? Whose fuckin' bright idea was that?'

'If we have a rapist in the camp I want to know who he is,' roared Eli John, scanning the men's faces. He had his own suspicions. There were probably just three men in the camp capable of such an act.

'Oh, I can tell you his name,' said Owen, blandly. Tracey had picked him out of a mugshot album. 'His name's Lemmy Wilson – he's the one who caused all this.'

Hostile eyes turned on Lemmy Wilson and the owners of the eyes knew he was well capable of such an act. 'That's bollocks!' he protested, savagely. 'I never been near the woman!'

But there were men in the camp to whom he'd boasted of his rape.

'That's not what I heard,' someone said.

Wilson's wife confronted him, her face contorted with fury. 'Is this true, Lemuel fuckin'

Wilson, ye big dirty shite?'

He wore and punched her in the face, knocking her to the ground. Owen should have arrested him for assault but the woman sprang to her feet and hurled herself at her husband, screeching, cursing, biting, scratching like a howling, insane harridan. Owen felt he could do no more so he went to his car and drove straight to the site where Sam was working. Of all the stupid and dangerous things Carew had done, this took the biscuit.

'I need you to tell me you had nothing to do with it.' Owen was shouting up from the ground.

'Nothing to do with what?' Sam was fixing a first floor window frame into place with help of Curly, a labourer. 'Do you know what he's on about Curly?'

'Why would I know what he's on about, boss?'

'I thought you might,' said Sam, 'with you both being of the Celtic persuasion.'

'There's a good few miles of muddy water between the Irish and the Welsh, boss. I've more chance of understandin' the Hindu.'

'I'll come down,' Sam called out. 'Give me a few minutes. Make us a brew in the cabin.'

Owen was pouring water from the kettle into the mugs when Sam opened the cabin door. It was a warm, July day and sweat was glistening on his skin.

'Warm one today, Owen,' he said, picking up his mug. 'Right, what can I do for you?'

Owen stared at his friend, trying to gauge his innocence. But innocence was a difficult thing to gauge in Sam Carew.

'Sam, we both know what I'm talking about. Last week I saw Jimmy O'Connor on this site. The next thing I know someone's set the Cenotaph Hill encampment on fire. From what you've told me about him in the past a job like that would be right up Jimmy's street.'

'Jimmy went back to Belfast a few days ago.'

'Did he now? How many days ago was that?'

'Two,' lied Sam, lighting a cigarette. He figured it wasn't a malicious lie, just a fib to make things easier for Owen. 'What's this all about, Owen? Am I being accused of conspiracy to commit arson? Which would carry a life sentence. Do I look stupid?'

'Don't tempt me to answer that one,' said Owen. 'What was Jimmy doing on this site?'

'Because he's the best electrician I've ever come across.'

'He's also one of the best explosives experts you've ever come across,' countered Owen.

Sam returned the Welshman's gaze with narrowed eyes. 'Owen, you only know about Jimmy because I told you about him in confidence. I assume you haven't mentioned anything about him down at the station?'

'You don't need to ask that, boyo,' replied Owen, tetchily. 'I know the man had a raw deal but that doesn't give him leave to go round creating mayhem.'

'Why? Are the Unsworth Police unhappy that it happened?'

'Does that mean it *was* Jimmy?'

'It doesn't mean anything,' said Sam. 'It was just a simple question. Will the coppers be happy to be rid of them?'

'You know the answer to that as well as I do.'

'In which case, even if I did know anything about the fires I wouldn't be doing you or the Unsworth Police any favours by compromising you with full knowledge of the facts. You love me too much to want to lock me up. The very existence of that camp threatened my life – through no fault of my own, I might add.' He sipped at his tea, looked out of the window and asked, casually, 'What are they going to do?'

'Well, they're apparently not insured. They've lost everything. Some of the women were in tears.'

'Oh dear, how sad – never mind.'

'You can be an unfeeling bugger at times, Carew.'

'Do you know, I find it really hard to have any sympathy for the foul-mouthed bunch who wrecked the Clog and Shovel last week and the Plasterers Arms the week before that. A man from that camp raped Tracey Ormerod and threatened to kill her son.'

'I know.'

Sam was surprised. 'You know? How do you know?'

'Because I went to see her with some questions regarding her husband. She told me what had happened and that she wasn't pressing charges against her attacker. She never told me she'd told you, but I guessed that she might have – especially after I saw what happened to the camp.'

'I don't think she wants it broadcast,' Sam said. 'There's a stigma to being a rape victim, that's why a lot of women don't report it.'

78

'I went back and got her to photo ID her assailant,' said Owen, 'hoping it might prompt her to press charges.'

'And?'

'And she ID'd a traveller called Lemmy Wilson. She still refused to press charges against him. The best I could do was to ID him to the camp so they know who to blame.'

'Really? You might well have passed a death sentence on him – mind you, he passed one of me so fair's fair.'

'I did nothing illegal, boyo, which is more than I can say for some.'

'Owen, there's kids scared to go to school, women scared to walk the streets, mayhem all over the place and the police were running around like headless chickens.'

'I know all of that.'

'And there's me. I'm a bit worried at having my life threatened. These people don't usually make idle threats, Owen.'

'I know about that as well. They reckon the damage amounts to half a million euros.'

Sam was unimpressed. 'Really? They'll have to lay a lot of crap drives to get that sort of money back.'

'They can't live there – unless they set up tents.' Owen watched Sam's eyes for a hint of worry over such a suggestion. There was none.

'They're travellers, not campers,' Sam said. 'Will they be travelling on?'

'I get the impression they'll be dispersing to friends and relatives.'

'Very wise of them. They can tell their friends

and relatives what happens to people who make life difficult for law abiding citizens. What's that old saying? *Justice should not only be done but should be seen to be done.*'

'I don't think that applies to vigilantes, boyo.'

'Doesn't it?' said Sam. He winked at his Welsh pal. 'I imagine Bowman wouldn't be sorry to see them go. Hey, maybe he set it all up – he's done worse in the past.'

Owen wasn't impressed. 'Apart from Tracey Ormerod the person who benefits most from them leaving is you, Sam.'

'Do any of the pikies think it's me?'

'Not as far as I know. They seem to think it's the work of the whole town. Is there any reason why they *should* think it's you?'

'None at all.'

'Apart from you putting two of them in to hospital. Sam if you had anything to do with this and you get nabbed for it–'

Sam interrupted him. 'Owen, have you any idea what it's like to have your life seriously threatened by people who live on your doorstep and who are more than capable of carrying it out? It's worrying, Owen. Believe me, it's very worrying.'

Owen picked up his tea mug and gulped the lot down in one go, despite it still being hot. 'Sam,' he asked, 'am I being asked to pursue this investigation with less diligence than usual?'

'Owen, you can pursue it with as much diligence as you like, just as long as your diligence doesn't involve me.'

'What about Jimmy O'Connor's direction?'

Sam stared at him for a full ten seconds. 'How's

80

Eileen?' he asked. 'You must have been with her what – two years now? How's she managed to put up with you all that time?'

At times like this Owen found him unbearably exasperating. He was tempted to tell him about the women who were weeping over the loss of their homes, and the despair on the faces of the men. But he knew that wouldn't be fair. Were the travellers to stay there was a good chance they'd come for Sam at some stage. A man had a right to protect his own life.

'DI Bowman's told me to follow a line of enquiry that it was an inside job,' Owen said. 'One of their own with a grievance.'

Sam nodded his agreement. 'That's exactly the line of enquiry I'd be taking if I wanted to get a grip on the rising level of crime in Unsworth. Mind you, I wouldn't mention it to any of the travellers that you're taking that line of enquiry.'

'Perhaps I should wait until the travellers have dispersed,' said Owen, 'and then begin my enquiries.'

'Unorthodox, but wise,' said Sam.

CHAPTER ELEVEN

There were five passengers on the Learjet that flew from Leeds and Bradford Airport to Schiphol, nine miles south-west of Amsterdam. Sam and Sally; Frances Fowler, the curator of the bicentennial exhibition in Unsworth Gallery;

Stuke White and Rudolph.

'I've organised a couple of armed security guards to escort us from the gallery to the plane,' said Stuke to Sam, without taking his eyes off the North Sea, three miles below. 'We go straight to the Rijksmuseum from Schiphol, take a look at the painting and you tell me if it's possible for a clever villain to steal it from under our noses. You've all night to think about it. We pick it up at ten in the morning, take off at eleven, back in Leeds and Bradford Airport at twelve, into a security van and back in Unsworth at one.'

'I'm guessing this security van will have your firm's name on it,' said Sam.

'It'll be one of our vans. Is that a problem?'

'And will there be a television camera at Leeds and Bradford Airport, by any chance?'

'Hopefully, both at the airport and Unsworth. That's part of the PR.'

'And that's part of what bothers me,' said Sam.

Three hours later they were in gallery 9 of the Rijksmuseum, standing in front of a Rembrandt painting entitled *Self Portrait as The Apostle Paul*.

Overall, including the fairly plain, darkwood frame, it was about three feet by four and behind glass. 'What do you think?' asked Stuke.

'Well, it's not something you could cut out with a Stanley knife and stuff up your jumper,' said Sam. 'Anyone planning to nick it will need to take the whole thing, frame and all.'

'It's being crated up tonight ready for us in the morning,' Stuke said, then added, 'Is there anything that *really* worries you about this?'

'Only the obvious.'

'Which is?'

'The fact that everyone and his brother seems to know about it. I noticed a picture of it in a paper called *De Telegraaf* at the airport. The *Unsworth Observer's* told everyone it's arriving tomorrow. If it's worth a zillion quid it could well tempt someone.' A thought struck him and he looked at Stuke with suspicion. 'You've heard a whisper, haven't you? I think you've heard a whisper, which is why you enlisted me at the last minute.'

Stuke hesitated, then nodded. 'It was no more than a whisper and it came from Unsworth police who picked it up from the Met. Just a warning to be extra vigilant, nothing more.'

'Extra vigilant at which end, here or Yorkshire?'

'There was nothing specific. Just a rumour from a snout in London that some Russian mafia character's interested in owning the painting. It was passed on so the Met could cover themselves. There's been some bad publicity lately about the police authorities not sharing information.'

'Right,' said Sam, 'so it's probably nothing, then?'

'Almost certainly nothing.'

'Easy money, then.'

'Money for old rope.'

'Good.'

Sam looked at the Rembrandt. 'He looks pretty fed up for an apostle. He looks like an old bloke who's trying to get on with reading his paper but he can't because his wife's giving him earache about something. What's that sticking out of his jacket?'

'It's a dagger,' said Sally, who had read up on the painting in a brochure, 'and it's not a jacket, it's a doublet. And it's not a paper it's a manuscript. And he's wearing a middle eastern turban instead of his more familiar painter's cap.'

Frances Fowler was impressed. 'The dagger and the manuscript he's holding are attributes of St Paul the Apostle, who was beheaded.'

'It's the first painting of himself as an historical figure,' added Sally. 'I don't think anyone's ever equalled his chiaroscuro effect.'

'You took the words right out of my mouth,' said Sam.

'Caravaggio, perhaps?' said Frances.

'Ah, yes, Caravaggio,' agreed Sally as if she'd momentarily forgotten Caravaggio and his chiaroscuro effects. Sam thought about asking her something about Caravaggio that might trip her up, but decided that might be churlish.

'I've got a *Mona Lisa* tea towel,' he said.

Sally glared at him.

'Why is it behind glass?' Sam wondered. 'I thought oil paintings were supposed to be displayed without glass. I've seen *The Haywain* in the National in London and that's not behind glass.'

'Ideally this shouldn't be behind glass,' Frances told him. 'This is a hundred and...' she did a mental calculation, 'and sixty years older than *The Haywain*. They obviously feel it needs the added protection.'

'How much is it worth?' he asked.

Frances shook her head. 'Hard to say. This is one of his major works. One of his lesser works, *A Portrait of a Lady*, sold a couple of years ago for

45 million euros.'

Sam whistled and looked at the painting with new eyes. 'So, I'm looking at 30 million quid minimum.'

'It's worth a lot more than that,' Stuke remarked. 'For the time this is away from this gallery it's insured for 80 million pounds. The Bickersdike Foundation has stumped up a fairly hefty premium. Two blokes from the insurance company will be travelling back with us to ensure we're looking after it properly.'

'I bet they will,' said Sam.

Someone cleared his throat behind them and a man's voice said, 'It's our duty to advise you that the terms and conditions of the police must be strictly adhered to, in order not to invalidate the insurance cover.'

Sam turned, as did the others. Two men in smart suits stood there. The one who had spoken held out his hand. 'John Frickers, Morgan Black-stone Insurance Company. This is my colleague, Alan Weston. We're just here to observe.'

'Observe away,' said Stuke, irritably. 'This job will be done by the book and then some.'

'Please make sure it is. Our underwriters are sticklers for such things.' Their job done the two men walked away.

'You can't put a price on charm like that,' said Sally.

'Morgan Blackstone have their own security company,' explained Stuke. 'I actually undercut them. I gather they're a bit cheesed off.'

'Has anyone checked these terms and con-ditions?' Sam asked.

Blank faces looked at blank faces. 'Surely it's the job of the insurance people,' Sally commented, 'to offer guidance on such matters. Or is their job restricted to making unhelpful comments and walking away?'

Sam walked right up to the painting and examined it intently for several minutes as the others looked on. Then he stepped back and said, 'It might be an idea not to advertise the exact day it's being returned. I think the Russian mafia might be a bit out of my league.'

There was an almost inaudible tinkle of a bell, then a bicycle, ridden by a young woman, brushed past Sam's elbow at a good 25 mph.

'Next one to do that goes into the canal,' he grumbled. 'I've never seen so many crap-looking bikes. And how come they get to ride on the footpath? They could do with fewer bikes and more street cleaners round here.'

'Sam, chill out, we're in Amsterdam.'

'And look at all this graffiti–'

'Sam, chill out.' She looked at him as they crossed a canal bridge, narrowly avoiding a group of chattering cyclists. 'You're worrying about something, aren't you?'

'I've got a funny feeling about this job. Trouble is, I can't put my finger on it.'

Sally knew that Sam's funny feelings were not to be taken lightly. There were times he blundered headlong into obvious danger, and other times when he had an almost psychic ability to see what no one else could see.

'Sam, I can't see there being any trouble at this

end. Not with an armed police escort.'

Sam said nothing, then he gave her a broad smile. 'You're quite right, Miss Grover. Here we are in Amsterdam and I'm being a miserable old sod.' He took a street map from his pocket and turned it sideways so that he could orientate himself, then he pointed to his right. 'Along this canal, left down ... Doelenstraat, and we're there.'

'Where?'

'The Rossebuurt.'

'Is it nice?'

'It's very nice,' he assured her. 'My guide book says there are some very nice sights in The Rossebuurt.'

'Good,' said Sally, happy that he was no longer grumbling. He took her hand as they strolled the side of the canal. It was late evening. They had wined and dined in some style at the hotel and had energetically road-tested the four-poster bed. She didn't want any bad thoughts clouding the nice time they were having. They walked down Doelenstraat and came to the next canal, on either side of which were many coloured lights reflecting on the murky water. Crowds of people strolled up and down either side of the canal. Men in dark suits stood in garish, neon-lit doorways from which blared a cacophony of jazz and soul music. Sally glanced up at the large, first floor windows. The glazing went from floor to ceiling and was ideal for displaying the wares on offer. Half-naked women stood in bored, but provocative, poses. Some much more than half naked. Sally wasn't amused.

'Sam Carew, you seedy old bugger!'

'Come off it, I'm no older than you.'

87

'You've brought me to the bloody red light district.'

'I told you where we were coming.'

'No, you didn't, you said it was the…' She tried to remember. Sam helped her out.

'Rossebuurt – the red neighbourhood.'

'How was I to know? I don't speak Dutch.'

'Oh, sorry. You seemed such an expert on Dutch paintings this afternoon I just assumed you were fluent in the language. Silly me, eh?'

She gave him a touché grin. 'Well, one of us had to sound knowledgeable. Anyway I'm surprised you need to visit a place like this after what we've just been doing.'

'Professional curiosity, Miss Grover. The world of crime is a twilight world – as is this.'

'Really?' An idea occurred to her. 'I wonder just how twilight you want this evening to be?'

'Well, I won't be knocking on any windows.'

'Perhaps you fancy a coffee?' said Sally.

'Perhaps I do.'

The man behind the counter was smiley and black and called Joe. In free and easy Amsterdam where everything is legal except murder, rape and Morris Dancing, the words Coffee Shop are a euphemism for *Get Your Weed Here*.

Joe served them two coffees and stood back in anticipation of a more lucrative order. There were four other customers, all of whom were smoking joints.

'I'm guessin' this is yo' first time.'

Joe's accent told them he had lived here long enough for The Netherlands to have affected his Jamaican patois.

'In Amsterdam, yes,' smiled Sally. 'Do you have a menu?'

Sam wondered why she needed a menu after the sumptuous meal they'd only recently had. He certainly wasn't hungry. From under the counter Joe brought out a laminated A4 card on which was written Weed Menu. Sam now wondered how Sally knew to ask for such a thing. He watched as she studied the various types and strengths of cannabis on offer: Red Lebanese, Bubble Trouble, Shark's Breath, Cherry Bomb, Polm Gold. She pointed to Polm Gold.

'Could you roll us one of these, please?'

'A wise choice,' smiled Joe. He rolled them a long, cone-shaped joint and gave them a tin ashtray to take to a table.

'What did he mean, wise choice?' whispered Sam.

'I think he means it's the mildest on the menu.'

'You only think?'

'Sam, you used to be a copper. How come you don't know? Don't tell me you've never smoked a joint before.'

'You know I haven't – have you?'

She lit up and took a deep drag. The other customers smoked away in contented silence. A young man looked at Sam and remarked, in an American accent, 'Hey, this sure is good skunk.'

Sam looked at Sally and whispered. 'Skunk? Are we smoking skunk? I thought you'd got the mild stuff.'

'No idea. You tell me.'

Sam took the joint from Sally and drew in a deep lungful of smoke. It was hot against his

89

throat and made him stifle a cough.

'What do you think?' said Sally, taking it off him.

'Tastes like a Capstan Full Strength that's been kept in a plumber's sock for six months. If it's skunk I know where they got the name from.'

'All part of the twilight experience.'

By the time they finished it they were both smiling stupidly at nothing in particular. Sam felt vaguely dizzy.

'Sal, do you feel dizzy?'

'A bit.'

'Yeah, so do I.'

He sat there in silence, sipping his coffee, waiting for the dizziness to go. He rested his elbows on the table as he waited. It got progressively worse. For some reason he began to think of infinity.

'Lasts a long time, dunnit?'

'What does?'

'Infinity.'

'Ages,' agreed Sally, earnestly.

The dizziness got worse. 'I can't get my er … head around it,' he said.

'Around what?'

'In … finity.' He looked at her. 'Hey, Grover … how come you're not as err … as dizzy as me?'

'No idea,' she said. 'It affects different people in different ways.'

Speech was becoming difficult so he decided to say nothing more until the dizziness went. That's if it ever went. He couldn't confidently guarantee that. Which was a worry. He went very quiet, alone with his thoughts. After a while Joe came across and asked Sally, 'Has he bin drinkin' much?'

'We had a couple of bottles of wine earlier –

well, Sam drank most of it. I'm more your gin and tonic.'

'Oh dear – and this is his first joint?'

'I think so.'

'But not you?'

'Well, first time as a responsible adult.'

Joe laughed out loud. 'There's nothin' responsible about smokin' weed, lady.' Sally laughed. Sam wondered what the hell was so funny. He had now lost almost every ounce of strength in his limbs and all they could do was laugh.

'He'll be all right, lady,' said Joe. 'Him got what we call very low weed tol'rance. Him on another planet right now.'

What bollocks! thought Sam. *I'm not on another planet. I'm in a scruffy café in Amsterdam, and I'm dizzy and weak. What's so bloody great about being dizzy and weak?*

He forced himself to his feet and staggered to the door. Sally threw some euros on the table and ran after him. She heard the bicycle bell but Sam didn't.

That night Sally ended up alone in their four-poster bed in the Amstel Hotel. Sam ended up in the Saint Lucas hospital, recovering from concussion. He was lucky he hadn't ended up in the canal.

At ten o'clock the next morning Sally, Frances Fowler and Stuke White were sitting in a Mercedes driven by Mr Bert Kromkamp, the head of security at the Rijksmuseum. Rudolph, along with two armed Dutch policemen and a museum security guard, was in a plain white security van in front of them which, in turn, was following two police motor cyclists. Behind the Mercedes was a Lexus carrying John Frickers and Alan Weston of Morgan Blackstone. The two armed policemen were in the back of the van, sitting on the wooden crate which had been specially made to house the Rembrandt. The van was being driven by the museum security guard, beside him was Rudolph.

They drove through the museum grounds, past the building work at the front. People stared, most of them knew exactly what was happening. There had been enough publicity about it. A battered, builder's van shot out from behind some scaffolding and drove straight past the convoy, giving the police motor cyclists a heart-stopping moment. Was this it? They sighed with relief as the van, pushing blue smoke from its exhaust, drove out of the gate and turned left along Stadthouderskade. The convoy turned right and then right again down Hobbemakade, where the road was blocked by a concrete lorry discharging its load.

'I don't know about you, but I'm beginning to get a bit jittery here,' said Sally. 'I wish Sam was with us.'

'I think Sam might have enough problems of his own without him bothering about us,' remarked Stuke.

After negotiating narrow city roads and canal bridges for ten nervous minutes they emerged on the A10. Stuke was visibly relieved.

'If anything was going to happen it would have happened by now,' he said. 'It's open road from here to the airport.'

The A10 became the A4 and ran into an underpass. Just beyond it two men stepped out of a 4x4 parked on the grass verge. They took up position behind the bridge pillars, holding rifles. They each fired a dart into a police motorcyclist. Within seconds the policemen began to wobble all over the road. The security van driver saw this happen and managed to drive around them without hitting them. The Mercedes had to brake sharply to avoid running over them as they fell off their machines. Other vehicles, unaware of what had happened, drove past and filled the road between the Mercedes and the security van, effectively breaking the contact between the van and the other two vehicles in the convoy. The gunmen jumped back into the 4x4, drove over the grass verge and headed back down the other carriageway. Inside the security van Rudolph was watching the mayhem through the wing mirror as the driver drove down a slip road.

The mobile phone rang. The driver answered in Dutch. He swung sharp right down into what looked like an industrial estate and after half a mile pulled to a halt. Rudolph looked around, wondering what the hell was happening. Then he noticed the driver pointing a gun at him.

'What the fu–?'

'Give me please your mobile telephone.'

'Phone? What d'yer want me phone for?'

In the back of the van the two armed policemen had been phoned by Bert Kromkamp and made aware that an attempt had been made to stop them. They were told that Kromkamp had contacted the driver and that the van had escaped the thieves and was heading for the airport. What the policemen didn't know was why the van had stopped.

In the front the driver's eyes narrowed with impatience as Rudolph made no move to give him the phone. 'Listen, big man. You had better know that I have no time to waste.' The driver stuck the barrel of the gun into Rudolph's face.

'OK, OK, take it easy man.' Rudolph took out his mobile and handed it to the man.

'Get out.'

Without a word of protest Rudolph opened the door and heaved his great bulk down on to the road. The van sped away leaving the big black man with no clue as to where he was and no means of contacting anyone. Shit! This had been very simple. Fat lot of good Carew had been. He hadn't even been there.

Back on the A4 Bert Kromkamp, after stopping to make sure the downed policemen were OK, drove the Mercedes on to the airport where they and the men in the Lexus were eventually given clearance to take the car straight to where the Learjet was parked. Sam was waiting for them. The news had reached him that the security van had now disappeared without trace; the two policemen in the back weren't answering their mobiles; neither was the driver; neither was Rudolph.

Sam helped Sally out of the car with obvious relief on his face. Her safety was of more value to him than the Rembrandt. His head was bandaged where he'd been concussed by a bicycle the previous night.

'You OK, Sal?'

'I'm OK. Does anyone know what happened to the security van?'

'Not yet, what happened?'

Stuke came around the car. 'The coppers on the motorbikes were shot with some sort of drugged darts. We nearly ran them over. The van just took off.'

'The van driver had to be in on it,' guessed Sam, looking at Kromkamp. 'Either that or Rudolph's got a gun to your man's head.'

'It won't be Rudolph,' said Stuke. 'He's not that smart or he wouldn't be a steroid junkie.' He looked at Sam. 'I assume you noticed?'

'I did wonder,' Sam admitted.

Kromkamp quickly absolved himself of all blame. 'Our driver is an employee, just like me. His credentials will have been scrutinised, but not by me.'

The three of them looked at the men getting out of the Lexus. Frickers had a face like thunder. 'Where's the bloody van with the painting?'

A police car skidded to a halt behind them. Two uniformed officers got out. One of them, an inspector, walked up to Kromkamp, who was the tallest and most important looking man there. Very agitated, the policeman took a deep breath and announced, 'The Rembrandt has been stolen!'

He made his announcement with the same solemnity as he would the assassination of Queen Beatrix. Frickers and Weston shook their heads.

Frickers took out his phone, let out a deep sigh and dialled a number as the inspector related what had happened.

'Our two officers were disarmed and forced out of the van at gunpoint, then the thieves drove away. We suspect we'll find it shortly, but sadly with its precious cargo missing.' He turned to Sam and Stuke and remarked, with a hint of censure, 'A British security man was found at the roadside.'

'A *Dutch* security man was driving the van,' retorted Stuke. 'We're guessing he's one of the gang.'

The inspector nodded. 'One of our men is unaccounted for. The others do not know what has happened to him.' He sighed, deeply. 'This theft will be regarded as a national tragedy.'

'And I think you'll find you've acted in contravention of the terms and conditions of the policy,' Alan Weston told them. Frickers was still on the phone, but nodding his confirmation of this.

Sam jabbed a thumb in the direction of the Learjet. 'In that case it's just as well it's in the plane,' he said, casually. He inclined his head in the direction of a builder's van parked nearby, the one that had worried the two policemen in the museum grounds. 'I brought it in that van. The precious cargo in the security van was an empty wooden crate. I'm guessing it'll be a bit of a bummer when the villains open it.'

Sally grinned, as did Frances, Stuke and Kromkamp. Frickers told whoever he was talking to to hold the line for a moment. The police inspector's face contorted into an odd mixture of relief, amazement and annoyance.

'The Rembrandt is not stolen?'

'No, it's in the plane.'

Frickers and Weston hurried over to the aircraft

to see for themselves. After a few seconds Frickers came to the door and called out, angrily.

'Why the hell didn't you tell us what you were doing?'

'Because we don't like you,' said Sally.

'The whole point of the plan,' Sam explained, reasonably, 'was that as many people as possible who were involved with the transfer of the painting would think it was in the security van. That way, if there was an inside man working with the would-be thieves he wouldn't smell a rat.'

'And there *was* an inside man,' said Sally.

'When did you think of that?' Frickers asked, sourly.

'It came to me last night,' Sam said, 'in a coffee bar.'

'So, who knew about it?'

'Just the four people in the Merc and the copper who came with me in the builder's van.'

'Do you realise how much anxiety you've put me and Mr Weston through?'

'I didn't, actually – that comes as an unexpected bonus.'

Sally, Stuke, Frances and Kromkamp all tried to hide smiles. Frickers opened his mouth to say something, thought better of it then went back inside the aircraft. The police inspector was struggling for something to say.

'So … do you know where our missing man is?'

'Ah, yes,' said Sam. 'He came with me. He had to get changed to look the part. He was the only one of your people who knew what was happening. Like I said, it was all done on a need-to-know basis.'

97

A sheepish-looking man in work clothes got out of the driver's side of the builder's van. 'Sorry, sir, I didn't have time to clear it with you.'

'It was all very last minute,' Sam explained. 'I got to the museum early this morning and got talking to some of the builders. I asked them if I could borrow their van for half a day. They charged two hundred euros – cheeky sods! Mind you, they'll have to come and pick it up themselves. I forgot to mention that.'

The Rembrandt was wrapped in a simple, white sheet. As the pilot warmed up the engines and waited for clearance Sam lifted up the sheet, rested the painting against the empty seat facing him and sat back to enjoy his own private eighty million pound art exhibition.

'I didn't realise you were that much of an art lover,' remarked Rudolph, sitting behind Sam. He'd been oddly effusive in his praise of Sam's ingenuity that day.

Sam smiled. 'It's just that I've had a bad feeling about this job and it hasn't gone away – it's probably just me. Anyway I just want to keep my eye on it if no one minds.'

'Well, so far you've saved someone eighty million quid,' Stuke said. He glanced back at the insurance men and added, 'Not sure who that someone is. It doesn't look like Morgan Blackstone would have coughed up.'

Frickers and Weston said nothing. They'd said too much already.

Sam didn't let the painting go out of his sight or his reach until it was safely handed over to Unsworth Museum of Art. The first part of his job was done, but he still felt uneasy. Before Sam left, Stuke handed over a cheque for £3,000, insisting that he had already earned his bonus.

The following day Mr Kromkamp rang Stuke to tell him that the Amsterdam police had found the van burnt out but they didn't hold out much hope of catching the perpetrators who had been highly organised and professional. But even the most highly organised and professional of criminal minds couldn't cater for the unorganised mind like that of Mr Carew who, incidentally, had had traces of marijuana in his blood, according to the Saint Lucas hospital.

CHAPTER TWELVE

Sam had his feet up on his desk. Sally hated this, especially as he'd just been visiting a muddy site to read the riot act to a new bricklaying gang who thought Sam's partner, Alec, was a soft touch. Alec wasn't a soft touch, but neither was he a brickie. As far as he was concerned if Sam wasn't available to lay bricks the least he could do was to call on site to hand out a necessary bollocking to the brickies who were replacing him. The phone rang. Sally answered it and immediately pressed the mute button.

'It's Mrs Ormerod, are you in?'

Sam gave it a couple of seconds' thought, then picked up his extension.

'Tracey.'

'Sam, I thought I was paying for your exclusive services.'

He had half expected this, and was therefore prepared. 'There's a connection.' A simple lie was better than an argument. No one had a right to his exclusive services. Being self-employed meant being free of such exclusivity.

'Oh, right.' There was hope in her voice. His lie had given her hope. Damn! She had made her own connection. 'Is it something to do with Rudolph?'

'No, it's nothing to do with Rudolph.'

'It's just that I read about Rudolph being involved, and with him being a friend of Jim I...' She paused. 'It *is* something to do with Rudolph, isn't it? Sam, if he had something to do with Ally's death I want to know.'

Sam reacted, sharply. 'As far as I know he had nothing to do with Alistair's death. Look, I don't want to appear rude, but I carry out investigations my own way and I'm answerable to no one.' He let a silence hang between them for a few moments, to let the implied ultimatum sink in, then he softened his tone. 'Tracey, because we're old mates I'll do you a special deal – no result no fee. If I get Jim out of the clink you pay me twenty grand, if not there's no charge.'

Sally raised a critical eyebrow at this. It was a most unprofessional way of working but it gave Sam the upper hand with his client. Tracey wouldn't want to irritate him now. He heard her giggle on the other end of the phone.

'Old mates? Is that what we are? I suppose it is. It was definitely the mating season when I went out with you.'

Sally looked up, even though she wasn't listening in. Sam figured she had a sixth sense about these things. He put on his business face. 'Apart from that, Mrs Ormerod, this investigation will be conducted on a strictly professional basis.'

'Mr Carew, I wouldn't dream of having it any other way.'

But there was no sincerity in Tracey's voice. She could be a worry, Sam thought. The Tracey Ormerods of this world would always be a bit much for him. He put the phone down and sensed Sally's eyes on him.

'She's still got the hots for you.'

'How...?' Sam didn't finish his question. There were some things that women like Sally just knew.

'When you told her there's a connection, what did you mean?'

He shook his head. 'She was going on about me going to Amsterdam on her time – it was a lame excuse.'

'You shouldn't have to make lame excuses. But that thing about there being a connection came out very readily, as if it had crossed your mind as being true.'

Sam looked up at her and wondered how the hell she knew such stuff. 'How the hell do you know these things?'

She gave a thoughtful shrug. 'You and I have been through some fairly extreme situations. Maybe that's given me an insight into how your mind works. Maybe it means that sometimes I know you better than you know yourself.'

I hope not, Sam thought. 'I don't know why I

think there's a connection,' he said. 'I mean, I *can* make a connection, but if you spread your net wide enough you can tie almost anyone in with any crime.'

'How wide do you have to spread this net?'

Sam puffed out his cheeks and shook his head. 'Not very wide as it happens. Rudolph's the obvious connection, then there's one of his Syndicate mates, Dave, he's some sort of art dealer, then there's the murder of another member, who happens to be a solicitor.'

'Maybe Alistair Waring was murdered because he found out what was planned and threatened to blow the whistle,' surmised Sally. 'Maybe Stuke was involved and managed to get word to Rudolph at the last minute that the Rembrandt wasn't in the security van, only not in time to stop the ambush, which turned out to be a bit lame, don't you think? Almost as if the van driver and Rudolph changed their version of the plans at the last minute?'

He allowed Sally to digest these theories as he lit a cigarette. He offered her one but she refused. She was stopping smoking again.

'I'm surprised *you* still smoke,' she commented, pointedly, 'after what happened.'

He studied the burning end of his cigarette, remembering. Then stubbed it out. 'You're quite right. I keep trying to stop – I'll use the memory as an incentive.'

The phone rang. It was Alec saying the brickies had taken umbrage at the way Sam had given them a bollocking and had walked off the site. They were on a tight schedule, would Sam fill in for a couple of days until he got proper replacements? He said it in such a way as to leave Sam with no option but to say he would. He swung his feet off the desk.

'Meanwhile,' he said, 'Sam Carew, ace detective and righter of wrongs is back on the tools. And you, Miss Grover, can get your shapely arse into gear and find a two and one gang who have actually worked on a building site before.'

'In the meantime Alec wants you to do the work of three men, does he?'

Sam held out his arms, expansively. 'Alec runs the building side of the Carew empire and he knows my true worth. What I need you to do is find two bricklayers and one labourer who can replace me.'

'And what about your theory regarding the murder connection?'

'I can expand on my theory as I lay one brick on top of the other. If Tracey rings tell her I'm in meditation mode.'

'I'll tell her nothing of the sort. By the way I think your theory had quite a few holes in it.'

'So do I, but it's the bits between the holes I need to think about. There's a connection there somewhere but it's so tenuous I can't quite grasp it. I need to keep digging. I need to investigate all the members of the Syndicate, and I need to go a bit deeper into Alistair's background.'

'Have you completely discounted the fact that Jim might have done it?'

'Nope, I haven't discounted anything. All I know is that a massive theft has been attempted and there's a connection with a murdered solicitor.'

'Will you mention this to Owen?'

'I certainly will, but there'll be no need to mention it to any other coppers, especially Bowman.'

'I thought things were OK between you and Bowman now.'

Sam grinned. 'Things will never be right between me and Bowman. It's the natural order of things.'

CHAPTER THIRTEEN

The Rembrandt took pride of place between an Atkinson Grimshawe and a Holman Hunt, both on loan from Leeds City Art Gallery.

It was on a small podium just feet away from the Dutch Master that Detective Inspector Bowman made a speech in his capacity as one of the gallery's trustees. The room was crowded to capacity with civic dignitaries, local businessmen and professional people, the local and national press and West Yorkshire Police Divisional Commander (Unsworth) – here on Bowman's personal invitation. It was designed to be the next step towards his regaining his rank as detective chief inspector. A rank he'd been relieved of the previous year. It could have been worse. Sam had once been demoted from detective sergeant to bricklayer as a result of his own stupidity – and Bowman's malice. Sam glanced, proprietorially, at the painting, which wouldn't have been there had it not been for him. On the journey back from Amsterdam he'd grown to really like it. He'd developed an empathy with it that few other people probably had over the years. The old guy in the picture didn't look like a world-famous artist, he looked like a vulnerable old man who needed a break. Like most old men he wouldn't have minded a shot at recapturing his youth for a while. He looked like old Billy Batley who used to sell the *Observer* outside Unsworth Town Hall. It was the look Billy gave you if you didn't give him the right money and then hung around, waiting for him to fiddle in his bag for change. He would fiddle about until you told him to keep it. Yes, Sam had grown to like the old man in the picture. Funny how he looked different today, hung on a wall in a favourable light, old man Rembrandt didn't look quite so appealing. No way would Sam let this old man keep the change.

'My Lord Mayor, distinguished guests, ladies and gentlemen,' began Bowman. Sam shuffled nearer the Rembrandt. He was moving along the edge of Bowman's vision and earned himself a reproachful glance from the officer who had been the reason Sam had to leave the force due to a misdemeanour, which had caused Bowman much electrical discomfort. Sam stopped moving and smiled at the DI, who continued his speech. 'It's a great honour to be asked to speak at the opening of this bicentennial exhibition to which galleries from the whole of Great Britain and Europe have contributed, such is the international esteem in which the Unsworth Museum of Art is held. Examples of almost every period of art are represented here from the Renaissance to

David Hockney.'

Sam felt like asking him a question about the Renaissance as he had a strong feeling that Bowman wouldn't know a Raphael from a Rolf Harris.

'But the pride of the exhibition has to be the Dutch masterpiece on the wall behind me.'

All eyes were now on the Rembrandt as Bowman began to describe it, using almost exactly the same words as Sally had used in Amsterdam. Sam guessed he'd read the same brochure.

'The title of the painting is *Self Portrait as the Apostle Paul* and is, of course, by Rembrandt van Rijn. It is the first painting of himself as an historical figure. Rembrandt was of course a master of the chiaroscuro effect...' He gave a contrived, apologetic smile. Sam figured he'd forgotten the rest of his spiel. 'But you don't need me rambling on when the evidence of this wonderful exhibition is right before your eyes. I need only add that until the exhibition comes to a close the Unsworth police will be ensuring that no harm comes to any of these priceless exhibits. As you know we almost lost the Rembrandt to thieves whilst it was in transit to this exhibition. But I would point out that had the Unsworth police been on the job it's doubtful if the thieves would have even bothered to make the attempt–'

'It's not the same painting.'

All eyes turned to Sam who had now approached to within inches of the Rembrandt. He shook his head and turned around, trying to locate Frances Fowler. She was excusing herself to the Lord Mayor of Unsworth as she pushed past him.

'It's not the same painting,' Sam repeated.

'What do you mean?' said Frances.

'I mean this isn't the painting we brought from Amsterdam. Look at the end of his nose. In the real painting there's a bit missing. I couldn't tell if it was a big pock-mark in Rembrandt's nose or just a bit of paint that had flaked off.'

Frances rubbed the back of her neck as she examined the painting. 'I really don't know,' she said.

'Carew, what the hell are you playing at?' seethed Bowman, whose moment had been stolen from him. 'Since when were you an art expert?'

Frances looked at Sam, whose judgement she'd learnt to respect. 'Are you sure, Sam? If it's not the real thing it's a hell of a good fake.'

'All I know is that this is not the painting I brought back from Amsterdam. Why not compare it with the reproduction in the brochure?'

'Good idea. That's definitely taken from the one in Amsterdam.'

A brochure was produced and both Frances and Sam made the comparison as the bemused crowd looked on. 'Feel free to take a look around the exhibition,' Bowman called out. 'And I don't mean the exhibition that Mr Carew is making of himself.' He waited for the laugh but none was forthcoming. Nobody moved. They all knew the implications if the painting borrowed from Amsterdam had been stolen. Frances walked to a chair and sat down, white-faced, as other gallery officials came through to examine the painting, comparing it to the brochure.

Sam stood back, awaiting what he knew to be the inevitable. On closer examination the two paintings were different in so many ways. Within minutes everyone had come to the same conclusion. The Rembrandt was a forgery. The Divisional Commander edged Bowman off the podium.

'Ladies and gentlemen,' he said, in a voice that boomed off the gallery walls. 'It appears we have a major problem that necessitates the closure of the gallery. Would you all kindly move out of this room and as soon as possible, but please remain in the gallery until we require you to leave.'

Sam stepped to the side of Frances. 'Do you want me to stay?' he enquired. She nodded. Sam looked at Bowman. 'I've been asked to stay,' he said.

'I'm telling you to leave,' Bowman snapped. He blamed this on Carew. Why? He didn't know. All he knew was that Carew was to blame for much that went wrong in his life.

'The curator wants me to stay,' Sam addressed himself to the divisional commander. 'I was in charge of security when it was brought here from Amsterdam.'

'Then stay.'

'He could be a suspect,' Bowman pointed out.

'In that case you won't want to let me out of your sight during the initial investigation,' said Sam, reasonably.

'I want every available detective put on this immediately,' ordered the commander, brusquely. He turned to face Bowman. 'God knows why you brought me here. It would have been far better for this to have happened without immediate police presence. This way it looks as if it's been taken from under our noses.'

Not for the first time Bowman could have cheerfully throttled Sam, who was looking at Rudolph, who was fairly obviously trying to avoid eye contact. Pieces of jigsaw whirled around in Sam's head. Rudolph's face was on one of them. He couldn't fit it in with the main picture, far too many pieces were missing – pretty much all of them. Rudolph shuffled his feet, uncomfortable as Sam's eyes bore into him. He weaved his way in and out of the departing guests and stood beside the large black man.

'Got to hand it to you, Rudolph,' he said in a low voice, from the side of his mouth. 'Your lot are far better than the amateurs in Amsterdam. How the hell did you do it?'

'Don't know what you're talking about.'

'Bad answer,' murmured Sam.

'What?'

'Rudolph, you're a security guard. Your integrity is paramount. You're supposed to be highly indignant at such a slanderous accusation. Livid even. You should make a complaint about my disgraceful behaviour to someone – maybe one of those nice policemen. Try DI Bowman, he hates my guts.'

'Fuck off, Sam,' muttered Rudolph.

'A more convincing answer,' said Sam, 'but it came too late. Where are you thinking of hanging it – over the fireplace? I thought you were more a "dogs-playing-pool" man myself.'

'Bollocks.'

'Let's see,' mused Sam, rubbing his chin, thoughtfully. He kept his voice low so that only Rudolph could hear. 'The frame would have been

109

easy to replicate – it was fairly plain. And there are quite a few artists about who can do impressive copies of fairly straightforward paintings such as this – there's only the face that'd require any real skill. And there was glass over the painting which would make it more difficult to see the brush-work. This is clever stuff, Rudolph. Hmm, I don't wish to insult you but I think someone a bit higher up the food chain thought this one up. How long did you think it would take before an art expert such as me rumbled you?'

Rudolph walked away from him, thinking, *Shit! How come he knows?* He ran the events of last night through his head, trying to see if there had been any slip ups.

The artist, who lived in Amsterdam, had been paid three thousand euros by a buyer who had ordered the copy painting over the phone. It had been collected by a courier. Dave had gone on the artist's reputation as a copyist and had taken the risk of buying it unseen but they all agreed it was the dog's bollocks. How anyone could spot it was a fake without giving it close examination, God only knows.

There were as many paintings in the basement storage rooms of the Unsworth Gallery as there were on display. Rudolph had let Dave and Shane in through a service entrance and led them to the bottom of the steps which would take them up to a gallery adjacent to the one where the Rembrandt hung. He had pointed out the main fuse box and, in particular, the one fusing the cables that powered the cameras.

'Like I said, the cameras have got their own

110

circuit,' he told them. 'It's a crap system but it suits us fine. Ya turn off dis switch and ya turn the cameras off. It takes a minute before the auxiliary power kicks in. Ya got one minute ter do the switch. I'll be watchin' the monitors wid me mate Carl and a couple of other guys. Well, we'll be playin' brag actually, but it'll be hard ter miss sixteen screens goin' blank. I'll do a bit o' cursin' an' I'll check the power from dat end. The auxiliary power kicks in after exactly one minute. But by dat time ya should be back down here and have switched the normal power back on.'

'What are you supposed to be doing right now?' Dave asked him.

'Me an' Carl are supposed ter be patrollin' the place. Dis is part of me patrol. We swap over wid the guys in control at midnight. There'll be at least fifteen minutes when there's no one in the gallery. All of us will be drinkin' tea and playin' a few hands o' brag. I'll send you a text just after midnight. Ya do the switch straight away. Ya got one minute ta do it. Like I told ya the paintin' is just hooked on to a long chain. One picture off, one picture on, one minute. It's a piece o' piss, man.'

'I hope you're right,' breathed Dave. His heart was picking up speed.

'Jus' make sure it's straight when ya leave it,' Rudolph warned. 'And make sure ya wear shoe covers, we don't want ter leave no footprints leadin' ter this door.'

'Rudolph, I know all about shoe covers and gloves and masks,' Dave said, irritably. 'All I'm worried about is time.' He glanced at the stop watch in his hand and flicked it on. All three

111

watched the seconds tick away as Rudolph talked them through the sequence of events. He had them back down the cellar steps by the time Dave had pressed for one minute.

'See, a minute's a long time, man,' grinned Rudolph. 'Just think of the last minute of extra time when Unsworth Town is tryin' ter defend a one goal lead. Man, dat minute lasts forever.'

'I can't remember the last time Unsworth Town had a one goal lead,' muttered Dave. 'Right, we'll be standing by to turn the power off at midnight. You prepare a text message and press *Send* when we're good to go.'

'No problem, man,' Rudolph assured him. 'Just remember ter lock the gallery door and the outside door behind ya wid the keys I had made and switch the power switch back when ya come back down here.'

'I know that as well,' said Dave, who was supposed to be running the show.

At five past twelve Dave was standing behind the unlocked door to the gallery, the fake painting was resting on the floor by his side – his mobile vibrated in his hand, the words Go, Go, Go came up on the screen. He and Shane both pulled balaclavas down over their faces – as a precaution in case the cameras came on. Dave nodded to Shane, who was standing by the fuse box at the bottom of the steps. Shane flicked the switch and ran up the stairs, Dave opened the door and within ten seconds he had leant the fake Rembrandt against the gallery wall and was helping Shane lift the real one off its hook. After thirty seconds the fake was in place and Shane was adjusting it to straight in accordance with Dave's guidance. After fifty seconds they were locking the door behind them and after sixty seconds Shane switched the power back on before the auxiliary power kicked in.

Up in the control room the screens came back to life, ending a minute of mild anxiety from the guards who had been watching Rudolph fiddle with the wall plugs.

'This whole place needs rewiring,' he was grumbling when the screens came back on. 'Ah – I tink it was maybe a power surge.' They all returned to their tea and the game of brag, the incident forgotten. Rudolph would be off duty at two. He would leave through a back door that didn't necessitate him going through the galleries or the storage basement. He needed to keep the finger of suspicion pointed as far away from him as possible.

So it came as a great source of shock to him when Sam Carew suspected him straight away. They'd carried out the perfect heist. What right did Carew have to suspect him?

CHAPTER FOURTEEN

'How the hell does he know?'

Rudolph answered Dave's question with a shrug of his huge shoulders, then added, 'Search me, man. He looks at you like he can read your mind. He sussed me out on the way back from Amsterdam. Told me I was lucky the painting wasn't snatched or the Dutch police would have had me in the frame.'

'Did he suspect you were one of the Amsterdam gang?'

'No, man, he did not. Told me I hadn't been behaving like a man involved. But I guessed he figured me for somethin'.'

'How d'you mean?'

'He's a friendly guy but he never got real friendly wid me. I always felt he had me figured for a thief, man.'

'Maybe he's a racist.'

'Nah, I can smell a racist a mile off, man. In the gallery dis guy spotted the switch before all the experts.'

'I must admit I thought it'd take 'em a bit longer,' admitted Dave. 'Still, it makes no difference in the long run.'

'When do we get our money?' enquired Shane.

'Before we let go of the painting,' Dave said. 'They've asked to see it and I've asked to see the money.'

The three of them were in Shane's flat. The robbery was currently the talk of West Yorkshire. The painting had been taken out of its frame, the canvas unpinned from the wooden stretcher and loosely rolled up in a 12" diameter cardboard tube. Anything tighter, Dave had said, might crack the heavy impasto. The tube was in a security deposit box in Leeds to which there were four keys, one for each of them. Alistair's key had been discussed. Should they be worried about it? Should they move the painting? No, was the unanimous decision. There was nothing on the

114

keys to identify the lock.

'These London blokes can be a bit dodgy,' Shane remarked. 'We still don't know if it was them who topped Ally – he was the one who made the contact with them. They think it's all cloth caps and stew up here. We definitely need to be ready for them.'

'Do you really tink them guys topped Ally?' Rudolph asked Dave. 'Personally I can't see anyone else in the frame.'

'If they did it doesn't make any sense,' said Dave. 'No sense at all.'

'Maybe they think we'll be a softer touch?' suggested Shane.

Dave shook his head. 'Shane, we've just nicked one of the world's most valuable paintings from under the noses of the filth – they're not gonna take us for a bunch of yokels.' He lit a cigar and gathered his thoughts. 'My plan is that both parties come three-handed, and first check that no one on either side is tooled up. The exchange will take place in a car park. The painting will be in the boot of one of the parked cars. I'll show them which one when the preliminaries have been taken care of and the money counted.

'You, Shane, will have parked the car an hour previously. Their team will probably include a heavy and an art expert, pretty much the same as ours. I'm guessing they'll want the deal to go smoothly. Just like us.'

'What about counting the money?' Rudolph asked. Now the hard work was done he was thinking about the practicalities. 'If we're asking for the money in used twenties it's gonna take a while to count out four million.'

'You and me go to the meeting in a van,' Dave said. 'I'll be taking a money counting machine. Me and Shane'll do the counting in the back. It won't take all that long. We count out one mil and check that there's three more piles the same size. We do a rough check on these piles to make sure they're all pukka twenties – I'm also taking a machine to check for dodgy notes. This, they know about. I've also told them I'm going to count every note. One dodgy note and the deal's off. I doubt they'll try anything on. They don't get to see the painting until the money's counted and agreed. The thing is, they want to buy the painting even more than we want to sell it. They'll want the deal to go smoothly.'

'What happens to Ally's share?'

'We split it,' Dave told Shane, without hesitation. 'With the best will in the world we can't be giving a mystery million to Ally's sister. Let's face it – it's what he would have done to us.'

'What about Jim and Manny?' Rudolph asked.

'What about them?'

Rudolph shrugged, he wasn't quite sure why he'd brought them up. 'Nuthin', man.'

'We kept them out of the team for good reason,' said Dave. 'Jim's got enough money to handle his own defence, and Manny's an idiot. He cheated with his score last Saturday – I don't know whether any of you noticed. He was hacking away in the rough on the sixth and when I asked him how many he'd taken he said five. He took at least seven to my knowledge.'

'He does it all the time,' Shane said. 'If he did

it playing with anyone else he'd get reported to the committee and booted out.'

'The man's a cheatin' bastard,' grumbled Rudolph. 'And he's tight. I don't know why we let him play with us.'

'He plays with us,' said Dave, 'because you asked him to make up a four-ball about three years ago and we can't shake the bugger off. I wouldn't trust him as far as I can throw him. Plus he hasn't got the bottle. No way could we have trusted him to be a part of this.'

'The reason I asked for this meet is because I got a call from London this morning.'

'So, the exchange is organised?' said Shane. It was the day after. They were back in his flat. Dave shook his head.

'The bastards are trying it on. They've reduced the price to three million.'

'Shit!' exploded Rudolph. 'I hope ya told him ter fuck off.'

'Pretty much. Trouble is it's pretty much a buyer's market and they know it. He told me it was because we'd lost one of our team and wouldn't need the extra million.'

'It's probably their fault we lost one of our team,' said Shane. 'Did you mention that to him?'

'I said we couldn't think of anyone but them who could have done it.'

'And?'

'He said they couldn't think of anyone but *us* who'd want to do it.'

'What? They think we did it?'

'I actually don't know what they think. Look, I

don't know these people. They've got my mobile number, that's the only contact I have.'

'Do they know who *we* are?' enquired Rudolph, nervously.

'Not as far as I know. But then again they weren't supposed to know who Alistair was. It was all done through this client of his who he helped get off a building society robbery charge.'

'Billy Hargrave,' remembered Rudolph. 'Two men went down, Billy walked – and none of the money was recovered.'

'Do we have any clues as to where Billy Hargrave is now?' Shane asked.

'Disappeared off the face of the earth as far as I can tell,' said Dave.

'Maybe he's six feet *under* the earth,' remarked Shane, ominously.

Rudolph gave him a wide-eyed stare. 'Shit, man! Dis puts us in a bad position. I never expected no shit like dis. Why don't we just go for the 3 million?'

Shane answered Rudolph's question. 'Because they've just proved their word means nothing.' He looked at Dave. 'I say we ring the bastards back and give them 24 hours to come up with the full 4 million or the deal's off and we take the reward off the insurance company.'

'Reward, what reward?' said Rudolph, hopefully.

'The reward they're bound to make,' said Dave. 'Shane's right, but the insurers won't offer a proper reward until there's no hope of the police getting it back. By the way, I can't ring them, I don't have a number.'

'Withheld their number?' guessed Shane.

Dave nodded and said, 'Always do. So, until they make contact we go about our normal business. If the filth comes sniffing round we obviously don't know anything. They've no need to pull any of us in, even you, Rudolph. If Sam Carew gives you any grief, just tell him to piss off.'

'Might give him a slap as well. He told me I should react more strongly to his accusations.'

CHAPTER FIFTEEN

It was raining as Billy Hargrave pulled up at traffic lights near his new home in Preston. The front and rear passenger doors opened and closed. Two men got in. It was done so casually that it aroused no suspicion or interest from the car behind.

'Bloody weather! By heck, yer took some trackin' down, Billy,' said the man in the front, cheerfully. 'We had ter get some friends in the West Yorkshire Police to look you up on their computer. Cost us a grand, that did. A grand that'll come out of our wages.'

'Who the fuck are you?'

'We're your business associates. Just drive on, Billy.'

'Look, if it's ter do with the buildin' society brass I've put the other shares ter one side. If the lads inside want me to hand it over to their wives, I will. So far they don't seem so keen.'

'We're not interested in yer little odd jobs, Billy. Our bosses are a bit more concerned about a

119

picture what's gone missing.'

'What are yer – insurance men or summat?' He turned to look at them. 'Yer don't look like no insurance men ter me. Anyroad, I don't know what yer talkin' about. What picture?'

The men laughed. 'That's the spirit, Billy, keep schtum. That's what we want. Yer the only link between our bosses and the thieves. Bad things, links, Billy. If there's one thing a boss hates it's a link. Yer see, our bosses know who the thieves are, but the thieves don't know who our bosses are. Trouble is, you know who both of 'em are. See the problem, Billy?'

'Well, they've no need to worry about me. I've said nowt ter nobody.'

'That's what we've heard, Billy Hargrave knows how ter keep his mouth shut.'

'That's right. I'm norra fuckin' amateur y'know. Been at this game too long ter go shootin' me mouth off.'

'We know that, Billy,' remarked Billy's front seat companion, amiably. 'In fact we know all sorts of things.'

They arrived at another set of lights. Billy stopped, pulled on his handbrake and asked, 'What sort of things?'

'Well, I'll tell yer one of the things we know. We know there are no CCTV cameras along this stretch of road? Did you know that, Billy?'

'No, I didn't.'

'It's the sort of thing we check on. Well, we have to in our line of business.' The man opened the door and began to get out. 'See you, Billy.'

Billy looked across at his departing passenger.

'What exactly is your line of busi–'

His query was cut short by the man behind him who held a silenced gun to the back of Billy's head and pulled the trigger. The bullet came out through his mouth and smashed into the radio, splattering the windscreen with blood and cutting off one of Terry Wogan's wisecracks. The two men got out of the car, waved fond farewells to the driver, closed the doors behind them and walked casually away before anyone in the queue of traffic noticed anything was wrong.

Billy's death had two purposes: it closed a security loophole and it sent a clear message to the art thieves about how serious their clients were. Contact would be made in two days, when these thick Yorkshire thieves would be ready to make any kind of deal.

CHAPTER SIXTEEN

'I got a text saying "Await instructions re: RVR. Hargrave was a warning",' said Dave.

'RVR?' queried Rudolph.

'Rembrandt van Rijn.'

They had all read the report on Billy's mysterious murder. 'I'm guessing they don't know who we are,' said Shane. 'If they did I reckon it would have been one of us who got topped.'

'That is some guess, man!' said Rudolph. 'But I don' want ter risk my life on one of your guesses. I want cast-iron certainties, man.'

'Them paying out three million isn't a cast-iron certainty,' said Dave. 'They've topped two men so far. What's to stop them topping two more? Whoever's left will hand over the painting just to save his skin? I know I would.'

'Supposing,' suggested Shane, 'you tell them only one of us knows where the painting is? Don't say why. But they'll know that if they top the wrong man, it's lost forever.'

Dave ran the idea through his mind, nodding eventually. 'It's actually quite an idea.'

'Would they believe it?' asked Rudolph.

'Can they afford *not* to believe it?' Dave said. 'I won't antagonise them. I'll settle for the three million and throw that piece of information in fairly casually. They'll ask who it is that knows, I'll ask them why they want to know.'

'When are they due to contact us again?' Shane asked.

'No idea. I think they'll let us stew for a while, with the memory of Billy Hargrave to think about.'

Manny's car lot was more of a fenced-off compound with an ancient caravan for an office. His most expensive car, a rusting 1993 Sierra, was marked up at £595 ono. Manny had bought it as a non-runner from the car auctions for £50. Not only did it now run but it also had a dodgy MOT certificate. As were all his cars it would be *sold as seen* with no come-backs on the vendor. Manny would take the prospective purchaser for a trial run along a nearby road which was unique for its lack of pot holes and speed bumps and offer to knock £200 off the price and sell at a loss because he was running short of space on his lot. With luck the car would run far enough to take the new owner beyond walking distance of Manny. Sam was browsing when Manny spotted him through the window.

'Nice little runner that, sir. Is it for the lady wife?'

Sam realised he was standing by a Polo that looked to have less life in it than the mint of the same name. It was marked up at £495 ono.

'What sort of an offer would you take?' he asked curiously.

Manny rubbed his face and stared at the car. 'Doubt if I could do much better than four fifty. It's got three months' tax and a bit of ticket left on it.'

'Ticket?'

'That's what we in the trade call MOT, sir. I don't think it expires until the end of next month, so it's a drive away bargain. Tell you what. Give me four and a half and I'll put it through its test. A full year's ticket. I can't say fairer than that. Would you like me to start her up, sir?'

'Not really.' He looked up from the car and gave Manny a broad smile. 'My name is Carew. I've been engaged by the Morgan Blackstone insurance company to investigate a theft.'

Manny's salesman's smile dropped from his face like the oil from the Polo's gearbox. 'A theft? Well I can assure you that none of my motors are stolen. I have all the documentation in my office.'

Sam maintained his own smile, but it was a smile that was designed to unnerve. 'I'm sure you have, Mr Green. But it's not a stolen car I'm investigating.' He was sure Manny would be mixed up in

123

all sorts of dodgy business. He already had form for receiving stolen goods – Owen had told Sam that much. Whether or not he was up to handling an eighty million pound painting was debatable. But maybe he'd had a hand in it.

Manny took a step back as Sam's slightly manic gaze bore into him. 'What?' he protested. 'What are you talking about?'

Sam watched Manny's eyes and took a step towards him. 'I'm talking about a Rembrandt painting, Manny.'

The guilt in Manny's eyes turned to relief. Sam could see that as clear as day. Then from relief to annoyance.

'Rembrandt painting? You mean the one what was lifted from the Unsworth Art Gallery last week? Are you pulling my plonker? Piss off, you dozy bastard! If you don't want to buy a motor just say. Have you any idea how many time-wasters I get every day?'

Sam waved a calming hand. 'Naturally I don't think you had anything to do with the theft. But I suspect one of the thieves might know you?'

Manny's face twitched like a curious bird. 'What? You think I might know who nicked it?'

Sam nodded. 'There's a big reward. Even con-tributing towards the painting's recovery would earn you big money – and I'm talking six figures.'

Manny's interest perked up several notches. 'You'd have ter point me in the right direction. I know lots of people. Many of them not too kosher. But I couldn't put a name to a face that might do such a job. If I can help I will.'

Sam considered throwing Rudolph's name into

the conversation then thought better of it. Six figure money might lead to Manny making up stories just on the off-chance that he might hit the jackpot. Sam needed Manny to come up with Rudolph's name without prompting. He needed him to come up with Rudolph's name plus a bit of evidence. All Sam had was a hunch. He gave Manny a card.

'Give me a ring if you think of anyone.'

Dave McLeish's shop was in an arcade in Unsworth town centre. He referred to himself as an art dealer but in fact he made most of his money from framing pictures and selling greetings cards and prints. Original artwork comprised less than a quarter of his turnover, which had been going down for two years since one of a national chain of art shops had opened not far away. Dave himself was an artist of reasonable ability and it was he who had located the Amsterdam copyist and selected the painting to be stolen. His idea in stealing a foreign-owned painting was that the British police might not pursue the thieves with as much enthusiasm as they would if it were a British owned Turner or Constable.

Alistair Waring had arranged the buyer. Dave was serving a customer when Sam walked in. He browsed through an array of prints as he waited. Apart from the other customer he was the only one in the shop. He'd just walked past the competition, which had been extremely busy. It was obvious that McLeish's shop was struggling to survive. The owner might well be in need of a large injection of cash. After Dave had served his

125

customer he called across to Sam.

'Anything in particular you're looking for, sir?'

'Actually, yes.'

Sam walked over to the counter. 'I'm looking for a Rembrandt self-portrait – in particular the one stolen from Unsworth Gallery last week.' As he spoke he watched Dave's eyes for the tell-tale flicker that had been disappointingly absent in Manny's. It wasn't absent in Dave's. His whole face went taut for a second. He frowned as he regained his composure.

'You don't have it, do you?' Sam asked him.

'You mean a copy?'

'Well, I hardly mean the original,' laughed Sam.

'Yes, of course. I er, I'm sure I can order you one. If you'd like to leave me your details I'll get in touch as soon as it comes in.'

'My name is Carew, Sam Carew. I imagine your friend Rudolph has mentioned me to you.'

Another flicker of alarm told Sam he'd probably now identified two of the thieves.

'Rudolph – you mean Rudolph Mace? Yes, we sometimes play golf together, and no, I er, I don't think he's ever mentioned you.'

'No? Then perhaps you might mention me to him,' said Sam, cheerfully. 'I suspect you'll have much to discuss.'

'Morgan Blackstone? Good morning, my name is Carew of the Carew Investigations Bureau. Could I speak to … Mr Michaelson please?'

Sam glanced across the desk at Sally to confirm he had the right name. She'd dug it out for him. Sally was an expert on digging out information in

126

a few minutes that Sam might take an age over. She nodded her confirmation.

'It's about the theft of the Rembrandt from the Unsworth Museum of Art... Yes, I'll hold.'

He tapped his fingers as *Greensleeves* was played down the phone to him. 'What makes them think I want to listen to *Greensleeves*. Why can't they play me a bit of Black Sabb– Ah, Mr Michaelson ... Carew Investigations Bureau... That's correct. Yes, I think I might be of some help in recovering the Rembrandt.' He pulled an angry face as he listened to Michaelson's adverse reaction. Sally waved her hands in a calming manner – telling him to stay cool. He winked at her and nodded.

'Mr Michaelson, despite what Mr Frickers and Mr Weston have to say I would point out that I have a good reputation, which the Unsworth Gallery is aware of.' Sally gave him an approving thumbs up as he continued, politely. 'They're also aware that had it not been for me the painting wouldn't even have reached Unsworth, despite it being accompanied by our Mr Frickers and Mr Weston.' As he listened to Michaelson's more positive response he gave Sally another wink. His words seemed to have hit home. 'My terms will be three per cent of the insurance valuation, plus VAT, and I will work on a no recovery, no fee basis... Good, if my terms are acceptable I'll have my solicitor send you a contract for signature... Yes, with something of this magnitude I think it's best to have a legally binding agreement, don't you?... The contract will have a clause saying that in the event of the painting's recovery, by whomsoever, if our involvement was crucial to its recovery we will be due the full amount. If we are only partly involved then a percentage will have to be decided by an independent arbitrator.'

Sam was quoting notes which Sally had written down for him. His professionalism seemed to impress Michaelson, who was provisionally agreeing to his terms. They discussed details for a while then Sam said his goodbye and put the phone down. He rubbed his hands.

'The tea leaves might have done us a big favour. Three per cent of eighty million is two point four mil.'

'I don't think the thieves will do you any favours, Sam. If they were clever enough to steal it, don't you think they'd have been clever enough to get rid of it straight away. It probably went straight out of the country.'

Sam gave this some thought, then he shook his head. 'No, I don't think so, somehow. I think they're sitting on it until the heat dies down. They haven't changed their daily routine.'

'Wouldn't that be part of their original plan?'

'Probably, but no one sticks rigidly to the original plan when they've suddenly come into a load of dosh. Things alter. I've checked on Rudolph and he hasn't acquired any expensive habits and it doesn't look as if McLeish has either.'

'Maybe that's because Rudolph and Dave weren't involved.'

'If they weren't involved then I'm wasting my time, Sal. But I'm prepared to waste a fair bit of time for a chance of two point four million.'

'Two point four million is a very good point,' agreed Sally. 'I suggest you check out the final member of the Syndicate – Shane Outhwaite.'

Forty minutes later there was a polite knock at the door. Sally went through to the outer office to answer it. The caller was a good-looking young man with perfect teeth and dressed in fashionably scruffy attire.

'Is Mr Crew in?'

'Mr Ca – rew.' Sally emphasised the first syllable, not sure if he'd got Sam's name wrong or whether it was just lazy, student-type speech.

'That's him, Mr Ca-rew. If he's in I'd like to have a word.'

'Who shall I say wants a word with him?'

'My name's Shane Outhwaite. I'm guessing he knows who I am.'

Sally took umbrage at his attitude. 'Is that what you're guessing Mr Outhwaite? I'm guessing I'd better ask him if he wants to speak to you.'

Shane stepped inside the office and sat on a chair. 'I'll wait here then, shall I?'

Sam heard what had been said. He came through. 'What can I do for you, Mr Outhwaite?'

Shane didn't get up. 'I was just passing and I thought I'd pop in and save you a journey.'

Sam remained standing. Sally went through into the main office to demonstrate her total lack of interest in this rude young man. She part closed the door and stood behind it, listening.

'That's very good of you,' Sam said. 'What journey was that?'

'The journey to see me.' Shane stood up now, realising he was at a disadvantage, with Sam towering over him.

129

'To see you? Why would I want to see you?'

Sam was now ahead of him. Shane was here to forestall the inevitable approach which might leave him looking as guilty as Dave and Rudolph, who both suspected they'd betrayed their guilt to him. He was obviously working on the 'attack is the best form of defence' theory. Sam knew it well. He was a great exponent of the art.

'I think we both know the answer to that, Mr Ca – rew.'

Shane mispronounced Sam's name with an insolence which had Sam retaliating. Sally winced at the childishness of this.

'Humour me, Mr Ow-thwaite. Let's pretend I haven't a clue what you're talking about. First of all, tell me who you are. I assume you're in the building trade, looking for work.'

Shane was immediately wrong-footed. He had assumed that Sam would mention the missing Rembrandt to him straight away. It wasn't part of his plan to have to mention it first. What the hell was all this about building work? He was temporarily lost for words.

'Or is it the private investigations side of our business?' Sam asked him. Shane remained mute, not sure how to handle this. 'You're going to have to give me a clue, Mr Outhwaite. I'm many things but I'm not a mind-reader. What brings you here?'

'You went to see Dave McLeish...'

'Dave McLeish, yes I went to see Mr McLeish. So...?'

Shane gathered himself. 'And you spoke to Rudolph Mace.'

'Rudolph? Yes I've spoken to Rudolph.'

130

'So I assumed you'd want to see me.'

'Right...' Sam lit a cigarette then asked, 'Why would I want to see you?'

'Because we're all part of the same group. We er, we play golf together.' Shane was dearly wishing he hadn't come.

'Never played golf,' Sam said. 'Football was my game – well it was until my knee went. Cartilage problems. Still get it, now and again.' He gave a puzzled shake of his head. 'Not sure why I'm supposed to want to see you.'

Sally was grinning gleefully. Sam occasionally played dumb with her. She found it infuriating. Shane would drop his guard any minute. In fact any second. 'You think we stole the Rembrandt,' he blurted.

Sam jumped straight down his throat with, 'How do you mean, I *think* you stole the Rembrandt? Of course you stole the Rembrandt. If you *hadn't* stolen the Rembrandt why on earth would you bother traipsing round here?'

'What?'

'You're trying to get the first one in before I start on you. I asked you what brought you here and now I'll tell you. Guilt brought you here, Mr Outhwaite.'

'What? How do you work that out?'

Sam smiled and held open the door. 'Goodbye, Mr Outhwaite. By the way, you should have got rid of it straight away.'

'How did–?'

Shane stopped himself but he'd said two words too many. He squeezed his eyes, angry with himself. He made to leave. Sam barred his way.

'Look, I can probably arrange for the owners to take no action, provided you return it undamaged. The longer you hang on to it the less likely that is to happen. If you get caught you'll get a massive, massive sentence – commensurate with the value of goods stolen.'

Shane looked at him, dumbfounded. This was not how it was supposed to be. Sam was supposed to back off – embarrassed at having made accusations he couldn't back up with evidence. How the hell did he know they hadn't got rid of it? He pushed his way past Sam and hurried out of the building. Sally came through.

'Wow! He practically admitted it. How the hell do you do that, Carew?'

Sam gave a modest shrug. 'It's a gift. Hey – did you notice he didn't mention the other Syndicate member – Manny Green. I went to see Manny, but I didn't suspect him. If they were *all* innocent, young Outhwaite would have mentioned me speaking to Manny as well as Dave and Rudolph. They obviously haven't asked Manny if we've been to see him, and Manny's seen no reason to mention it to them.'

Sally tried to unravel his logic. 'Carew, you have a strange way of thinking, but you're quite right ... I think.'

'Let's get that contract drawn up with Morgan Blackstone – today if possible.'

Sally clicked her heels and saluted. 'Will do, your highness.'

'Sal, as your boss, your lover and your employer, is there any chance of you treating me with due respect?'

'Don't be ridiculous. Look, there's something I've been meaning to ask you. I've lost track of our on/off betrothal. Are we engaged at the moment?' She gave a wince and added, 'If we are, I think I've lost the ring.'

Sam gave this some thought then shook his head. 'You broke it off just before Easter. You accused me of getting you drunk and you got all silly. You're a very badly behaved drunk if you must know.'

'Did I give you the ring back?'

'No idea what happened to it. I'd had a bit to drink myself. Actually, I think you threw it at me and missed.'

'Blast! I only get drunk once a flood. Did I really do that?'

'Sal, it was two months ago, why bring it up now?'

'If you must know I couldn't remember what had happened to it and I didn't like to ask – it was a very nice ring.'

'It's lost. Sal, the Morgan Blackstone contract. If we get the painting back I'll buy you another ring.'

'Yes, your highness.'

CHAPTER SEVENTEEN

'Jim, long time no see.'

Jim Ormerod wore a yellow plastic sash to identify him as an inmate. 'Two and a half years. I did some snagging work for you on the Beamsley Court job. You had some right cowboys working on that site.'

'That's right,' remembered Sam. 'They only worked for us a few days but they did us a lot of damage – and I remember you doing a good job putting things right.'

Jim sat down in the chair opposite Sam. The visits room in Armley was crowded as usual. 'I'm hoping yer've come to do a bit of snagging fer *me*, Sam. I gather Tracey's offering twenty grand if yer can sort this out. By the way, just so yer know, I didn't kill Alistair.'

'That's the theory I'm working on.'

Jim stuck out his hand, unexpectedly. 'I gather she was having a problem with the gippoes as well.' He spoke in a low voice, for which Sam was grateful. As he shook Jim's hand he wondered if Tracey had told him she'd been raped.

'They'd been giving her trouble.'

'And you sorted it. I just want ter say thanks fer that. They'd got my lad shittin' green snowballs. Too scared ter go ter school.'

Sam decided Jim didn't know about the rape. Perhaps just as well. 'It wasn't me who sorted it, Jim. I had nothing to do with it.'

'Nothing?'

'Nothing.'

'Fair enough. Thanks, anyway.'

'Don't mention it. In fact don't mention it ever again.'

'I won't.'

'Good,' said Sam. 'Right, I'm trying to fathom out why Alistair Waring was killed.' He allowed a benevolent gaze to rest on Jim's face. 'And I want

134

you to tell me if you think there was anything dodgy about him?'

Jim screwed his eyes up, quizzically. 'Anything dodgy about Ally? Are you kidding? He was screwing my wife.'

'Sorry, I'm not making myself clear. What I mean is – well, screwing your wife isn't illegal – do you think he was capable of doing anything illegal?'

'He's arranged quite a few bent mortgages for me in the past.'

'And why would you need bent mortgages?' Sam asked him, curiously.

'I do a bit of buying and selling houses. It's cheaper to get a bent mortgage than pay the interest on a proper business loan – even if I could get a business loan. On top of which you can get 90% finance – but you need a bent solicitor to do it.' Jim gave a dry laugh. 'He used to say he was a man of principle – Ally was as bent as a nine bob note.'

'Would he get mixed up in anything big?'

'Such as?'

'The theft of a valuable painting.'

'What?' Jim shook his head, trying to unravel Sam's thinking. 'You don't mean the one from Unsworth Gallery?'

Sam nodded.

'Bloody hell! You think Ally had something to do with that?'

'Well, I've an idea the thieves knew Alistair.'

'So, you know who the thieves are, do you?'

'Don't you?' Sam asked him, casually, watching his face for a reaction.

135

'Me? How the hell should I know?' Jim looked around the room, then back at Sam. 'What? You think I might have heard something in here?'

'Look, forget it, Jim. It's just a lead, one of many.'

Jim's thoughts were so far off track it was obvious to Sam he knew nothing about the robbery, and he therefore saw no benefit in mentioning his suspicion of Dave, Rudolph or Shane. At least he knew that Alistair Waring hadn't been whiter than white. He had no criminal record, but he sounded as bent as the other three. He had already eliminated Manny as a suspect. He now eliminated Jim but brought Alistair Waring into the frame. The four of them had been involved, probably working for a pre-arranged buyer. He was also fairly confident that the painting hadn't been moved on to the buyer, and with the seed of worry he'd sown into Shane and Rudolph's minds, they might not be in too much of a rush to get rid of it. Last night he'd spoken to Rudolph and told him that once the thieves passed the painting on to the buyer their own future was in the buyer's hands, so what if the buyer got careless? If he did the odds were that he'd take them down with him. All their possessions would be confiscated by the courts and they'd be kicking their heels for thirty years wondering why they hadn't accepted Sam's offer of help. *You know it makes sense, Rudolph,* Sam had told him. Rudolph had told him to fuck off, but it was a very half-hearted fuck off.

Sam also knew that Ally's murder was in some way connected to the theft. Solve one crime, you get two for the price of one. Trouble was, which one first? It might be an idea to have a chat with

Owen. See how far the police had got with their investigations.

'You haven't got much ter say for a man who's come ter pay me a visit,' Jim was saying.

Sam realised he had been lost in thought for a while. 'Sorry, I was miles away.' He got to his feet, as did Jim. 'Well, Jim, it was short, sweet and productive.'

'Was it?' said Jim. 'I hadn't noticed.'

CHAPTER EIGHTEEN

'DC Price, could I interest you in a swift half?'

A mint imperial rattled around in Owen's teeth as he thought of a witty riposte. He couldn't think of one. 'Go on, then boyo. I'll have a small pint of Bootham's.'

They'd just met in the Clog and Shovel. Owen, since Sam's departure from the force, had acted as a reluctant inside man for his private eye friend. Unfortunately, apart from their friendship, he owed Sam many favours. In fact Sam also owed Owen many favours but Sam was much more adept at calling such favours in. As Dave, the barman pulled the drinks, Owen eyed Sam with suspicion. 'I gather you're working on the art thefts.'

'It's a living,' said Sam.

'You know the insurance companies are reluctant to pay out large rewards or ransom money because it encourages more thefts.'

'I have a bona fide contract with the insurers,

based on my track record which, I might add, is quite glowing.'

'For God's sake don't turn your back to me, Carew – the sun shining out of your arse might blind me.'

Owen allowed himself a rare smile as a reward for his own witticism. Sam granted him a like reward and handed his friend his pint and asked, 'Where are the police up to with the art theft?'

'Search me, boyo. It was handed straight to the Met. We've had the Art Theft Squad sniffing round but they're assuming us yokels won't know much so they don't ask much which suits us down to the ground. Apparently there's all sorts of agencies taking an interest. The Dutch National Police Agency, Interpol, the FBI, the Sûreté, the Carabinieri, the Man from Uncle – Tom Cobbleigh and all.'

'Owen, knowing you, you have bent someone's ear to get as much info as possible. Tell me what you know.'

Owen took a gulp of his pint that left no more than a couple of inches swilling around in the bottom of the glass. 'Well, I did have an informal chat with one of the investigating officers.'

'And...?'

'And I know that art theft is quite unique. If, for example, the Rembrandt had been stolen from the Rijksmuseum store room its theft might never have been made public.'

'Why on earth not?'

'Because galleries don't wish to call attention to the inadequate security of their collection. Many minor works of stolen art eventually end up on

138

the legitimate art market. The big experts are Interpol. Art theft's quite a thriving business in France and Italy.'

'It's hardly likely that this Rembrandt's going to end up in the legitimate art market.'

'No,' agreed Owen. 'The Rembrandt will most probably have been stolen to order by a private collector who'll get a real kick out of having it on his lavatory wall – and I do not jest.'

'Oh, I know you don't,' agreed Sam, whole-heartedly. 'So, does the Art Theft Squad have any clues?'

'Apparently there's a Serbian gang been operating on the Continent. Word is that they've moved over here.'

'Really?' said Sam. 'They don't think it's anyone local, then?'

Owen shrugged and finished off the rest of his pint. He put the glass down on the bar and looked at Sam, keenly. 'Why?'

Sam's police background urged him to tell Owen everything he knew, but Owen's association with him was known about and very much frowned upon down in Unsworth nick, especially by DI Bowman. Then again, Owen was his best mate.

'I have a few suspicions,' he said. 'Do you want to get involved?'

Owen shook his head without having to think about it. Getting involved with Sam Carew was a dangerous pastime.

'Fair enough,' conceded Sam. He pondered for a while, then said, 'Would you be interested if I told you I thought there was a link between the Rembrandt and Alistair Waring's murder?'

'Oh, bloody hell, Carew! Don't do this to me. If you know anything, report it to the police.'

'Owen, I don't actually *know* anything at this stage. Nothing that wouldn't have Bowman sneering at me – you know what he's like.'

Owen stuck his hand into the pocket of his voluminous trousers and brought out a handful of change from which he selected the exact sum to pay for another round. 'The police aren't looking for anyone else in connection with the Waring murder,' he said, as he placed a neatly stacked pile of coins on the bar and signalled the barman to pull another two drinks.

'I am,' said Sam, in a voice low enough for only Owen to hear. Then in a louder voice he called out, 'Leave mine in the pump, Dave. I'll have it later.'

The barman nodded, pulled Owen a pint, picked up the money and wandered off to the till.

'I think Waring was mixed up in the robbery, along with three others.'

'Sam, this sounds so far-fetched. If it wasn't you I wouldn't give the idea house room. Who are the three others?'

Sam smiled to himself. Not for the first time he'd got Owen hooked. He led his Welsh friend over to a quiet table.

'David McLeish, Rudolph Mace and Shane Outhwaite.'

'What? I interviewed them all as part of the Waring murder investigation.'

'And...?' asked Sam.

'And they've all got form. Mace has done a three stretch for GBH, McLeish has done time

140

for receiving stolen goods and Outhwaite's been fined a few times – possession of illegal substances and obtaining goods by deception.'

'Well remembered.'

'It's a gift,' said Owen. 'I only interviewed them a week ago, to see if they might make credible prosecution witnesses against Ormerod.'

'A half decent barrister'd take them apart.'

'True. I doubt if the prosecution will use them.'

'Has Jim Ormerod got any form?'

'No.'

'So,' summed up Sam, 'his guilt isn't all that cut and dried.'

'It is as far as Bowman's concerned – apparently he knew Waring quite well.'

'Now, why doesn't that surprise me,' said Sam. 'According to Jim Ormerod, Waring was as bent as a nine bob note. Look, Owen, it would do your standing down at the station no harm if you were instrumental in bringing the real killer – or killers, to justice.'

'Sam, you're assuming I have a standing down at the station.'

'You will have when this is over.'

CHAPTER NINETEEN

The young woman in the VW Golf clicked off her mobile and looked up at the window of Sam's second floor flat, wondering if he'd be up yet. It was 7.20 a.m. She'd give it another ten minutes.

7.30 seemed an optimum time for this sort of thing.

Sam was in the shower when his bell rang. He wrapped a towel around himself and picked up the intercom phone.

'Hello?'

'Mr Carew?'

Sam looked at the CCTV monitor which showed who was at the door. His visitor was in her mid-twenties and was dressed in a smart, business two-piece. Her fair hair was tied back and she wore tinted, designer spectacles.

'Yes.'

'Sorry to disturb you at this time but I wonder if I could talk to you. I'm from Morgan Blackstone Insurance.'

'Oh, right.' He buzzed the entrance door open and went to get a dressing gown. When he got back she was ringing the bell on his flat door. Sam opened it and was met with an efficient smile which he returned. She held out a hand.

'Penny Martin.'

'Pleased to meet you,' said Sam.

'I'm really sorry to disturb you at this time, Mr Carew, but I was passing and thought I'd take the opportunity to have a quick word about the missing Rembrandt.'

'Oh, I see – look, why don't you come in? I'll put some coffee on.'

'Thank you.' The woman entered, looked around the flat and gave it her seal of approval. 'This is what a man's flat should look like. Interesting and untidy.'

'Oh, right,' said Sam. 'I have a woman who

142

comes in and cleans twice a week.' Then he wondered why he was making excuses to this young woman who had called, uninvited, at this early hour. If he allowed himself to admit it, it was because beneath her sober attire she was obviously a cracker. 'So, while I'm doing the coffee, why don't you tell me what this is all about?'

She sat down and arranged her tanned legs in a provocative way which had Sam doing a double take of them before going into the kitchen area of his living room.

'Well, it's almost embarrassing, really. You see, there's one of these mass emails going round saying that you stole the painting yourself, just to get the insurance money.'

Sam stopped what he was doing and called out, 'What? That's ridiculous.'

'Exactly, but it puts us in a very bad light. I just wanted to have a chat with you before going back to my line manager to see how to handle it.'

A car door slammed outside. Penny stood up, went to the window and looked down. 'Oh dear! There's a very angry woman down there. Looks like she's coming into this building.' The entrance bell rang. Sam looked at the CCTV and picked up the intercom phone.

'Sal?'

'Can I come up?'

'Yeah, of course.' He pressed the switch to open the outside door.

'Friend of yours?' said Penny.

'Yeah, she's my assistant and er…' he shrugged as he tried to think of a fuller description.

'Your girlfriend?'

'Er, yeah.'

'Oh, dear! Then it might not be a good idea for her to find me here at this time on a morning, especially with you in your dressing gown.'

'What? Oh yeah – you're definitely right there.'

'Shall I wait in the bedroom until she's gone?'

'If you would – er, thanks.'

Penny disappeared into the bedroom as Sally was ringing the doorbell. Sam opened the door and immediately stepped back as Sally burst past him.

'Do you have a woman in here?'

'What?'

She squared up to him. 'Do you have a woman in here?'

'Woma–? Of course not.'

'Don't lie to me, Sam.'

'Sal, what the hell is this all about?' The convincing innocence on his face diffused Sally's anger to the point where she felt slightly embarrassed by her own actions. She sat down.

'Sam, I've had a stupid phone call from a woman. She reckons she saw you bring a prostitute in here last night and that she's still here – at least she was twenty minutes ago. I'm sorry to be so suspicious Sam but she sounded really irate, as though she was a neighbour or something. I just want you to prove her wrong so I can apologise for being so untrusting.'

Sam had no option but to go on the attack. 'What? So, you've come around at half past seven in the morning to search my flat for prostitutes? Sal, I don't think so. I think we need to have a bit more trust in each other than this. Anyway, how

144

would one of my neighbours know your phone number? I hardly speak to them.'

Sally shook her head, now disgusted with herself for what she was doing. An awkward silence hung between them, then she looked up, apologetically. 'You're right. Look, I'm sorry. I shouldn't have come round. I'll go, and you can finish getting ready.'

'You must be Sally, I've heard so much about you.'

Sam and Sally turned to see Penny leaning against the bedroom door. Her spectacles were gone and her fair hair tumbled luxuriantly across her shoulders. She was wearing one of Sam's shirts, unashamedly hanging open at the front, scarcely hiding her nakedness beneath. For a second Sam wondered how she'd managed the transformation so quickly.

'I gather you're his secretary,' said Penny. 'Don't worry, I've nearly finished with him. I'll make sure he gets to work on time.'

Sally stared at Penny with a mixture of dismay and rage. Sam's mouth was forming the words, *it's not how it looks,* but he didn't allow the words to come out. It would have sounded so lame. Sally's face went white. She sprang to her feet and unleashed her fury on Sam in the form of a slap to his face, which sent him staggering backwards. By the time he'd regained his senses she'd gone. He followed her down the stairs, shouting.

'Sal, it was a set up. She only got here five minutes ago.'

Sally turned to face him, her face streaming tears. 'Why the hell would anyone want to set you

145

up like this, Sam? Credit me with a bit more sense. I asked you if you had a woman in your flat and you said no.'

'I know I did, but...'

He couldn't think of anything to say. How the hell had this happened? One minute he was in the shower, the next minute his world had turned upside down. He stood in the doorway and watched her drive off, concerned that she'd drive safely in her unbalanced state.

As he went back upstairs he didn't notice the lift coming down. The woman who had called herself Penny Martin was walking out of the building just as Sam was walking back into his flat. He checked the rooms to ask her what the hell this had all been about. And he wasn't surprised that he couldn't find her.

As a set-up this had been expertly done. Right now he couldn't even think of a way to persuade Sally that it *had* been a set-up. What she needed was a bit of time. Time enough to feel so bereft at what had happened that she'd be just *wanting* to believe Sam's story, so that everything could get to how it was. The trouble was, would *he* believe such a story if he were in her place? It was all a bit incriminating. Then he brightened. The thing he had going for him was the anonymous phone call. If Sally thought about it hard enough she'd realise the anonymous phone call gave the game away. The anonymous phone call stank of a set-up. He smiled and poured himself a coffee. No problem. Whoever had done this had failed miserably.

She wasn't at the office when he arrived there an hour later, which was no great surprise. His phone was telling him he'd missed four calls. He rang the first caller back. It was the accounts department of a plumber's merchants.

'Hello, this is Sam Carew of Carew and Sons, returning your call.'

'Ah, Mr Carew, erm, I rang because I was obviously concerned about the notice in this morning's *Unsworth Observer.*'

'Notice? What notice is that?'

'I thought you'd be aware of it. It's a notice applying for a winding-up order on your company.'

For a second Sam was no more than puzzled. 'Winding-up order? How do you mean a winding-up order?'

'It means that someone is applying to the courts to put your company into liquidation due to your insolvency – and with your account with us standing at just short of £22,000 it's obviously a bit worrying.'

Sam was completely lost for words.

'Hello? Are you still there, Mr Carew?'

'What? Yes, I'm still here. Look, I know nothing about this. I can assure you we're far from being insolvent and to prove it I'll write out a cheque for your money here and now.'

'We'd be grateful if you would, Mr Carew.'

Sam put the phone down, rang one of the other numbers and ended up having a similar conversation. Five minutes later he got a call from his bank telling him that the company accounts had been temporarily frozen.

'How do you mean, temporarily frozen?'

'It's bank policy during liquidation proceedings, Mr Carew.'

147

'But there aren't any liquidation proceedings. The notice in the paper is a mistake.'

The man from the bank sounded unconvinced, as though he'd heard it all before. 'I'm sorry, but we have to follow procedures. If it's a mistake I'm sure it can be sorted out quickly.' His very tone suggested he thought there was very little chance of that happening.

'And when it is,' said Sam, petulantly, 'I'll be taking Carew and Son's accounts elsewhere.'

Within the next hour the phone rang continuously, with worried suppliers and sub contractors asking what was going on. Eventually Sam unplugged the phones and went out to buy an *Unsworth Observer*. The application for a winding-up order had been made by a company called Halstead and Grove Ltd, of whom Sam had never heard. He rang up the classified ads section of the paper and was told the notice would have been put in by the court, so he rang Derek Armitage, his solicitor, who said he'd check into it.

Half an hour later the solicitor rang Sam back to confirm that, according to the court records, Carew and Son had a High Court judgement against them for £187,000, owed to Halstead and Grove Ltd, and that an application for a winding-up order had been lodged with the courts.

'This is ridiculous!' said Sam. 'I've never heard of them – and we've never run up debts for that amount with anyone. It's got to be a mistake.'

'Well, I must admit I've never heard of such a mistake,' said the solicitor. 'Look, all I've been told is what's on the court computer. I'll send someone down there to check on the paperwork.'

148

'I'd appreciate it if you'd do it personally. Ring me on my mobile. I've had to unplug the office phone. If we can't sort this out in the next couple of days we can't pay the wages on Friday.'

Sam's next port of call was to the Plessington's site where Carew and Son was working on the construction of three units in a retail park. It was the biggest job they had ever undertaken and there was a very strict penalty clause in the contract. Alec Brownlow was already worried.

'I've just tried to order some bricks from Whitakers. They told me we're on the bloody stop list. What the hell's going on, Sam?'

Sam related what had happened that morning, including the part about Sally, which he was only now beginning to link with the whole thing. He was being set up, bigtime. Alec could scarcely contain his frustration.

'Jesus, Sam! It's got to be the private bloody eye side of things that's causing this. I wish yer'd just pack it in an' get on with what yer know best. If we can't get supplies and we can't pay the men we'll have to start laying them off on Friday, which means we'll soon be into penalties in this job – we're struggling to keep up with the schedule as it is. If we're not on site when they invoke the penalty clause they can terminate our contract and bring someone else in to finish the whole job – and they don't have to pay us owt until the job's finished. And if the new contractor's price is more than ours – which you can guarantee it bloody well will be – it'll come out of our pocket. And if they finish after our completion date the penalties are taken out of what they owe us. In fact we could end up owing them. We could go out of business, Sam.'

'Alec, you're panicking over nothing.'

'I'm being bloody realistic, Sam. If word's got round that we're insolvent, that's all it needs. Everybody comes banging on the door for their money and if the banks have frozen us out and the developer's not paying us, we're up Shit Creek without a paddle. Whoever's behind this knows exactly what they're doing. Before we know it we'll be in genuine liquidation.'

Sam knew that Alec had once run his own company which had been forced into bankruptcy by bad payers, so he knew what he was talking about. He also knew that every penny they had, including most of the money from his private eye firm, was invested in this contract.

'Look, I've got a solicitor checking things out with the court.' His mobile rang. It was Derek Armitage.

'Sam, I'm down at the court now. At the moment no one can turn up any papers to back up what's on the computer. They're sure it's around somewhere, but they can't put their hands on it.'

'Derek, they can't put their hands on it because it's not around anywhere,' said Sam, confidently. 'I'm being set up by someone.'

'If there are no papers, no action can be taken against you,' said the solicitor, reassuringly. 'I'm checking on Halstead and Grove Ltd.'

'You'll find it's an off-the-peg company that hasn't traded yet,' forecast Sam. 'This is a very elaborate set-up. If I'm right, which I am, how long will it take for the court to withdraw the action, and for the *Unsworth Observer* to publish a retraction? Can this be done quickly?'

Derek Armitage sighed. 'Well, the courts don't rush into things.'

Sam tried to contain his exasperation. 'In the meantime, do you think I could get a letter from the court saying that the application to wind me up was bogus?'

'The short answer is – I don't know. What I do know is we're talking very serious bureaucracy. I've never come across anything like this before and I suspect neither have the people down at the Unsworth Courthouse; responsibility's going to be batted about like a ping-pong ball. If what you're saying about it being set up is true it means someone's hacked into the court computer to do it. And that someone's got enough savvy to get a notice put in the paper. God knows how they did that. I doubt if the courts will do anything without a thorough investigation, which might involve you being questioned.'

Sam exploded. 'So, I'd have to go bust while they contemplate their bloody navels? I need this sorting out now!'

'I'll do what I can, but even assuming you're right about it being a set-up, I can't see a quick way around this.'

'Bloody hell!' Sam hurled his phone at a pile of sand, then looked at Alec, and shook his head and said, 'Looks like being a long job.'

Alec spun on his heel and walked away. His forty-nine per cent share of the business had been virtually given to him by Sam, in exchange for him running it. Now it was being taken away from him. Sam went over to the sand pile, picked up his phone, rubbed the sand off it and checked that it was still working. He needed to ring Sally. If nothing else this was further proof that someone was out to get him. There was no reply. She was the one person he needed right now. He drove round to her house but she wasn't in, nor was her car in the drive. A woman came out of the house next door and called over to him.

'I think she's gone on holiday or something, love. I saw her putting a suitcase in the car and she said she was going away for a bit.'

'Right, thank you.'

He rang Owen Price.

CHAPTER TWENTY

The Welsh DC was waiting for Sam in the Clog and Shovel. He had always regarded Sam with suspicion and affectionate animosity, but when the chips were down the two of them always closed ranks. But it didn't stop Owen being the indelicate bearer of bad news.

'There's an email that's going around about you, boyo. Do you know about it?'

'Email?' Sam remembered the woman from early that morning. 'It's not about me stealing the painting for the insurance money is it?'

'It's exactly about that, boyo. I don't know how many people have received it but there's been quite a lot of phone calls to the station about it.'

Sam picked up the pint which was waiting for him on the bar, took out his mobile and rang Morgan Blackstone Insurance.

'Hello, my name is Sam Carew, I'd like to speak to Mr Michaelson ... yes, I'll hold.' He took the phone and his drink across to a table which Owen had found for them. 'Mr Michaelson ... yes, I know about the email. Look, at the moment I'm being victimised on all sides and I'm sure it's to do with the painting: someone's placed a bogus liquidation notice in the *Unsworth Observer* that the courts can't find any paperwork for; and this morning I had a visit from a woman calling herself Penny Martin; she said she works for Morgan Blackstone and she really dropped me in it with my fiancée... What, your secretary?... Look, before you ask her I'd better describe the woman who came to see me. She was early twenties, fair hair... Not her? I thought not. Look, this email has been circulated to a lot of people, including the police, who will no doubt investigate the hell out of me. If you like I'll come off the case but I can assure you that I may be many things but I'm not a thief.'

Owen looked on as Sam went quiet, listening to Michaleson's reply. Eventually Sam said, 'I understand, Mr Michaelson,' and switched the phone off. He took a swig of his pint and looked, ruefully, at Owen.

'Well, whoever's doing this has pulled it off. Morgan Blackstone have kicked me into touch. It seems that some computer nerd has put me completely out of business.' He told Owen the full story of what had happened so far that day.

153

The Welshman seemed more concerned about Sally than Sam's business.

'Where do you think she's gone, boyo?'

'Not sure. To her parents in Bournemouth, possibly. If she's not there, I don't know where she'll be.'

'Well, she should be your first priority.'

'Owen, my first priority is to unfreeze my bank accounts. They've frozen my personal account as well.'

'What about the private detective account? That's a separate business, isn't it?'

'It is, but with this building contract being such a big one I did a temporary loan transfer to the Carew and Son account. There's only loose change in the detective account at the moment. The only money I've got is what's on me, and that's not much. I can't even use my debit card.'

'Don't you have a credit card?'

'Ah.' Sam's mind had been so cluttered up, he didn't think of that. 'Credit card, yes. Rarely use it, but it might see me through. That's if it hasn't been stopped.' He took the platinum card from his wallet and got to his feet. 'Might as well try it out now. There's a cash point just around the corner, back in a minute.' He came back five minutes later looking marginally more cheerful.

'One problem solved. If I draw out the maximum over the next few days I should be able to pay the men their wages.'

'What about you and Alec?'

'I can go back on the tools until it's sorted, so can Alec. Trouble is, by the time it's sorted there might not be a Carew and Son left.'

154

'That bad?'

Sam nodded. 'The news is out that we're in trouble and the vultures have already started circling. The fact that we're far from being insolvent is neither here nor there. Every penny we've got's going into this retail park site. We're due a big stage payment next week, if that doesn't come through we're in massive trouble.' He thought about this and gave a wry smile. 'Even if it does come through it'll be paid straight into our bank, who won't let us touch it.'

'What sort of terms are you on with the bank manager?'

Sam looked at him and shook his head. 'What bank manager? Owen, there aren't any bank managers nowadays. It's all press this bloody number and that number until you get through to someone in a call centre in Delhi who's working for buttons and doesn't know you from Adam and cares about you even less. We live in an automated world which can pull the rug from under you at the press of a button.'

'Why don't you just contact all your suppliers and tell them what's happening?' suggested Owen. 'They could always ring the court themselves to check you're telling the truth.'

'Oh, I intend doing just that,' said Sam. 'Problem is, I doubt if the court will tell them anything until they know for certain what's happened – and I've no idea how long that will be. Could be days, could be weeks, could be months.'

He sipped his drink, meditatively. His thoughts switched back to Sally. He took out his mobile and brought up her number, then had second thoughts. 'I won't ring Sal straight away, she might think I want to sponge off her. I know she's not short of cash – and she knows I know she's not short.'

'Sally doesn't think like that.'

'Owen, you didn't see how mad she was this morning. She'll see the truth of it, all in good time – I hope, but right now she might take some convincing.'

'I could have a word if you like. She knows I don't lie to her.'

Sam turned this idea over for a while then rejected it. 'No, she seems to think I have some sort of mystical influence over you. You know, and I know it's rubbish, but that's the way she thinks. She thinks I take advantage of you.'

'Carew, you do take advantage of me.'

'Bloody hell, Owen, not you as well!'

CHAPTER TWENTY-ONE

Unsworth: 1972

He was seven years old and had been living with foster parents for four years. They were the only parents he had ever known. He knew they were his foster parents because he'd been told, but it meant nothing. They were his mam and dad, that's all he knew, that's all he'd ever known since he could remember.

His mam was called Vera and his dad was called

156

Mike. At first there were two other kids in the house, both girls, both older. He didn't refer to them as his sisters, nor did they call him brother, but they were OK to him. Then they went away. He couldn't recall the exact time they went, it just happened, that's all he knew about them. No one told him anything, not even his mam and dad. After that it was just the three of them and as far as he knew he was happy. His mam was the one he loved the most. She was funny and always smiling. He had few really solid memories of her – his mam showing him how to shine his shoes was one. She tickled him and made his hand slip, so he put polish on her nose and he howled with laughter. She dipped her finger in the polish and gave him a moustache. They both looked in the mirror and pulled funny faces. Then she picked him up and hugged him and they laughed together. The memory always made him smile. It was a memory he treasured. His dad could be a bit grumpy and he wasn't around much. He did something called 'shifts' and slept a lot during the day. But he was OK. No one ever smacked him, he remembered that much.

He went to a school called Quarry Place Primary, where he did well. He had an aptitude for learning. He was at school when his dad died in a mining accident. He had been called from class and taken home by a policeman who didn't tell him anything. His mam was at home, but all she did was cry. He cried as well but he didn't know why. When your mam cries it's as good a reason as any to have a good weep yourself. It wasn't his mam who told him about his dad. She wouldn't stop crying. A policewoman eventually told him.

'I've got some bad news. There's been a nasty accident and Mike's dead.'

It didn't register at first. Shooey never called him Mike. He was Dad, always had been as long as he could remember.

'Can I see my dad?' he asked. He needed one of them, and Mam wasn't much use right now.

The policewoman got up and went to speak to Vera, then she came back, now aware of where she'd gone wrong.

'I'm sorry, love. It's your dad I was talking about. I'm afraid he's dead. That's why Vera – that's why your mam's crying.'

It wasn't easy to take it in. It never is when you're seven years old. 'Oh,' he said. 'Does that mean he won't be coming home, then?'

'I'm afraid so.'

For the next few weeks he remembered his mam getting quieter and quieter until she hardly spoke to him at all. He could hear her crying at night in her bed and he didn't know what to do, so he did nothing. Then one morning she came into his bedroom and told him she was going into hospital for a few days and he would be going to a nice home where there were lots of other children to play with. She gave him a toy car and a box of Bassett's Liquorice Allsorts. 'I'll be back before you know it,' she assured him. And he believed her. As far as he knew, she'd never lied to him.

A week later one of the women in charge of the home told him that Vera had died and that he'd be staying there for good. And that was that. It was as if they didn't realise that Vera was his mam

158

and he wondered if he should have told them. When he did pluck up courage to tell them they told him he wrong – she had been his *foster* mother which was an entirely different thing. No one even thought to take him to her funeral.

He was immensely sad for quite some time but no one seemed to notice. He was taken out of Quarry Place Primary and moved to another school where the kids poked fun at him. Being from a home was apparently something to be ashamed of – a shame he would have to live with for many years and many children's homes. He saw no sense in trying hard at his lessons; being seen as clever would have put an even greater barrier between him and the other kids.

He found out, several years later, that his mam had taken a bottle of Librium. At first he hated her for that. He called her a rotten coward and wished he'd never been sent to live with her. Then he forgave her because she was the only woman he had ever loved.

As soon as he was old enough he joined the army. There was nothing shameful about being a soldier. He kept his shoes beautifully shiny in memory of his mother and they all called him Shooey.

His first killing had left him disturbed. Londonderry, 1987. He'd been on patrol with three other squaddies and a corporal. They'd stopped to chat with three of their mates guarding a check-point when a car pulled up with screeching brakes, all but knocking one of the guards down. His corporal shot the nearside tyres out and the eight of them surrounded the car at a distance, wary of occupants with Armalites or nail bombs or hand grenades. The driver got out much too quickly. He'd been told to act slowly, with hands well away from his body. Maybe he hadn't heard. He was seventeen and they'd stolen the car. There were four of them, all aged under twenty. All had been drinking heavily. It was later discovered that all were unarmed, but who was to know?

None of the commands the squaddies were shouting to the youths were being obeyed. The driver pointed at Shooey and suddenly shrieked with laughter, then he lunged forward. Maybe it was a deliberate act of drunken aggression or maybe he was simply off balance. The enquiry was told it was the former. In any event Shooey wiped the grin from the youth's face with a single shot which went straight through his chest, coming to rest in the front seat passenger's right shoulder.

The dead youth seemed to hang in the air for an age. He had time to look down at his wound, then up at Shooey. His eyes widened with sudden tears, before the light behind them died away and he dropped to the ground. Inside the car the injured youth was screaming with pain and fear. He was sent to hospital and the other two youths taken to the police barracks. Without collusion all three told different versions of the same story, as drunks always do. This helped Shooey at the enquiry.

His mates had backed him up, reluctantly. To have done otherwise would have caused both them and the army problems they didn't need. They'd got their stories straight. Each told of how he'd been on the verge of firing himself but

Shooey had beaten him to it. It could have been any one of them being investigated, they said. The army found there were no charges to answer. The Coroner returned a verdict of death by misadventure. Sinn Fein called it murder. His so-called pals had frozen him out. He was given a medical discharge. No counselling, no words of sympathy, just a medical pension and a lift to the station in the back of a truck, which happened to be going that way anyway. He was also told, on the quiet, that he was damned lucky not to have been charged with murder.

Killing affects different people in different ways. He had never got over it, until he killed Alistair Waring. There had been something cathartic about that. Private Shooey was back, but this time he was feeling good.

The killing of the youth had affected his nervous system and his metabolism. His weight had gone down from fourteen stones to ten stone two. For a six foot man, that was thin. It had also left him with a bottled-up anger. The cork had flown out of that bottle the second he'd swung the golf club at Alistair's head. And the anger had poured out with every blow he struck. Until there was no more anger and no more blows.

But now he was putting weight back on. There was a hint of colour in his cheeks that hadn't been there for over twenty years. Killing people wasn't so bad after all. In fact it was going to be very profitable. It was going to change his life. He was now up to ten stone eight pounds and he knew that the anger had been replaced by another of the deadly sins – lust. A lust for blood.

A lust to do it again. Just once. One that was properly planned.

Three people stood in his way, although they didn't know it. Ally had paved the way; killing him hadn't been so bad, in fact it had been easy, easy and exciting – especially when he thought about it afterwards. So, why not do it again? Yeah, why not do it again?

Doing another would make the rest of the bastards stop and think before coming for him and his money – when he got it. Money bought power. OK, one more, then cash in and take the others on if they came for him. Or maybe he'd take out all of them just for the hell of it. Let's see how it goes. He just couldn't see a way to cash in on his potential fortune while any of the others were still around. He'd been entitled to just one share, but they'd tried to deny him that, the bastards. Now he'd have the lot. All of them could do him damage if they found out he'd taken it from under their noses – especially Rudolph. He hated to think what Rudolph might do to him if he found out. Cashing in was easy. The money would be handed over in London in great secrecy, but what then? He couldn't live in Unsworth, that's for sure. No one could become an overnight millionaire in Unsworth without someone asking questions. He'd have to move away, maybe even abroad. That would be no problem except maybe the language.

CHAPTER TWENTY-TWO

The golf had carried on. In fact it was handy, in a way, that they'd lost two of the six players – they now had a regular four-ball. Much of the conversation was about Jim, and was he guilty? Manny was on the 'not guilty' side, so was Shane. The others weren't so sure. None of the other three ever talked about the painting theft, which made Manny wonder whether they *were* mixed up in it. If he'd been questioned, surely they must have been, so why did they never mention it? It was a suspicion that didn't last long. No way could those three plonkers have pulled off something so clever. Besides, if they'd done it, where was the money they'd got for it?

Sam calling to see Manny about the painting theft had unnerved the car dealer somewhat. His dealings weren't exactly kosher and being part of the investigation into something so high profile might have people nosing around where they shouldn't. Shortly after Sam called to see him a couple of coppers had followed suit. They were spreading their net and he was linked to Rudolph, who was linked to the painting. Manny couldn't see Rudolph being mixed up in anything so ambitious. It would suit Manny down to the ground if they could catch whoever had nicked the bloody painting – having coppers sniffing round was bad for business. He definitely couldn't see it being

Rudolph, though. Rudolph was many things, but an international art thief wasn't one of them.

Rudolph always walked home from the Queen of Clubs when he was working the door. It was usually around three in the morning, which suited him. The later the better. He got double bubble for every hour after twelve and he'd need double bubble until they got that bloody painting sold. That night he'd heard about all the shit Carew was in and Rudolph had scarcely stopped smiling. Carew had been to see Manny, which meant he suspected the whole Syndicate, which wasn't good. Too close for comfort. Anyway he had something else to worry about now. According to Dave, shit like this could put Carew out of business. And that suited Rudolph down to the ground.

Unsworth had its own red light area – Ragley Road – which was on Rudolph's way home. If Delicious Alicia was about he might invest a tenner in a quick hand job, as he often did. No way would he stick it anywhere inside her. He had a wife who took care of that for him. The Ragley Road girls carried no health certificates.

Rudolph might have kept his fondness for Alicia's hand-jobs from his wife, but there were those who knew about this flaw in his character – Shooey for one. Rudolph was big and strong and needed to be taken at his weakest moment. Having one off the wrist with Alicia was such a moment. A more precise moment would be what Rudolph coarsely referred to as, the vinegar stroke. The very idea brought a smile to Shooey's face as he waited in the shadows.

Rudolph didn't see her at first, then she got out of a punter's car right in front of him. The car drove off at speed, as they usually did. Alicia turned, and in the dim light recognised Rudolph's bulk before she recognised his face.

'Rudolph, is that you?'

'Who else?' His white teeth gleamed at her.

'One off the wrist or d'yer fancy something different ternight?'

'Nothing different darlin'. Yer know me – faithful husband.'

'Rudolph, yer have a strange way of bein' faithful.'

'Not screwin' other wimmin is bein' faithful, darlin'. Quick hand job and I won't have ter disturb me missis when I get home. Fer which she ought ter be very grateful.'

Alicia led him into Wineway's doorway, unzipped his trousers and took him in her hand. Rudolph lit a cigarette to add to his brief moment of hedonism as Alice worked away, industriously.

'D'yer know what I sometimes wish?' he said.

'No, what do you wish?'

'I sometimes wish,' he said, 'that I had a ten inch dick, instead of this big bastard.'

Alicia screamed with laughter as she pulled away at him. Rudolph laughed as well. His laughter turned to grunts of ecstasy when the big moment arrived. As though signalled by the grunts, a knife appeared over his shoulder and glinted in the light of a distant street lamp. In one quick movement it slashed his throat. The cut was deep and wide and opened up like a sliced melon as his head jerked backwards. Blood

165

sprayed over the prostitute, whose screams of laughter turned to screams of terror. Soaked with Rudolph's blood she turned her back to him, awaiting a similar fate herself. Rudolph slowly sank to his knees as Shooey walked, quickly, away. Smiling broadly. That had been so easy.

There had been a man in one of his so-called care homes whose throat he'd always wanted to slit. He was big as well – bit and loud and disgusting. It was appropriate that Rudolph had died whilst engaged in such an act. Shooey had often imagined slitting the care-home man's throat during the times that such an act – and sometimes worse – had been forced on him. Joining the army had been the great escape. He should have stuck it out. Had he known then how easy killing could be he would have done. All those wasted years, tormenting himself over killing that youth. If only he'd known.

CHAPTER TWENTY-THREE

Sam had no trouble finding work. He'd got a job for a local road contractor, building brick manholes. It was two weeks since the notice had gone in the paper and much had happened. Carew and Son (Builders) Ltd had had their Plessington Holdings contract terminated in accordance with clause 7b, and all moneys due to them were being held back, pending the contract's completion – which pretty much meant they could wave bye-

bye to it. Sam had pointed out, via his solicitor, that they weren't in violation of clause 7b which gave Plessington Holdings the right to terminate the contract should Carew and Son become insolvent.

The site had been closed and the men laid off, eventually paid, courtesy of Sam's credit card. He had notified all the creditors of the true situation but didn't get too much sympathy for his plight; the creditors had plights of their own to worry about.

He was then officially notified that the contract had been re-let to a Castleford building company and any excess in the final contract cost would be deducted from the money owed to Carew and Son.

He'd tried Sally at her parents in Bournemouth. They'd said she wasn't there, and had expressed enough worry about their daughter's whereabouts to convince Sam that they were telling the truth.

Sam realised he was more worried about Sally than he was about his business. Money was something he could always earn by laying one brick on top of another. But where the hell was Sal? He was six feet below ground level, building a manhole when Owen's head peered down at him.

'They told me I'd find you down there, boyo.'

'Did they?' said Sam, slapping compo on the side of a brick and placing it in position with accomplished ease.

'There's been another murder.'

Sam tried to raise some enthusiasm for this. All morning he'd been trying to figure out a way to track down Sally. Her clearing off for a few days was one thing. This was getting beyond a joke.

'Owen, you're a copper,' he said, eventually. 'When there's a murder you're usually the first to know.'

'Well, this was Rudolph Mace, see.'

'Ah.' Sam's trowel paused in mid-air. He looked up at the Welsh detective, then back down at his work. Then he scraped the comp from his trowel back on to his hand-hawk.

'Rudolph,' he said.

'Throat cut as he was engaged in a carnal exchange with a prostitute.'

Carnal exchange? Sam often wondered where Owen got his terminology from. He climbed out of the manhole workings.

'Did the prostitute do it?'

'According to her she was giving him hand relief when someone came up from behind and cut his throat. Nasty business. His todger was still out when we arrived on the scene. If you ask me it was a bit on the small side for a black man, which I found quite reassuring – unless some of it shrinks post-mortem. Mid you, they say steroids does that to you. Some of these body builders have testicles the size of peanuts, look you.' He looked at Sam as though inviting him to enter the discussion about the size of Rudolph's genitalia. Sam didn't take the bait. Owen was a very odd man at times.

'Are the police making a connection between this and the Alistair Waring killing?' Sam asked.

'Not really. We already have Waring's killer awaiting trial, and there's no similarity in MO.'

'No,' conceded Sam, 'but there doesn't have to

168

be for it to be the same killer.'

'Well, at the moment the police are treating it either as a random killing or someone who's got a grudge against a big rough doorman.'

'But you think differently,' said Sam, pointedly, 'or you wouldn't be here.'

'I'm here because it's Rudolph Mace and you've had dealings with him.'

'Please tell me I'm not a suspect, I probably haven't got an alibi. What time did it happen?'

'Around 3 a.m.'

'I haven't got an alibi, unless you count Michelle Pfieffer. About three o'clock this morning she was trying to have her wicked way with me in the Clog and Shovel car park. I was fighting her off, then I woke up.'

'You're not a suspect, boyo, as far as I know.'

'Whose case it is? Bowman's or Seager's?'

'DI Seager's been given it. A Murder Incident Room's been set up – I'm doing the legwork as usual.'

Sam nodded his approval of DI Janet Seager being assigned the case. 'Tell Janet I think it's definitely tied in with the Alistair Waring murder and the Rembrandt theft. Tell her that I don't think Jim Ormerod is involved in any way, shape or form and tell her to take a close look at Dave McLeish and Shane Outhwaite.' Sam waited as Owen scribbled a few notes down in his book. In the distance the site foreman was looking his way, wondering why he wasn't working. 'I'd love to get involved in this, Owen, but I've got a living to earn.' He made to climb back down into the manhole, then he paused and turned back.

'You haven't heard from Sally, have you?'
'Not yet.'
'If you hear anything…'
'You don't have to ask, boyo.'

CHAPTER TWENTY-FOUR

Manny was waiting on the tee when Dave and Shane arrived, separately. 'I was going to ring you both,' he said. 'I didn't know whether it was right playin' golf after what happened to Rudolph – I suppose you've heard.'

'From the horse's mouth,' said Dave. 'I had a bobby round last night.'

'Yeah, and me,' said Shane. 'What about you, Manny? Did you get a visit?'

Manny looked at them both then shook his head. 'Me? Why should they visit me? Oh, because of that painting thing? What is it with these coppers and the stolen bloody painting? Do they honestly think we're international bleeding art thieves? Is that why they came to see you?'

'They came to see us because we all spend a lot of time together on the golf course,' explained Shane, quickly. 'They asked us if we knew anyone who might want to kill him.'

'Right, yeah. Well, I reckon quite a few people might hold a grudge against Rudolph,' remarked Manny. 'He can get a bit rough when he's workin' the doors.'

'I think that's the line the police are following,'

170

Dave said. 'Still, I reckon yer might get a visit from 'em.'

Manny shrugged and made a practice swing. 'I wish I could help them. Personally I reckon it'll turn out to be one of the whore's punters. Fancy getting knifed when you're having it off with a whore. It's an embarrasin' way to go. I bet his wife's delighted.'

'She's under sedation apparently,' Dave told him.

'Poor cow,' said Manny, teeing his ball up.

He drove into the rough. Dave and Shane both knocked their balls straight down the fairway. Shane made to help Manny look for his ball when Dave tugged his elbow.

'It's got to be the London crowd.'

'That's what I was thinking,' Shane said. 'But why would they kill Rudolph?'

'Dunno. Same reason they killed Alistair. They're seriously weird bastards, them London lot. I got a call last night just after the bobby left. They want to deal for two million quid.'

'Two million, now? I see. Did they mention Rudolph?'

'They didn't have to. They want to do the deal at eleven o'clock tonight, Leicester Forest Services on the M1.'

Manny found his ball without their help and chipped back on to the fairway. He looked across at his playing partners and wondered what they were talking so intensely about.

'Bollocks ter that!' said Shane. 'I'm not going to no meeting. Wait 'til they ring back, then do it on our terms.'

171

Dave sliced a 6 iron into a bush. His thoughts were a million miles from golf. 'To be honest, Shane, I'm shittin' meself. I wish I'd never taken this bloody thing on.'

'Mebbe we should just give the painting back,' Shane suggested. 'If we haven't got the painting, they'll leave us alone.'

'I've been thinking of that myself – and then I think of the two million and I wish I wasn't such a greedy bastard.'

'It could be that it *wasn't* them who killed Rudolph,' said Shane.

'What? You think Rudolph and Ally were just two random, senseless murders? Nothing to do with the London crowd dropping the money by a million every time one of us gets wasted?'

'What bothers me,' Shane said, 'is that whoever killed them seemed to know stuff about them – well, Rudolph anyway. And the cops reckon Ally was killed by someone who knew him. Which doesn't tally with the London crowd.'

Manny was calling out to them. 'Look, lads. When we're on the course we're supposed to put everything else behind us and concentrate on the game. Buck your bloody ideas up, will you? Rudolph's gone. He wouldn't want us to stop playing just for his benefit.'

CHAPTER TWENTY-FIVE

Sam was leaving work. Tracey Ormerod's car was parked in front of his. She watched him approach through her wing mirror and got out.

'How come you're working here and not for me?'

'Ah, Tracey.'

'So?'

Sam clicked the remote on his key fob to open his car. 'So, I'm having a few problems and I need to earn some money to keep myself alive.'

'So I've heard.'

'Who from?'

'Sam, for a private detective you're not a very private person. I heard a rumour and checked up on it.'

'You mean with Owen Price, the town gossip,' Sam guessed, accurately.

'I forget who it was. Are you having any luck sorting things out?'

'I'm waiting for the court to admit they've been taken for a ride by some computer hacker who's got a grudge against me. Which means someone's got to accept responsibility. There's a lot of buck passing goes on down at the courthouse.'

'I can imagine,' said Tracey. 'So, why aren't you keeping yourself alive by working for me?'

'Tracey, my arrangement with you is payment by results. My first priority is to stick food in my

173

mouth, keep a roof over my head and pay maintenance for my boys – not necessarily in that order. These people pay cash wages straight into my hand every Friday, which is how things should be done.'

'So, come and work for me on wages.'

Sam looked at her, giving her suggestion due consideration. It was tempting. 'You might be throwing good money down the drain.'

'That's my problem. Come round and see me when you've got yourself cleaned up. We'll sort something out. This Rudolph thing's got Jim really worried – me as well.'

'Jim thinks they're connected, does he?'

'Jim thinks there's a lot of shit going on that he doesn't understand.'

'Jim's not on his own,' said Sam.

The site agent drove past in his van. Sam waved him down. 'I'll work 'til Friday, then I'm away.'

The agent frowned his disappointment but there was little he could do. Sam turned back to Tracey. Somehow her turning up had brightened his day. Made him realise he still had plenty of things going for him. As he investigated Ally's murder he'd also do some checking on whoever had set him up. Highly likely the two were connected. He might even track down the art thieves, which would be a hell of a bonus.

'I'll be round at eight,' he said, getting into his car.

Tracey watched him drive away. Her mind wasn't entirely confined to her having Sam work on Jim's case. Before that night was over she'd have him working on her case – a case of severe, post-rape ... sexual turmoil.

As Sam drove it crossed his mind that there might be more to his meeting with Tracey than simply discussing Jim's case. He felt a twinge of guilt because the thought excited him. Do no harm to ring Sally's parents to find out what the score was. If she was still playing silly beggars it might assuage his guilt.

'Hello, Mrs Grover ... Sam Carew. I was wondering if you'd heard from Sally...' The answer was brief but affirmative. 'You have? Good, er, did she say where she was?...' This answer was brief but uninformative. Sally would prefer he never knew where she was – ever apparently. In view of his innocence, this annoyed Sam somewhat.

'Right,' he snapped. 'Then if she's not interested in hearing the truth from me perhaps she'd care to ring Owen Price. If nothing else she knows he'll be honest with her.' He clicked the phone off before Mrs Grover could react to this. It gave him some satisfaction for a few moments, then he wished he hadn't been so rude. She was only protecting her daughter – and maybe Sally had good reason to suspect him. In the time they'd been together he'd slipped the leash on more than one occasion. The most significant being Kathy Sturridge, to whom he'd been engaged until she'd died saving his life. If he were honest with himself, Kathy was the reason he'd never got seriously engaged to Sal. So why the hell did he miss her so much?

CHAPTER TWENTY-SIX

As Sam drove to Tracey Ormerod's house he didn't notice the car following him. It was an insignificant-looking, dark blue, slightly tatty Vauxhall Astra – not a car you'd pay much attention to in your rear-view mirror. It parked fifty yards up the street from where Sam was ringing Tracey's bell. The door opened as if on its own. Tracey's head peeped around from behind it. A welcoming smile on her face.

'You've just caught me unawares. I haven't got too many clothes on.'

'Right.'

'You can come in if you like.'

Sam stepped inside. Tracey closed the door, taking care not to reveal herself to the street, as she was completely naked. Sam gave her an approving glance and tried not to look shocked.

'You're right about not having too many clothes on.'

He walked through to the living room as if her nakedness was having no effect on him. She was saddened that he hadn't been overcome with passion, but that wasn't Sam's style. She remembered now. Sam had always been a bit backward in coming forward in that department. She followed him through.

'Well,' she demanded. 'What do you think?'

'Are we talking about your body or Jim's case?'

176

'Sam, if you're trying to demoralise me you're doing a good job. Do I look good or not?'

'Tracey, if you didn't think you looked great you wouldn't be standing there starkers.'

'So, you think I look great?'

Having been thus invited he allowed himself a longer look at her. 'Yep, I can safely say you look great. Mind you, you always did.'

'If I remember rightly, I was the first woman you saw in the nude.'

'You remember rightly.'

'That's why I don't feel humiliated at having to do this. You've seen me like this before.'

He noticed the tears in her eyes.

'How do you mean, *having to do this?* Tracey, what's the matter?'

'Sam, I want you to take me to bed and I don't want to stand on ceremony. The last sex I had was when I was raped and it's really beginning to get to me – as if that was the only sex I've ever had. I can't explain it. It's like needing to climb back on a horse after you've fallen off – sorry, that's a crap analogy. It's – it's like I need a good man to purge that bloody rapist from my system or I'll never want to have sex again, not with anyone. I don't want an affair. I'm not going to fall madly in love with you. I just want honest, real sex. After which we can talk business.'

Sam felt his resistance failing. At the back of his mind he'd suspected they might end up in bed but it hadn't stopped him coming. She'd had that look about her back on the site. Something of a desperate look. He'd probably been looking a bit desperate himself. Maybe she'd picked up on that. Women can pick up on such things. His mind went back over twenty years. To a scene indelibly printed on his memory.

'I remember you doing a striptease in Wyke Valley woods,' he said.

'I remember that day too, Sam.'

'You brought a portable radio with you and danced to T-Rex, *Get It On.*'

'God, that was a golden oldie, even back then. I seem to remember we got it on that afternoon, Sam.'

Sam nodded, to indicate that he too remembered that afternoon. 'If you must know, I remember that as one of my beautiful times.'

'Was it, Sam? Did I give you a beautiful time?'

'You did – and we don't get many of them.'

Tracey happily stretched herself and thrust out her breasts, quite brazenly. Her waning self-confidence was returning. She had an all-over tan which suited her. 'I've got a Marc Bolan CD if you want to try and recreate the moment.'

Sam sat back and examined his conscience. The fact that Sally had left him for something he hadn't done might well assuage any guilt he might feel. To all intents and purposes he was single, unattached, and sitting opposite a beautiful, naked woman who wanted him to make love to her.

'If you're going to recreate the moment you'll have to put a few clothes on, so you can take them off,' he pointed out.

'I can do that. And if we're going to recreate the moment accurately you have to end up naked as well.'

'I think I know the rules.'

178

'There's one more rule,' she said, earnestly.

'What's that?'

'I need to be in control.'

'What's new?' said Sam, who understood.

They didn't end up in bed, they ended up on the carpet, from where they transferred their lust to the settee until, mutually satiated, they lit cigarettes and drank Tracey's malt whisky.

'Do you feel purged at all?' Sam asked.

'Well and truly. I'm once more a woman in control.'

'That's good. My therapy worked, then.'

She laughed. 'I often think about you ... about that time in the woods. And I laugh when I hear them call you Mad Carew. It kind of fitted you that afternoon. You were made for it, Sam. Mad and clumsy as hell, but, do you know...'

'What?'

Tracey drew deeply on her cigarette and let the smoke drift out of her partly open mouth. She was lying with her head on Sam's lap and was wearing a shirt and nothing else.

'You said it was one of your beautiful times. Well, I remember it as my *most* beautiful time ever. Ask me anything about it and I can tell you. You were wearing brand new jeans and a white T-shirt with a tear in the front and dark blue Y-fronts that you were a bit ashamed of because they were your dad's and you'd started wearing boxers.'

'And you were wearing a smile and a ruby ring.'

'It was my grandmother's. I didn't go there intending to do a strip, it's just that I knew that if ever I was to do one I wouldn't get a more appreciative audience.'

'You were my first,' he told her. 'You know that, don't you?'

'You didn't say, but it was fairly obvious.'

'What about you – was I your first?'

'If I had a pound for every time I've heard that...'

'Sorry.'

'I can remember your face,' she said, 'when I was stripping off. Blimey! I thought you were going to pass out.'

Sam remembered it well. 'Well, it's a memory I treasure.'

'Well, I hope you mention that in your memoirs.'

'If I live long enough to write any memoirs.'

There was a long pause before Tracey sat up and said, 'Will seven fifty a week be enough? I'll give you the balance of the twenty grand if you get a result.'

'That's fine,' said Sam, 'but there is something I'd better mention. It's a question of professional ethics.'

'Ah, you mean you don't screw clients' wives?'

'Something like that.'

'It never bothered Alistair.'

'And look what happened to him.'

'That only counts if you think Jim killed him, which you don't.'

'Let's just say it'd be better if you kept your clothes on during our weekly conferences.'

'I'll do my best... Sam.'

'What?'

'I've just had my second most beautiful time.'

CHAPTER TWENTY-SEVEN

He had just unlocked his car when the man pointed a gun at him. The man was wearing a balaclava with just his eyes showing. This told Sam that the man expected him to live to tell the tale, but Sam was ever the optimist. He held up his hands as the man barked out an order.

'Get in the car and don't start it 'till I tell yer.'

Sam got in. The man got into the backseat. Sam could smell drink on his breath. It was almost midnight and the street was deserted.

'Do you mind if I ask what this is about?'

'Shut the fuck up and drive.'

A thought crossed Sam's mind. 'Is it you who's been setting me up? If so, why?'

'Shut the fuck up an' drive.'

He directed Sam out of town with a series of monosyllabic grunts. The absence of information as to why all this was happening began to worry Sam. His expectations about surviving this were now dwindling. He was out in the country at the dead of night. Behind him was a man with a gun and a belly full of drink. That was all he knew and it wasn't enough.

'Look mate, if you're going to shoot me, the least you can do is tell me why. I thought you might have been satisfied with what you've already done without shooting me.'

The man answered by prodding the gun into the

nape of Sam's neck. Then Sam realised that he recognised the voice. He was one of his three attackers, but this man had been doing the most shouting. Would Sam be signing his death warrant if he revealed to the masked man that he knew who he was? Tracey's rapist, Lemmy Wilson, saved him the trouble. He took off his balaclava and rasped.

'They left me crippled fer life, the bastards.'

Sam glanced at him in the rear-view mirror. Lemmy was sitting in the nearside backseat, his face spasmodically lit by passing lights. Head shaven, neck tattooed, ring through one eyebrow. It was a face engraved with deep anger; anger and innate stupidity, a dangerous combination.

'You mean the men from the camp?' Sam said. 'That was nothing to do with me. I never met any of them.'

'Me woman's left me an' gone back to 'em – taken the boy, an' good riddance.'

Sam felt he couldn't blame her, but telling him this wouldn't help his cause. A decent lie might help, though.

'The woman you assaulted wanted to report you to the police. I persuaded her not to.'

'No, because ye thought ye'd burn the fuckin' camp down instead.'

'Like I said, that was nothing to do with me. Why would I do that? I hardly know the woman.'

'Ye seem ter know her well enough now. Ye were in her house long enough. She's a great shag, is she not?'

This last remark aroused an anger in Sam that he knew he had to control. 'If she'd reported you to the police you've have been sent down for life for rape,' he pointed out.

Lemmy laughed out loud. 'Maybe she didn't report me because she enjoyed it too much. She fought like a fuckin' vixen at first, but I left her screamin' fer more.'

He began to sing, one of Sam's favourite songs – nothing to do with Liverpool football supporters, who rarely sang it in tune; more to do with one of his favourite films, *Carousel*. The situation was now quite surreal because the man had a sweet and powerful voice. Had he been on at Unsworth Labour Club he'd have gone down a treat. It seemed so unjust that such a sweet sound should come out of such a vile mouth. It was when he came to the end of the song that Sam shuddered with the reality of the situation. Instead of ending the song with the original words, he sang 'You'll never walk again,' and exploded into fits of humourless laughter, which gave Sam a pretty good idea of what was in store for him. Lemmy decided to give him a graphic description of his fate.

'I have nine bullets in this gun. That's four in each leg an' one in the bollocks. IRA trained. I know how ter do it without ye dyin' – although maybe ye'll wish ye was dead.' He cackled again. 'There'll be no more runnin' around an' shaggin' fer you, Mr Carew.'

'You'll get life for this.'

'How can I get life when I'm not even here? How are ye goin' ter prove I did it, Mr Detective? No one'll ever get any of that forensic shite off this car, because no one'll ever see it again. An' I've got one of them alibi things. Great things, them alibis. All ye've got ter do is scare the shite out of someone, an' they'll give ye one fer free. I'm a scary fuckin' man, Mr Detective. Which is somethin' ye lads will find out in due course.'

Sam's heart almost stopped beating. Was he hearing correctly?

'Lads, what lads?'

'I mean them two sons of yours. Ye lost me my boy, it's only right an' proper, Mr Detective – and ye'll be able te do fuck all to help 'em. A cripple with no bollocks. I don't think they'll be lookin' ter you fer protection. Ye see I've planned it, just like you planned burnin' down the fuckin' camp. Only I'm doin' you more damage than ye ever did ter me. I'm cripplin' ye whole fuckin' family, Mr Detective. Ye can tell 'em I'm goin' ter do it if ye like – give 'em somethin' ter look forward to. It won't stop it happenin'. One day – a day of my choosin' – they be out and about on two good legs and then bang, bang, bang, bang. No more kneecaps – and they'll blame you fer it, just like I got the blame fer the camp burnin' down. Naturally I'll have a lovely alibi.'

Sam said nothing. He was almost choking with fear for his boys. This bastard definitely meant what he said – and he was right about the boys blaming him. Christ! He'd blame himself if anything happened to them. Why, oh why did he get mixed up in all this crap? Why didn't he just stick to laying bricks?

He realised his heart was racing faster than he'd ever known it, almost bursting through his chest. He was controlling himself by taking short breaths. He must try to put the threat to his boys

184

right out of his mind. His panicking on their behalf wouldn't do anyone any good. If he knew anything he knew he must keep control of his wits. It was the only advantage he had over this drunken didicoy in the back seat. There was always something. The man would have a destination in mind where he would carry out the first part of his threat. Somewhere isolated. What did Sam have in his favour? The bulb in his petrol gauge had gone. He'd bought a bulb to replace it, but replacing dashboard bulbs in modern cars isn't straightforward. It was still in his glove compartment. Sam's whirring brain turned it into an idea.

'How far are we going? There's not a lot of petrol in this thing.'

He was lying but Lemmy had no way of knowing. The didicoy leant forward to try and look at the gauge. Then he sat back. There was hesitation before the answer came, which was good. He'd sown a seed of uncertainty in Lemmy's mind. Running out of petrol would cock up his plan.

'Just keep drivin'. There'll be petrol enough for where we're going.'

Sam pushed his luck. 'The gauge is showing empty. Shoot me here, pal, and you're stuck out in the sticks with a dead body and a car that won't go. So much for your alibi.'

'I'll manage.'

Shit! Sam inwardly moaned. All this was just talk and bluff. He needed something more concrete. As he rounded a corner his headlights picked out what looked like a stone monument, maybe twenty feet high with a cross on the top. He glanced at Lemmy through his rear-view

185

mirror and worked out his plan in an instant. In situations like this, instants were all he ever had to work with. Given time he'd have had second thoughts about such a drastic plan.

At the last second he swung the wheel and drove into the base of the monument, on which was inscribed *In God We Trust.* Sam was placing his trust in his seat belt and airbag. He struck the monument at around forty miles an hour. His seat belt held and the airbag inflated. Lemmy, who wasn't wearing a seatbelt, hit the headrest of the front passenger seat with sufficient force to knock him cold. Sam blacked out for a few seconds and found himself trapped behind the steering wheel which had been forced back into his chest by the impact. The airbag had quickly deflated but he still couldn't move. His biggest fear was still in the backseat. He held his own breath for a few seconds and listened for Lemmy's breathing. If the man was conscious he was very quiet. He was either dead or waiting for the right moment to take his retribution. Sam was in no position to turn his head and look round. It would be great if another car came along and the driver stopped to investigate. More than one car, hopefully.

But it was a quiet road, and late at night. Lemmy had chosen well. Sam heard a moan from behind him, and the sound of movement. And he knew this was no place to sit around waiting for help that might not come.

He reached down with his right hand, pulled up the seat recliner lever, then pushed himself backwards, away from the steering wheel. The force of the impact had sprung the driver's door open, which was a help. He unfastened his seat belt, eased himself sideways, out from behind the steering wheel and virtually fell out of the car on to the grass verge, where he lay for a few seconds, assessing his injuries.

His right knee hurt like hell and he thought he might have either broken or dislocated his left shoulder. He'd had both injuries in the past and both were as painful. His ribs felt sore where the seat belt had locked on impact and secured him. Maybe he had a broken rib or two but he'd settle for these injuries when compared to what Lemmy had had in store for him.

An intensely loud bang almost deafened him. A bullet clipped his left ear and embedded itself into the ground. Sam looked up and saw Lemmy's bloodied face in the car window, eerily lit by moonlight and partially obscured by the bullet hole he'd just made.

Sam instinctively rolled over and over as more shots followed until he reached a point around the front of the car where Lemmy couldn't get a bead on him. Blood was streaming down Sam's neck from the wound to his ear. He had counted four shots altogether. He could hear Lemmy swearing and trying to get the back door open. The crash had buckled the frame.

Sam dodged around the back of the monument and looked about to see if there were any houses in the vicinity where he might seek some sort of sanctuary. He couldn't see any. Lemmy was now climbing over the seat and getting out through the driver's door. Sam turned and ran.

The road was lined with trees which afforded

him some cover, but he was severely hampered by the pain in his right knee. It didn't help that his right shoe was missing. It meant he couldn't run at any great speed.

Another shot rang out. The bullet ripped through Sam's sleeve but didn't touch his skin. He worked out that Lemmy had maybe four bullets left – unless of course he also had spare ammo with which to reload. There was always that. Best not to rely on the empty gun theory.

Ahead was a broad oak, its trunk silhouetted by the moon. He could hear Lemmy's heavy breathing as he gave chase. Lemmy wasn't far behind. For a cripple he was moving well. Sam ran past the oak until he figured he was out of Lemmy's sight, then he doubled back and hid behind its trunk.

As Lemmy ran past Sam flung himself at him, trying to wrest the gun from the didicoy's hand. His only weapons were his right first and his head, his left arm was useless. Lemmy swung the gun towards Sam and fired, point blank. Sam moved his head out of the way a split second before a bullet buried itself in the tree trunk. The nearness and violence of sound numbed his senses for a second, causing him to wonder if he'd been hit and, if so, how badly? Instinctively his hand had gripped the wrist holding the gun and locked like a vice as Sam shook his head trying to clear it. As far as he could tell he was OK. He rammed his head into Lemmy's face with a ferocity that caused the didicoy to howl in pain and drop to his knees clutching his broken nose with one hand and waving the gun, in Sam's vague direction, with the other. He fired twice and missed causing Sam to take cover as Lemmy staggered to his feet, with the gun held out in front of him. Sam ran around the back of the tree as Lemmy screamed out a string of obscenities. There was a metallic rattling which Sam recognised as the magazine being ejected and another one slammed into the gun, and he cursed his ill judgement. He should have fought it out while he had the man at close quarters, with his gun nearly empty.

Sam was breathing heavily, whatever pain he felt was obscured by the extreme anxiety of his situation. Lemmy began to scream with manic laughter. He fired shots either side of the tree to show Sam he had no avenue of escape.

'Ye fuckin' done for, Carew! Ye dead meat! An' when I've settled you, I'll cripple them two bastards ye spawned. But I'll frighten the shite out of 'em before I do it. I'll make sure the little bastards know what's comin' to 'em. I'll have 'em weepin' and beggin' fer mercy. And d'ye know what mercy I'll show 'em Carew? I'll let the little bastards live the rest of their lives out in wheel-chairs. That's how much mercy they'll get.'

Sam tried to gauge the direction of his voice and edged around the tree, keeping it between him and the didicoy. If the drunken bastard was going to kill him Sam wasn't going to make it easy for him. It could be that a car would come along, and investigate the wreck just down the road. It might give him a chance. Lemmy kept up his obscene tirade. Both men were bad on their feet but Sam found he could negotiate the narrow perimeter of the tree a lot quicker than Lemmy could encircle it from a distance. But it was a game which couldn't go on forever.

'Shit!'

He winced and cursed as he trod on a large, sharp stone with his shoeless foot. He picked it up, wondering, at first, whether to risk throwing it at Lemmy. The odds were he'd miss and even if he hit he didn't have the strength to throw it very hard. It would also present him as an easy target. So, sod that for an idea.

Lemmy stopped his ranting. The silence was broken only by a midnight wind rustling the tree branches and the hoot of an owl and the distant grumble of Sam's car engine, which he hadn't switched off. Once again he held his breath to locate his adversary. His heart raced when he realised Lemmy had closed in and was right at the other side of the tree. On his way to make a kill. Edging around the tree trunk.

Sam judged Lemmy's approach to be from his left. He edged to his right, glancing from side to side all the time to check that he was guessing correctly. He saw Lemmy's gun appear, low and to his left. Sam's fist tightened on the stone in his right hand as the gun arm appeared. He took a quick step to his left and swung his arm around in a wide arc, with all the force he could muster.

The stone smashed into Lemmy's already broken nose. The intense pain caused the didicoy to cry out, giving Sam the split second he needed to drop the stone and grab the didicoy's gun hand, twisting inwards with all his strength. Lemmy, with blood pouring out of his nose, used two hands to try and force the weapon back in Sam's direction. Spitting out words of violence and venom. Anything to hurt Sam, whether it was word or deed.

'What I'll fuckin' do, Carew, is ter capture your lads and sell 'em to a gang o' pervs what I know. They'll pay me good money.'

Sam felt the gun turning in his direction. Once again he jammed his head into Lemmy's face, again and again. He had no idea where the gun was pointing when it went off. He felt the force of the blast and stopped fighting for the second it took for him to realise he hadn't been shot. The gun dropped from Lemmy's hands. The didicoy tried to cling on to Sam as he slumped, slowly, to the ground. Sam kicked him away, then he did the same with the gun.

The moon cast a speckled light through the branches of the tree as Lemmy sank to the ground and rolled over on his back. Looking up and coughing blood. A dark stain was spread across his chest where the bullet had entered. From that close range Sam figured there would be an even bigger stain on his back. But his rage and hatred of Lemmy hadn't gone. This man's threats against his sons were still ringing in his ears. He knelt down beside the didicoy, who was glaring at him, with hate in his dying eyes.

'I win, you lose,' Sam hissed. 'You're on your way to hell, you stinking rapist bastard.'

Lemmy's vicious glare turned to abject fear. It was as if he hadn't realised he was dying until Sam told him. Sam got to his feet and walked away. Condemning this foul man, who had threatened his sons so obscenely, to die alone.

A car's headlights appeared in the distance.

Sam limped out into the road and held up his good arm for the driver to stop. Such was his bloodied and frightening appearance that the driver, understandably, went straight past him and didn't pull up until he saw the crashed car.

By the time the driver turned around and had driven back, Sam was sitting, exhausted, by the side of the road. The headlights picked out the corpse of Lemmy Wilson and the driver chose to stay in his car, with his engine running, as he dialled 999. Sam struggled to his feet and limped back to his own car to try and find his shoe.

It was all he could think to do.

CHAPTER TWENTY-EIGHT

'Does this one belong to you?' enquired the nurse as she examined Sam's chart.

It took Tracey a few seconds to realise the nurse was talking about Sam, whom she was visiting.

'What? No, I'm just a friend.'

'He probably needs friends. I've just been looking through his medical records. I've read shorter Stephen King books. Is he a trainee suicide bomber or something?'

'I *am* here,' protested Sam. 'And are you supposed to discuss my medical history with all and sundry?'

The nurse gave Tracey an old-fashioned look. 'All and sundry, eh? He thinks you're all and sundry.'

Sam had spent the night in Leeds General Infirmary – not one of his favourite hospitals. Too big and impersonal. The nurse went on her way. Sam watched her go, then turned his attention to Tracey.

'Did they tell you who it was in the car?'

She nodded. 'Lemmy Wilson. Don't know whether to feel guilty or relieved.'

'Try relieved.'

'Did I see the police leaving as I came in?'

'You did,' Sam grumbled. 'I was honoured with a visit by an inspector and a sergeant from Leeds Police Headquarters in Millgarth Street. It seems my reputation has preceded me. They all but accused me of being the cause of his death because I purposely crashed my car, causing him so much injury that he eventually shot himself because he wasn't thinking straight. I suggested that their theory might not stand up in court, which didn't go down well. It'll be Bowman's doing. He'll have poisoned their minds against me.' He muttered the last bit almost to himself.

'Who's Bowman?'

'A DI down at Unsworth nick. Me and him have a bit of history.'

'You seem to have a bit of history with a lot of people,' Tracey commented, then added, 'Do you think it was Lemmy who's been setting you up?'

Sam shook his head. 'It crossed my mind when he held a gun on me, then I realised who he was.' He tapped his temple with a finger. 'Whoever set me up's got a bit more up here than Lemmy Wilson ever had.'

'He could have got someone else to do it.'

'Possible, but very doubtful. The Lemmy Wilsons of this world tend not to mix with intelligent people – unless it's to mug them.'

She nodded her head in agreement, then asked, 'So, how are you?'

'Happy to be alive,' said Sam. 'One dislocated shoulder, one knackered knee, two cracked ribs and one missing earlobe. Luckily for me there's a bed shortage so they're letting me go home as soon as a doctor's given me the all clear.'

'Going home? To Sally?'

'She's not around, as I think you probably know.'

'I thought she might be back. I can drop by and help you out if you like.'

Sam met her innocent gaze with an admonishing gaze of his own.

'What?' she said, innocently.

'Tracey, if you start trying to help me out Sally'll never come back. And I might lose my enthusiasm to get Jim out of the clink.'

'Ah, I see the problem. It's just that last night wa–'

'Tracey, last night didn't happen. What we need now is to get Jim and Sally back.'

'Yes, of course we do.'

Sam thought she sounded more patronising than sincere. 'Tracey,' he said, 'me and you will never happen.'

'Hey, listen to old bighead. Who says I want it to happen? Jim's my husband. All I want is to get him out.' She took one of the mint imperials which Owen had brought for Sam and popped it in her mouth. Her gaze rested on a cleaner who was polishing a chrome bedhead.

194

'Do you know,' he said, 'there's something been nagging at me and I've only just realised what it was.'

'What's that?'

'That clean golf club in Jim's bag. Why would he clean one golf club? He never cleaned the others. Not big on cleaning stuff, my Jim.'

Sam remembered something Sally had said. 'Maybe it's a club he never used.'

Tracey nodded. 'Yeah, but there's unused, and there's highly polished.' She watched the cleaner rub a cloth along the rail. 'That club looked as if it had just been polished up. Jim's not a big one for polish. It takes him all his time to clean his teeth.'

'Have you asked him about it?'

She looked from the cleaner to Sam and shrugged. 'It's as much a mystery to him as it is to me. It's probably something or nothing. I just thought it was odd, that's all.'

'Actually, I don't see what it has to do with anything,' remarked Sam. 'It's not as though it's clean because the killer rubbed his prints off it. Apart from the one that killed Alistair, none of Jim's clubs were at the crime scene, including the clean one. They were all in the locker room at his golf club.'

'That's odd as well,' said Tracey. 'Why would he leave his clubs in the locker room and just take one with him to kill Alistair? It seems a very odd thing to do.'

'Maybe he just had that particular club in his car boot for some reason,' Sam suggested.

'Whose side are you on?' protested Tracey.

'It's called playing devil's advocate. If you're

looking for someone to tell you what you want to hear, you've come to the wrong person.'

'What? Oh, right.'

'But I'd like you to keep coming up with ideas like that. It's the bits of stuff which don't make sense that solve mysteries.' Sam helped himself to a mint imperial. 'Tell you what, I'll take another look at the clean golf club.'

'And do what?'

'I'll try and make sense of it – try and think of a scenario that would lead to it being pristine clean. In fact you should do the same. The fewer scenarios we can think of, the more chance we have of one of them being right. I might ask his golfing pals.'

'You'd better be quick while there's any left.'

CHAPTER TWENTY-NINE

Sam was in his office, sitting with his right leg resting on a chair. His wounded ear had a huge plaster on it and his ribs were strapped up. His shoulder had been popped back into place but it still ached. All in all he was happy to be alive. He'd made a random list of things to do. At the top of the list it said, *Get hold of Sal and sort things out, you idiot.* This was followed by: Insurance claim on car; check contract with Morgan Blackstone; check building contract; see Shane Outhwaite, see David McLeish, Stuke White, Manny Green, anybody else connected with these people

196

– wives, girlfriends etc etc; send golf club to forensic lab in Wetherby; ring *Unsworth Observer* and sell them the story about the set-ups and the attempt on my life; ring the court to check on progress; tell court I'm contacting the *Observer*.

This last idea brought a smile to his face. Courts hated all public accusations of incompetence – especially ones they couldn't defend. He should have done this straight away. It was the kick up the arse they needed. It would probably have been the first thing Sally thought of. It was as if whoever had done this to him knew of the important part Sally played in his life. He sat back in his chair and wracked his brains. Who the hell would know such a thing?

Owen Price knocked and entered just as the thought was occupying Sam's mind and it instantly occurred to him that Owen was one of the few people who would know such a thing. Then, a nanosecond later, he mentally rebuked himself for even thinking this.

The Welshman's mouth chewed on a sweet as his eyes travelled over Sam's various injuries. 'You know, boyo, there's only so much luck in the world and I'd say you've got it all.'

'You call this luck?'

'After what I've heard I call you being alive luck.' Owen swallowed whatever he'd been chewing. 'Sally not put an appearance in yet, boyo?'

'I wish you wouldn't call me boyo. It's like an Irishman saying begorra. They just don't do it.'

Owen looked bemused, wondering what sort of an answer this was to a perfectly reasonable question. Sam's grumpy mood gave him the answer.

'I'll take that as a no, then.'

'I don't even know if she *is* coming back,' said Sam.

'I've heard from the Leeds police, look you, that the CPS are taking no action against you regarding the violent death of Lemmy Wilson.'

'That was quick, they usually like to keep you dangling.'

'It was the word of a live lunatic against the reputation of a dead didicoy with a sheet as long as your arm,' said Owen. 'It was a close decision, but you scraped home by a nose.'

'I had a couple of uniforms come to see me in hospital,' Sam said. 'They knew Lemmy was from the camp that burnt down, so naturally they put two and two together and got five. Accused me of starting the fire and giving him reason to harm me. What sort of minds do these coppers have? My alibi for that night is Sally, who thinks I'm two-timing her, so maybe it's a good job I don't have to rely on her.'

'You could always rely on Sally,' said Owen.

Sam nodded. 'Whoever set me up stuffed me good and proper. I don't think I'd have believed me if I'd have been her. If I could talk to her I'd make her see sense in five minutes.'

Owen unravelled this in his mind. He was secretly impressed that Sally walking out seemed to be bothering him more than his other troubles. But they were troubles which required his attention.

'I think Sally will come back in her own time – unless she's met someone else.'

Sam gave his possibility a few seconds' thought,

198

then dismissed it with a shake of his head. 'Yeah, you're probably right, she'll come back in her own time.' He lit a cigarette and studied his list.

'I thought you were trying to stop,' Owen said.

'I don't smoke in pubs any more.'

'You're not allowed to smoke in pubs any more.'

Sam studied the lit end of his cigarette. 'I've cut down to only smoking in times of great stress.'

'Your whole life's a time of great stress.'

Sam ignored this. 'My car's a write-off,' he said. 'Do you think the insurance company will give me any grief if they suspect I crashed it on purpose?'

'Did you tell uniform you crashed it on purpose?'

'No – I told them I was panicked into crashing it. You know the drill. If I told them I'd crashed it on purpose it would have set unnecessary wheels in motion – especially with it being me.'

'So, why would the insurers think you crashed it on purpose?'

'I don't know. Maybe it makes no difference. I'll have to check my policy.' He looked at Owen. 'He wasn't only going to cripple me, he was going to kneecap my boys as well – he also threatened to hand them over to some pervy pals of his, and I believe he'd have done it. The man was a complete psycho.'

'Bloody hell, Sam! Did you tell the uniforms that?'

Sam lowered his voice. 'No, I didn't. This is between me and you. I don't want the boys ever to know the danger their stupid dad put them in.'

Owen placed a hand on his friend's shoulder. 'No problem, boyo.'

Sam touched Owen's hand, briefly, then said, 'I keep wondering if there was a way of sorting it without him getting killed. No matter how vile they are it always sickens me when someone gets killed because of me – even if it wasn't my fault.'

'The man was truly vile,' said Owen.

'Yes he was,' said Sam, 'but there'll have been a time when he was just a kid, like any other kid – like you and me. That's what I keep thinking about. Then he went down the wrong road because he wasn't taught any different.'

'Sam, you could say the same about Adolf Hitler. Lemmy did mankind a favour by removing himself from our midst. The man would have been a constant threat had he lived. As it happens I think you approached the problem in the only way possible – if in a typical Carew manner.'

'Well, I didn't think it through, I must admit. When you've only got two seconds thinking time it's not easy to think things through.' He gave Owen a sudden smile. 'Anyway, it's done and dusted. No need to worry about it any more. There'll be an inquest, I'll give my evidence and that will be that.'

He got up, hobbled to a filing cabinet, took out a file marked Morgan Blackstone then sat down again. 'Morgan Blackstone cancelled my contract,' he said, opening the file. 'They cancelled it because of an anonymous email that said I'd stolen the painting for the insurance money. I don't think they can do that.'

Owen sat down opposite him and took a Mars Bar out of his pocket. 'I shouldn't have thought it'd make much difference now. I should have thought you had more important things to worry about, like restoring your reputation – such as it is.' He took the wrapping off his chocolate bar and bit into it. With his mouth full, he mumbled, 'Did you know that you can get deep-fried Mars Bars in Scotland. I wonder why they don't do that down here?'

'What?'

'I imagine a deep-fried Mars bar would taste quite exotic.'

Sam's eyes scanned the wording in the contract as his ears picked up Owen's culinary observation. 'To a Welshman a deep-fried turd would taste quite exotic,' he said, without looking up.

'Careful, boyo, your inbred Yorkshire coarseness is showing. Did you know that the only instance of genocide in Britain was in 1069 when William the Conqueror killed off eighty per cent of all Yorkshiremen because he considered them to be a pain in the arse? He obviously didn't catch up with the Carews.'

Sam was usually up for such banter but his mind was now elsewhere. 'Do no harm to let my solicitor take a look at this,' he said. 'There's nothing in here that gives them permission to terminate the contract like they did.'

The Welshman took the contract from him and read it through as Sam finished his cigarette and examined his sore knee. 'They should have put one of those pressure bandages on this,' he commented. 'They would at Unsworth General. I've always had first class service at Unsworth General.'

'You're probably right about this,' Owen said,

giving him the document back, 'but there's no point spending money on solicitors until you actually find the painting – and correct me if I'm wrong, but isn't Mrs Ormerod paying for your exclusive services right now?'

'She is indeed,' conceded Sam, 'but the painting theft and Alistair Waring's murder are linked – as is Rudolph's murder. If I find the painting, everything else will fall into place.'

'And you'll collect a fat fee from Morgan Blackstone as well as wages from Tracey.'

'If I make this contract stick. I'm going to have to be really careful here. If I find the painting and don't hand it over to its rightful owner because Morgan Blackstone won't stick to their contract I could be in trouble with the law. Not sure what the charge would be but Bowman will think of one, no doubt about that.' He rubbed his chin, thoughtfully. 'I'll have to tread very carefully. Not actually tell them in so many words. Just let them know that if they went the painting back I can get it for them.'

'You make it sound as if you know where it is already.'

'Wish I did – but I'm fairly certain I know a man who does.'

'By the way,' said Owen, 'Bowman's taken over the Rudolph Mace enquiry. DI Seager was getting snowed under.'

'Has he now?' Sam looked at Owen and grinned. 'Can you imagine the look on Bowman's face when he finds out we were right all along about the painting theft and the murders being linked?'

'How do you mean *we* were right? It's *your*

theory, boyo.'

'Ah, but you'll be telling Bowman there's a connection, because you know I'm right and you won't be able to resist telling him.'

'And Bowman will tell me not to be such an idiot.'

'He'll probably assume you got the idea from me.'

'Carew, he'll *know* I got the idea from you.' Owen became thoughtful. 'The DCI's been on sick for a week and he's just been taken into hospital this morning. If the prognosis is bad someone's going to be made up to acting DCI.'

'That's either Janet Seager or Bowman,' Sam guessed. 'Most likely Bowman.'

'Most certainly Bowman,' said Owen.

Sam went quiet, as though his mind had switched to more important matters. He looked at Owen. 'Sally hasn't rung you, has she?'

The Welshman shrugged and shook his head. 'Why should she ring me?'

'Just something I said to her mother. If she rings you, you will put her straight, won't you? None of your lame attempts at jocularity. Just put her straight. Tell her what's happened to me.'

'Will I tell her you're missing her, boyo?'

'What? Oh, yeah, tell her that.'

CHAPTER THIRTY

Detective Inspector Bowman glared at DC Owen Price. 'Do you know what I smell, Price?' he said.

'Sir?'

'I smell the fetid odour of Carew.'

'Carew, sir?'

'Yes, Carew. This association you've made between the murders of Waring and Mace, and the art theft. This isn't *your* association, this is Carew's association. It's his thinking. I know Carew's thinking. It gives off an unmistakable aroma.'

Bowman had called Owen into his office. With Owen knowing as much as Janet Seager about the Rudolph Mace enquiry he'd been asked to bring Bowman up to speed.

One of the many things that bugged Bowman was that Janet Seager, his detective sergeant of only twelve months ago, had been promoted to detective inspector, while he himself had been reduced to that same rank because of a serious misdemeanour. She had risen from being a distant subordinate to being of the same rank within a few weeks. What bugged him even more was that DC Owen Price worked almost exclusively within her team. And what bugged him about that was that Owen Price was still closely connected with former DS Sam Carew whose career in the force had been foreshortened when he electrocuted Bowman in a prank gone wrong. Since then, Carew had been a pain in Bowman's side. Making him look a fool on more than one occasion.

'I admit the theory is his, sir,' Owen said, 'but there is an element of credence to it when you come to think of it.'

'But I *don't* come to think of it, Price. The last thing I want to think of in this world is Carew. If I lent Carew ten thousand pounds and never saw him again it would be money well spent. Do you understand me, Price?'

'I understand there are issues between you and Mr Carew, sir, but it would be wrong to let them hamper the possible solving of a crime,' said Owen, bravely. Much of his courage came from the fact that he considered himself the property of DI Seager who also valued Sam's unofficial input on crime.

Bowman got to his feet, walked around his desk and positioned his face just a few inches from Owen's. Then he spoke in a low but menacing voice.

'Listen to me, Price. Disaster clings to Carew like the smell of drains. People die, people commit murder, people steal priceless works of art. You cling to Carew, Price, and that smell will stick to you like shit to a blanket. It will follow you around until it sucks you in and spits you out. One day you will become one of Carew's casualties. I don't much like you, Price, but I like Carew even less which is why I'm giving you this valuable advice.'

'That's very kind of you, sir. I'll bear it in mind.'

Owen didn't need Bowman to tell him that Sam

was a walking disaster area. He had always known that. But he also knew that Sam was an irresponsible, irresistible star, illuminating a murky universe. Owen reluctantly orbited that star, suffering the odd minor catastrophe in exchange for its warmth, its light, its adventure, its friendship and its humour. Also in its orbit were Sally, Sam's two sons and one or two minor satellites, such as Alec and DI Janet Seager, if they cared to admit it. 'Will that be all, sir?' he added politely.

'For now,' snapped Bowman picking up his newspaper.

The *Unsworth Observer* always considered Sam to be worth a few column inches. His hard luck story about being set up to get him off the trail of the murderer was given sympathetic treatment. Sam hadn't mentioned his theory about the killings being connected with the art theft; he had no proof and it might put the thieves on their guard. The journalist who covered the story had been reporting Sam's exploits for years. At the end of his piece he added a personal opinion:

...knowing Sam Carew's reputation and his uncanny ability to sniff out villains it's my guess that the killer will be more worried about Sam Carew than he will the police.

Bowman read it and threw the paper across his office before storming out to vent his spleen on Owen who was, fortunately for Owen, no longer around.

Shooey read the same article with a mixture of

consternation and excitement. Logically his next victim should be Carew, but Carew wouldn't present an easy target. If he got the others out of the way it would mean Carew had nothing to work on. They were the only links to him. Carew would arrive at a dead end. On top of which the others wouldn't be laying claim to their shares – on account of them being dead. It would all be his and he could pick up the money without looking over his shoulder. Ever.

CHAPTER THIRTY-ONE

The chapel at Unsworth crematorium was barely a quarter full. Rudolph's wife and two daughters sat together in the front pews with their heads bowed as Stuke White read out Rudolph's eulogy. The pews behind Mrs Mace and her daughters were empty, apart from Sam and Owen, sitting on the back row. They half expected a bitter outburst from Rudolph's widow when Stuke came to the part about Rudolph being a loving husband and father. She'd apparently taken the circumstances of her husband's death very badly and had refused to fork out any money for his funeral. Stuke had generously stepped in and paid for a hearse, a standard service and a basic cremation in a bottom-of-the-range coffin.

On the other side of the chapel sat Rudolph's grieving mother and various younger relatives, plus a row of shaven-headed, thick-necked bouncers. Also in the chapel were Manny Green, Shane Outhwaite and Dave McLeish; the latter two had an aura of shock about them. Shane kept looking around the chapel with a look on his face that Sam recognised as fearful. Shane's gaze travelled to the row behind him and settled on a man to whom he nodded. He then turned back and said something to Dave, who also looked at the man, before nodding to him. Sam was now interested in this man, mainly because there was no one else here to take his interest. He nudged Owen and whispered, 'Do you know that bloke?'

'How do I know? I can only see the back of his head,' said Owen. 'All I can tell from here is that he doesn't own a comb.'

A chaplain got up and led the congregation in the Lord's Prayer. He then said something about Rudolph going to a better place and Mrs Mace burst into a loud sob so the chaplain curtailed his discourse and nodded to a man who switched on a tape player which played 'Abide With Me'. Owen began to sing, but his voice soon dwindled out when he realised he was on his own and that people were looking at him. As the hymn drew to a close a conveyor belt took the coffin through a pair of purple velvet curtains which had scarcely closed when Mrs Mace got to her feet and urged her daughters back down the aisle. Without a single glance to anyone in the chapel the small family hurried out.

Owen muttered, 'Bugger!' as he dropped his hymn book to the floor. He was retrieving it when the lone man followed. Sam examined the man's face for future reference. It was the face of a man on the verge of something. Permanently crumpled, as though on the verge of tears. On the other hand, thought Sam, this was a funeral. Leaving Owen in his wake, he quickly followed the man out, then stepped in front of Manny who was a few paces in front of Dave and Shane.

'Who's that bloke who's just gone out?'

'Oh, what's his name? – Gerald something or other,' said Manny, walking straight past. He called out over his shoulder. 'Bloody weirdo if you ask me. Wouldn't surprise me if he's the bloke you're after.'

'His name's Gerald Rothwell,' said Dave, pausing beside Sam, as did Shane. 'He plays golf at Bostrop Park.'

'Is that how he knew Rudolph?'

Dave shrugged. 'Prob'ly. He's a very odd bugger – used to work for Alistair. Not a bad golfer, actually, but he's an odd bugger.'

'In what way odd?'

'Hard ter put yer finger on,' Dave said. 'For a start he's a hell of a lot younger than he looks. I played with him in a four-ball once. He walked off on the ninth – reckoned he were playin' crap an' he didn't want ter play any more. Yer don't do that in a four-ball. I reported him ter the committee.'

'Really?' said Sam, who never failed to be amazed by the singular devotion of golfers to the laws and courtesies of the game.

'No point playin' if yer partner walks off halfway through,' Dave explained. 'It's like a goalie pissin' off to the pub at half time and not comin' back.'

Sam could empathise with this, he'd once

known such a goalie.

'He apologised,' said Dave, 'but I never had him as a partner since.'

'Does he still work at Alistair's firm?'

'No,' chipped in Shane. 'I heard that he's working for a car park firm now. No idea what doing. Prob'ly handing out parking tickets, knowing Gerald.'

'He's harmless enough' said Dave. 'Still lives with his mother – that type.'

'Anybody know where he lives?' Sam asked.

'Why? D'yer think he's the killer?'

'Do you?' asked Sam.

Dave immediately shook his head. 'If he's a killer,' he said, 'I'll show my arse in Woolworth's window for a week.'

Shooey heard most of their conversation from his position around the corner after watching the service from a pew near the back. He lit up a cigarette and decided on his next victim.

Dave McLeish watched his tee shot sail down the centre of the sixteenth fairway. It was turned eight in the evening and as far as he could see he was the only one on the golf course. This was one of the great joys of his life. Finding out that he was a diabetic had been a right bastard; in many ways even worse than finding out his second wife, on whom he had doted, had been having it off behind his back with an estate agent from Wakefield. The divorce had cleaned him out, despite him being the innocent party. Both his ex-wives were financially OK but that hadn't stopped them setting the CSA onto him. The fact that he was self-employed made them easier to cope with as they couldn't order the money to be deducted from his salary.

He'd started out with a small picture framing business and when he moved from his backstreet premises into a shop he'd started selling a few pictures and art materials. From there he'd taken a real interest in art, buying paintings from auctions and house clearances and selling them in his shop. He had put on exhibitions for local artists and had even done a course in Fine Arts at Unsworth College. The idea to steal the Rembrandt had been his. The Unsworth Museum of Art had asked him to organise a few local artists to exhibit at the bicentenary art festival and had told him about various old masters coming to town. He hadn't been serious when he'd mooted it to Alistair, but the solicitor saw the possibilities in such a caper. Rudolph had been recruited because of his connections with the security firm and Shane simply because he was a bright and agile young man who wasn't averse to breaking the law. The other two members of the golfing group, Jim and Manny, had been left out as surplus to requirements.

The organisation had all been down to Dave and Alistair, with Alistair finding the London buyers and the intermediary, Billy Hargrave; and Dave using his association with the gallery to check the place out – or 'case the joint', as Shane had put it. Dave had also been to check on the three paintings they had short-listed for the theft: Rossetti's *Beata Beatrix* in the Tate London, Renoir's *The Theatre Box* at the Courtauld Institute in London, and the Rembrandt in Amsterdam, all being loaned for the exhibition. Dave had selected the Rembrandt because of its handy size, because the plain frame was easy to copy and because it was behind glass which would help hide fraudulent brushstrokes from expert eyes.

At first, as far as Dave was concerned, Alistair's murder had been nothing to do with the theft. But when Billy Hargrave and Rudolph were also murdered it seemed pretty obvious to him that it was the London men who were behind it. He'd got the idea in his mind that they intended leaving just one of them alive. The survivor would be so scared he'd hand over the painting for nothing. But it seemed such a flaky way for organised criminals to behave; risking capture every time they took someone out. The painting was worth twenty times what they'd originally agreed to pay for it, so why all this? Maybe they weren't organised criminals. Maybe they were just a clumsy gang.

He knocked another ball down the fairway as these thoughts went through his mind. An empty course was the ideal place to practise his drives.

The London men hadn't been in contact since he'd failed to turn up for the meeting at the M1 service station, and he didn't know whether this was a good or bad thing. Shane had the idea of hanging on until a reward was put up. This didn't seem like a bad idea at all – providing the London men had lost all interest. The alternative was to wait and see if they killed either him or Shane, then the survivor could make the final decision. It wasn't much of an alternative.

He knocked away another couple of drives, both

of them sliced, viciously, to the right. It was time to pack it in. A man with his head full of worries can't play golf. There was this saying: Golf is a game of inches – the five inches between the ears. Golfers have many self-deprecating sayings, which make the non-golfer wonder why they bother.

He heard the shotgun blast as he was pulling the headcover on to his driver. The noise passed away a millisecond after Dave passed away. He heard the beginning but not the end. Shooey had crept up behind him from the cover of nearby bushes and blasted him from point blank range, blowing a hole straight through Dave's body and splattering his internal organs all over the tee-box. Early the next morning he would be found by an assistant greenkeeper who would add to the visceral mess with a more bilious mess of his own.

Shooey picked up the spent cartridge case, calmly climbed over a boundary wall, got into his car and drove away, amazed at how quick and simple it had all been. He would, of course, need to get rid of the gun and destroy every article of clothing he was wearing, including his footwear, which was why he had turned up in his oldest gear – watching American detective programmes had taught him that. He had left no cigarette butts or anything with incriminating DNA or fingerprints; his car was parked on a road where he'd leave no tyre tracks, and he'd attached temporary false number plates for the benefit of any CCTV cameras. Each of his killings had been different. Variety is the spice of life – or death in this case. It would further confuse the police – make them wonder if it was the same killer who had killed all three friends. It was a game. It was the most exciting game he'd played in his life and the rewards would be considerable.

CHAPTER THIRTY-TWO

Owen was standing at the bar with the *Daily Mail* propped up on an empty pint glass when Sam walked into the Clog and Shovel. In Owen's other hand was a half-full pint. He was also chewing what Sam suspected, going on the crumpled evidence by his elbow, was a Mars Bar. The woman behind the bar asked Sam if he wanted a pint of the usual. Sam nodded, then inclined his head towards Owen, 'Is he eating a Mars Bar? How can anybody drink beer and eat Mars Bars?'

'Hey, don't ask me – he's your pal.'

Owen didn't look up. He stabbed a finger at a photograph in the newspaper. 'Look at this, look you, they've had wanted pictures of this Manchester rapist all over the papers and the telly for weeks. Now they've caught him they cover his head with a blanket – what's that all about?'

'Look at this look you?' said Sam, 'What sort of talk's that?'

Owen shook his head at the picture. Sam watched his pint being expertly pulled. There was something civilised and British about a hand-pulled pint, something that was lacking in electric beer. The Welshman folded his paper and finished his drink in two enormous gulps. 'Bowman's been made acting DCI,' he said, pushing his empty glass towards the barmaid, saying he would like another please and that Sam would pay.

Sam nodded his consent to this, then he picked up his own pint and took an appreciative sip. 'Only to be expected. So, who's doing what?'

'Another DI's coming in on a temporary from Wakefield. Janet's got the Mace and McLeish murders.'

'And you're doing the leg work for her?' asked Sam, hopefully.

'Some of it, unless Bowman says differently – I'm just going to keep out of his way.' He looked at Sam, carefully. 'That chap at the crematorium...'

'What chap?'

'You know better than that, Sam. You don't do your job at the expense of ours. You could save me a bit of time if you gave me his details. I know you've got them.'

'His name's Gerald Rothwell. Unmarried. He lives with his mother at number 117 Ashburton Road and he works at the new NCP multi-storey in town. Something to with security, although I've never anyone who looks less like a security man – present company excepted.'

Owen ignored Sam's jibe. 'Have you spoken to him?'

'Nope. If he's the man we're looking for it makes no sense to put him on his guard. If you must know I fully intended handing it over to you lot. This isn't work for a private eye. If he is our man I need you to nail him for the Alistair Waring killing as well. Do that and my job for Tracey

Ormerod is done. He used to work for Waring.'

'So, you think he might also have been involved in the Rembrandt theft?'

Sam had been thinking about this for some time. He shrugged and said, 'Your guess is as good as mine. If he is I want my important part in this noted for when I claim my fee from Morgan Blackstone.' He eyed Owen. 'No matter what Bowman says.'

'That's no problem,' Owen promised. Sam knew he would never renege on such a promise.

'What does Rothwell look like?' Owen asked. 'I only saw him from behind.'

'He's sort of emaciated. I'm told he's in his mid-forties,' said Sam, 'but he has a complexion that somehow doesn't match the rest of him, podgy yet wrinkled, like a scrotum.'

'You have a poetic way with words, Carew.'

'He's not a relative of yours, is he? He did have a Welsh look about him.'

'I'll ignore that.'

'Ah, but you won't be able to ignore him. The man could use a gallon of Botox.' Sam studied Owen's face. 'Have you thought about Botox, Owen?'

'I'll think about it when I get to your age.'

'You're attempting humour again, Owen. I've told you before. Welshmen shouldn't attempt humour. It's against their nature.'

CHAPTER THIRTY-THREE

Shane scarcely dared leave his flat. Every time the phone rang he jumped, although he couldn't figure, for the life of him, how the London crowd might have got his number. He just wanted out and his only way out, without being locked up, was Carew.

He'd thought of leaving the painting somewhere and ringing the police up to tell them where it was. But supposing someone else picked it up and didn't hand it in? He'd be worse off than ever. He needed the painting's return to be cast-iron safe and recorded in newspapers. The London crowd must be made aware of its return and therefore leave him alone. Carew was the only way he could think of. He would tell Carew the problem, the whole story, and let him handle things. That was Carew's job. He'd do it because he'd get paid from the insurance company. Shane knew about Carew's contract. Shane knew about many things to do with Sam. In fact he smiled to himself as he thought of how much help he could be to Sam Carew. What the hell? Maybe he could get a piece of the action. After what he'd been through he deserved a piece of the action. Some of the insurance money which Sam would no doubt collect. No harm in trying. In any case this needed doing properly. It needed some thought or he could land inside doing a very long stretch.

Sam was still in his office. Owen had just left to track down and question Gerald Rothwell. It would be a real feather in the Welshman's cap if he captured a triple murderer and major art thief, single handed. The phone rang.

'Mr Carew?'

'Yes.'

'This is Shane Outhwaite.'

Sam swung his foot off the chair and sat up. This was going to be a call worth taking.

'I need you to help me, Mr Carew. I think it'll be worth your while.'

'Really? How's that?'

'I wonder if you could come to me? I, er, I think you can guess why I don't want to show my face too much.'

'Yes. I suspect you must be worried. Have you mentioned your worries to the police?'

'Er, what? No, I haven't. I, er, I thought I'd ring you. There are things I need to, erm–'

Sam interrupted him. 'Give me your address, I'll be over there this afternoon.'

He put the phone down and wished, not for the first time, that Sally had been sitting opposite him. He needed to bounce stuff off her. Exchange insults and ideas. Let's face it, Carew. You just want to hold her and squeeze her and kiss her and – he dismissed the more carnal of his desires from his mind as being insulting to Sal.

Sam could have gone to Shane's that very minute, but committing himself to immediate action when it wasn't absolutely necessary was something which often caused problems in this line of work. In this line of work if there's time to think, take it. Sam took the time and was pleased he had. When he arrived at Shane's flat he'd be prepared.

His train of thought was broken by the rattle of his letter box as the post arrived. He heaved himself from his chair and went to pick it up.

One of the letters was from Plessington Holdings informing him that substantial remedial works were being carried out by the new contractors and the cost would be deducted from his final payment. It was the second such letter he'd had in a few days. He strongly suspected that a deal had been done between Plessingtons and the new builders which would stiff him for all the money Carew and Son were due. There was nothing he could do about it. He opened another envelope to see if it contained better news. It didn't.

Shane lived in a two-bedroomed council flat on the Roberstown estate. It was just Sam's luck that it was a second floor flat. His knee was creasing him as he knocked on Shane's door. There was a delay as he sensed himself being examined through the spy hole. Two bolts rattled, a key turned, and a safety chain was unhooked. The door opened. Shane ushered Sam inside, then relocked.

They sat inside a comfortably furnished living room which, to Sam's mind, had a woman's touch about it. Net curtains, pot plants, ornaments, a fluffy rug. Shane glanced at the elbow crutch which Sam had been using, then at his bandages.

'You look to have been in the wars, Mr Carew. I read about what happened with the gippo. Near thing by the sound of it.'

'The job has its risky side. Do you live here on your own?'

'I do now. Split up from my girlfriend a few days ago. I guess you know how it is.'

'Really? You seem to know a lot about my private life. How come?'

Shane stared at him, then he took out a packet of Marlboros. 'Smoke?'

'Thanks.' Sam took one and accepted a light. Then he sat back. 'Tell me how this is going to be worth my while, Shane.'

'I know the insurance company hired you to find the missing painting.'

'The insurance company sacked me,' Sam said, 'when someone sent them a malicious email.'

'I can clear all that up,' said Shane.

Sam gave him a long, cold stare that had Shane shifting, uncomfortably.

'So, that was you, was it?'

Shane gave a shrug.

'Some sort of computer expert are you, Shane?'

Another shrug.

'I need some sort of immunity.'

'That's not what I think you need,' said Sam. 'Why would you need immunity?'

Shane puffed, nervously, on his cigarette, then stubbed it out in an ash tray. 'Look, Mr Carew, I'm shit-scared of being killed. They've killed Alistair, Rudolph and Dave. I'm the only one left. I've got something you want and I'll give you it, if you'll help keep me out of jail.'

'Would this something be a picture of an old man, Shane?'

'You know what it is – I'm prepared to do a deal with you.'

'What sort of deal?'

'I'll tell you where it is in exchange for a half share of the insurance money – plus I don't go to jail.'

'But I've just told you I've been sacked by the insurance company. At the moment there is no money. And if I do get any there'll be none coming you way.'

'OK, a quarter share,' said Shane.

'A quarter of nothing's nothing.'

'What if I square things with the insurers?'

'What if I just get up and walk out of here?'

Shane let out a sigh. 'OK, forget the money. I just need to give the painting back so the bastards who are killing us will know I haven't got it.'

'Was it you who set me up with the woman, Shane?'

This drew a grin from the young man. 'Hey, it was nothing personal. I gather you got a pretty good eyeful, at my expense. I just had to give you something else to think about. You were on our tail. It was all part of the game.'

'A game – really?' Sam was fighting hard not to betray his feelings but Shane's answer had him boiling. No way would this smug little shit get away with ruining his private life. 'I understand,' he said, 'and all the other stuff – was that all part of your game?'

'I suppose so.'

'What about the limited company we're sup-posed to have owed money to?'

'We already had it,' Shane said. 'Ally set it up

with bogus directors. He thought it might come in handy somewhere along the line. He liked to have a Plan B, did Ally. The winding-up order was my idea – sorry. The company wasn't actually trading as anything but that didn't matter. All I needed was for it to be registered at Companies House and it was enough to fool the court computers. Once you fool the computers you throw the whole system into bloody chaos. I've got a first class honours degree in IT – apparently I've got a bit of flair for hacking. You'd be amazed at how easy it is to get into some of these antiquated systems. The court computer was an absolute pissball, so was the *Unsworth Observer*. They should be better protected.'

'Maybe after this is all over you could get a job doing just that.'

The words 'after this is all over' brought a smirk of relief to Shane's face. 'Yeah, maybe some good might come out of it.' He lit another cigarette; Sam was still on his first. 'Just as a matter of interest, Mr Carew, did I slow you down much? I'd no real way of knowing how much effect it all had?'

'It had the desired effect,' said Sam. He fully intended having the desired effect on Shane, who was grinning.

'Well, I guess the insurance money will make things right – once I've squared things with Morgan Blackstone.'

'How do you propose doing that?' Sam asked him.

The young man took a handkerchief from his pocket. Inside it was a 35mm film canister which he handed to Sam. 'Excuse me being cautious,' he said. 'I'm just a bit wary of my fingerprints being on this. There's a film in here with a photo of the Rembrandt on it, alongside a copy of the *Daily Express* dated the day after the robbery. It was our buyers' idea, to prove we had it. The film isn't developed so it can't have been tampered with. We've already sent them one roll. We took this one for insurance, just in case the deal went sour.'

'Plan B, eh?'

Shane shrugged, 'Something like that.'

Sam took the canister and pondered on what Shane had told him so far. It left many unanswered questions.

'Why would they kill Alistair *before* you did the robbery?'

Shane shook his head. 'Your guess is as good as mine. Because they're a bunch of psycho shysters? They offered four million at first, then three after Alistair got killed, then two mil after Rudolph. I guess it's down to one mil now.'

'Have they contacted you?'

'Not me. As far as I know they don't have my number.'

'What about your address?'

'No idea. But they won't have that after today. I'm moving out.'

'A wise move,' said Sam. 'I don't suppose you have anything to prove to the cops that Jim Ormerod didn't murder Alistair?' He was wondering if he sensed hesitation here.

'Jim wasn't involved in the robbery, neither was Skinny Bollocks,' Shane said.

'Skinny Bollocks?'

'It's what we call Manny – tight as a duck's arse

is Manny. He must have plenty of money, he doesn't spend much on clothes.'

Sam fixed him with a steady gaze. 'Shane, you've already proved that you're a master of setting people up. Did the killers get you to set Jim up?'

'What? No! Bloody hell! I wouldn't do a thing like that. Jim's a mate. I only set you up because I knew you'd get out of it, eventually.'

'How kind of you.'

Sam allowed his gaze to rest on Shane's eyes as he gauged the truth of what the young thief was saying. He seemed genuine.

'What about this Gerald Rothwell bloke?'

'What about him?'

'He once worked for Alistair. Could he be connected with the killers?'

Shane smiled and shook his head. 'Never in a million years, mate. The people we were dealing with are hard men from London.'

'That's not a very convincing answer, Shane. Whoever the killers are they've been keeping tabs on you. It's hard to do that when you're 200 miles away in London.' He stubbed his cigarette out. 'Look, the only way to catch these people is for the police to stake out this flat. Which means you moving out right now.'

'What? You're going to shop me to the cops? I'll just deny everything.'

'I didn't say I was going to shop you. I'm saying your life is in danger right now. When the painting's handed back you'll probably be safe. But the safest thing is to catch them. I imagine you want the people who killed your friends to be caught, don't you?'

224

'What? Oh yeah, course I do.'

Shane thought about it for a while. 'OK,' he said. 'At the moment what I've given you is proof that I know where the painting is, but there's nothing to prove that photo comes from me – or that I'm in any way connected with the theft.'

'You're a sharp lad.'

'I like to keep one step ahead. So, what you and the police and the insurers will want to know is where the painting is.'

'Right, I see where this is going,' said Sam. 'The secret location of an eighty million pound painting is your ticket to immunity. That's a hell of a good ticket, if you don't mind me saying so.'

'It's just a pity I can't cash in on it,' said Shane.

'You're going to come out of this with your life,' Sam reminded him, 'which is more than your pals did.'

'There is that,' admitted Shane.

'Do you have somewhere to go?'

'I've got a mate who'll put me up overnight.'

'OK. Pack a bag, I'll make sure you get there safely, without being followed.'

'God! Am I in so much danger?'

'You tell me, Shane – as the sole survivor of the gang, who do you think they'll come for next?'

'Oh shit!'

'I'll need your mobile number.'

'OK. When will you contact me?'

'Give me twenty-four hours to set things up with the police and the insurers.'

Within the hour Sam had tailed Shane to his friend's house, ensuring no one had followed him.

An hour later he was in Morgan Blackstone's offices in Leeds, sitting opposite Mr Michaelson. He had just placed the film canister on the desk.

'I'm taking a bit of a flier her, Mr Michaelson. But I have reason to believe that when you develop this film there will be a photograph of the stolen Rembrandt on it, alongside a newspaper printed the day after it was stolen. If this is the case, I have no doubt you will contact me with regard to reinstating my contract.'

'If this is the case, how do I know you're not one of the thieves?' retorted Michaelson, pompously.

'Because I can prove it, Mr Michaelson. And as soon as my contract is legally reinstated I will invite the police to recover the painting.'

'So, you know where it is.'

'I haven't got the foggiest, but I know how to get it back to you. I urge you not to mess me about Mr Michaelson. You need my full cooperation to recover this painting. I trust you know someone who does quick film developing. I'll meet you in Unsworth Gallery at 10 a.m. tomorrow. I would appreciate it if you didn't bring in the police at this stage.'

CHAPTER THIRTY-FOUR

Sam was talking to Frances Fowler when Michaelson arrived at the gallery, along with acting DCI Bowman and two uniformed constables.

Michaelson gave a nod. Bowman was looking

226

at Sam's injuries, smirking. 'No wonder the NHS is running out of money.'

Sam paid no heed to him. His attention remained focussed on Michaelson. 'Why have you brought the police?'

'Why shouldn't I? This is a police matter.'

'Good, let the police find the painting.' Sam made to leave. Bowman put a hand on his shoulder and asked, 'Where did you get that film, Carew?'

'A man gave it to me in a pub – didn't catch his name.'

'You're lying.'

'Prove it – and while you're trying to prove it, the painting might disappear forever, all because Mr Michaelson here is a shyster who won't honour his contract with my firm.' Sam turned to Frances. 'Do you think he should honour his contract, Miss Fowler?'

'If it means getting the Rembrandt back, of course,' said Frances. 'That's why the Bickersdike Foundation paid the insurance premium.'

'Well,' said Sam, 'the longer these two prat about, the more chance there is of the Rembrandt disappearing for good.'

'OK,' said Michaelson to Frances. 'I'll honour his contract providing he can prove he's not connected with the robbery.'

Bowman smirked and winked at the insurance man. As he saw it, possession of the film was very incriminating. Carew would have a tough time proving such a thing.

'I think my contract needs updating,' Sam said. 'I need to make it shyster-proof.' He called out to

227

a man admiring one of the nearby paintings.

'Derek, could you come and sort this contract out please.' To Michaelson he added, 'This is Mr Armitage, my solicitor. He's here to make things so watertight that even Morgan Blackstone Insurance can't wriggle out of it.'

Armitage took a document from his briefcase and gave it to Michaelson. 'If you'd read this and sign both copies here, and here ... and perhaps if acting DCI Bowman could be witness...'

'I'm signing nothing more,' said Michaelson.

'Right, I'm out of here,' said Sam, turning to go. Bowman put a hand on his arm to stop him. Sam removed it. 'If you arrest me, Bowman, you can say goodbye to the Rembrandt – and cop for all the bad publicity that I will make sure comes your way. I imagine the Divisional Commander will just love you.'

Bowman motioned for the two constables to step away. With some reluctance, Michaelson signed both copies, with Bowman as a witness, as did Sam and Frances Fowler. Then Sam said, 'Right, the bad news is I've got no idea where the painting is. The good news is, I know a man who does.'

'And will this man be so grateful to you for shopping him to the police that he'll swear you'd nothing to do with the robbery?' sneered Bowman.

Sam snapped. 'Trying to be clever doesn't suit you, Bowman!'

Bowman was slightly taken aback. Carew was one for odd, clever remarks, but he was rarely if ever downright nasty. 'Just remember who you're talking to, Carew,' he warned.

Sam glared at him. His nerves were frayed. The last few days hadn't been easy but he swallowed his next caustic comment and collected his thoughts. 'This man might well deny having anything to do with the robbery, with me squealing on him when he thought I was acting on his behalf to do a deal with you. And there's nothing to connect him to this film. No fingerprints or anything.'

'But there's something to connect *you* to this film,' pointed out Bowman. 'It's something called possession.'

'Do you think I don't know that, Bowman?' Sam shook his head, scornfully. 'Do you honestly think I haven't covered myself from that angle?' Bowman scowled darkly as Sam went on. 'Maybe he'll come clean when you show him this.' He took a laptop computer from a case, rested it on a seat and switched it on. It played a full sound and vision recording of Sam's conversation with Shane. Totally exonerating Sam from any involvement. Frances found herself smiling. Bowman and Michaelson remained impassive.

'His name's Shane Outhwaite,' Sam told them. He took out a DVD from the laptop and handed it to Bowman. 'Honours graduate in IT – which explains many things. Pleasant enough lad, very bright in his own limited field, but otherwise as thick as two short planks. Not very observant for an IT expert. I recorded the whole thing on a pinhole camera with a lens sticking through a buttonhole in my shirt. I imagine,' he suggested, 'that if you put an obbo on his flat you might picked up a few murderers, including Alistair Waring's real killer.'

'Where's Outhwaite now?' muttered Bowman, deeply unhappy that Carew had solved a case that had been baffling both him and the National Crime Squad for weeks.

'At his mate's house, waiting for me to ring him,' said Sam. 'He'll tell you where the painting is, with you having him bang to rights with this recording. All he really wants is to get the killers off his back. I suppose he might be a bit more amenable if you offer him some sort of deal in exchange for him giving you the painting back.'

'He'll get no deal from us,' sniffed Bowman. 'And he'll be well pleased with you for dropping him in it like this. I got the impression from that video that he's expecting you to arrange some sort of immunity for him. With something of this value a devious bugger like you might have had a chance, but you didn't even try. Why was that?'

'Never intended to try. Tell him I might have tried to keep him out of prison if he hadn't made the big mistake when he set me up.'

'What big mistake?' asked Bowman

'Well, setting me up with the court and my bank was bad enough,' Sam explained. 'But the other thing was bang out of order.'

'What other thing?'

'He deliberately knackered my private life,' said Sam. 'Thought it was a big joke.'

'Well, it's a joke that's going to cost him a long stretch in prison,' remarked Bowman. He smirked at the prospect in store. 'Yes, I'll be sure to tell him where he went wrong.'

'By the way,' Sam said to Michaelson. 'If you check the working on the new contract you'll find that I've already done my bit, and I'll be due payment in full on recovery of the painting.'

Owen was waiting on the gallery steps as Sam limped out. His knee was now killing him, his ribs were still sore and his ear hurt like hell. The expression on his face was not one of the triumphant man who was due a payout of two point four million from an insurance company.

'I got wind that Bowman was coming down here to stick you for the robbery,' said Owen. 'What happened? Are you OK?'

'Yeah, I'm fine,' Sam told him. 'I nailed the thief. They should pick the painting up today and I should get the insurance money. It's the same bloke who set me up with the winding-up order and all that crap – Shane Outhwaite.'

'Well, that's brilliant, Sam. Back on your feet again eh, boyo?'

'Well, something like that.' Sam stared, unfocussed, into the middle distance, then said, 'I got a letter from Sal, yesterday.'

'Sal? That's good – isn't it?'

'Not really. She's not coming back.'

'Not coming back?'

'She's found herself a bloke.'

It took Owen a while to find his tongue. 'Oh, I see. What was it – a holiday romance?'

'She didn't go into details. It's just some really nice bloke. Never got the chance to tell her I'd been set up. Not much point now.' He forced out a smile and turned to his pal. 'I can't compete with someone who's a really nice bloke. Sounds right out of my league.'

'I reckon if you went after her she'd come back.'

Sam shrugged. 'Maybe you're right, but it wouldn't be fair on her. I mean, look at the state of me. I'm trouble, Owen. I'm not what she needs. She needs a husband and a family.'

'What – wedding bells already? It all sounds a bit whirlwind to me.'

'Well, maybe I was reading between the lines. She sounds very taken with him. I've done all the husband stuff and made a hash of it. She'll make a great mum will Sal. The kindest thing I can do is wish her well.'

'Fair enough,' conceded Owen, who had no argument with that. 'I could meet you in the Clog at lunchtime if you like. We could talk about football and villains and put the world to rights.'

'No, I'm going round to see my boys. It's the school holidays. I haven't been seeing enough of them, according to their mother. They've just got their GCSE results. Nineteen between two of them. Tom pipped Jake by one, but Jake got one more A grade. They obviously take after their dad.'

'Obviously,' said Owen, without much conviction.

CHAPTER THIRTY-FIVE

Sue Kingsley came to the door as Sam got out of his rental car. He had been a disgrace to the word 'husband' and it annoyed the hell out of her that she still had feelings for him. Luckily for her sons

232

their dad wasn't a disgrace to the word 'father'. They thought the sun shone out of him. Jake appeared around the side of her.

'Is that a Subaru, Dad?'

Sam glanced back at the car. 'I think so. That's nearly what your mum used to be called.'

That had always amused Sam – much more than it ever amused the former Sue Carew. Her sounding like a Japanese car had done nothing to prop up their ailing marriage. Getting married to Jonathan Kingsley had been tantamount to a passport back into polite, non-sniggering, society. Jonathan was OK with the boys and didn't try to compete with Sam for their affections – he had more sense than to do that. Non identical twins, they were both 16 now and had taken their GCSEs two months ago.

Sue strolled down the path with her arms folded, studying his latest injuries. 'Anything potentially fatal?' she asked.

'Not this time, I'm afraid.'

'She *is* joking dad,' called out Tom, from the doorway. 'We didn't come and see you in hospital because you'd been discharged by the time we heard.'

'I understand congratulations are in order,' said Sam. 'I've no doubt your mother reckons you got your brains from her side.'

'Looking at the state of you I hardly think there's any doubt,' remarked Sue. 'No sane person gets into as much trouble as you.'

'Point taken,' conceded Sam. 'You've apparently *not* got your father's brains, boys – anyway, well done.'

'Is your ear going to heal up properly,' asked Tom, 'or will you end up with a bullet hole in it?'

It sounded to Sam as if the latter would be preferable. A dad with a visible bullet hole was worth a lot of kudos in teenage society.

'I'm told it'll have a bit missing – maybe just the lobe.'

Jake grinned. 'You could get a prosthetic lobe.'

'He'd be better off with a prosthetic brain,' said Sue. 'It wouldn't be any worse than the one he's got now.'

Jonathan came to the door and gave Sam a nod. 'Sam.'

'Jonathan – not at work today?'

'Well, I was going to go to the one day match at Headingley with the boys, but...'

'But me ringing up has put the kibosh on it?' Sam said. 'Look, it's not a problem. I just called in to say "well done" to them.'

'No, it's OK. I thought you might like to take them. I'm not as keen on cricket as you lot. I've got tickets, by the way.'

'It'll also give Jonathan and me a day to ourselves,' said Sue, slipping her arm through her husband's, as if to establish where her allegiance now lay. Sam looked from the excited faces of the boys to the faces of his ex-wife and Jonathan. They were the nearest he had to a family. He cursed under his breath as he felt himself filling up. The roller coaster ride of the past few days had got to him at last. This was normality. This was how life could have been for him and Sally, had he been normal.

'Are you OK, Dad?' Tom asked.

'Take no notice, I'm fine, son,' said Sam. 'I've

just had a tricky few days. Stuff gets to me after a while.'

'I remember,' said Sue. 'Your stuff got to me as well.'

'Everything's sorted now.'

'What about Sally?'

She had heard she'd gone, but she wouldn't know about the letter. Sam squeezed his eyes shut, as if trying to remember what had happened to Sally; in fact he was fighting back tears.

'She's, erm, she's OK. She's actually gone off to do her own thing. Y'know, new feller and all that.'

'Oh, I see,' said Sue.

There was an awkward silence. Even the boys knew the significance of what he'd just said. Jonathan made an excuse about going back inside to get the tickets. This was a moment for the four of them, despite Sue being his wife. His marriage to her was successful because he knew when to leave well alone.

She folded her arms and studied Sam. 'I'm sorry, Sam, but I don't blame Sally. You're a very hard man for any woman to love. There are too many uncertainties with you. You attract trouble like a magnet.'

'Hey, I don't go out looking for trouble. If I see trouble heading my way I take quick steps in the opposite direction.'

A note of censure crept into her voice. 'That's the problem, though – you can never see trouble coming. Trouble always comes to you as a consequence of your own behaviour, but you just can't see it. You spend more time in A&E than most nurses.'

Sam was at a loss for an answer, especially as she was probably right.

'I'm out of it now,' she went on, 'but it's not fair on Tom and Jake. They joke about it now but, honestly, it's no joke at the time these things happen to you.'

Sam looked at the boys, whose sheepish expressions told him they agreed with their mother. He wiped his eyes with the heel of his hand and managed the smile they deserved. 'Hey, I'm not here to argue with you lot. As a matter of fact today's been a good day, so far, and it can only get better – especially if England beat the West Indies.'

Jonathan appeared at the door with the tickets. Sam stepped forward to take them. He shook Jonathan's hand. 'Thanks ... oh and thanks for looking after this lot,' he inclined his head towards Sue and the boys. 'I wasn't much good at it, as you've no doubt heard.'

It was the longest conversation he'd ever had with his ex-wife's husband.

CHAPTER THIRTY-SIX

Gordon Plessington, the son of the founder of Plessington Holdings, was sitting at his desk, opposite Sam; Derek Armitage, Sam's solicitor, was sitting on Sam's right and Alec Brownlow to his left. The three of them had travelled over to Manchester that morning after Derek Armitage had alerted Plessington that his company would be sued for breach of contract if he didn't agree to settle out of court.

'My clients did inform you in writing that there was no valid winding-up order against their company. This leaves you in breach of contract,' said Armitage.

Plessington had chosen to conduct the meeting without legal help. He took his time to light a cigar, as if to show just how unconcerned he was.

'Mr Armitage, how was I supposed to know the winding-up order wasn't valid? Not even the courts knew what was happening.'

'You were informed by us of the court's confusion over the matter, and yet you still went ahead and terminated my client's contract.' Sam's solicitor spoke coolly, without any emotion.

Plessington took a steady drag on his cigar, which had an expensive aroma. 'The application to wind the company up was in the Public Notices column of the *Unsworth Observer* – that's all I needed to know.' He looked at his watch. 'Is this going to take long, I have much more pressing things to take care of.'

Derek Armitage glanced down at the contract he had on his knee. 'At the moment you have brought another builder on to the site. According to the terms of the contract all monies due on any work done is to be paid to my client, who has no obligation to pay any money on to the new builder.'

Plessington's studied mask of boredom slipped a little. 'What? Don't be ridiculous.'

Armitage gave the MD a sad smile. 'Contract Law is very clear on this. As soon as you were told there was doubt about the order you would have been well advised to wait for the court's verification. Did you seek legal advice on this?'

Armitage knew the answer. If this man didn't think he needed legal advice at this moment he was damned sure the man hadn't bothered when he cancelled Carew and Son's contract.

'Why would I have needed legal advice? Time's money in this business. I see a notice in the paper that this man's firm's about to be shut down and you expect me to ignore it?'

Armitage gave a nonchalant shrug, which earned him Sam's admiration. 'All I'm saying is you would have been wise to investigate the truth of the matter.'

'Our lawyers confirmed that there was a winding-up order registered with the court.'

'Had they investigated further they'd have found it wasn't supported by any court judgement. It was obviously an anomaly at the very least. The action you took was drastic. In any event the facts are that my clients were not insolvent at the time you invoked clause 7b of the contract, which action put you in breach of contract. You are also in breach for not making an agreed stage payment and barring them access to the site – plus various other breaches. I suggest you take legal advice, Mr Plessington. My client will claim payment for all work done on the site until its completion in accordance with the contract. This will include any work carried out by the new builder. They will also claim damages for late payments. I suspect when you do get legal advice it will be for you to cancel the current contract and restore my client to the site.'

The solicitor now had Plessington's full attention. 'How the hell can I do that? The new builder's on the same contract as Carew.'

Armitage looked first at Alec, then at Sam, who had now taken the bandage off his ear to reveal a missing lobe. It was something he'd have to live without. Recent events had made Gordon Plessington, MD of Plessington Holdings PLC, seem to him like an insignificant being, who was unworthy of respect. He leant forward on Plessington's desk and spoke in a low voice, which was just short of menacing.

'I've heard the new builder's on a much better price than us, Mr Plessington – at least his price is a lot better *on paper*, with his extra money being taken off our contract price.'

'You'll never be able to prove that.'

'I know that,' said Sam. 'It's what you were relying on. But as things stand now we don't have to prove it. We have a valid contract, which we haven't broken. All we have to do is sit back and watch the new blokes doing the job for us. We're good contractors with a good reputation but when this thing blew up you wouldn't give us the time of day. If this mess hadn't been sorted you'd have shuffled the paperwork around to make sure every penny you owed us would have been taken up. I know this because we've started getting the bills from you for remedial work that didn't need doing, but we couldn't prove it because we didn't have access to the site. By the time the job was finished these bills plus the money paid to the other builder would have added up to what you owe us. I know the way it works, Mr Plessington.

I know how wealthy businessmen like you make their money. Our firm ends up with a genuine winding-up order from some creditor who runs out of patience and we go into liquidation. If we go into liquidation any assets we have will be shared by the preferential predators.'

'You mean preferential creditors.'

'I know what I mean, Mr Plessington. I mean the taxman, vatman, liquidator, solicitors, bank – the genuine creditors might have a few scraps to fight over but there'll be no money left for us to fight you in court. You know this as well as I do. To you it's just hard-nosed business. To my men – and to our trade creditors – it's their livelihood.'

'Just so you know how things stand,' chipped in Armitage, evenly, 'any building costs, remedial or otherwise, which you have incurred are not my client's responsibility.'

'You are taking the piss!' blustered Plessington.

Sam took out an envelope and placed it on the desk. 'This is an account for the work completed, plus stock on site, plus work in progress at the time we were denied access to the site, plus an additional £50,000 for miscellaneous damages and loss of profit caused by your breach of contract. For every week you don't pay it goes up by £10,000. The alternative is to sort it all out in court.'

'Which means it probably won't be decided until the contract is finished by your new builders,' added Armitage. 'Which means you'll be paying both them and Carew and Son the full contract price, plus all damages, plus costs.'

'Like hell we will!'

Sam shrugged and got to his feet. It was now common knowledge that he was due a massive payout from Morgan Blackstone Insurance for his part in recovering the Rembrandt. It would certainly have reached the ears of Plessington. Some anonymous hand at the bank had re-activated his accounts and the *Unsworth Observer* had published a front page apology.

'Fortunately I can afford to wait,' yawned Sam. 'I've been advised that it will be more profitable in the long run to settle in court – especially with Plessingtons paying the costs. I just thought it only fair to give you a cheap get-out.' He tapped his watch. 'The clock's ticking, Mr Plessington. Ten grand a week might not be much to you, but it'll suit me just fine. I suspect your father might not be too pleased with his son tarnishing the firm's reputation – I know my dad wouldn't.'

CHAPTER THIRTY-SEVEN

'What about the killer?'

'That's a good question,' said Sam. Tracey had called into his office after seeing his new car parked outside. In anticipation of vast incoming wealth he'd bought a Jaguar XKR on credit. 'Shane Outhwaite is convinced it's the men from London who had arranged to buy the Rem-brandt. It's certainly a line the police are follow-ing. They put an obbo on Shane's flat in the hope they might come for him but no one turned up.

241

The police have sent a file down to the Met. If it is them they'll have gone to ground when they heard the Rembrandt had been recovered, which won't do Jim any good.'

'What about you?' Tracey asked. 'You're still on wages, remember? But are you still on the case or are you busy playing with your new toy?'

She was looking out of the window at the Jag, and she was looking good. There were light flashes in her hair, which she hadn't had the last time he saw her, and her skin looked much fresher than that of your usual woman in her late thirties. She was wearing a dark blue cotton blouse with the top three buttons undone, revealing the start of an admirable cleavage. A short, fashionably distressed, denim skirt and dangerously high heels showed off her tanned legs to their full advantage. Around her hips hung a loose, tooled leather cowboy belt, adorned with fake bullets. The brass buckle formed the word HOTSHOT. Sexy bordering on tarty, but just the right side of the border. Sam reckoned she'd made an effort, maybe for him. He joined her.

'Always wanted one,' he said, looking at the car. 'Got a good deal on it. It's a couple of years old but it's only done 10,000 miles.'

'Do you think you'll get it up to 20,000 before you wreck it?'

She had a point. Sam had a theory that if he bought a car he treasured he might also end up treasuring its driver, thereby reducing his habit of taking undue motoring risks. It was a theory open to flaws.

'I'm not sure that these mystery men from The

Smoke had anything to do with the Unsworth killings,' he said. 'There's something that doesn't make sense about the whole thing. Waring, Mace and McLeish were all killed by an amateur – or amateurs, but there's another murder which ties in to them. Just after the robbery a bloke called Billy Hargrave took a professional hit. He had connections with Waring and, according to Shane, he was part of the gang – the middle-man between them and the London people.'

'So, what you're saying,' summed up Tracey, after giving it some thought, 'is that the killings were done by a mixture of amateur and professional hit men. Which doesn't help Jim one bit, unless you can get proof that he's not one of the amateurs. Couldn't it be just one amateur?'

'Possibly,' said Sam, 'but the MO in each case was totally different. Different weapon, different type of location. The only thing the last three killings have in common is the lack of evidence. Whereas Alistair's killers left a mountain of evidence behind – all pointing at Jim.'

'What about the police? Are they looking at Jim's case again?'

Sam shrugged. 'All I know is that they've questioned him about the other two Unsworth murders. I guess they're working on the theory that he might know who the killer or killers are.'

'Even if he did kill Alistair,' said Tracey, 'how could he know who killed the others? He was locked up at the time.'

Sam went back to his desk and sat down. Tracey sat down opposite. 'I'm disadvantaged,' he said, 'because I'm working on a criminal case without police authority. On the other hand the police are disadvantaged because they're looking at three murders which are definitely connected, but two were committed while the chief suspect for the first murder was locked up.' He was speaking his thoughts out loud. 'If they hadn't already collared Jim they'd have assumed they were looking for just one killer – due to the close association of the victims.'

'I think you're losing me,' said Tracey.

'I might be losing myself,' conceded Sam. He pressed his palms to the sides of his head, as if to keep in any escaping ideas. 'Maybe it's me, maybe I can't see the wood for the trees. What I must do is ignore the Mace and McLeish murders and concentrate solely on what we have about the Alistair Waring killing.'

'Which is what?' asked Tracey.

'First I have to work on the theory that Waring's murder was nothing to do with the art robbery; second I need to find out why one of the clubs in Jim's golf bag was pristine clean; third I need to check on Jim's story that he stopped to change a wheel on his way to Alistair's; fourth I need to know how the murder weapon – one of his other clubs – got into Waring's dustbin, which seems an odd place for a ruthless killer to hide a weapon covered with his fingerprints, and fifth I need to check on Alistair's friends and relations. Did he have many relatives?'

'Just a mother and a sister as far as I know. The case goes to court in three weeks, so if there's anything I can do to help..?'

'Are you any good at secretarial work?'

244

'Not really. I used to be a hairdresser.' She paused, then said, 'I gather Sally's found someone else.'

He pulled a face and nodded. 'Yeah – I can hardly blame her. She's down in Bournemouth at the moment, living with her parents.'

'And he lives down there as well, does he?'

He tried to sound disinterested. 'I think she said he lives in Bath. She met him on holiday.'

'Bath, eh?' Tracey said. 'I've got posh relations who live in Bath – not that we have anything to do with each other. They're much too good for us common lot up here in Unsworth. They spell shit with a Y in Bath.'

This vaguely amused Sam but he knew Sally would never have come out with a coarse crack like that. She could curse with the best of them but there was nothing coarse about Sally.

'I doubt if he's like that or Sally wouldn't have anything to do with him.'

Their eyes met and Sam remembered their recent encounter. 'I'm always here,' she said. She crossed her legs, allowing her skirt to inch up her thighs.

'It'd be unprofessional,' said Sam, without much conviction, 'with Jim being my client.'

'I know, but it's maybe what we both need. Sounds like Sally's getting her share. It's not as if you're being unfaithful.'

Getting her share. Her words cut into him. Sally with another man. He didn't want to think about it.

'What about you?' he asked.

She shrugged. 'I was never faithful. Jim might

245

appreciate me having a lover who got him out of clink. Which reminds me…'

'Reminds you of what?' asked Sam.

'I've been asked to be a prosecution witness. The police know I was having a fling with Alistair, which gave Jim his motive.'

'You can refuse to testify against your husband.'

'I already have. I think you should take me for a spin in your fancy car.'

The XKR was a bright red convertible – the colour of a pathologist's apron, to quote Owen – and hardly the ideal car for an undercover PI. But Sam figured that if Magnum PI could drive around Hawaii in a Ferrari then he could drive around Yorkshire in a fancy Jag. There was always an unmarked firm's van for when he needed to be incognito.

'Have you bought this as compensation for losing Sally?' enquired Tracey.

They were on the A1 heading north. North Yorkshire was pretty much speed camera free, which was just as well. Sam gave Tracey's question due consideration, then said, 'Possibly.'

'And is it any compensation?'

'It is a bit.'

'You can't take it to bed. I could help out with that part of the compensation if you like.'

'Tracey, are you a nymphomaniac?'

'Hardly. I've had it once in six weeks and that was with you. I need some excitement in my life.'

Sam put his foot down. The supercharge kicked in. The car shot from eighty to a hundred and forty. Sam felt a surge of excitement as the seat

246

pushed into his back. He gave a loud whoop.

'Wow! Did you feel that?'

Tracey screamed and clutched her hands to her groin. 'I sure felt something. Sam Carew, take me to a hotel room this minute!'

Fifteen minutes later they were in a hotel in Boroughbridge. Twenty minutes later they were in bed. An hour later Sam was exhausted, Tracey was happy, Sally was forgotten and Jim was forgotten. It crossed both their minds that they could have a lot of fun together if they simply said goodbye to the world and went off to play. It would come to an end but what a time they'd have. Tracey leant up on one elbow and said.

'Are you thinking what I'm thinking?'

'I do believe I could be.'

'Fancy car, pots of money, sexually compatible, both approaching middle age. We could take off around the world and have a mad year to remember.'

'It's tempting,' Sam admitted, thinking back to the few weeks he'd just had.

They were both naked, she moved on top of him, straddling him, arousing him once more. She felt his arousal and smiled, coquettishly. 'A year of unashamed stupidity and hedonism. Sam, when I leave this world I want to have nothing to come back for. I want to have done it all. We like each other but we don't love each other – that's a great combination. No tears, no heartbreak, just plain, good old-fashioned filthy fun. The question is, are you up for it, Mr Carew? Oops! I suspect you are.'

An hour later Sam was in the shower and Tracey

was lying on top of the bed with her eyes closed. He came through to the bedroom as he towelled himself dry. He looked down at her and wondered what the hell he had been thinking about. If he was going to spend a mad year with any woman it would have to be Sally. He wouldn't last five minutes with Tracey. She was too much for him. She opened her eyes and read his thoughts. Women could do that with Sam Carew.

'Wow, has a whole year gone by already, Sam?'

He smiled and nodded. 'Time flies when you're having fun.'

CHAPTER THIRTY-EIGHT

Sam stared at his benefactor and his benefactor gave him a sorrowful look which said, *Get a grip of yourself, Mr Carew. Life is not so easy.*

'Behave yourself, Billy,' murmured Sam.

The security guard, standing beside the painting, glanced at Sam, wondering if he was talking to him. He wished someone would talk to him, this was a very boring job.

Rembrandt's self-portrait still looked like old Billy Batley who used to sell papers outside Unsworth Town Hall. The pockmark at the end of his nose still looked as if a piece of paint had flaked off and Sam could not believe this old man was about to make him rich. Right out of the blue, with hardly any effort involved. Unearned income in many ways.

248

The painting had been recovered, undamaged, from the safety deposit box, examined by experts flown in from The Rijksmuseum, who after much wrangling and discussion, had agreed to let the painting remain until the end of the exhibition provided it was kept under 24 hour guard. The original frame had been recovered from Dave McLeish's store room, something that Sam had kicked himself for not checking. He had assumed that McLeish wouldn't have been so stupid as to hide the painting there but it was odds on it had been taken from the frame, which Sam would have recognised in an instant. Shane Outhwaite was languishing in Armley prison on remand, cursing Sam for reneging on his promise. Sam felt no guilt about this whatsoever.

It was just after 9 a.m. The gallery had only been open ten minutes and was almost deserted. Half an hour ago Frances Fowler had rung and asked Sam to meet her there. He heard the sound of high heels click-clacking against parquet flooring. He turned and smiled at her. She didn't return his smile.

'Everything OK?' he asked. 'This *is* the right Rembrandt, isn't it?' He was joking. Sam knew this painting as well as anyone.

'Yes, it is, and once again we thank you, Mr Carew, for its safe return.'

'There's a big, "but" in there somewhere?' Sam observed. 'Are you OK? There hasn't been any come-back on you has there?'

'Oh no, nothing like that. In fact we're more grateful than you can imagine for getting the

Rembrandt back for us. Had we not got it back it might well have been catastrophic.'

Sam looked at her through narrowed eyes. There was bad news coming. 'Why catastrophic?' he asked. 'I mean the painting's insured.'

'Nothing's certain yet,' she told him, 'but we've been advised that there may be a problem with the insurance company.'

Sam felt himself go a little cold.

'I see.'

Frances looked at him, almost embarrassed.

'Actually I don't see,' Sam said. 'I think you'd better tell me what you know, Frances.'

She sat down on an upholstered leather bench. 'It came like a bolt from the blue when I got in this morning,' she told him. 'It's apparently very hush hush at the moment but I think you're entitled to know.'

'Know what?'

She winced and took a deep breath. 'Apparently Morgan Blackstone Insurance are about to be investigated for serious fraud.'

Sam went quiet for a moment, then asked, 'And do Morgan Blackstone know this?'

'Not as far as I know. I've been told to keep it to myself but we owe you such a great debt of gratitude and I know this affects you enormously.'

'You could say that,' said Sam. 'Trouble is, I'm not sure me being forewarned can do me any good. Do you know when the balloon's due to go up?'

'What? Oh, I see what you mean. I believe it's imminent. Our office was given a tip-off by someone in the Serious Fraud Squad.'

'Really?'

'We've been warned not to do anything which might alert Morgan Blackstone. I believe the police have applied for a warrant to search their offices in Leeds and London.'

'What, today?'

'I don't know. I've just been told to close the gallery and double the security until we resolve the insurance problem. It could be that none of the exhibition paintings are insured.'

'What about the rest of the paintings?'

'They're not insured, anyway. It would be too costly. It's easier just to suffer the loss.' She looked up at him. 'I daren't ask you what this might cost you.'

'No,' said Sam, 'and I daren't tell you. Talk about here today gone tomorrow.' He thought about the fifty grand car he had parked outside and winced. He hadn't seen this one coming. An insurance company going bump on him.

'Don't all these insurance companies have things called underwriters to guarantee things?' he asked her.

'I'm not sure what happens in the case of fraud,' she said. 'I think the claims might be underwritten, but you haven't got a claim. You're an unsecured creditor.'

'So I am,' he said, nodding away two point four million. 'Very unsecured. Still, you can't win 'em all.'

'Mr Carew, I'm desperately sorry for your loss.'

'I've had worse losses.'

'Really?'

'Not of the financial kind.'

251

'I assume you're talking about Sally. I was quite surprised to hear she'd left you.'

'Why's that? You hardly knew her.'

'I saw enough of her. You two were a couple.'

'All twos are couples.'

'All right, you were two halves of something.'

'Something better?'

'Something good.'

Sam went quiet, then said, 'Are you sure I'm going to get stuffed for this money?'

'It seems like there's a very good chance of it.'

'Jesus. I'm not sure how to react. I mean, it's not like losing a loved one or a leg, but it's a hell of a lot of dosh. How would you react if you'd just lost two point four million?'

'I've got no idea. I've never had two point four million.'

'Neither have I.'

'Well then, what you've never had you won't miss.'

'Simple as that, eh?'

'No point looking upon it any differently. You should forget the money and get Sally back.'

'She's got another feller.'

Frances shrugged. 'They won't belong together.'

Sam looked at her, then he turned to the Rembrandt and shrugged. 'You were right, Billy.'

Frances raised an eyebrow. 'Billy?'

Sam smiled. 'I call him Billy. He thinks I need to get a grip.' Then a thought struck him. 'Jesus! I really do need to get a grip.'

CHAPTER THIRTY-NINE

It was misty over the Pennines as Sam drove along the M62 towards Manchester. His mind had been spinning out plans from the second he'd left the gallery. He'd discarded one as being unworkable at short notice and another as just plain stupid. This one was workable and not quite so stupid. He switched on the handsfree and dialled the number of Plessington Holdings.

'Mr Plessington, this is Sam Carew.'

'Good morning, Mr Carew.'

'This is actually a courtesy call, Mr Plessington. Personally I wouldn't bother, but my solicitor says it's the right thing to do, which is why I'm recording this call. I tell you what, there's some fancy gadgets in this XKR. Fancy a car phone being able to record calls. Do you like Jags, Mr Plessington? Never thought I'd be able to afford one.'

'Hmm, I don't need to ask if you've received your insurance fee.'

'How did you guess? Two point four million smackers from an insurance company who are ever so grateful that I saved them an eighty million payout.'

'Would you get to the point, Mr Carew?'

'Oh, right, erm, the *Daily Mail* have asked me to tell the story of the Rembrandt theft and the way the thieves tried to discredit me, and all the

253

trouble that caused me. I'm on my way to their Manchester offices now to meet a journalist. I've given them a brief breakdown over the phone.' Sam didn't know if the *Daily Mail* had a Manchester office, but it was a fair bet that Plessington didn't know either.

'I see.'

'According to my solicitor,' Sam went on, 'your part in it, that is, your refusal to honour your contract, does Plessington Holdings no credit. There are bad guys and good guys in this story, Mr Plessington, and at the moment Plessington Holdings are among the bad guys.'

'Tell the *Daily Mail* we'll sue them if they discredit Plessington Holdings.'

'The *Daily Mail* will be including a disclaimer pointing out that they're not giving an opinion, Mr Plessington, they're simply telling my story. It's me you'll have to sue.' Sam had no idea if this was how newspapers worked, but it sounded as if he'd explored that aspect of things.

'Then we'll sue you.'

'Oh yeah? Then you'll have to prove I'm lying. How can you do that when you know I'm not?'

Plessington didn't reply. Sam pressed on, adopting a reasonable tone. 'Look, the reason I'm ringing you is that I'm told bad publicity like this might have an impact on Plessington's stock market value, which will affect thousands of shareholders who haven't done me any harm, which is not what I'm after. Hey, I myself might want to invest the odd few quid in your company – you obviously don't throw money away too easily. I just want what's right. The amount you owe us is a drop in the ocean compared to what it might cost your company.'

'If it's not what you're after, don't do it.'

Sam didn't answer straight away. He waited until Plessington said, 'Hello, are you still there?' There was anxiety in his voice.

'Mr Plessington,' said Sam patronisingly, 'to be honest it'll suit me down to the ground if you don't pay up, then I can expose your company for the financial bullies you are. It's one of the joys of having a nice few quid in the bank. Like I said, this is a courtesy call. The story goes out tomorrow and you can be either the good guys or the bad guys. Maybe you'd like to check my offer with your dad or some of the other board members. You'll now have my mobile number on your phone. I'll be in Manchester in half an hour. If I don't hear from you I'll take it that you don't want to pay what you owe.'

Sam switched off the phone, took a deep breath and began worrying. The more he thought about it the more he couldn't believe this hair-brained plan would work. Surely Plessington would have twigged what he was up to the minute he put the phone down. Carew you are such an idiot. Mad Carew, no wonder they call you that.

Ten minutes later he was approaching Scammonden Dam. The road was clear for half a mile in front, unusual for the M62. He kept his foot down and took the car up to a hundred and forty five, the fastest he'd ever driven. Maybe the fastest he'd ever drive if they took the Jag off him for non-payment. In less than a minute he was back in traffic, foot off the accelerator, slowing down through one hundred, ninety, eighty. He knew about the speed camera half a mile ahead, back into the middle lane as an impatient Porsche 911 came from nowhere, right behind him, sounding its horn and hurrying past. The camera flashed, costing the Porsche driver three points and ninety quid. Sam looked at the phone, willing it to ring.

The bank had freed his accounts, leaving Carew and Son with just enough to pay off its creditors and for Sam to put a deposit on his car. Alec had looked down his nose at that, but the money was Sam's and nothing to do with the building company. He'd promised Alec he'd get Carew and Son up and running as soon as the insurance money came through. Meanwhile Alec was chasing up work.

And now, well, without pots of insurance money he knew he couldn't hope to win an action against Plessingtons, much less get the building firm up and running again. It was the world's oldest story. Money begets money. They should have put that in the bible along with all the begats and begottens listed in Genesis.

His only hope would be a solicitor who would work on a no win no fee basis. Derek Armitage had already mentioned that his firm wouldn't do that and he didn't know a solicitor who would. If Plessington didn't fall for this bluff, Carew and Son were stuffed. Might as well take the car back tomorrow.

He was in the centre of Manchester now, driving along Deansgate with nowhere to go but back to Unsworth if the phone didn't ring. Should he ring Plessington back? No, it would show weakness. If

Plessington suspected he was bluffing that would prove what he must already suspect. Maybe Plessington had rung the *Daily Mail* to see if what Sam had said was true. Would anyone at the *Mail* even know what every single journalist was working on? Sam had no idea. With his mind bunged up with negative thoughts he turned down a side road, found an empty parking bay and pulled in. He lit a cigarette and had been there for several minutes when he spotted a parking meter attendant hurrying towards him. The man looked as if he'd relish slapping a ticket on this fancy Jag – all the better if the driver was still inside it. Sam sighed, just what he needed. This was turning out to be some day. First he loses two point four million, then this. He certainly wasn't going to pick up a parking ticket to add to his woes.

He was outside the car, trying to find some change for the meter when his mobile rang. It was a Manchester number on the screen. He collected his composure.

'Hello?'

'This is Plessington.'

'Oh, right.'

Sam tried to sound disappointed. He held a staying hand up to the impatient meter attendant as he listened to what Plessington had to say:

'I've had a discussion with my directors and you can have your damned money!'

Sam could have howled with delight but he managed to inject a degree of reprimand into his voice. 'Hey, don't do me any favours, Plessington. We're talking about money you rightly owe.'

There was a silence, which Sam suspected was

Plessington controlling his temper. The meter attendant had his pad out and biro poised. Sam stuck some coins into the slot a split second before the ballpoint touched the paper. The meter clicked Sam into two hours credit and the foiled attendant trudged on. Plessington spoke. 'I'll arrange to transfer the money to your bank.'

Sam made a triumphant fist, suppressed a scream of *Yesss* and said, 'Don't bother. I'm in Manchester right now. I'll pick up the money before I call in to the *Mail* offices. I want a banker's draft for the full amount.'

'Carew, we live in a computer age. We can transfer the money direct to your account.'

Sam was ahead of him. Agreeing to this meant he might well lose control of the situation, and when you're working a scam, control of the situation is paramount. Plessington might well decide to play for time, because time often throws up unexpected advantages. For certain Sam would have to check his account at some stage that afternoon to see if the money was there, and if it wasn't he would have to ring Plessington back. If Plessington *was* playing for time he'd make sure he was in a meeting and unavailable, so Sam would be put through to accounts. He knew the routine. Accounts would assure him the money would be transferred within twenty four hours, by which time the news about Morgan Blackstone Insurance might well be out – plus no story in the *Mail*. Sam would lose the edge he had over Plessington. And the edge was worth one hundred and sixty three thousand, seven hundred and forty one pounds, plus VAT.

258

'You'll understand if I have a mistrust of computers, Mr Plessington. Computers have all but ruined my life. I'll be round in fifteen minutes to pick up a banker's draft for the full amount including VAT.'

An hour later Sam was depositing a banker's draft for one hundred and ninety two thousand three hundred and ninety-five pounds into the Manchester branch of his bank. At six o'clock that evening he was back home in Unsworth where he caught an item on the BBC news about Morgan Blackstone being investigated for fraud. There was film of men carrying boxes of papers out of the company's London and Leeds offices.

He opened the fridge and took out a celebratory can of Bootham's Smooth. That day he'd lost a large fortune, which he hadn't really earned, but he'd gone on to rescue money which *had* been properly earned. Rescued it in the nick of time as well. Frances Fowler had more than repaid the debt she and the gallery owed him. He must thank her very kindly – well, not too kindly. She was a very pleasant and personable lady, but she was twenty years older than Sam. Maybe Owen might be interested.

Despite the disparity in amounts the victory had somehow cancelled out the massive loss. It had been a David and Goliath victory. Good over evil. Such battles were worth winning. The victory over Lemmy Wilson had been a much more rewarding one – in fact he'd been rewarded with his life, not to mention keeping his boys safe.

As he sipped his beer he allowed himself a rueful smile. Keep going, Carew. Keep thinking like that

259

and you might even convince yourself you're better off without the two point four million.

Jesus! That sort of money would have been ever so nice.

Within thirty minutes he'd had three phone calls. One from Alec, one from Owen and one from Derek Armitage. All were amazed at how well he'd taken the Morgan Blackstone news. Derek warned him to expect the worst, then he tentatively asked Sam if he'd had time to think about how it might affect his dealings with Plessingtons.

Sam arranged to meet all three men in the Clog and Shovel where he'd buy them a drink and tell them a great story. Then his mind turned to Sally and to what Frances Fowler had said that morning. *Two halves of something good.*

CHAPTER FORTY

Shooey read about the painting being recovered and Shane Outhwaite being remanded in custody. Rumour had it that Shane had coughed to the police about Alistair, Rudolph and Dave being in on it as well but not Jim or Manny. Did the police suspect they'd been in on it, though? Suspicious bastards, the police. He cursed because he had planned on killing Shane, if only to complete the job he'd started. Then he laughed. What a bunch of morons! They do the hard work in stealing the painting and then they make a mess of moving it on. He'd have moved it on in five minutes – and he'd have got more than £4 million for it. Ironically they'd have been better off dealing directly with him – a nice profit could have been made all round. He allowed himself a smile. But that wouldn't have worked. No way would they have dealt with him, not under the circumstances.

He was fairly confident that the police wouldn't track him down. His main problem was this bastard Carew. Carew definitely worried him. He had a record of solving crimes the police couldn't fathom. Carew was a definite danger to his plans. He needed to get rid of Carew before he made his final move. The very thought cheered him up and he smiled because he already had a plan to dispose of Sam. A chance meeting with an old acquaintance in an Unsworth pub had thrown up the idea. He knew about the trouble Carew had had with the pikies, so it would make sense for the pikies to come back and take their revenge. Sometimes a killer has to delegate; just like the British Army delegated him to do their dirty work for them.

CHAPTER FORTY-ONE

Imogen Waring lived in Derbyshire. Her husband, Alistair's father, had died three years previously. She had reservations about Sam coming to visit her but he had sounded OK over the phone so she agreed to it. She came to the door in response to his ring and looked over his shoulder.

'Nice car.'

'Nice house.'

He reckoned it was worth close on a million and he also reckoned she lived alone.

'Won't you come in?'

'Thank you.'

He followed her to a living room that had been tastefully and expensively furnished back in the 1970s, including a 26" television in a walnut cabinet. She invited him to sit in one of the two chesterfields.

'Would you like coffee, Mr Carew?'

He could smell it simmering somewhere. Proper coffee. It would make a change from the instant he had at home.

'Oh, yes, please.'

As she left the room he took a piece of paper from his pocket with a list of questions on it. He didn't want to come away without asking her everything, nor did he want to consult it while she was there. She came back with a tray laden with a cafetière, china cups, sugar bowl, milk jug and a plate of assorted biscuits. It impressed Sam enough for him to make up his mind to treat his own guests like this from now on. It put to shame his own habit of serving cups of instant and a packet of Jammie Dodgers.

'This looks great, Mrs Waring.'

'I don't get many guests.'

As Sam sipped his coffee he allowed his eyes to wander around the room in search of a tell-tale ashtray. There were none. To Sam, coffee and cigarettes went together like bacon and eggs.

'You may smoke if you want.'

'I'm trying to stop, Mrs Waring.'

It would be rude to pollute a non-smoker's house with cigarette fumes.

'Thank you for not offering your condolences,' she said. Sam tried to figure out if she was being sarcastic, but she wasn't. 'It gets a bit wearing after a while. In fact it gets very wearing when people are offering endless sympathy. It makes one seem so ungrateful.'

'I know,' said Sam. 'I lost my dad and my fiancée a few years ago. It seems to go on forever.'

'I did love him, you know.' She said it as though it was her duty to have loved him, with her being his mother.

'I'm sure you did, Mrs Waring.'

'Burying one's child is the hardest thing.'

'Some people say it's fate.'

'Do you believe in fate, Mr Carew?'

Sam shrugged. 'I call it the luck of the draw. But I believe in making my own luck.'

She laughed and Sam guessed she hadn't done much of that recently. 'I've checked up on you, Mr Carew. You seem to tempt fate quite a lot.'

'Fate definitely seems to smile on me, Mrs Waring, but I'm sure she'll have her wicked way with me in the end.'

'What about Alistair? Do you think he tempted fate by having an affair with a married woman?' she asked him.

Sam put his coffee down and leant towards her. 'Actually, I don't think he was killed by that woman's husband.'

'Which is why you've come to see me.'

'It is.'

'Do you know who killed him?'

'I'm afraid not.'

'Was he involved with that art theft?'

'I think his death might possibly be connected to the art theft, Mrs Waring. The CPS have ruled it out – I haven't.'

She sipped her coffee and took a biscuit from the plate. 'So, do you think the theft went wrong because my Alistair wasn't there to organise things?'

'Well,' said Sam, truthfully, 'they certainly ended up running round in circles.'

'You know, Alistair was a singular boy, quite pompous and irritating at times – never had any really close friends – but he had a clever head on his shoulders. I don't condone theft of any kind, but this was amazingly ambitious and well planned, don't you think, Mr Carew?'

'Well, had they pulled it off they'd have had unspoken public admiration,' Sam said. 'The public appreciate a good clean theft that doesn't involve violence or loss to any individual.'

'I would have been blazing mad at him had I known.'

'Ah, but would you have turned him in to the police?'

She thought about this, then decided, 'I would have insisted on him sending the painting back.'

The conversation was drifting off track. Sam took out his piece of paper and glanced at it before putting it back in his pocket. 'I understand Alistair was involved in gambling.'

'Why do you say that?'

'Just keeping an open mind, that's all.'

'He played poker. I know this because I taught

264

him. Unfortunately he wasn't a very good player, he was more of a gambler. There's much more to poker than gambling. Poker's all to do with working out the odds and being able to figure out your opponent's style of play. Alistair was no good at the latter.'

'Do you think he might've had gambling debts?'

'I wouldn't rule it out – but this is England, Mr Carew, not the Wild West. Gambling debts are settled honourably or not at all.'

'I've known people who collect gambling debts without using too much honour.'

'So, you think my son might have been killed over a gambling debt, do you?'

'I'm exploring every avenue. Would it be possible for me to have a look through his papers?'

'What sort of papers?'

'Well, gamblers quite often keep records. Does he have any ledgers, diaries, notebooks?'

She sighed. 'Everything of that nature is in a box in the garage. I haven't looked at any of it, but you must help yourself. He always kept a journal, if that's of any help. If you wish to take anything away please do. All I ask is that you return it.'

'Thank you for trusting me,' said Sam. 'Could you tell me the names of any of his friends up in Yorkshire. I know about his golfing friends and a few work colleagues but not much else.'

'There's a man called Gerald Rothwell.'

'Really? Now there's a name that keeps cropping up. What do you know about him?'

'I know Alistair played cards with him. He was connected to Alistair through work, not sure how. Harmless enough man. I doubt if he was involved

265

in my son's death. If I thought he was I'd throttle him myself. I know his name because Alistair took me along to a Leeds casino once when I went to visit him. They had a private poker school and I was allowed to join in. Gerald's the only one I remember, mainly because he was the best player there – and maybe because he was a bit odd-looking. Not a handsome man by a long stretch.'

'Did Alistair win or lose?'

'I seem to remember he lost about as much as I won, which was around three hundred pounds. I'm trying to think if he had any other friends, but I can't bring a name to mind.'

'Just before he died, did he give you the impression that he had money worries?'

She shook her head. 'He had a well paid job. If he had money worries he'd have worked them out.' She nibbled on a biscuit and eyed Sam. 'Aren't you leaving your investigations a bit late. The trial starts on Monday.'

'I know. I've, er, I've had one or two other distractions.'

'I imagine a man like you will have many distractions, Mr Carew.'

CHAPTER FORTY-TWO

Owen had never been a comfortable witness. Sam thought he always looked more guilty than the accused. Roger Figgis QC, for the Crown, looked up from his papers after Owen had taken the oath, and smiled at the Welsh constable.

'DC Price, I have only a couple of questions for you.'

The gratitude was evident in Owen's face. He glanced across at the defence counsel, Delia Knowles QC, hoping she'd be easy on him as well.

'You were present during the search of Mr Alistair Waring's house shortly after his body was found, were you not?'

'I was, sir, yes.'

'In fact it was you who found the golf club which we'll prove to be the murder weapon, was it not?'

'Yes sir, it was in the wheelie bin around the back of the house.'

'What state was this golf club in?'

'State?'

'Condition, DC Price. What condition was it in?'

'It was covered in blood, sir.'

'And what did you do with the golf club?'

'I didn't do anything with it. I left it for forensics. They photographed it, then they bagged it and tagged it and took it away for testing.'

The judge cleared his throat to alert the court that he had something to add. 'I assume this golf club will be introduced in evidence.'

'It will, my Lord. I intend calling an expert witness to confirm what was found on the club.'

'Might we be let into that secret right now, Mr Figgis?' The judge raised a questioning eyebrow at Mrs Knowles, who shrugged her consent.

Figgis looked at Owen. 'Could you tell the court the result of the forensic resting?'

'DNA and forensic testing proved that it was covered in James Ormerod's fingerprints and Mr

267

Waring's blood, sir.'

'And presumably it was this damning evidence that prompted you to arrest James Ormerod on a charge of murder.'

Delia Knowles glared at the judge. It wasn't his place to speak of damning evidence. It was up to the jury to decide if evidence was damning or not.

'It was, sir,' said Owen.

'No further questions, my Lord,' said Figgis.

He sat down as the defence barrister got slowly to her feet. She was in her thirties with a stern face that matched her reputation. Jim Ormerod had laid out every penny he could get his hands on to hire her.

'DC Price,' she enquired, without deigning to look at him. She was looking at the jury to gauge their reaction to her question. 'Why do you think Mr Ormerod put the alleged murder weapon in the wheelie bin?'

'I don't know. Maybe he hoped the binmen would empty the bin before the body was found.'

Sam, sitting in the public gallery, wondered if Owen had prepared himself for this odd statement to be examined by defence counsel.

'Ah, now that's a possibility that hadn't occurred to me DC Price.' Mrs Knowles now turned to look at him. 'Was there much rubbish in the wheelie bin?'

'As a matter of fact, no – it was nearly empty.'

'Could this have been because the wheelie bin had been emptied on the Friday, just two days previously?'

'I'm sure I don't know what day the bins are emptied.'

'I should have thought such a simple enquiry might have formed part of your investigation.'

The judge cleared his throat once more. 'Is there a point to all this, Mrs Knowles?'

'There is indeed, m'Lord. I'm struggling to understand why my client'd commit such a monstrous crime then attempt to conceal the murder weapon, covered in his fingerprints, in an almost empty dustbin outside the back door. He might just as well have left it by the side of the body with his card attached. It's almost as if the person who put it there actually *wanted* it to be found.'

The judge looked at the prosecuting barrister. 'Do you have any observations on this, Mr Figgis?'

'I do indeed, my Lord. We intend to prove that this crime was committed in a fit of jealous rage. In such circumstances we would hardly expect the accused to be thinking clearly.'

'Yes, I'm inclined to agree with you, Mr Figgis. When a man's emotions are out of control it's unreasonable to expect him to act rationally.'

'What?' exclaimed Mrs Knowles, furiously. 'M'Lord, it seems that you are leading the jury, rather than have them form their own opinion. You're assuming that the murder was committed by my client in a fit of jealousy. This has yet to be proved. The murder may well have been carried out in cold blood by someone wishing to point the blame at my client.'

'I am allowed an opinion, Mrs Knowles.'

'Only when you've heard all the evidence m'Lord, and even then your opinion must be very carefully considered.'

'Pedantic, but strictly correct,' accepted the

judge, sourly. 'The jury will disregard my last comment. Any further questions of this witness, Mrs Knowles?'

Delia Knowles scowled. 'No, m'Lord.'

Delia Knowles QC walked into a secure conference room below the courts. She wasn't pleased.

'Pedantic, but strictly correct? What sort of stupid fucking comment is that? This is a court of law, we're supposed to be strictly correct. If this judge takes one more step over the line I'm going for a mistrial!'

'What does that mean?' asked Jim, hopefully.

'It means she'll ask for the case to be retried by another judge,' Sam explained. He'd been allowed in on a special request from Delia, with him being an 'indispensable part of the defence team'. She took off her wig and threw it on a chair. Sam thought it a shame to cover such beautiful hair with a horsehair wig. In fact, without the wig, she looked quite fanciable. He glanced at her ring finger. The fact that she called herself Mrs didn't mean she was still married. But the gold band was there, along with an engagement ring with a huge solitaire diamond.

Just as well. If he got involved with her she'd probably make mincemeat of him. She smiled at the two men then rubbed an eye with her finger.

'Don't mind me,' she said. 'The silly old sod's past his sell-by date and he knows it. He also knows I won't take any shit from him, so maybe he'll behave himself from now on. Oh, and please excuse my language. These courtrooms are such stuffy places I need to let rip now and again. My husband's a Born Again fucking Christian, so I can't swear at home either. Just my luck. When I met him he was an embezzler with a way with words and a dazzling smile that charmed his defence counsel all the way to the alter – well, after he served two years.'

'So, you didn't get him off the charge, then?' said Sam.

'Get him off? I got him off a ten stretch. He'd still be inside but for me.'

'Is there anything I can do that might help?' Sam asked.

'We need to throw a spanner in the prosecution's works,' said Delia. 'Whoever did this left the murder weapon in the wheelie bin covered in Jim's fingerprints.' She looked at Jim. 'I know we've been through this a hundred times, Jim, but have you no idea who might do a thing like that? Who would deliberately set you up? Where would he get the club from?'

For the hundredth time Jim shook his head. 'I left my bag in the locker room. The club was in the bag the last time I saw it.'

'The 5 iron was the only clean club in the bag,' Sam said, 'why was that?'

'No reason I can think of,' said Jim. 'It should have been as filthy as the rest of them.'

'Jim, think carefully. Have you ever annoyed anyone sufficiently for them to set you up like this?' Sam knew that were he asking himself that question he'd have to make a list, but Jim was shaking his head.

'Any vengeful husbands?' asked Delia. 'Anyone you've owed money to ? Does anyone, anywhere,

271

have that much reason to hate you?'

Jim continued to shake his head. 'Honestly, I'm just an ordinary bloke. I just do ordinary stuff.'

'Well, there's someone out there who's had it in for you,' Sam said. 'All we need to do is find out who it is.'

'And do you have any ideas?' Delia asked Sam.

'I've got one, but I don't know where it will lead. I'll get back to you in a couple of days.'

CHAPTER FORTY-THREE

'I had this 5 iron tested at a private forensic lab,' Sam told Delia.

Delia looked at the golf club inside the poly-thene bag, and took an official-looking envelope from Sam. He'd come to see her in her chambers in Leeds.

'It's the one found in Jim's golf bag. I thought it stood out from the rest because it was as clean as a whistle so I had it tested. Cost an arm and a leg. These private forensic people must make a fortune.'

'All forensic people costs a fortune,' said Delia. 'Mind you, so do some people in my profession.' She looked up at Sam. 'So, if it was as clean as a whistle why did you spend this fortune?'

'Well, I always figure these forensic people earn their fortunes by working miracles.'

'And did they?'

'I wouldn't call it a miracle,' Sam told her. 'I'd

272

call it carelessness on the part of the killer. It seems that some blood had seeped down the shaft under a split in the grip – enough to take a DNA sample, apparently. Can it be offered in evidence at this late stage?'

'If it's Waring's DNA they daren't refuse. What's your take on this?'

'If it's Waring's DNA,' Sam said, 'my guess is that this is the club that killed him. The killer took another club out of Jim's golf bag, one that was naturally covered in Jim's fingerprints, wiped it in Waring's blood and put it in the wheelie bin. He then cleaned off the real murder weapon, put it in the golf bag and took the golf bag back to the golf club.'

'How did the killer get access to Jim's golf bag?'

'No idea. I'm guessing the golf bag was in Waring's house for some perfectly plausible reason. Could be that Waring had spotted it lying around in the locker room and brought it home so it wouldn't get nicked.'

'And, after the murder, the killer took it back to the golf club for the police to find?'

'Yeah, something like that,' agreed Sam. 'In fact it was Shane Outhwaite who found it.'

'So, we're looking at a golfer, not some London mobster?'

'I think so,' conceded Sam. 'To get in the locker room you need to key in a code. In fact you need a code just to get into the car park.'

'Does the car park have CCTV?'

'Even if it does I'm guessing the tapes will have been recorded over half a dozen times since then. It's a pity the coppers picked Jim up so early with-

273

out carrying out an extensive investigation. When the golf bag turned up at the club it should have been automatic procedure to check any tapes.'

'Or is that just the benefit of hindsight?'

'Maybe,' admitted Sam, but he was sure he'd have checked. 'I also think whoever rang it in was the killer.'

'Why do you think that?'

Sam's explanation was simple and made Delia smile. If he was correct she would ensure that the police pathologist confirmed his theory in court.

'If the DNA on this club turns out to be Waring's,' she told him 'I'll have it entered as a defence exhibit. The pathologist's up tomorrow, we should be able to turn him to our advantage.'

CHAPTER FORTY-FOUR

Professor Alan McNulty took the stand with the arrogance of the professional expert. Sam had little time for professional experts and their expert opinions. To Sam, expert opinions were no less fallible than his own opinions – and he'd made the odd cock-up in his time. There was obvious deference in Figgis's manner as he addressed the learned professor.

'Professor McNulty, you have been asked to appear for the prosecution in your capacity as an expert in the field of Forensic pathology. Could you briefly enlighten this court as to your qualifications.'

274

'Well,' said McNulty, 'I'm a fellow of the Royal College of Pathologists.'

He stopped there, as if this was enough. He'd repeated his qualifications in court so many times it had got boring. But Figgis felt the court needed more enlightenment.

'And to become a Fellow you need to have been a Member of the Royal College of Pathologists and held in good standing for a minimum of eight years.'

'Yes, that is correct. I've been an FRCPath for about twenty-three years and for most of that time I've been a practising forensic pathologist. I'm also a Master of Science, a Doctor of Philosophy, a Member of the Worshipful Society of Apothecaries – would you like me to go on?'

Figgis fixed a smile to his face and turned his head from McNulty to the jury. 'So it's safe to say that you're an eminent forensic pathologist.'

Which is nothing to go on, Sam was thinking. The professor shrugged away Figgis's compliment as if in a hurry to get on with things.'

'And you did an autopsy on Alistair Waring.'

'I did.'

'Could you tell the court the cause of Mr Waring's death?'

'I attributed the cause of death to the inhalation of blood as a result of head and facial injuries.'

'I see,' said Figgis. 'And what do you think was the cause of these injuries?'

'The deceased was struck eighteen times with a blunt instrument, the shape of which was not inconsistent with the head of a golf club.'

'Could the witness be shown exhibit 6?' said

275

Figgis to the clerk of the court.

McNulty was shown Jim's 3 iron. 'Professor McNulty, this is the golf club which was shown to you during the autopsy. Can you confirm that you ascertained the injuries to Mr Waring to be an exact match to the head of this club?'

'Yes, I can. It was either this very club or one very much like it.'

'May it be noted that the witness was shown a golf club belonging to the defendant which was found in a wheelie bin on Mr Waring's premises shortly after the crime was committed. We will prove that on this club were traces of Mr Waring's blood, plus the defendant's fingerprints – and no one else's. Thank you, Professor. No more questions of this witness, my Lord.'

The judge nodded and turned his head in Delia's direction.

'Mrs Knowles?'

'Thank you, m'Lord.' Delia got to her feet and smiled at McNulty, whom she knew of old.

'Professor McNulty, I accept your eminence in the field of forensic medicine and in particular your ability to often determine the precise sequence of events leading up to death – in this case, the sequence of the blows.' McNulty was nodding, interested.

'Well,' he said, 'I couldn't give you the sequence of the blows except to say that they were delivered with some force and in quick succession.'

'The only blow I'm interested in, Professor, is the first one.'

'Ah, I think I can help you with that. From the injuries, I detected that there was just a single blow

276

delivered from immediately behind the deceased, when he was most probably standing upright.'

'Would this have been the first blow?'

'Almost certainly, yes. The rest of the blows were delivered from above the body as it lay on the floor.'

'Tell me about this first blow, Professor. Was it a severe blow?'

'Very severe, yes. It was a heavy blow to the right temple, penetrating through to the brain.'

'Would it have killed him?'

'Not necessarily. It would certainly have disabled him and caused him to fall to the floor.'

'Would he have been unconscious?'

'Probably. With an injury like that he would have been deprived of most of his faculties. He may have had some sense of awareness, but not much.'

'What about his voice, Professor? Would he have been able to scream?'

McNulty shook his head. 'He wouldn't have had the strength to scream, even if he knew what he was screaming about. I doubt if he knew what had happened to him.'

'So would it surprise you, Professor, that the anonymous caller who dialled 999 did so because he said he'd heard screaming coming from Mr Waring's house?'

The judge leaned forward. 'Mrs Knowles, Professor McNulty is a pathologist. I doubt if screaming comes under his area of expertise.'

Figgis smirked. This irritated McNulty who addressed himself to Delia. 'Well, I don't know who was supposed to have been screaming, but I very much doubt it was Alistair Waring.'

The judge scowled, Delia smiled. 'Thank you, Professor.' She turned to the judge. 'The point I am making, m'Lord, is that the person who killed Alistair Waring is quite possibly the same person who made the anonymous 999 calls. Perhaps we could call in Mr Waring's neighbours as witnesses to testify if they heard any screaming that day. If there were no screams it leaves a very big question mark over how the caller knew a crime had been committed – unless he actually witnessed it? And if he did witness it, why did he lie about walking past the house and hearing screams? And who is he?'

The judge mulled this over, then said, 'Could it be that the accused made the call in order to baffle us all.'

Delia nodded her appreciation of this observation. In truth, she thought it would do no harm to flatter the old duffer.

'That's an excellent point, m'Lord. Fortunately such calls are recorded. With the court's permission we could always bring in a voice expert. If the caller was my client then it would indeed be most incriminating.' She looked across at Jim who seemed completely unperturbed. 'But as you can see, he doesn't seem unduly worried by such a prospect.'

Figgis was on his feet. 'Neighbours? Voice experts? My Lord, surely this should all have been arranged before the trial started.'

'How could I?' protested Delia. 'M'Lord, I've only just heard the defence expert give testimony which has brought me to this conclusion. It's obvious that the murder of Alistair Waring is but one of three closely connected murders, two of which were committed while my client was in prison. M'Lord, there's much more to this case than a single, isolated murder.'

'Well done,' said Sam.

'It was your idea,' Delia said.

'But it was you who turned the anonymous caller into the real killer. I was looking at the Jury. You had them in the palm of your hand.'

'Does this mean we're winning?' Jim asked.

'It means all is not yet lost, Jim,' Delia told him.

Sam turned to the young police constable who was standing by the door. 'What do you think, Mark?'

The constable shrugged. He knew Sam well and liked him. 'I'd sooner have your barrister than his. He's a slimy bugger is Figgis. He's just swapped his wig for one about ten years older to make it look as if he's been in the job a long time.'

'I noticed,' said Delia, taking off her own wig. 'He can have this bloody thing if he wants. I keep finding spiders in it.'

'You couldn't get us a cup of tea, could you, Mark?' said Sam.

'No, I couldn't,' said the constable. 'I'm not a tea boy.'

Sam looked at Delia and shook his head. 'They soon grow up, don't they? It doesn't seem two minutes ago that I was showing him how to get his boots really shiny.'

CHAPTER FORTY-FIVE

Eli John sat on the boundary fence of the field that still housed the twenty three burnt out caravans and mobile homes. In his mouth was a slender, hand-rolled cigarette that he could somehow transfer from one side of his mouth to the other, using only his tongue. It was something he did whilst he was thinking. The man standing in front of him had given him plenty to think about.

'I knew he was the feller what battered Lemmy and the other two gobshites,' Eli said, 'and I knew he was the feller what did fer Lemmy in the end – but I also knew the rapist gobshite had it comin'.'

'Take it from me, Carew's the one who arranged for this camp to be burnt down,' said Shooey. 'Lemmy Wilson threatened him, and Carew doesn't take kindly to threats.'

'Jesus Christ, ye fuckin' tellin' me!' said Eli, looking around the camp. 'This is some piece o' work! How can one man do all this?'

'It wasn't Carew who did it, he just arranged it.'

'So it was a gang?'

'No, it was one man, his name's Jimmy O'Connor.'

'And where have I heard that name before?'

'He was given eight years for burning down a Catholic presbytery in Derry back in the Eighties. The army handed him over. He swore he'd been acting under orders, but the army denied it.'

'Jesus, I remember it.'

'So do I,' said Shooey. 'I were in the army meself back then. Guarded him to and from the court during the trial. Got to know him well. I believed his story, but he had no chance with that court.'

'So, why would he do this to us?'

'He were mates with Carew – used ter work for him. In fact he were working for him just before your camp went up. I saw him in a pub in town. We got talking.'

'And did he mention that he was thinkin' o' firin' this camp?'

Shooey shook his head. 'He's hardly gonna tell me a thing like that, but he told me he owed Carew a favour and that Carew was having trouble with some of your people. I'll tell yer what, he's the only man I've ever heard of who could do this on his own.'

Eli John's dark, glittering eyes fixed themselves on Shooey. 'An' why are you tellin' me all this?'

'I saw one of the fliers yer've been putting about to get information on who did the job. That's how I got yer number. I could do with that £1,000 reward right now.'

'Could ye now? And maybe ye've made all this shite up just te get the reward.'

'Maybe I have – but you'll be able to find that out for yourself when yer nailing Carew's bollocks to this fence. I'm sure you'll be able to get the truth out of him.'

'Oh, ye can be sure o' that,' said Eli. 'Don't you worry, mister. An' when I get him to part with the truth I'll get him to part with his money. Someone owes us half a million euros and this

281

Carew feller sounds the hot favourite te have that sort o' cash.'

'And then what will you do to him?'

Eli surveyed the stricken campsite for several seconds before deciding. 'Well, maybe we'll splash him with a gallon of unleaded an' see how well *he* fuckin' burns.'

Shooey nodded his approval. 'If you let him live he'll come after you agin. Very tenacious man is Carew.'

Eli flicked his cigarette end away and spat out a piece of tobacco. 'Ye don't get too many tenacious corpses,' he said. 'We have a good woman dead because of this.'

'What? A woman died in the fire. I never heard anything about it.'

Eli got down off the fence. 'It wasn't the fire what kilt her. It was the loss. She was a wild woman whose man and child were killed in a car smash only a year gone. There's just so much loss a body can take. She got herself steamed with the drink and drove her Harley Davidson straight into a quarry. It'd have been handy for her to have had Carew riding pillion. She'd have liked that.'

CHAPTER FORTY-SIX

Manny Green fidgeted, nervously, in the witness box. He was wearing a dark suit, white shirt and a plain, blue tie, the outfit usually worn by the accused, on the advice of their lawyers. It was a

282

mystery to Sam, and to Delia Knowles, why he'd been called at short notice by the prosecution. But they could hardly protest. They had several last-minute witnesses of their own to call.

'Mr Green,' said Figgis, 'on the day of Mr Waring's death you gave a statement to the police.'

'Yes, that's right, I did.'

'You told the police that you had come round to Mr Waring's house in response to a telephone call from him, asking you to go round.'

'That's right, I did.'

'Did Mr Waring tell you what it was about?'

'No, he never told me what it was. He were like that, were Ally.'

Jim felt himself nodding his agreement, although, like Sam and Delia, he had no idea where this was going.

'Indeed.' Figgis cleared his throat and looked up at Manny. 'Mr Green, the police officer was obviously under the impression that you had only just arrived at Mr Waring's house in response to this call. Would that be correct?'

Manny squirmed. 'Well, I had and I hadn't if you know what I mean.'

The judge glared at him. 'No, we don't know what you mean, Mr Green. Had you just arrived on the scene or not?'

'Well, not as such, no. I'd actually been round a bit earlier. I live round the back y'see, so I can walk there if I cut down the ginnel.'

'How much earlier did you arrive, compared with the time the police officer interviewed you?' Figgis asked.

'About twenty minutes.'

'And could you tell the court what happened during those twenty minutes?'

Manny looked apologetically at Jim, who returned his stare with one of bemusement.

'I were just comin' down the ginnel when I saw Jim dash out of Ally's side door. He was in a right state.'

'What do you mean by, right state?' enquired Figgis.

'Well, he was covered in blood. It bloody shook me, I can tell you.'

'Please refrain from using obscenities in this court, Mr Green,' grumbled the judge.

'Sorry sir.'

'Then what did Mr Ormerod do?' asked Figgis.

'Well, he jumped in his car and drove off like a bat out of hell.' He glanced nervously at the judge, wondering if he'd just used another obscenity.

'What did you do then?'

'To be honest I didn't know what to do. It were fairly plain the blood wasn't Jim's. He'd never have been able to move so fast if it were his own blood. So I assumed it were Ally's.'

'Why would you assume it was Mr Waring's?'

'Well, he lived on his own and I knew he was in because he'd just rung me so...' He stopped, not knowing what else to add.

Figgis helped him out. 'So assuming it was Mr Waring's was a reasonable assumption.'

'I thought so, yes. No way were I goin' in that house, I can tell you.'

'So, what did you do, Mr Green?'

'Well, to be honest I didn't do nowt for a bit. I should have done, I know I should, but I didn't

284

know what to do. Then I dialled 999 and told 'em I'd heard screams coming from the house.'

'And had you heard screams?'

'Well, no. I didn't know what to say. I wasn't gonna tell 'em I'd just seen me mate running out covered in blood.'

Figgis glanced at the jury, 'Mystery solved I believe. Then what happened, Mr Green?'

'I went home and came back ten minutes later. That's when the copper interviewed me. Jim must have gone back to the house and the coppers arrested him. God knows why he went back.'

'And why didn't you tell the officer about what you'd seen earlier?'

'Well, Jim's me mate. You don't split on your mates. But I've thought about it since, and Ally was a mate as well, so I thought it's as well to tell the whole story.'

'Thank you, Mr Green. No further questions, my Lord.'

Figgis sat down. Delia got to her feet. 'Mr Green, think carefully. Are you absolutely sure it was Jim Ormerod who came out of the house?'

'Well, I were standing as close to him as I am to you.'

'But wasn't he covered in blood?'

'Oh yeah, absolutely lathered.'

'Was there blood on his face?'

'Covered in it.'

'So, how can you be so sure it was him?'

'What?'

'Could it have been someone who simply looked like Mr Ormerod covered in blood? When people are covered in blood, Mr Green, they do

285

take on a different appearance.'

'Do they? Well, I wouldn't know about that. All I can say is I'd swear blind it were Jim.'

'Bloody hell, Manny, it wasn't me!' Jim shouted.

Manny shrugged and looked down. Delia hadn't finished with him.

'Mr Green, you say Jim got into his car.'

'Yes.'

'From where you were standing could you see Mr Ormerod's car?'

'From where I were standing...?' he hesitated.

'Mr Green, you either saw his car or you didn't, which one is it? Are you sure the car was visible from where you were standing? Obviously this can be checked.'

'Well, maybe I didn't see his car. I definitely heard him drive away, though.'

'So, you heard him drive away, but you couldn't see his car. Is that what you're telling the court?'

'Yes.'

'So it might not have been his car and if he was covered in blood it might not have been him.'

'I was sure it was him,' said Manny, now uncertain.

'Hmm, a minute ago you were sure it was his car,' said Delia Knowles, cynically. 'And you rang the emergency services to say you'd heard screams when you hadn't – and you also failed to tell the police about what you now say you saw.' She shook her head, dismissively. 'What are we to believe, Mr Green?'

'I said I heard screams because I didn't want ter get me mate into bother – I'm sorry.' He looked up at Jim. 'Sorry Jim, I thought it were you.'

286

Manny wilted as Delia gave him a withering glare. 'I understand that Mr Waring – the victim; Mr Ormerod – the accused; Mr Mace – a man recently murdered; Mr McLeish – another man recently murdered, and Mr Outhwaite – a man recently arrested on a major theft charge, and you, were all members of a six man golf society, were you not?'

'What? Er, yeah.'

'Does this society have a name?'

'What?'

'A name, Mr Green. Does this golf society have a name?'

'Er, we're called the Syndicate.'

'The Syndicate? That's very formal for a golf society – did you have any other activities which might merit such a name?'

'Activities?'

'Was golf the only thing you six men did collectively?'

'Well … yes.'

'Thank you, Mr Green.'

Delia and Sam were alone in a conference room. 'Where the hell did Green come from?' she seethed. 'Is he for real?'

'To be honest, I'm not sure what to make of him,' said Sam. 'If he's telling porkies we've got to ask ourselves why? The only thing I can think of is that *he's* the real killer, trying to fit Jim up good and proper.'

'If he's the real killer, why would he expose himself like that?' pondered Delia. 'Why didn't he just keep his mouth shut about seeing Jim Ormerod?'

'Not sure,' said Sam. 'I must admit, Manny was never in the frame. I never suspected him.'

'Suppose,' suggested Delia, 'he's telling the truth about believing it was Jim who came out of the house? His reactions to that seem all very plausible – I know the jury bought it.'

Sam snapped his fingers to announce the arrival of a better idea. 'Or he could have heard about you bringing the 999 caller into the frame and he wants to jump in and discredit that theory before they find out the caller was him.'

She gave this idea some thought, and nodded that it was a possibility, then added another thought of her own. 'Or,' she said, 'maybe it *was* Jim he saw.'

'What? And the other two murders are unconnected? I don't think so. There has to be a connection.'

'OK,' Delia conceded, 'so, this brings us back to my original question – do we believe Mr Green is for real? Is he telling the truth – or what he thinks to be the truth – or is he lying in his teeth?'

'I definitely believe all three murders were connected in some way,' insisted Sam.

'But we know Manny had no involvement in the art robbery,' Delia pointed out.

Sam nodded. 'Well, I think we've pretty much established that Waring was killed by a golfer from Bostrop Pay and Play – which puts Manny in the frame – so maybe it was something else. Something he *was* involved in.'

'Are we saying Manny Green killed all three men?' asked Delia, quietly.

'What?'

'Are we saying Manny Green killed all three of them for reasons unconnected with the art robbery?'

Sam shook his head as he cast his mind back to the inoffensive, ordinary looking car dealer in the witness box. Appearances often deceive, but Manny Green didn't look much like a multiple murderer to him. Delia interrupted his thoughts.

'Look, I wouldn't mind getting Green back into court and pulling him to pieces. Do you think you could get something for me to pull him to pieces with?'

'I'm not sure,' Sam said, 'but I know a man who might.'

CHAPTER FORTY-SEVEN

The man in the car park office was easily identifiable by his unusual ugliness. He swung his feet off a table, put down his *Telegraph* and came to the window.

'Mr Rothwell?' said Sam.

'Yes?'

'My name's Carew. I'm a private investigator.' He handed Rothwell his card through the hatch. 'I wonder if I could ask you a few questions about Alistair Waring.' He kept his eyes fixed on Rothwell's for signs of uneasiness. There would never be a better time for Rothwell to show his hand – the man was apparently a fine poker player. Once on his guard Sam knew his face would display nothing. It displayed nothing now.

'You might as well come inside,' Rothwell said. 'I doubt if this is the sort of thing you wish to talk about in public.' He was looking beyond Sam towards the exit barrier when an irate-looking motorist was getting out of his car. Rothwell was opening the office door to allow Sam inside as the man arrived at the window.

'Yer machine's took me money but I never got me ticket back. Where does that bloody leave me?'

'I will let you out, sir.'

Rothwell pressed a button that raised the barrier. The man muttered something and went back to his car.

'Must remember that the next time I've got no money for the car park,' said Sam.

'I'm not paid enough to argue with people,' said Rothwell. 'The man coming on next would have argued with him and we'd have had cars backing up to level four.'

Rothwell sat down at the table. Sam glanced at the newspaper and noticed the crossword was filled in. Sally would have been impressed, she liked to do the *Telegraph* crossword. How come she was in his thoughts so often? There had only ever been one love in his life, Kathy Sturridge, and she was dead.

'I assume it's to do with the murder case, Mr Carew. What is it you wish to know?'

'I'm part of the defence team. It's becoming more and more obvious to us that Alistair wasn't killed by a jealous husband. Did you know Jim Ormerod?'

Rothwell ran his fingers through an unruly

mass of greying hair. 'In ten years I've played golf with him seven times.'

Seven times, how precise, Sam thought.

'He never struck me as a man of passion, Mr Carew, but you never can tell.'

'We think his murder is connected with those of Rudolph Mace and Dave McLeish. Would you be able to throw any light on this?'

'You think Alistair was part of the Rembrandt theft gang?'

'We know he was,' Sam assured him, 'but that might not have any connection with his murder.'

'Really?'

'I gather you played poker with him. Do you think his murder might have had something to do with his gambling? Did he have any gambling debts?'

Rothwell gave a short laugh. 'I imagine he had considerable gambling debts, Mr Carew. He owed me over four thousand pounds, but murdering your creditors is a most inefficient method of collecting, do you not think? The odd thing is that on the morning of the murder he rang me to say he would be honouring his debt within five days. I gather he said the same to his other creditors.'

Sam was wondering how the hell the police hadn't picked up on this. And was it a significant fact to bring up at the trial?

'I understand you used to work with Alistair Waring but you left around the time of the murder.'

'I actually left three weeks before Alistair's murder. I was a general dogsbody and they took advantage. They had me working late at night,

291

which interfered with my other profession.'

'Really? Which is?'

'Professional gambler, Mr Carew.'

'Ah – presumably a poker player.'

'Correct.'

'I'm told you're good.'

'Whoever told you that was right. I *am* good. This job is simply a safety net. I need to know that whatever happens at the card table I will never be without a roof over my head. I never play on credit. The money I win from gambling stays separate, and it's very considerable. I am not a married man, Mr Carew. I apparently lack the required sexual magnetism – having a face like mine doesn't help. However, I have an unusual brain. I will never climb very far up the ladder of any normal profession but I have a more than useful aptitude for poker. One day I will buy a big house and the ladies will love me for my money and for my elephantine penis.' He smiled, ruefully, 'The Good Lord compensated me for my cosmetic deficiency, but I would rather have had the handsome face. I'd even settle for your face.' He treated Sam to an unappealing smile. 'Tell me, Mr Carew, would you care to swap your face for a gigantic member?'

Sam couldn't think of anything to say to this. This man was odd. He got to the reason he'd come. 'Do you know much about Manny Green?'

'Such as?'

'Would you consider him a trustworthy man.'

'No, I would not. Manny Green is a dodgy car dealer.'

'Which is the dodgy part, him or the cars?'

292

'Both, from what I hear.'

'Do you know anything specific about him?'

'Why do you ask?'

No harm in telling him, thought Sam. 'He's a key witness against Jim Ormerod.'

'And you need to discredit him.'

'Something like that.'

Rothwell frowned, as though he was wrestling with a difficult decision. 'Actually, I do know something,' he said, 'and the reason I didn't tell the police is that had I informed on him to the police it might have caused me aggravation at the golf club. Bostrop Pay and Play isn't exactly *The Belfry*. A lot of rough types play there – the types that most golf clubs wouldn't allow over the threshold.'

'I'm not the police,' Sam said.

Rothwell paused as he got his thoughts in order. 'It happened a few weeks ago. I was up in the car park security room watching the CCTV monitor and I saw a Citroën Xantia come in. I know it was a pre-1998 model because I have one myself. Only this one had a V registration, which is the registration for a 2000 model at the earliest.'

'So it was a false plate?'

'Without question.'

'Did you report it to anyone?'

'That would have caused me aggravation. I'm not in this job for aggravation.'

'Fair enough,' said Sam, who wasn't here to judge.'

'Ten minutes later what looked to be the same car came out, only this one had P plates on.'

'Are you sure it was the same car?'

'It was the same model, same colour and same condition. I took the cassette out and saved it so I could have another look later. I went off shift straight after that.'

'And did you have another look?'

'Yes, there's a video machine at my lodgings.'

'As a gambling man, what are the odds on it being the same car?'

Rothwell screwed his eyes. True gamblers always take such challenges seriously. 'I'm more than ninety-five per cent certain it was the same car.'

'And what's the connection with Manny Green? Was it him driving it?'

'Our CCTV's a bit Charlie Chaplin, to quote one of our security people. You can't see who's driving, but I think it was him.'

'What makes you think that?'

'I saw him in it the next day, up at the golf club.'

'Presumably you'd written the number down and checked it?'

Rothwell tapped his temple. 'I didn't need to. I remember all numbers of any significance to me.' He gave Sam a broad grin. 'I'm not just a pretty face, you know.'

'Where's the video cassette now?'

'It's in my locker.'

'And can I have it?'

'Of course. In fact, if I can be of any help I'm at your disposal.'

'If we pursue it you may be needed to give evidence against Manny Green in court.'

'I'll do that. I never liked the man.'

'What about the, er, the rough types at the golf club?'

'I'm not frightened of these people, Mr Carew. I just don't see the sense in looking for trouble.'

'Your bosses might say you should have handed this video straight to them as soon as you took it out of the VCR. This won't jeopardise your job, will it?'

'I'm a car park attendant, not a captain of industry. What's to jeopardise?'

Sam smiled, but as he smiled his mind mulled over just how useful this would be in discrediting Manny's evidence. To make this stick it would probably take time they didn't have. Police enquiries etcetera, etcetera. It would also require Rothwell to give evidence in court, and Rothwell might prove not to be a great witness. Delia needed something much more immediate.

Rothswell obliged. He snapped his fingers, loudly.

'I've just realised, there is something else that just might be of interest.'

'Anything will do. We're clutching at straws at the moment.'

'Well,' said Rothwell, 'I don't know how significant this is, or even if there's any connection, but the number plates were switched on the same day poor David McLeish was murdered.'

'What? – exactly what time did the car come in and out of the car park?'

'It arrived at 20.33 and left at 20.42.'

Sam knew that the time of Dave's death had been narrowed down to between 7.30pm and 9.00pm. It was a pity Rothwell had seen fit to keep this to himself. Bloody annoying even.

'And still you didn't think to report it?'

295

Rothwell looked hurt. 'Mr Carew, *I've only just realised it.* My brain is inefficient in more ways than it's efficient. Have you any idea how frustrating it is for me to be intelligent enough to realise how stupid I am?'

'You're not stupid, Mr Rothwell.'

'I feel stupid. Things that jump out at you sometimes don't register with me until something triggers the connection, which in this case is you coming here. I remember seeing Manny arrived at the golf club in the Citroën about two minutes before I went into the clubhouse and found out about poor David. One thing put the other thing right out of my mind – until now.'

'I imagine it would,' conceded Sam. 'Anyway, it's probably no more than a coincidence.' He was trying to remain ultra-calm as he said it. He didn't want to alert Rothwell to the possibility that they might well have just unearthed the real murderer. Gerald Rothwell had a strange mind. Could he be trusted not to blab to all and sundry? Putting Manny on his guard.

'Mr Rothwell, can I trust you not to say anything to anyone about this conversation?'

'What would happen if I did?'

'It might cause you a lot of aggravation.'

'In that case you can trust me. As you know, I don't go looking for aggravation, Mr Carew.'

'No one likes aggravation. Can you think of anything else?'

Rothwell gave this question a lot of thought. 'No,' he said, eventually. 'I'll get you that tape.'

CHAPTER FORTY-EIGHT

The CCTV tape Sam was playing to Delia was a copy of the one he'd given to Owen that morning. Both shots were from the same camera and picked up cars entering and leaving the car park. The image was monochrome and grainy but the number plates were clearly visible, as was a missing nearside door mirror. This, plus something light coloured stuffed behind the passenger side windscreen – perhaps a cloth – pretty much identified the two cars as being one and the same vehicle. The timing was incriminating and exactly as Rothwell had remembered: 20.33 hours entering, 20.42 hours leaving.

'Why would he use a car park to swap his number plates?' Delia wondered.

'Because he's not the sharpest tool in the box,' Sam said. 'Stupidity catches nine out of ten villains. He probably thought it was as quiet a place as any to swap plates. I'm guessing he went to the top level where it will have been pretty empty, then drove straight back down. He wouldn't have figured on being sussed out by an eagle eyed car park attendant, much less one who knew him.'

'Where is he now?'

'The police picked him up just after I showed them the tape. I gather from DC Owen Price that there's some DNA evidence been found at the scene of Dave McLeish's murder.'

'DNA?'

'They found some human hairs caught in the bushes where the suspect will have evidently hidden after climbing over a wall from the road. If they can tie that in with Manny he's got big problems.' He looked at her, hopefully. 'How's it going to affect this case?'

She laughed and shook her head. 'Well, I must admit, Sam, when I asked you to bring me something to pull Manny to bits with, I never expected anything this strong. For a start I'll make damned sure his evidence about seeing Jim coming out of Waring's house covered in blood is totally discredited, and it wouldn't surprise me if he's in the frame for the Waring and Mace murders. We're about to hole the prosecution well below the water-line. It's already fairly obvious that he was at the scene of Waring's killing. That little turd Figgis will be really struggling.'

CHAPTER FORTY-NINE

DI Janet Seager looked at Manny Green sitting at the other side of the table from her and Owen. 'Mr Green,' she began, 'let's start at the beginning. Why on earth would you want to kill your friend Dave McLeish?'

'I hardly think that's the beginning, Detective Inspector,' said Manny's solicitor. 'You appear to have jumped a few questions.'

'OK, do you own a Citroën Xantia registration number P714SLD?'

'I'm a car dealer. I own many cars, but I don't have a Xantia at the moment.'

'Did you own such a car on August 12th of this year?'

'Yes, I believe I did.'

'And were you using this car as your personal vehicle on that date?'

Both she and Owen saw a brief flash of shock on Manny's face. 'I don't remember.'

Janet smiled sweetly. 'Oh I think you do remember, Mr Green. We know you drove it to Bostrop Park Golf Club the following morning.'

'That doesn't mean I were driving it the night before. In fact I know I wasn't. I lent it out to a customer on approval the day before. He brought it back just before I went up to the golf club.'

'Do you have this customer's name?'

Manny stoked his wispy beard as he gave the question some thought. 'As a matter of fact I do,' he said. 'It was a bloke who plays golf at Bostrop – Gerald Rothwell.'

Janet and Owen looked at each other. 'Can you prove this?' Owen asked him.

'I don't know. What sort of proof do you need?'

'Can anyone verify that you lent him the car?' Janet said.

Manny shook his head. 'Not really. I'm only a one man band. I don't have anyone working for me. He just took it out on approval. Left his own car, which was the same model only older, with me.'

Janet had suspended the interview. She was outside in the corridor talking to Owen.

'You spoke to Rothwell, what's he like?'

'Weird.'

'We need to bring him in. Check on his background. Has he got any previous? – and find out how long this bloody DNA job will take. If it matches Rothwell or Green, he's the one we'll keep.'

'Mr Rothwell,' said Owen, 'you have supplied the police with a video tape showing cars entering and leaving the Radcliffe Road car park in Unsworth on the evening of the 12th of August this year.'

'I did.'

'In particular, this tape showed a car entering with what appear to be false number plates and leaving with different ones.'

'The Citroën Xantia,' said Rothwell, who looked decidedly uncomfortable in the interview room. He had been given a female duty solicitor with whom he had exchanged the bare minimum of words.

'Could you tell us what you were doing at this time?'

'I was working, watching the video monitor. That's how I could tell the plates had been switched.'

'Can anyone verify this?' Janet asked him.

Rothwell thought for a few seconds. 'I don't think so. I was on my own.'

'The owner of the car said he'd lent it to you on approval.'

Rothwell looked genuinely bemused. 'Approval? I don't understand. Why would I want it on approval? I've got exactly the same car myself only mine's in better condition.'

'So, you're saying the owner of that car is lying?'

'DI Seager, the owner of that car, as we both know, is Manny Green, and of course I'm saying he's lying.'

Janet sighed. 'Mr Rothwell, you say you were working alone. If you had left your post, for whatever reason, that evening, who would have noticed?'

'The first car to need my help. You get one stuck at a barrier the next thing you know there's a dozen backed up, all with horns honking.'

'Only if the barriers are down,' said Owen. 'But from what I could see on the video the barriers were permanently open, allowing cars in and out without paying.'

Rothwell stared at him for a while as though waiting for his memory to travel back to that night. 'That's right,' he said, eventually. 'I remember, now. There was a problem with the barriers. We had to leave them open for a while until an engineer got there.'

'So, you could have left your post without anyone noticing,' said Janet.

Rothwell shrugged. 'I suppose I could – but I didn't. Why do you ask? I thought I was just here to help with your enquiries.'

'And I'm afraid we'll have to keep you overnight until our enquiries are complete,' said Janet.

For the first time Rothwell lost his composure.

He looked at his solicitor, then back at Janet Seager. 'You can't do that!'

'Yes we can, Mr Rothwell.'

CHAPTER FIFTY

Sam was on his own, throwing darts at the board, when Owen walked in to the Clog and Shovel. It was early doors on Thursday and the place was barely a quarter full. As the Welshman reached the bar Sam called out to him.

'There's a pint in the pump for you.'

He continued throwing, allowing himself a murmur of self-congratulation as one of his darts hit treble 20. Owen brought his pint over, picked up another set of darts and stood with his feet sideways to the oche. His first dart hit the wire outside double 5 and bounced on to the floor. He looked around to see if anyone might be within earshot. No one was.

'We're holding both Manny Green and Rothwell for the McLeish murder.'

'Both of them?' said Sam. 'Why Rothwell?'

'Manny Green reckons Rothwell was driving the Xantia that evening. Rothwell says he wasn't. Anyway, we're still waiting to see if there's a DNA match from the hairs in the bushes. If there's no match we'll have to release them both. The CPS say we haven't got enough to hold either of them.'

'Aw, bloody hell!' grumbled Sam. 'That's all we

need. Who mentioned Rothwell's name first, you or Manny Green?'

'Green brought it up first, without any hint from us, boyo. We're not that stupid.'

'Who's we – you and Janet?'

Owen nodded. He pulled his two darts out of the board and picked the other up from the floor.

'Did he say why Rothwell was driving it?' Sam asked him.

'According to Manny Green he was thinking of buying it. Manny says he lent him it overnight. It's also quite possible that Rothwell could have gone absent from his work, killed McLeish, and got back in time.'

'So, why didn't he just keep quiet about it? Why did he tell me about the videos?'

'I dunno,' said Owen. 'Maybe he had a grudge against Manny Green. Maybe he had a grudge against all three dead men. You have to admit, he's a bit of an oddball.'

'Yeah, there is that,' conceded Sam. 'Hey – are you telling me the police are now linking all three murders. If so, how come Jim Ormerod's still in the frame?'

'Whoa, steady on, boyo! It's just that we had a forensic profiler look at the Mace and McLeish murders. Janet Seager asked him – unofficially, look you – to look at the Waring murder as well. He described a killer that fitted Rothwell to a T.'

'Hmm, is there some way we can use this in court?'

'Not without dropping me in the brown smelly stuff – mind you, that never stopped you before.'

'Have you checked on Rothwell's background?'

'It's all a bit obscure. He has no previous and since he left the army in the Eighties he's had pretty low paid jobs.'

'Army? I'm amazed they took him.'

'Maybe they weren't so fussy back then.'

'I think they were,' Sam said.

'Anyway, we're waiting for his army record to come through. It could be that something happened to him back then that sent him over the edge.'

'He's apparently a good poker player. Makes a lot of money at it – according to him, anyway.'

'I wonder what Rothwell's idea of a lot of money is,' Owen commented.

Sam sighed and threw a dart with some force. 'Talk about one step forward two steps back. Delia's gonna be really pissed off. She's opening for the defence on Monday.'

Owen gave him an exaggerated wink. 'Delia eh? I reckon she'll be opening for you if you play your cards right?'

Sam ignored him. He threw his other two darts into the 20 and issued a challenge to his Welsh pal. '501 up? Best of three for a fiver?'

'You're on, boyo.'

'By the way,' Sam said, retrieving his darts. 'I've heard from Sally.'

'I knew she'd relent in the end.'

'I wouldn't call it relenting. She's coming back up tomorrow – staying for a few days to sort out her house sale.'

'Is she still with her new bloke?'

'They're setting up house together down in Bath – it's all very serious. She sounded really

304

happy, Owen.'

Owen couldn't fail to miss the note of despondency in Sam's voice. 'Tell you what, boyo. When she comes up to sort out her house sale, if you play your cards right I reckon you could sort her out good and proper.'

'Are you being seedy again, DC Price?'

'I was merely offering helpful advice, boyo. Is the boyfriend coming with her?'

'I don't think so.'

'Oh dear! Now there's ever so foolish of him. I'm guessing she hasn't told him too much about you, if anything at all, or he'd be up here riding shotgun on her. I suggest you invite her out for a drink for old time's sake. Get her feeling guilty for the way she walked out on you in your hour of need. Before you know it she'll be making you your breakfast.'

'As a matter of fact I have a better plan,' said Sam, aiming at double twenty and hitting double one. 'My plan is *not* to make her feel guilty – in fact I might even apologise for creating a situation that caused her to walk out on me. I will tell her I don't blame her. Then I will do something to really gain her sympathy.'

'Such as?'

'I don't know yet, but it will be something she can't resist. In my experience there's no one more sympathetic than Sally.'

'Or pathetic than you.'

CHAPTER FIFTY-ONE

The following morning Sam was in his office studying the books, which hadn't been touched since Sally left. If nothing else there was a VAT return to sort out. It wasn't a job that Sam relished. He was thumbing the Temp Agency section of the *Yellow Pages* when the phone rang.

'Good morning – Carew's,' said Sam. It covered both companies. Sally had used it as her standard telephone greeting.

'Could I speak to Mr Sam Carew please?' It was a woman's voice. Efficient and businesslike. Someone's secretary.

'Speaking.'

'Good morning, Mr Carew. This is Plessington Holdings, I have Mr Plessington for you.'

Sam was inclined to put the phone down, but curiosity got the better of him. He hadn't heard from Plessington since he'd tricked the hard-nosed businessman into paying what he owed. He braced himself to give at least as good as he got. Plessington came on the line.

'Mr Carew, no point beating about the bush, I'd like your company back on the job.'

Sam said nothing for a long time, then, 'Really?' was all he could think to say. It wasn't what he'd been expecting.

'Yes, really. Business is business, Mr Carew. I don't hold a grudge against you for the little

306

scam you pulled on us. In fact I like to think I'd have done the same under the circumstances.'

'Mr Plessington, do I detect a note of admiration in your voice?'

'Call it what you like. Do you want to come back on site or not?'

'I assume the replacement contractors have let you down.'

'The replacement contractors have let no one down but themselves, Mr Carew. Suffice to say their contract has been terminated.'

'The contract will have to be re-negotiated,' Sam told him.

'You haven't got us over a barrel, Mr Carew. There are other contractors in the area.'

'I know, you've just tried one of them. What there aren't too many of, Mr Plessington, are good, reliable contractors. My partner, Alec Brownlow, is the best site manager I've ever come across – excluding my dad – and I think you know that.'

'We're prepared to re-negotiate on fair and reasonable terms.'

'I'll have to ask Alec, then I'll get back to you.'

'I need an answer by tomorrow night.'

'You'll have one, Mr Plessington.'

Sam sat back and beamed at the telephone. This would get him back in Alec's good books. His partner had told him they'd have trouble finding any work as good as the Plessington's job. He was still beaming when Eli John walked into his office carrying a sawn-off shotgun. By the look on his face he was prepared to use it. Sam looked at him, shook his head and moaned.

'Why can't I have just one day when everything goes right?'

Eli fixed him with an angry stare and sat in the chair at the opposite side of the desk. He pointed the weapon at Sam, but Sam instinctively knew that this was a scare tactic rather than a prelude to murder. Murderers have a different look in their eyes. In a murderer's eyes there is either unbalanced hatred or no emotion whatsoever. There is no middle ground for a murderer.

'I remember thinkin' the same thing meself the day I got the call te say the camp was burnt down.'

'Ah, you're one of the travellers.'

'Travellers eh? How polite ye can be when it suits ye. I've no doubt we're all pikies behind our backs.'

'What happened to your camp was nothing to do with me.'

'I'm thinkin' otherwise, Mr Carew. I'm thinkin' the deed was done by Jimmy O'Connor, and I'm thinkin' it was done at your behest.'

The mention of Jimmy's name took Sam aback somewhat, but there was no point claiming he didn't know the man. In this situation telling an obvious lie would do him nothing but harm.

'If it was Jimmy who burnt your camp down it was nothing to do with me. What makes you think it was him?'

'What I know about yer man is that he felt he had an obligation ter ye. Dat's all I need to know.'

'Obligation?' said Sam. 'You're making this up as you go along.'

Eli's mouth formed into a thin, humourless

308

grin. 'Yer man Jimmy is no better than the rest of us when he's in drink. Him and one of his old army buddies got together over a few pints. He has a loose tongue on him. It's his loose tongue dat's got ye into dis shite.'

Sam couldn't believe Jimmy, even in drink, would blab about something like that. He figured Eli was fishing for the truth.

'Maybe he had a grudge against someone at your camp.'

Eli shook his head. 'No, I tink the grudge was all yours, Mr Carew. It cost one of our people their life, did ye know that?'

'I know no one was in the camp at the time of the fire. Lemmy Wilson died by his own hand as he was trying to kill me.'

'I've no interest in Lemmy Wilson. I talk of a fine woman who took her own life because of what she lost in the fire.'

Sam wasn't sure he believed him, but this was no time to contradict the man. 'I'm sorry to hear that,' he said.

'Yer sympathy pays no bills. I'm here te collect payment in full.'

'Which is what?' asked Sam.

'Half a million euros.'

Sam gave a slow nod. What he knew was that he had time. What he didn't have was half a million euros, but this man wouldn't expect him to have that sort of money readily available.

'Will you take a cheque?' he asked.

'Yer a funny man, Mr Carew. I've heard that about ye.'

'If you've heard things about me you'll have

heard I've got serious money problems.'

'I've heard yer a slippery customer. I've heard I need te keep me eye on ye – which is why ye'll be comin' wid me.'

There was sufficient menace in his voice to convince Sam he meant what he said.

'There's a van parked outside the door. Ye'll get inside the back of it and please don't tink ye can make a break. The first notion I get that ye not doin' as yer told I'll put a fuckin' hole in yer big enough ter kick a football through.'

Sam's office was originally a shop and fronted on to Ackersfield Lane. With the shotgun at his back he opened the door.

'Hold it!' commanded Eli.

Sam held it.

'Look up and down the street. Is there anyone within fifty yards of ye? If there is, and ye lie to me, they'll get caught up in the fuckin' bloodshed.'

Sam looked to his right. The street was clear for a good fifty yards. To his left a woman was looking into a shop window about thirty yards away.

'There's a woman to my left.'

The woman disappeared into the shop.

Sam thought about not mentioning this, and playing for time. Sometimes buying time is a good means of defence. He stood there for a full minute. The woman didn't emerge. Nor did any ideas. He felt the gun prod into his back.

'I'm losin' me patience.'

'All clear now,' Sam said. 'She's gone into a shop.'

In front of him was a dirty blue Ford Transit

310

van with the sliding, side door open. Inside the van he could see another man pointing a handgun in his direction.

'If ye fancy yer chances,' said Eli, 'go for it.'

Sam fancied his chances against the man in the van. He reckoned he could dart to one side, out of the man's limited field of vision, before he fired. It was the man behind him he didn't fancy his chances against. He stepped across the pavement, climbed into the van and was immediately clubbed unconscious.

CHAPTER FIFTY-TWO

Sally hesitated when she arrived at Sam's office door. For three years she had regarded that door as pretty much her own. But now it wasn't, nor was anything behind it – or any*one* for that matter. She scarcely dared admit to herself that her heart was fluttering in anticipation of seeing him once again. She hadn't told him she was coming but Alec told her he'd be in the office about now – doing the books. The thought of Sam doing books made her smile. This she had to see.

Him she had to see.

For heaven's sake, Sally Grover, pull yourself together! There was no future with Carew. Calling him Carew had helped her get a grip on the reality of the situation. Carew was very bad for her. Carew had almost got her killed – twice. It wouldn't be long before he got himself killed and

311

she didn't want to be around when that happened. She would go to his funeral and weep buckets. Then she would mourn his passing from a safe distance – from the safety of her home in Bath. With her new man, who was kind and loving *and safe*.

She tapped on the door and pushed it open. It led into what would have been a reception area had they ever had a receptionist. Sally had been the only staff they had ever had. Both Sam and Alec would pop in to deal with orders and tenders and signing cheques and suchlike, but this had been her domain. The Monet and Degas prints on the wall had been of her choosing. So had the carpet and wallpaper and the bench seat under the side window. The door to the main office was partially open with no sign of life beyond.

'Sam?'

The office was pretty much as she had left it, right down to the intray full of unfiled correspondence and the vase of now dead flowers on the window sill. It was odd that he'd gone out and left the office unlocked. That was very unlike Sam. She picked up the phone and rang Alec on his mobile.

'Alec, it's Sally… I'm at the office but Sam's not here. He's left it unlocked… I know, I thought the same thing myself. Look I've still got a key on my key ring, do you want me to lock up?… Right. If you need me you've got my mobile number… Yes, tell him I called round. See you, bye.'

She blew out a disappointed breath and looked at Sam's chair, which was inferior to hers. She pictured him sitting there with his muddy boots on the desk, smoking and telling her grossly exaggerated stories about the police or his escapades on the building sites. It made her smile and wish he was here right now. If nothing else, Sam Carew could tell a good lie.

But the lie she thought he'd told her about the woman in his flat hadn't been a lie after all. Both Owen and Alec had confirmed that. Is that why she was here? Had she come to apologise? Apologising to Sam would be a novel experience. Up to now it had always been Sam apologising to her.

CHAPTER FIFTY-THREE

Sam came round in what he assumed was a cellar. It wasn't immediately apparent that it was a cellar because it was pitch black. No hint of light anywhere, which was unusual, Sam thought. Light was like water, it crept through the tiniest of cracks and crevices.

He assumed it was a cellar because it smelt like a cellar. It smelt damp and musty. And it was bloody cold. Before the advent of the damp-proof course a cellar was the only efficient way of keeping the ground floors of houses dry. Trap all the damp in the cellar.

He could hear water in pipes and the rumbling of distant traffic. All the noise came from above where he was lying on cold flags. His feet and hands were tied together behind his back, which was bloody uncomfortable. Why do people who

313

tie you up always make it so uncomfortable? The idea of tying someone up is simply to immobilise them. It's quite possible to do that without it hurting quite so much. This was the tangle of thoughts in his head when he first came round. His head was throbbing with pain as he tried to collect his senses. Where was he and why was he here? He couldn't figure out how he'd come to be here. He tried to piece together the events of that day. Jesus! What day was it? Was it day or night? It must be night with this much darkness. So, what day or night was it? Friday. That was something. He knew it was Friday. Or at least his last memory had been Friday. It must be Friday night – or maybe Saturday morning. He remembered Friday because Sally was coming back on Friday and he'd had plans for her. So, what the hell was he doing in this cellar? A thought struck him. Was it just very dark or was he blind? He'd never known inky darkness like this. It was like being locked inside a tin of black boot polish. This type of darkness must mean he's blind. He'd been hit on the head, he knew that. He'd probably been hit on the head so hard he'd been blinded. Oh Jesus! Please Jesus, no, not blinded! Who the hell had done this to him? Why had they done it?

He felt tears tumbling down his cheeks. He didn't want to be blind. He was too old to be blind. He was too old to learn how to be blind. He remembered the man with the gun; the man with the brown, wizened face who wanted money. Then he had a brief image of the van with the man pointing a handgun at him. Then nothing. Well they wouldn't be getting any money.

314

They'd already done their worst to him, if they wanted to shoot him they might as well. He drew in a deep breath and let out all his anguish in one strident, piercing scream that would let anyone within a hundred feet, inside or outside the building, know what he was there; that he was conscious; and that maybe he was blind.

But no one came.

CHAPTER FIFTY-FOUR

Delia Knowles looked up at Janet Seager who had just taken the oath.

'Detective Inspector Seager, I'm obliged to you for coming to court at such short notice but I called you for good reason. You see I did intend recalling Emmanuel Green as I had further questions for him, but he's apparently unable to attend court because he's in custody. Could you tell me why that is, DI Seager?'

Figgis got to his feet. 'My Lord I must protest. Mr Green has been detained on an unrelated matter.'

'M'Lord,' said Delia. 'The prosecution's case rests very largely on Mr Green's integrity.'

'And is it your intention to question Mr Green's integrity, Mrs Knowles?'

'That's for the jury to decide, m'Lord. I simply want to put them in the picture regarding this witness – and why I'm unable to question him further.'

The judge turned to Janet. 'Very well, you may answer the question, DI Seager.'

'He's being held in connection with the murder of David McLeish.'

'And has he been charged?'

'Not yet, my Lord. He's been arrested on suspicion and is being held pending the results of DNA testing.'

Delia turned to the jury. 'David McLeish was a close associate of Alistair Waring and Rudolph Mace – all three murdered within weeks of each other, so it's incorrect to suggest that these murders were unrelated. It adds weight to the theory that whoever killed Alistair Waring also killed David McLeish and Rudolph Mace, the last two murders being committed while my client was in custody.' She remained silent as she allowed the implication of what she had told them to sink in. The silence was broken by the judge.

'Do you have any further questions of this witness, Mrs Knowles?'

'I do, m'Lord. I wish to bring to the court's attention to defence exhibit 9.'

A plastic bag containing a golf club was produced by one of the court ushers. The club was taken out of the bag and shown to DI Seager.

'Do you know what this is, Detective Inspector?' asked Delia.

Janet was ready for this. 'It looks like a 5 iron from Mr Ormerod's golf set.'

'M'Lord,' said Delia, 'might the accused be allowed to look at it for further identification?'

'I don't see why not.'

The club was shown to Jim who looked at it and

nodded. 'That's definitely mine. I can tell from the way the grip's split. I was meaning to have them all re-gripped, but I never got round to it.'

'It's perhaps as well you didn't,' said Delia, watching as the club was handed to the judge. She returned her attention to Janet. 'DI Seager, I understand the alleged murder weapon – a 3 iron from the same set as this – was found in a wheelie bin at the back of the victim's house. It was assumed to be the murder weapon because it was found to have blood on it belonging to the victim and fingerprints belonging to the accused.'

'That's correct.'

'Were you aware that the remainder of the golf club set was found in a golf bag at the Bostrop Park Gold Club where the accused played golf?'

'I was.'

'Did you examine the golf bag?'

'Not personally, but it was thoroughly examined by other officers.'

'Did these other officers notice anything odd about it?'

'Nothing odd. I understand it was noticed that one of the clubs was a lot cleaner than the others. At the time we attached no significance to it.'

The judge intervened. 'If this is going to be of significance to the case, shouldn't the person who actually examined the clubs be made to give evidence?'

'If necessary, m'Lord,' smiled Delia. 'I will also be questioning the accused to find out why it was so clean.'

'It wasn't clean when I left it,' shouted Jim. 'It was as mucky as the rest of them.'

'Mr Ormerod,' said the judge, sourly, 'please do not interrupt this court's proceedings with such outbursts.'

'So,' continued Delia, who was happy with Jim's contribution, 'the club weren't sent for forensic examination?'

Janet Seager shook her head, guiltily. 'No, they weren't at the crime scene, so it was considered unnecessary.'

'Was this a misjudgement on your part?'

'It would seem so.'

'What happened to the bag of clubs?'

'They were returned to the accused's wife.'

'Do you now see any significance in the unusually clean club?'

'Possibly,' said Janet, uncomfortably.

From her file Delia took a sheet of paper and addressed herself to the judge. 'M'Lord, a private investigator, working for the defence, took this golf club to a private forensic laboratory who found traces of blood under the grip. The blood was then sent for DNA testing. This is a copy of the DNA results taken from the club by the Goven Clarke DNA testing service – my learned friend has been supplied with a copy. We passed this on to the police, along with the golf club.' She returned her attention to Janet. 'DI Seager, using these DNA results were you able to identify whose blood it is?'

'Yes, the DNA matches the DNA of Alistair Waring.'

'And have you been able to come up with any reasons why Alistair Waring's blood came to be on this club, one that had been meticulously cleaned by persons or person unknown?'

'We have theories, nothing concrete.'

'Would one of the theories be that the killer wiped the real murder weapon clean of his finger-prints and Mr Waring's blood, put it back in the bag and took out another club which he correctly presumed would be covered in Mr Ormerod's fingerprints and liberally coated it with the victim's blood before hiding it where it could easily be found and then taking the bag of clubs, complete with the actual murder weapon, up to the golf club and leave it in the locker room?'

Delia rattled her theory off so quickly that Figgis had no opportunity to intervene. He was now on his feet.

'My Lord, this is outrageous. I must protest. She is not simply leading the witness she is driving her towards a conclusion not of her own making.'

'I agree. Detective Inspector, you will not answer that question and Mrs Knowles you should know better.'

'I do apologise, m'Lord. It's simply that I could see no other explanation. No doubt the jury will be able to think of a thousand reasons for this mysteriously clean golf club to have traces of the victim's blood on it.' She knew full well that the jury would be able to think of no explanation other than the one she'd just given.

'Mrs Knowles!' warned the judge.

'M'Lord?' said Delia, innocently.

'Do you have any further questions of this witness?'

'Not at this moment, m'Lord.'

'Mr Figgis?'

Figgis got slowly to his feet. He wore a look on his face that he hoped would register his contempt for the defence's cheap chicanery.

'Thank you, my Lord.' He smiled at Janet. 'Detective Inspector Seager – this, er, this theory that my learned friend has mentioned – is it a theory that the police are actually working on?'

'Not at the moment, no.'

'No, I didn't think so. Thank you, DI Seager.'

Figgis sat down. Delia got up. 'One further question, if it pleases, m'Lord.'

The judge sighed. 'Yes, go ahead, Mrs Knowles.'

'Detective Inspector, have the police completely discounted the theory that all three murders are connected?'

'We're not discounting anything at the moment.'

'No further questions, m'Lord.'

'In that case I think we'll adjourn for lunch.'

CHAPTER FIFTY-FIVE

Sam had been without food or water for 72 hours and he was now hallucinating. His mouth had completely dried out and was coated with some thick, unpleasant gunge; his lips were parched and cracked; his tongue was swollen; what urine left in his body was highly concentrated and burning his bladder; the lining of his stomach had dried out – this was causing dry heaves and vomiting; his body temperature was high, with no

320

sweat to cool it. In his lucid moments he was quite sure he was dying and this was a most unpleasant way to die.

CHAPTER FIFTY-SIX

'Where the bloody hell's Carew?' Delia had found Owen in the corridor outside the court.

'Your guess is as good as mine,' said Owen. 'He hasn't been seen or heard of since Thursday night. Sally went to his office on Friday. The place was unlocked but Sam wasn't around. His car's still in its parking spot and what makes it really odd is that he wasn't around when Sally showed up. He knew she was coming.'

'What's the significance of that? Who's Sally?'

'It's a long story – suffice to say that Sam would definitely have wanted to see her. To be right honest I'm a bit worried about him. I was actually hoping he'd be here.'

'Well, he isn't,' grumbled Delia. 'What – you think something's happened to him? Something connected with this case maybe?'

'It could be something connected with any number of things,' said Owen, mournfully. 'A lot of very undesirable characters bear grudges against Sam Carew.'

'What about our friend Manny Green? Has he confessed to murdering David McLeish yet?'

Owen shook his head. 'He reckons if the hairs we found in the bushes are from his head it won't

321

make him the murderer.'

Delia shook her head in exasperation. 'Oh yes, so, what was he doing in the bushes?'

'Well, he also plays golf there. According to him he has a weak bladder and he often takes a pee in those very bushes.'

'Bloody great!' said Delia. 'All he needs are a couple of his little bloody golfing pals to verify this and any DNA evidence is useless. How come golfers have such weak bladders?'

Owen shrugged, although he, according to Sam, had a bladder the size of a peanut. The whole situation was frustrating Delia, who was allowing her temper to get the better of her.

'My husband's a golfer, did you know that, Owen? Born Again Christian and golfer – what a combination. I hate golf, do you know that, Owen? I think it's the most stupid fucking game ever invented! If all the fucking golf courses in the world were dying of some disease caused by lack of fertiliser and I had all the world's fertiliser inside my body, I wouldn't give a shit – what do you think of that?'

'I'm more of a rugby man myself,' said Owen.

CHAPTER FIFTY-SEVEN

It was only a dim bulb that went on in the cellar but to Sam it was as though someone was shining a one thousand watt searchlight in his face. And with it came the joyous realisation that he wasn't blind. There wasn't much to be joyous about in his situation but he'd take this.

His eyes focused on the man at the cellar door. Eli was grimacing at the stink emanating from Sam who had been lying in his own urine for at least forty eight of the seventy two hours he'd been down there. Luckily for him his bowels hadn't betrayed him. It was a small mercy, but one for which he was grateful. Eli approached and unscrewed the cap off a litre bottle of water. He poured it over Sam's upturned face and Sam captured as much as he could in his mouth, choking and coughing but coming back for more. Eli put down the bottle and untied his captive's bonds. He put the bottle into Sam's hands and Sam drank the rest of the water greedily and collapsed back on to the cellar floor as the life-giving liquid seeped through his cramped body. He tried to say, 'thank you' but all that came out was an animal grunt. He had reason to detest and despise this man, but right now he had more reason to be grateful.

His limbs burnt with pain as blood began to properly circulate through his body. Eli watched, curiously, as his victim groaned in agony, trying to stretch the cramp from his arms and legs. The fingers of both hands were clenched, clawlike. He tried to open them by pressing his palms down on the floor, but when he lifted them up they went back into spasm. He lifted them up to his face, wondering what the hell had happened to them. Eli went out of the cellar and came back with a bucket, something wrapped in a news-paper, and a black plastic bag.

'There's clothes in the bag for ye an' a bucket ter save yer stinkin' the place out. Put yer old clothes in the bag and tie it up. It'll be collected. If ye need more water there's a tap over there.'

Sam turned his head and saw an old, brass tap poking out of the wall only a few feet away from where he'd been dying of thirst. Maybe, had he been able to see it and not reach it, it would have been worse. Right now it was the centre of his universe.

'I'll be leaving the light on,' said Eli. 'I want ye ter dwell on how decent and friendly I'm bein' – an' if I get dis friendship thrown in me face when we do business I'll tie ye up again, turn off the fuckin' light, an' leave ye there ter rot.' He kicked whatever was wrapped in the newspaper over to Sam.

'Here, there's some pig food for ye. Once a pig always a pig.'

Slices of bread sprang out and scattered all over the dirty floor. Sam picked one up and gnawed at it, hungrily. He didn't notice the green bits that told of it being well past its sell-by date. It was food. Eli closed the door and Sam heard bolts being slammed on the other side.

Still sitting on the floor Sam looked around his prison. On the floor were stone flags and on one wall was an old, brick boiler, with a narrow, chimney breast leading up through the ceiling. There were no windows, the walls had been whitewashed many generations ago and the ceiling plastered over around the same time. It had no doubt been used as a washroom in years past. On another wall was a row of hooks on which would probably have

324

hung a tin bath, a rubbing board, a ladling can for transferring hot water from the boiler into a peggy tub, and a posser for pressing and stirring the washing. There would no doubt have been a mangle somewhere and a workbench where the man of the house would have cobbled the family shoes. A picture of all this passed through Sam's re-energising brain. He knew these things because such tales had been passed down from grandfather to father to son, and he'd worked in many buildings that contained such relics of the past. He felt himself smiling, stupidly; still enveloped in a cloud of euphoria; knowing he wasn't blind; knowing he now had food and water; and knowing he had hope of freedom and life – no matter how much it was going to cost him. All the money he had, probably.

Still unable to get to his feet he crawled over to the tap. His fingers were still in spasm and had no strength in them, certainly not enough to turn the tap on. Having failed in that endeavour he sat with his back against the wall, concentrating all his attention on his hands. Trying to open and close his fingers. Hoping they wouldn't stay like this for good. If they did he'd never be able to turn the tap on and God knows when that little bloody Irish gnome would be back. He had no idea how long he'd been down there. Having lapsed in and out of sleep it was hard to tell. He knew a fit man could last no more than four or five days without water and he'd definitely been on his last legs. He reckoned three to four days, which made it Monday or Tuesday.

He'd missed seeing Sally. She'd probably gone

back to her boyfriend in Bath by now. He'd missed the deadline for agreeing the Plessington contract – which meant he'd let Alec down. He had also let Delia down; she'd struggle in court without the evidence he'd been working on. If it were Tuesday he'd be due to give his evidence today. He'd let Jim down and he'd let Tracey down. He shook his head at the number of people who relied on him – placed their misguided faith in him. He'd probably let Owen down as well only he couldn't think why. No doubt Owen would be able to give him a reason. He was getting more movement in his fingers, which was a relief. What he needed now was his voice back. He tried to sing a cheeky song from his youth, moving his fingers in time:

Auntie Mary had a canary up the leg of her
  drawers,
When she farted it departed down the leg of her
  drawers.

His voice was little more than a croak but his fingers were getting very slightly more nimble, so he thought he'd give them a real workout to the rugby club version of the Eton Boating Song:

The sexual life of a camel is stranger than some
  people think,
In the height of the mating season, it tries to bugger
  the Sphinx,
But the Sphinx's posterior orifice, is filled with the
  sands of the Nile,
Which accounts for the hump on the camel, and the
  Spinx's inscrutable smile.

He knew enough verses of this to exercise his fingers into the mobility they needed to make another attempt on the tap. He finished the song in good voice and tried again, this time with success. He stuck his mouth underneath and drank. Not too long ago he had hallucinated about this delicious moment; about never-ending water pouring into his mouth, trying to drown him but it couldn't because he could drink faster than the water could choke him to death. Only this time the water got the better of him. He pulled his mouth away, coughed and spluttered and let the water run over the back of his head, then he filled his bottle and crawled back to where the bread was scattered on the floor and he ate every crumb of it, washing it down liberally with more water. Shit! You idiot, Carew! You've drunk too much too quickly. He was getting stomach cramps and wanted desperately to pee, and he knew it would be red hot and painful. He pulled off his reeking jeans and boxers, forced himself to his knees, and peed in the bucket. Moaning in agony as it came out like molten lava.

He then opened the plastic bag to find he'd been supplied with green, *Help The Aged* trousers and a red T-shirt, both of which would have fitted Luciano Pavarotti and left room to grow. He pulled the trousers on, took the belt out of his jeans, threaded it through the belt loops and pulled in the surplus ten inches of waistline. The T-shirt he discarded – his own polo shirt might be getting a bit whiffy by now but he didn't have to wear every bit of rubbish they threw at him.

He made his way back to the tap and washed his jeans and shorts. Then he wrung as much water from them as he could, forced himself to his feet for the first time and hung them on the wall-hooks to dry. This might take some time, but time, it seemed, was something he probably had plenty of right now. No way was he going to deal with these bastards looking like Coco the Clown.

Now, weak from his exertions, he sat down again and allowed himself the luxury of doing what he did best – dreaming up a plan.

Plan A was not to antagonise his captors into returning him to the condition he was recovering from. He didn't want to have to go through that again. The odds were that he wouldn't recover next time. Plan B was to give them whatever they wanted in exchange for his freedom, even if it left him skint. These were not very imaginative plans but they'd have to do for the time being.

His planning complete, Sam settled back to read the sheet of the *Unsworth Observer* in which his meal had been wrapped. A short item took his attention. It was an innocent item, totally unrelated to any crime, unless you had a mind like that of Sam Carew. His was a mind that retained odd scraps of information which normal people might well disregard. In fact, under normal circumstances Sam might well have scanned over the item, but given one piece of newspaper and nothing else to do he had time to read and digest every word. The item brought to his mind something he'd seen written down in the late Alistair Waring's journal. The chances of it leading to anything were extremely minimal but it would do no harm to

328

save it and check it out when he was freed.

He would have been most disappointed to learn that freedom didn't figure in the plan Eli John had for him.

CHAPTER FIFTY-EIGHT

Sally walked to the front window of her house. In three weeks it wouldn't be hers any longer. In three weeks she'd have cut her ties with Unsworth altogether. In three weeks she'd be living with Robert in Bath. He had been expecting her back on Sunday evening but she'd told him she had some loose ends to tie up. Sam was her only loose end. Where the hell was he? She half suspected that he'd made himself scarce to avoid her. Maybe he was mad at her for not believing him. Then she reminded herself that Sam wasn't like that. He couldn't bear a grudge for more than ten minutes unless it was against someone who had hurt the people he loved or who was threatening his life. Owen had told her about the travellers' camp, and about the man who had threatened Sam's boys, and about Shane Outhwaite who had set Sam up with the half naked woman. Was Outhwaite paying the price for hurting *someone Sam loved?* Owen thought so. Sam could be very unreasonable when he wanted. The house phone rang. She desperately hoped it would be Sam.

'Sally?'

'Oh, hello Owen.'

'Don't sound so excited. I was wondering if you'd heard from Sam?'

'Not a peep.'

'When are you due to go back?'

'Yesterday.'

'What? – are you waiting for Sam to show his face or something?'

'Oh, I don't know… Owen, do you mind if I ask you an awkward question?'

'I'll let you know when you ask it.'

'How did Sam take it when he found out I was going to live with Robert?'

'Robert?'

'My boyfriend – I thought Sam would have told you.'

A silence hung between them for a moment. Owen had a great affection for Sally and wished her a good life. He also doubted very much if Sam could give her that life. But he also had an inexplicable affection for Sam and, what was worse, an even more inexplicable loyalty to the man. He knew Sam didn't want to lose Sally.

'He did mention something, but not in any detail. The truth is he's never been one to cry on my shoulder – or anyone's shoulder for that matter. He's had a tricky time recently. I know for sure he misses you like hell.'

'Misses me like hell? Did he actually say that?'

'Yes.'

Owen said it without hesitation because even if Sam hadn't actually said those words it was how Sam felt. Sally paused for a long while then asked, 'You don't think there's anything to worry about with Sam going missing, do you?'

'Sally, if I wasted my time worrying about Sam Carew I wouldn't have time to do anything else.'

'Yes, that's what I thought you'd say. But isn't it odd of him to vanish just when he's needed to give evidence in a case he's working on?'

'Sam's an odd character, but yes, it is odd.'

'I know but ... hang on...'

A car just like Sam's pulled up outside. Her heart skipped a proverbial beat, then a woman got out and went into a house across the street and Sally remembered Sam didn't have his Mondeo any more. Just for a second she hated that woman.

'What?'

She collected herself. 'Nothing ... look there is something that occurred to me, only I'm not sure if Sam would think I'm poking my nose in where it doesn't belong.'

'And what's that?'

'Well, he had a security camera fixed into his office doorway so he could check his visitors. Quite often my job was to tell them he wasn't in.'

'I know about the camera. I suspect you told me he wasn't in when he was, on quite a few occasions.'

'He never did it to you, Owen. He never avoided his friends.'

'I'm pleased to hear it.'

'Anyway I got to wondering if there was a tape in the machine last Friday morning. If there was it might give us an idea what happened to him – what do you think? Do you think I'm being silly?'

'I think it's worth a shot, my lovely. Why don't I meet you down there? I assume you have a key?'

'I have. I'd better square it with Alec first. I

331

don't want to go treading on any toes.'

The tape in the VCR had run itself out. Sally ran it back to the beginning. The timer said it was switched on at 08.49 the previous Friday. She ran it on fast forward until she saw someone on the screen – Sam. He appeared at 10.14. The shot was just of Sam and maybe three feet either side of him. This included some brick wall and part of the street. He was standing in profile looking to his left and to his right.

'His lips are moving,' Owen observed, 'he's talking to someone.'

Sally was hoping that certain someone wouldn't be Tracey Ormerod. She knew Tracey of old and wouldn't put it past her to have got her talons into Sam. After a minute Sam stepped out of the frame, another man entered the shot from behind and quickly followed him.

'Run it back and freeze it,' said Owen.

Sally did as he asked. Owen cursed. 'Oh, bloody hell, no!'

'What? Who is it?'

'His name is Elias John Higgins, better known as Eli John. He's the leader of the gypsies whose camp was burnt down. If he thinks Sam was responsible he'll have a rare grudge against him.'

'And how do we get hold of this Eli John?' asked an alarmed Sally.

'I've no idea. He's an Irish gypsy. He could be anywhere in the country – so could Sam.'

'How do we track him down?'

'Sally I wouldn't know where to start. I'll report what I know and set a few wheels in motion but we haven't the resources to go chasing shadows. It looks to me like Sam might have to rely on his own resources.'

Sally felt sick with worry. 'He *is* a resourceful man, isn't he Owen?' She sought reassurance. Owen put an arm around her shoulder.

'Sally, he's the most resourceful person I've ever come across. He'll turn up like a bad penny, just as he always does.'

But Owen wasn't sure if Sam could get out of this one. He also felt that the wisest advice he could give to Sally would be for her to go back to Bath and to her new man; to try and forget Sam Carew and to get on with the rest of her life – and to do that now.

'I think I'll hang around until he turns up,' she said.

'OK,' said Owen.

CHAPTER FIFTY-NINE

It was Tuesday morning. By this time Delia had hoped to have had Sam in the witness box. Most of the jurors couldn't have helped but know who he was and any testimony he gave favouring Jim Ormerod would have weighed heavily in her client's favour. Sam Carew was regarded as something of a people's hero, a fact which got right up the nose of Acting DCI Bowman and many others down at Unsworth nick. As it was, Delia had to make do with Cassie Blake, Tracey, Shane Outhwaite and Rothwell. The nearest she could get to character witnesses. Cassie had just taken the oath.

'Miss Blake, do people call you Cassandra or Cassie?'

'Most people call me Cassie.'

Delia nodded and looked down at her notes. 'Right, erm, look I'm going to ask you a very personal question which I expect you to answer truthfully.'

Cassie shrugged. 'If it's about me and Jim I don't mind.'

'Miss Blake, at the time of Alistair Waring's death were you having an affair with James Ormerod?'

Cassie was pretty and in her late twenties. She gave a toss of her newly flashed auburn hair, and smiled up at Jim, who returned it with a thin smile of his own.

'I were his girlfriend, yeah.'

'I assume you knew he was married?'

'He were gonna leave her. He doesn't love her, he can't stand her. She's a right selfish cow – doesn't deserve him.'

'So, when you heard he'd been arrested for killing Alistair Waring, what did you think?'

'What did I think? Well, I just laughed ter be honest. Jim wouldn't hurt a fly. I mean we both knew Tracey were havin' it off with Ally, but Jim weren't bothered. I honestly didn't think they'd keep him in overnight when they realised how daft it all were.'

'Not bothered?'

'What?'

'You said Jim wasn't bothered about his wife's

334

affair with Alistair Waring.'

'Why should he be? He had me.'

'So, why were they still together?'

'Well, it weren't quite as easy as that. Y'see she's got a son and Jim thinks the world of him. If it had been just him and her he'd have left her like a shot, but he loves that boy even if he's not his real dad.'

Delia pressed home her point. 'So when you heard that Jim had been charged with murdering Alistair Waring in a fit of jealous rage because of their affair, how did you react?'

Cassie laughed. 'Well, like I said, that were just a joke. Everybody who knows Jim thinks that's a joke.'

Figgis sprang to his feet. 'Objection, my Lord – far too much supposition here.'

'Sustained, the jury will disregard the witness's opinion.'

But Delia knew that the jury would form opinions of their own. 'Thank you, Miss Blake,' she said. 'No further questions.'

Figgis stood up, very slowly, and peered at Cassie, distastefully. 'Miss Blake, are you madly in love with James Ormerod?'

'What?'

'Let me rephrase it. Was your relationship with Mr Ormerod based on sex or was it something more pure and spiritual?' He pressed on before Cassie could find an answer. 'Miss Blake, are you in another relationship right now, or are you still remaining faithful and true to Mr Ormerod?'

Cassie squirmed under his gaze. Delia wished she'd never called her. It was obvious that Figgis had found something out that Cassie hadn't mentioned.

'Well, nowt lasts forever, does it,' Cassie blurted.

'The truth is that you now have another boyfriend – I believe he's a bus driver by the name of Andy. In fact I believe you were seeing Andy at the same time as you were seeing the accused.'

Cassie became indignant. 'What's that got ter bleedin' do wi' you? Hey, if you've messed things up wi' me an' Andy I'll not be best pleased!'

'Basically, Miss Blake, you were Mr Ormerod's bit on the side, nothing more.' Figgis glanced up at the jury. 'Having a bit on the side doesn't preclude a man from having a fit of jealous rage over his wife's infidelity. No further questions of this witness, my Lord.'

'Shit!' murmured Delia, under her breath.

CHAPTER SIXTY

Sam was desperately hungry and in extreme discomfort. He had now used the bucket and had placed it as far away from him as he could. There was a grate under the tap so at least there was no smell of personal pee. The worst thing was that he didn't know what was happening. Was this little Irish bastard going to starve him half to death before coming back or what? He had now lost all track of time. The light hadn't gone out since it had been first switched on, whenever that was. He had dozed, fitfully, maybe even nodded off for a few hours at a time. There was no way he could tell, not having a watch to look at. It wasn't until the man had gone that he realised his watch had been taken from him – as had his mobile phone. Just leaving him with his watch would have been handy. It would have given him the time and the date – a grip on reality, albeit very tenuous. This little bastard knew exactly what he was doing. Sam had no sense of time, place, if he'd ever eat again, if he'd ever get out of here, see the sky, see his boys, see Sally, was he going to die in here? Was this it? He had no way of knowing. All he could do was wait.

But for what?

He figured his jeans would take 24 hours to dry down here so he tried them, periodically. They were still damp when he heard footsteps outside. Bolts being drawn. The door was kicked open as if trouble was expected from Sam. But he wasn't in any condition to be dishing out trouble.

Eli John and another man stood there. The other man was wearing a smart suit and was carrying what looked like a laptop. Eli was pointing a gun at Sam's head. Sam shook it by way of conveying his disgust at the inhumane way they were treating him. Eli sneered.

'Don't tell me yer unhappy with our hospitality, Mr Carew. It's a fuckin' improvement to the hospitality ye showed to my people.'

My people? thought Sam. *Jesus, who does this bloke think he is – the king of the gypsies?* He didn't speak. His eyes were fixed on the laptop which the man placed on the floor in front of him.

'Just in case ye've forgotten yer account numbers,' said Eli, 'we've done ye the favour of diggin' them out of ye files. All ye need is yer codes and passwords which I'm sure ye'll have in her head.'

'What?'

'Ye buyin' yeself out of jail, Mr Carew. Yer goin' ter transfer all the money in yer bank accounts into an account me man will tell ye about.' Eli cackled. 'Me man's figured out it can all be done electronically – as of course ye know yeself. Now isn't that just the dog's bollocks? Doesn't that just take all the risk and aggravation out of the blackmail business?'

'I'm not sure I can remember my passwords,' lied Sam.

'Well, if ye can't that's a pity, because if ye can't come up with them we'll switch out the light, turn off the water, tie ye up ter fuck and leave ye here ter stew in yer own shite. What d'yer tink o' that?'

'I think you've won me over with your Irish charm.'

It was his habitual bravado. He certainly didn't feel very funny. They had brought the account numbers for his Carew and Son business account, Carew Investigations Bureau account, and for his private account. They obviously hadn't worked out that he'd got a VAT account and a business investment account. Still, most of the money was in the three accounts they'd brought details of. He brought up the statements on the screen. The total available funds added up to just over one hundred and seventy six thousand pounds which Sam figured to be a round a quarter of a million euros. He sensed

338

that the man might be disappointed.

'What's that in euros?' rasped Eli. His crony stabbed the numbers into a calculator. 'At a euro forty five to the pound it's two hundred and fifty five thousand euros.'

'That'll only pay fer half the damage.'

'It's all there is,' Sam pointed out, wearily. He was figuring that he and Alec could limp along on the money from the other accounts until things got better. Eli slapped him with considerable force, knocking him to the ground. In his weakened state Sam couldn't get up.

'Best to leave him be, Eli,' murmured the other man. 'We want him sensible not senseless.'

He sat on the floor beside Sam and opened the Home Page of Sam's bank. The man knew his stuff. Sam's passwords and codes were all birthdays and the name of the dog he'd had as a boy. Hard to forget stuff. Within fifteen minutes the three accounts were empty of funds. All Sam could think about was getting out of this awful hole. He looked up at Eli.

'Can I go now, please?'

'Not so fast, mister. I have ter move this money right out of yer reach. I'll be makin' meself a banker's draft an' takin' the money where you and ye copper pals can't find it. In fact you and ye copper pals will never be able ter prove I've taken it.'

'How long will that take?' Sam asked, despondently. He didn't really care about the money. He just wanted to go home.

'As long as I want it ter fuckin' take!' rasped Eli.

A loaf of stale bread was produced. Sam ripped off the plastic wrapping as his captors left the cellar and bolted the door behind them. As he ate and drank he found himself weeping with humiliation and desperation and defeat. Then, just as he was cramming the last crumb into his mouth the light went out. He shouted to tell them, but his voice probably wasn't strong enough. His normal optimism would have told him the bulb had simply gone. Right now, however, he knew such optimism was probably misplaced and there was a way to find out. He felt his way round the walls to the tap. He turned it on. Nothing.

He knew for sure that they'd left him there to die.

CHAPTER SIXTY-ONE

Delia sat across the table from Jim in the secure, conference room. 'This is not going great, Jim.'

'I can see that – problem is I didn't do it. How can they find me guilty of a murder I didn't do?'

'Because someone's set you up. It wouldn't surprise me if that someone has got Sam Carew right now, preventing him from giving evidence.'

'What good would Sam have done me?'

'He wouldn't have done you any harm, put it that way. Men like Sam Carew can sway a jury without the jury knowing it.' She thought about this, then looked, hopefully, at Jim. 'Do you know of anything that might discredit Manny Green's testimony? I'm delaying getting him back on the stand as long as possible.'

Jim shook his head. 'I can't honestly see Manny being mixed up in it. He's just a dozy sod. He probably did think it was me coming out of the house.'

'His doziness could get you sent down.'

'What am I supposed to do?'

'Well,' said Delia, 'he was showing signs of doubt towards the end of his testimony for the prosecution. Maybe I can work on that.'

'That other golf club that had Alistair's blood on it – surely the jury will wonder about that?'

'It's the best thing you've got in your favour – that and the fact that Waring was just one of the three murdered friends who were involved in the Rembrandt theft. What's going against you is the club found in the wheelie bin, the fact that Waring was having an affair with your wife, Manny Green saying he saw you running away from the scene and the police finding you in the house kneeling over the body.'

'Why would I run away then come back?' Jim asked.

'They'll say you ran away because you panicked, then, when you came to your senses, you went back because you'd told your wife you were going to his house.' She looked at him, appraisingly. 'Another thing that might go in your favour is the way you behave when I call you tomorrow. You must act bemused and shocked at being accused of a murder you haven't committed. Don't annoy the judge, don't be flippant, take as much time as you like before answering the prosecution's questions – the jury likes a considered answer. You're a genuine bloke, Jim – if the jury

341

see that it'll go in your favour. If Figgis interrupts you, let him, don't protest, look a bit affronted at his rudeness if you like. If he doesn't give you a chance to answer a question before asking you another one you can ask him, politely, if he wants you to finish answering his previous question first. It'll throw the little turd. Remember, you are the victim in this – act like one. If he insults you, raise your voice to him if you like, but don't lose your temper. He might want to prove to the jury that you easily lose control.'

'That's a lot to remember.'

'I'll write it all down for you if you like.'

'It's OK, I get the gist of it all.'

CHAPTER SIXTY-TWO

Eli had gone off with the man with the laptop in whose Swiss bank account Sam's money was now legally deposited. Swiss banks are required to know their clients well enough to be confident that funds deposited are unlikely to come from criminal sources. The man with the laptop was known to be a respectable client. In fact, being a respectable client on behalf of his own, less respectable, clients formed a large part of his export business. Swiss banking laws make it a grave offence to divulge any information about a bank customer to a third party, including official requests from police or foreign governments. The man was doing his job as a family favour to his

342

cousin Eli. The favour would cost Eli ten per cent of Sam's money, which was considerably less than his cousin usually charged for money laundering.

Eli had gone with his cousin to collect his ninety per cent in cash. Sam had been left in the care of Henry Smith, one of Eli's fellow travellers; a man with an additional grudge against Sam, being one of the men who had suffered at Sam's hands outside Tracey Ormerod's house, as well as losing his home. Henry was looking forward to carrying out Eli's instructions regarding Sam's fate. He looked at his watch, wondering what was so special about four-thirty, the time when he'd been instructed to do the job. He had already been paid his two grand, why didn't he just do it now and be done with it? He knew full well why. Annoying Eli John was always a bad thing to do. The prisoner in the cellar would vouch for that. Henry put his feet up and nodded off. Half past four was two hours away.

Sam had now stopped feeling sorry for himself and was examining his options. It was pitch black, he was locked inside a cellar and he was physically done in. In all probability there were no plans to release him from here so it was up to him to do something. He examined his options once again and they didn't add up to much. This time he wasn't tied up, which was something. The other thing was he fancied he could break through the door. It was an old, ledged and braced type door, popular in cellars. The horizontal ledges and angled braces were on the inside which meant the vertical battens were nailed from outside. Probably the nails were as old as the door and would

343

respond well to a good kicking.

He knew he was as strong now as he ever would be whilst down here. He could hear no one moving about upstairs so maybe they'd cleared off and simply left him there to die. Fair enough. At least they wouldn't worry about the noise he made. What might he find outside this cellar door? Probably a narrow passage, off which would lead another room, maybe two. One of the other rooms may well have been a coal cellar. If so there would be a grate leading to the outside, maybe even a window.

He pushed himself to his feet and made his way to the door. Then he sat down, facing it and felt with his feet for the triangular area of battens between the bottom ledge and brace. He gave it a kick with the sole of his shoe and felt a batten give a little. A second kick and the batten sprang away from the bottom ledge. He knew then that he could at least get out of this room. It took him just five minutes to loosen sufficient battens and push them to one side far enough to give him room to squeeze through. He sat down on the cold floor to catch his breath. A door at the top of the cellar steps opened. There was a rattling as Henry stuck a fuse back in the fuse box. The lights came on, blinding Sam for a few seconds. When he opened his eyes Henry was standing over him. He drew his legs back to kick Sam but Sam saw it coming and flung himself forward, wrapping his arms around Henry's legs, and bringing him to the floor. Sam was on top of him, punching wildly, knowing this was all he could give. If he couldn't knock the man out with this

344

assault he would be finished.

Henry rolled away and got to his feet, leaving Sam panting for breath on the floor. There was no fight left in him. There hadn't been much to start with. Henry kicked at him until he was unconscious, with blood pouring from his head. The traveller looked at his watch. Twenty past three. Maybe he should do it now. Fuck it! Do as Eli says, it's only another hour. This bastard won't be causing any grief.

It took exactly an hour for Sam to regain consciousness. Every square inch of his head and body was hurting and he knew he was caked in blood. The lights were out again and his assailant gone. It was a fair bet that if he did manage to climb up the cellar steps that door would be bolted. Come on, Carew, you're still alive, that's half the battle. There must be a plan, there's always a plan.

The intense pain made it a struggle to stretch his imagination. He knew that his only hope was to find a window or a coal grate that the man guarding him didn't know about. He had looked like a man who wouldn't know much about cellar windows or coal grates. Sam pushed himself to his knees and felt for the walls either side of him, not knowing which way he was facing. He crawled forward a few feet and felt the stone steps in front of him. This wasn't where he wanted to be. He'd come the wrong bloody way. Get a grip, Carew! If there's a coal cellar it'll be at the far end of this passage. What was that smell? He sniffed the stale air and picked up the unmistakable smell of petrol. It was a very strong smell so there was a lot of petrol. Jesus! It didn't take much imagination for him to figure what was happening. The bastards were going to torch the place – with him in it!

CHAPTER SIXTY-THREE

Delia smiled up at Jim, who was pale-faced from his incarceration and his general ordeal. In her view he had done well. She had got the impression that the jury believed him and why shouldn't they? She believed him, which was more than she could say about a good half of the villains she defended.

'Just one final question, Mr Ormerod. After the murder your golf bag was found on a bench in the men's locker room at the Bostrop Pay and Play Golf Club. Why do you think that is?'

Jim shrugged. 'I suppose I forgot to bring it home. It's not the safest place to leave anything.'

'But if the prosecution case is to be credible, on the day before Mr Waring was killed, you must have removed a 3 iron from the bag with the sole intention of committing murder with it and then promptly forgot to bring the bag itself. One would have thought that the very act of selecting a murder weapon would have concentrated the mind sufficiently for you to have not forgotten the very bag from which you took it. On top of which, preparing yourself thus would mean that the murder was premeditated – which contradicts the

346

prosecution's theory that this was a crime committed whilst you were not thinking clearly. If you were thinking clearly you would hardly have hidden the murder weapon where it was found.'

'Well,' said Jim, 'I didn't do it, so I don't really know what to say.'

It was the answer Delia wanted. 'No further questions, m'Lord.'

'Mr Figgis?' droned the judge.

'Thank you, my Lord. I just have a couple of questions of the accused.'

Delia looked up from her notes. *Just a couple of questions?* She was fully expecting her client to be given a merciless grilling.

'Mr Ormerod, on the day of Mr Waring's murder, you say you arrived at his house no more than a minute before the police.'

'That's right. I was going to ring them meself, then they turned up.'

'So, if you had only just arrived you could have hardly committed such a prolonged act of violence and mayhem.'

Delia was on her guard. Jim was relaxed at such friendly questioning. Maybe the prosecution had had a change of heart.

'Like I said, I didn't do it.'

'Unless of course you are lying!' Figgis's manner was firm but controlled. He was looking down at his notes as he spoke, then he looked up, clasped his hands together and held Jim in an accusatory gaze. 'You *are* lying, aren't you, Mr Ormerod?'

'No,' said Jim.

'Mr Ormerod, your house is just two miles from Mr Waring's. You left at 11.15 and arrived at

347

Mr Waring's at 11.37. Twenty two minutes to do a five minute journey. What were you doing during the other seventeen minutes, Mr Ormerod?'

'Like I told the police, I had a puncture on the way.'

'Ah, the puncture. I have it in my notes, Mr Ormerod. You were questioned as to why you had clean hands when changing a wheel would have made them dirty and your answer was that you had been to the toilet and washed your hands.'

'That's right – that's what happened.'

'I have something else in my notes, Mr Ormerod. No doubt your counsel will have a copy of this in her notes as well. After the incident your car was taken to the police compound and an inventory of its contents taken – a copy of which I have here.'

Delia was rifling through her notes. What the hell was happening? Had she missed something?

'One of the items refers to the spare wheel, which is described as, "Michelin, part worn, fully inflated".'

Delia was reading it from her notes as Figgis spoke. She closed her eyes and cursed herself for such lack of diligence. She didn't drive and had little interest in cars, but she knew enough to spot the implications here. 'Bollocks!' she murmured under her breath.

'Mrs Knowles?' said the judge who wondered if he'd heard her correctly. Figgis had, and he smirked.

'Mr Ormerod,' he said, 'if you stopped to change a wheel, as you maintain, perhaps you can explain to the court how the spare wheel found in your car did *not* have a punctured tyre?'

Jim's mouth opened and shut. He wondered what the hell was happening. One minute everything was going well, next minute he was in deep trouble.

'I – I've just re – remembered,' he stammered. 'I couldn't get the wheel nuts loose so I pumped it up instead – there's a foot pump in the boot. I think it was the valve that was a bit dodgy – honest, that's the truth.'

'From a puncture to a dodgy valve? My word, you are indeed an inventive man, Mr Ormerod – as demonstrated by your charade when the police found you hovering over Mr Waring's body. Surely you don't expect the jury to believe any more of your off the cuff lies. The truth is that those seventeen missing minutes were spent bludgeoning Mr Waring to death, running away, then going back to cover yourself. I suggest that when you saw the full horror of what you had done you panicked, despite it being pre-planned. You panicked, you threw the murder weapon into the wheelie bin, you ran from the house – as witnessed by Mr Green – then, when you remembered that you were actually supposed to have gone to his house, you turned around and got back just before the police arrived. Isn't that the truth of what happened, Mr Ormerod?'

CHAPTER SIXTY-FOUR

Henry had emptied a five gallon drum of petrol, liberally dousing all the floors, furniture and staircase. One flame and it would go up like a bomb. He had also doused a ten foot length of soft rope, one end of which he laid inside a pool of petrol in the hallway, the other end led outside and down the steps. He knew it would take about three minutes to burn from end to end and it was now twenty-five-past four. What he didn't know, as he struck the match, was that Eli, at that very moment, was landing in Dublin airport with his suitcase stuffed with two hundred and twenty-five thousand euros. He would have a worrying twenty minutes or so hoping his luggage would arrive safe and sound through the rubber curtains. He had well and truly secured the case and made it easily identifiable with a red band tied around it. He smiled as the plane touched down. It was his only worry. Carew, on the other hand, had more to worry about.

Sam crawled, at snail's pace, back along the dusty, cold floor of the passage, occasionally reaching with his right hand to check for a door. The first he came to was the one through which he had recently escaped. His knee pushed against some-thing metallic. He reached down for it and his hopes of rescue soared. It was a mobile phone, probably Henry's, dropped during their scuffle – which would make this pain worthwhile, hopefully.

He experimented with the buttons and got it switched on. All the numbers illuminated as well as the screen. The bars showed it to be well charged and giving a signal. He rang Owen.

'Owen, it's Sam.'

'Where the bloody hell are you, Sam? Are you still with Eli John?'

'Who's Eli John?'

'He's the leader of the travellers. We saw you and him on video leaving your office. How are you?'

'How am I? Owen, I'm locked in a cellar. Some thug's just knocked seven bells out of me, he's soaked the place with petrol and I'm pretty sure he's going to burn the place down. Apart from that I'm as right as rain.'

'Oh, bloody hell, boyo. What cellar? Where are you?'

'I've got no idea. They took me last Friday. I'm in bad shape. I could do with a bit of help.'

'And you don't know where you are?'

'Not a clue. Look Owen, this is pretty urgent. I could be toast in half an hour. Where are you?'

'I've just come out of court. The case against Jim's looking strong. Delia's getting worried.'

'Owen, I've got other things on my mind. Can you get someone to take a fix on this phone? I'll leave it switched on. You'll have this number on your phone. Get hold of Janet, she knows what to do. She's done it before.'

'I'll do it now, there's some public phones here.

351

Don't switch off.'

Sam leant against the wall to regain some of his strength. He wasn't out of this by a long way. Two minutes later Owen's voice came over the phone. 'Sam … are you there?'

'Yeah, only just.'

'Janet's on to the phone tracking service. They can get a GPS fix to within fifty yards. Is there anything you can give us to identify which house you're in?'

'Yes,' said Sam. 'The bloody thing's on fire.'

There had been a *whoosh* above his head and he could see fire between the cracks in the floorboards. It looked as though the whole floor was on fire. In the short term the fire would work its way upwards, but it would take away his oxygen and eventually the whole house would collapse into the cellar.

'Owen, I'm going to upgrade my situation to really bloody urgent! I'm going to struggle to survive this.'

It crossed his mind to ring Sue and maybe have a word with his boys, but he dismissed that as pure self-indulgence – no point scaring them unnecessarily. He would have rung Sally but he couldn't remember her number. Such a call might well have put him back in her good books – if he survived. Then he pushed such plans from his mind when he realised that he had other things to think about.

He made his way to the end of the passage, which was now partially illuminated from above. The heat was getting through and a thin layer of smoke billowed across the cellar ceiling. There was another door, he got to his feet, undid the latch and staggered in. Above him he could see thin lines of bright fire between the floorboards, and he could hear the roaring of flames as the fire above him took hold. The heat was becoming unbearable. The pain from his kicking was forgotten. Survival was the thing. How could he survive until they got to him? How long would it take to get a fix on the phone? He had no idea. How long would it take for a fire engine to get here. He had no idea how far away from a fire station he was. For all he knew he might not even be in Yorkshire.

On the far wall he could see six pinpricks of light. Proper daylight, not firelight. It had to be a coal grate. He made his way towards it. As he got there his feet kicked against something that felt like a brick buttress sloping up towards the grate. But it wasn't a buttress, it was a coal chute. Sam knew that. He felt around. It had been built of bricks and rendered over with a sand and cement mortar which was cracking and coming away in his hands.

He clambered upwards until the grate was directly in front of him. He stuck his fingers into the holes and tried to push it upwards, but it was jammed solid. Rusted. No hope of shifting it. No strength. No way could he kick at it. No way could he open it. He put his eye to one of the holes and tried to see out, but all he saw were what looked to be bushes, illuminated by the fire raging above him. He placed the phone on the ledge by the grate where he figured it might give a better signal for those tracking it, then he shouted 'Help' several times and got the distinct impression that there was no one outside within earshot. Surely someone must be able to see the house is on fire. What's wrong with people?

He pressed his mouth against the hole, sucking in fresh air, but the heat around him was intense and he couldn't stay there forever. It was just three minutes since he'd spoken to Owen and he doubted if he could last another three minutes.

CHAPTER SIXTY-FIVE

Janet had been given a GPS fix on Sam's location by the phone tracking company. He was in an area just off the Leeds Road, five miles from the centre of Unsworth, four miles from the nearest fire station. The fire station had given an ETA of ten minutes. Three callers had already rung the fire in. The police now knew exactly which house it was. Owen rang Sally. She was in her car within seconds. They arrived at pretty much the same time.

The house was an inferno. It was quite large and detached, in the middle of a big overgrown garden. Two fire engines had already arrived. Firefighters from one were fixing a hose to a hydrant. Men from the other were directing water from its own tank at the flames. Nobody was making any attempt to enter the blazing building, such was its intensity. People were standing around watching from a distance.

'There's a man in there!' shouted Owen.

Sally screamed Sam's name and ran around the

perimeter of the blaze, knowing no one could survive in such a conflagration. The roof was caving in, flames and sparks were shooting high in the air, windows were exploding and huge balls of fire bursting out. She was in tears as she ran. She tripped and fell.

Owen was close on her heels. He realised she had tripped over the prone body of a man, lying face down in bright green, baggy trousers. The man gave a moan. Owen pulled him well clear of the heat then knelt down and turned him over, gently. Sally got to her feet and came over, watching in abject despair, wishing this could be Sam, but she knew it wasn't. Not in those trousers. The man's face was unrecognisable, caked in blood and soot. He opened his eyes and looked around. At Sally then at Owen.

'You took your bloody time!' he croaked.

Sally gave a deafening screech.

'Sam!'

She flung herself at him, hugging and kissing his smoke blackened face. Sam looked up at Owen and winked.

'The plan worked,' he said.

CHAPTER SIXTY-SIX

'We wish you wouldn't do this, Dad,' Jake said.

It was 9 a.m. the following day and Sam was in Unsworth General Hospital attached to a couple of tubes. He still felt woozy from sedatives. Now

355

he felt guilty. Tom and Jake were standing by his bed, as they had so often in the past. Just behind them stood Sue.

'Their words, not mine,' she said. 'I didn't put them up to it.'

'We're sixteen, Dad, we don't need Mum to put us up to anything,' said Tom.

'I'm not badly injured,' Sam told them. 'I'm just not at my best, that's all.'

'Dad, you were seconds away from being burnt alive.'

Sam needed no reminding. His life had been saved by a putlog – a five foot length of scaffold tube with a flattened end, used for attaching scaffold to a joint in the brickwork – precisely the same thing that had ended his dad's life three years previously, There had been a couple of them in the cellar. Not unusual. Putlogs were often taken from sites and put to various uses. Sam had used this one like a battering ram to knock out the coal grate. It took him less than a minute. Had it taken a minute and a half he would have been dead – that's what Jake had been on about. That's what one of the firemen had told Jake and Tom. Sam had clambered out using whatever strength he had left and had collapsed where Sally had tripped over him. He had felt the searing heat on his back and had staggered as far as he could. Self-preservation is a wonderful motivator and Sam had motivated himself to the outer limits of his endurance. And maybe a few feet beyond.

He had no words of excuse for his boys. Sally hadn't been back yet. She'd come with him to hospital, as had Owen, but she'd left shortly after he'd been transferred to a ward. He looked at his ex-wife. 'Have you heard from Sal?'

She shrugged. 'Sam, this won't do your cause much good. You're a target for every villain around – it'll only serve to remind her what's in store if she signs on with you again. Let's face it, I'm the expert.'

'Sue, I didn't volunteer to be burnt alive,' said Sam. 'I'm sitting at my desk in the office. A man walks in with a gun and I had to go with him. It happens.'

'Only to you.'

At ten o'clock Delia arrived at the hospital. 'Shouldn't you be in court?' Sam said.

'I've got the whole thing adjourned until Monday.'

'How's that?'

'You – I told the judge you were my main witness. He knew what had happened – you made the local news.'

'Not the national news? It was definitely a national news event. Honestly, Wayne Rooney breaks his toe and makes world headlines. I'm almost burnt alive and get Radio Unsworth.'

'Radio Leeds picked it up – anyway, when can you be up and about? You don't look too ill.'

Sally appeared behind her. Delia turned. Sam did the introductions.

'Delia – Sally, Sally – Delia.'

Delia gave Sally a look of appraisal. 'So, you're what all the fuss is about.'

'Fuss?'

Delia jabbed a thumb in Sam's direction. 'He's

357

besotted with you. I hope you're not besotted with him. There's no future in being besotted with a man like him.'

'Delia, you're not helping,' Sam hissed. He smiled at Sally. 'Delia likes to stir things. It's OK when you're trying to shake a witness, but a bad idea in a hospital. Thank God she chose the law and not medicine.'

'Hello, Delia,' said Sally. 'You seem to know Sam well.'

Sam butted in. 'I might have an idea that will help the case – if I'm right you won't need me to give evidence.' He really hated courts, plus, he didn't want these two putting their heads together to conspire against him. He had in mind what Sue had said.

Delia brightened. 'What idea?' The case had been looking increasingly hopeless. She had been pitting character witnesses against hard evidence and some of the witnesses weren't exactly people of character themselves. Cassie Blake had been a disaster, Shane Outhwaite a waste of time, and Tracey had been torn to pieces over her affair with Alistair Waring. She needed a contribution from Sam.

'I just need to tie a few facts together,' he said. 'I learnt something in that cellar that might be useful.'

'What? There were things in that cellar that were useful to the case?' said Delia. 'It's a pity the cellar's not there any more.'

'Are you being deliberately stupid?' Sam asked her.

Delia grinned. 'Absolutely,' she said. 'What

358

have you got for me?'

'Right this second, nothing. If we've got until Monday I might have something substantial.'

'Does it mean bringing in undisclosed evidence?'

Sam looked at her, uncertainly. 'Yes, will this be a problem?'

'Could be. But if it's crucial evidence that couldn't be produced earlier we might be able to talk the judge into allowing it. Figgis will no doubt object. Either way someone will have to give a witness statement to tell the court how we came to be in possession of this evidence.'

'That someone meaning me,' guessed Sam.

'Who else?'

'Bugger!'

'Is it to do with the art theft?' Delia asked, with understandable curiosity.

'No – if I'm right about this, I'm wrong about the art theft connection. I should have ignored that from the word go – it's that what's been throwing me.'

'Sam, why the bloody hell can't you just tell me?' asked Delia.

'It's the way his brain works,' explained Sally, who knew him of old. 'He doesn't want outside influences interfering with his train of thought.'

Sam looked at her and wondered how she'd figured that one out. Her explanation had never occurred to him, but she was right. She knew him better than he knew himself.

'First I need to get to a phone,' he said.

Exasperated, Delia produced a mobile. Sam looked at it then at her. 'You're not supposed to use them in here, it affects the equipment, or something.' He was very wary of breaking hospital rules, having spent so much time at the mercy of A&E nurses.

'That's just hospital propaganda,' said Delia. 'It does no such thing. They ban them because of the potential annoyance they cause, which would make a hospital stay even worse than it is. Here, take this and use it under the bedclothes when sister's not looking.'

Sam took the phone then looked at Sally. 'I need Jimmy O'Connor's phone number, can you get it for me?'

He knew he was killing two birds with one stone here. He was enlisting her help and he was re-enlisting her affection for him. For a second she seemed hesitant. Had she declined he wouldn't have pressed her. There were others who could have helped him.

'It's on the computer in the office,' she said. 'Why do you need it?'

'Because someone set me up for this – someone who wanted me out of the way, permanently. I think Jimmy might know who that someone is, and I think that someone is the man who killed Alistair Waring.'

'What makes you think that?' asked Delia.

'I suppose you might call it a hunch.'

It was enough for Sally; she'd been drawn into his net. She made up her mind that she would stay with this just until it was concluded and not a minute longer. 'Anything else you want me to do?' she asked.

'Yeah, there's a maroon journal in the cupboard

in the office. It's Alistair Waring's.'

'Legally obtained?' enquired Delia.

'What? Oh, yeah, his mother lent it to me. Anyway, I just want to check a few things before I start getting anyone's hopes up.' He looked Delia in the eye. 'Even yours.'

Delia looked at Sally. 'I understand he's good at these hunches.'

'At hunches he's a world beater,' said Sally, 'at anything else he's a pain in the arse.'

Delia looked down at Sam. 'I'm putting Manny Green back in the witness box first thing on Monday. I want to have a second go at discrediting his witness statement.'

'How?'

'I don't know yet – I may have to rely on personal inspiration, unless you come up with something good. From where we're standing it's our only hope. My other mobile number's in that phone. Ring me with anything you have, as and when you get it.' She turned to go. Sam called her back.

'What?'

'Haven't you forgotten something?'

'Such as?'

'I'm in hospital, an injured man, recently rescued from death's door. Shouldn't you have enquired after my current state of health?'

'How are you feeling?'

'I think I might be dying.'

'You must cling on until this case is over. Your time's your own, then.'

'You can go now,' said Sam, who should have known better.

CHAPTER SIXTY-SEVEN

'Jimmy, it's Sam. How is everything?'

'Shouldn't I be asking you that? Am I cool with the polis?'

'Everything's cool here as far as the police are concerned. Not too cool as far as the travellers are concerned. They captured me and cleaned me out to pay for the damage.' Sam was speaking from a gent's toilet in the hospital. 'Over a quarter of a million euros – transferred at the press of a computer key.'

'Jeez! Dem computers can be little bastards. Any chance of ye gettin' it back?'

'I'm not even going to risk my neck trying. They're bad people to have as enemies.'

The dead traveller woman had been preying on Sam's conscience. He'd got Owen to check and had found it to be true that she'd committed suicide, probably in despair after the loss of her home. He knew such things happened as a result of his activities. It went with the job. Maybe he deserved to lose the money.

'Holly Mudder, Sam! I never knowed they'd take ye money.'

'Neither did I, but they did. They fingered you for it as well.'

'Jeez, Sam – was it you what telled 'em?'

'You know better than that Jimmy. It was you who told them.'

362

'Away wid ye! Why would I do that?'

'Because you'd had a bit to drink one time in Unsworth and you got talking to some old army pal of yours about the trouble I was having with the travellers and how you owed me, and how you were going to repay me. I'm guessing this man knew who you were and what you were capable of. Am I right?'

There was a long pause, then Sam heard Jimmy mutter, 'Holy Mudder o' Christ – it must have been yer man Shooey.'

'Shooey?'

'I knew him in the army. He was one of the fellers guardin' me when I was appearin' in front of her Majesty's kangaroo fuckin' court. I saw him in a pub in Unsworth. We got a bit pissed an' I remember sayin' somethin' about owin' you a big favour. Maybe we talked about the pikies, I'm not sure. Jeez! Yer man knew what I could do. He'll have known it was me who torched the fuckin' camp.'

'And what do you say his name was?'

'Back in the army days I heard the other guards callin' him Shooey, but that wasn't his real name.'

'Do you know what it was?'

'Jeez, I knew because he told me, but I can't remember. I heard he'd been kicked out for shooting a young feller in Londonderry. It was covered up but they got rid of him. I heard it sent him a bit loony, but he seemed OK when I spoke to him. Mind you, I'd had a fair bit ter drink, I grant ye. Now, what was his real name. Jeez, it's on the tip of me tongue.'

Sam had to prompt him with several names

363

before one of them rang a bell with Jimmy. The more Jimmy repeated it to himself the more certain he became. The name wasn't at the top of Sam's short list of suspects. He asked Jimmy for a description of Shooey. It fitted the man well, even twenty years on.

'Will the travellers be comin' after me?' Jimmy asked.

'Dunno. Could be that they got all they needed from me. Still, it'd do no harm for you to disappear off the scene.'

'It's what I'm good at, Sam. I'll disappear, then.'

'See you, Jimmy.'

'Not if I can help it, Sam.'

Jimmy's phone clicked off. Sam knew he'd be OK. Right now he needed to speak to Tracey. She might have a piece of information he needed to complete his jigsaw. Failing her he'd have to ask either Jim or Shane.

CHAPTER SIXTY-EIGHT

Tracey came up with the information he needed but it didn't quite tie in with what he'd read in the newspaper in the cellar. Miraculously he'd brought the newspaper out with him, scrunched up in the pocket of his voluminous green trousers. The discrepancy confused Sam. It was very near in too many ways for it to be a coincidence, but not spot on – and it had to be spot on or the whole idea was a non starter. It was Sally who figured out the reason for the discrepancies. 'I think it's all to do with ages,' she told him. 'Ages?'

'Yes.'

She showed him how she'd worked it out. She'd double-checked it with notes Alistair had written down in his journal. It explained many things. By this time Sam was out of hospital and keeping Sally heavily involved in solving the mystery. He knew she could never resist a mystery. What she didn't tell him was if she was staying or going back to Bath. It was a subject he felt he had no right to broach. Sue had been quite right. His recent predicament should have warned Sally to stay clear of him. He was not a good bet for long-term security.

Monday morning. Sally was still in Unsworth, working with Sam in his office, which was a good sign. On the downside Alec rang to say he was gutted that all their working capital had been snatched away for the second time in a few weeks. 'I can't work like this,' he told Sam. Gordon Plessington had contacted him when Sam dropped off the radar, and in Sam's absence the Plessington contract was back on – only they had no capital to fund it.

'I'll raise money against my flat,' said Sam. 'If I can't put all the money back I'll give you the difference in shares of the company. In the short term I'll give you the extra two per cent that gives you control – it means I'll never be able to do this again without your agreement. In the meantime you must keep going. Where you get the money from is up to you. You might have to keep the

VATman waiting for a few weeks and maybe squeeze some up-front money out of Plessington. They need us more than we need them right now. I know you can do it, Alec.' It salved Sam's conscience and he hoped his dad wouldn't look down on him too harshly for giving away fifty one percent of the family firm. There was another call from his bank asking him if he would come in and see a manager, of whom Sam had never heard, to discuss his business account.

'My partner's taken control of the company, I'll ask him to get in touch.'

'If you would, Mr Carew.'

Two minutes later the phone rang again and Sam winced at the prospect of more aggro. Sally picked it up.

'Hello, Carew's?'

Sam felt himself smiling. Old times. Sally said, 'One moment please, Mr White,' then pressed the mute button. 'It's er, it's Mr White.'

'Really?' Sam raised his eyebrows and hesitated for a second, 'It's OK, I'll take it.'

'Yes, he's here, I'll put him on, Mr White.'

Sam took the phone. 'Stuke, what can I do for you?'

'Just checking that you're OK to take the Rembrandt back to Amsterdam at the end of the next month?'

'Why wouldn't I be OK?'

'I do read the papers, Sam.'

'I'm OK. Same deal?'

'Same deal. Two grand, private jet, luxury hotel and all the trimmings. Is it still for two?'

'Just me, this time.'

'So, how are things?' Stuke asked. He was trying to make conversation.'

'So, so.'

'Any joy with this murder case? Bloody bad business all round, if you ask me.'

'There might be developments,' said Sam.

'Really? What sort of developments?'

'Well, not the sort I can discuss with anyone not connected with the case.'

'That's told me,' said Stuke.

'No offence. I'll ring you nearer the time about the Rembrandt.'

'That's great. See you, Sam.'

Sam put the phone down. Sally looked at him. 'Now why would he be asking you about the case?'

'You tell me – he wants me to take the Rembrandt back to Amsterdam next month.'

'So I gather.'

He looked at his watch. It was 9.30. 'Curtain up in one hour. Are you coming to see the show?'

'Yes please.'

They went down to the courthouse in the Jaguar. Keeping up the payments on the car might pose a problem, but he'd overcome bigger obstacles recently. The Jag was becoming a symbol of his survival; it would tell the world he was doing OK despite the rumours. On the way they picked up a man called Freddie Lightfoot who seemed to have a bad habit of bumping into people. In fact Freddie bumped into Manny Green, not once but twice, in the space of ten minutes – once in the street and once in the courthouse. Manny was too pre-occupied with his approaching ordeal to notice it was the same man. Being questioned in court, even if you're only a witness, can be an intimidating experience – especially if the questioner is Delia Knowles. He'd already told her everything he knew, why did she want to question him again? Surely even she could see that Jim was guilty.

CHAPTER SIXTY-NINE

'M'Lord I would like to call Mr Sam Carew,' said Delia.

There was a murmur of anticipation in the courtroom. 'Ah, the redoubtable Mr Carew,' said the judge. 'We shall be fascinated to hear from him.'

Sam was called and took the oath. He was asked if he'd like to sit down and was grateful to accept, considering the condition he was still in.

'M'Lord,' said Delia, 'I have called Mr Carew as he has produced evidence that would have been impossible to disclose at an earlier date.'

'Really? What form does this evidence take?'

'It's three pieces of documentary evidence, m'Lord.'

'I see – and your witness has a statement to explain the late arrival of this evidence, does he?'

'He does, m'Lord. Mr Carew would you tell the judge how you came about this evidence and how it could not be produced until now.'

Sam got to his feet and began his prepared statement. 'I am being retained by the defendant as an investigator and recently I was the victim of an unlawful abduction...'

'Yes, I believe we probably all know about that,' interrupted the judge, nodding as he spoke. There was a murmur of agreement around the court.

Sam looked at the judge, then continued. 'The incident was unrelated to this case, but while I was locked up in a cellar I found an old newspaper that contained an article that made sense of my hitherto unfruitful investigation.'

'And this old newspaper is the new evidence is it?'

'Not quite, my Lord,' said Sam. 'But when put along with two other pieces of evidence it throws a lot of light on this case.'

'Does it indeed? Well, light is what we crave. We do not wish to live in the dark, which is what I believe happened to you, Mr Carew.'

'It did, my Lord,' smiled Sam.

Figgis was on his feet but the judge waved away his objection. 'Would both counsels approach the bench?'

Delia and Figgis did as requested. There was a murmured discussion resulting in the judge announcing a short recession while the matter was discussed in his room.

Sam remained seated in the witness box under the gaze of interested reporters. The court artist was sketching him and Sam deliberately kept moving his head to a different angle so as to make life difficult for the man. Ten minutes later the two barristers came back and it was obvious from Delia's face that she'd got her own way, as Sam knew she would. The judge sat down and turned to Figgis.

'Mr Figgis, do you have any questions of this witness?'

Figgis could think of plenty but he knew that Sam was a local hero and any adversarial questions would probably alienate the jury.

'No, my Lord.'

'In that case the evidence is allowed and you are free to leave Mr Carew. Are you ready to call your next witness, Mrs Knowles?'

'Yes, m'Lord. I wish to recall Mr Emmanuel Green.'

Manny trudged in, looking irritated. He was reminded that he was still under oath. Delia got to her feet.

'Mr Green, since we last spoke I believe you were held for questioning by the police regarding another murder. Is this correct?'

The judge looked as if he was about to intervene, but Figgis looked at ease with the question. If it went any further he was ready to jump in and demand that relevance be proved.

'Yes, me and another feller. We've both been bailed but they don't bail you if they've got proper evidence, which they haven't. Dave McLeish were me mate. Why would I kill me mate? They found some of me hairs on a bush just where he was murdered.'

'But you explained this because you often relieved yourself in that very bush when playing golf yourself and the CPS found this a plausible explanation.'

'Well, it's true,' said Manny.

'I'm sure it is, Mr Green. I'm sure it's just a coincidence. Just like the coincidence of the number plates on your car being swapped just after Mr McLeish was murdered.'

'I've already told the police. I'm a car dealer, I wasn't driving that car at the time.'

Delia looked at her notes. 'Yes, you've successfully shifted the burden of blame for that on to someone else.' Before he could answer, Delia asked him another, seemingly innocent question. Her eyes burnt into his as she asked it, as did the eyes of Sam and Sally, watching from the public gallery.

'Tell me, Mr Green, do you do the National Lottery?'

Figgis half rose to his feet. 'My Lord, so far I haven't heard a single question that has any relevance to this case.'

'M'Lord, the relevance will become abundantly clear very shortly,' cut in Delia.

'Do I have your solemn word on that, Mrs Knowles?' sighed the judge.

'You do, m'Lord.' Delia looked at Manny, expectantly. 'Well?'

'Well what?'

'Do you do the Lottery?'

'Not every week, no.'

'I'll rephrase the question in greater detail. Did you and your golfing friends have a Lottery syndicate?'

Manny hesitated, looking at his barrister for help. Figgis shrugged as if to say, *Answer the question, it's harmless enough. If she asks any more*

371

damned stupid questions I'll put a stop to it.

'Well, yeah, we used to.'

'You used to – so you don't any more?'

'Well, no – not under the circumstances.'

'Quite. Is it not true, Mr Green, that the last Lottery ticket the syndicate bought was for the Lottery drawn the day before Mr Waring's death?'

'If you say so.'

'Let me assure you, it was,' said Delia. 'Mr Green, the last time you were in this witness box I asked you if the group you call the Syndicate were involved in any activities other than golf – you said, no.'

'Well, I didn't think the Lottery counted.'

'Oh, but it does count, Mr Green. Are you aware that an unclaimed winning jackpot ticket worth over five million pounds was bought in Unsworth for the Lottery drawn the day before Mr Waring died?'

Manny shook his head, warily.

'Well, it was,' Delia assured him. 'Only last week it was in the local paper, along with the winning numbers – advising the winner to come forward.' From her notes she took Sam's crumpled page from the *Unsworth Observer*, the one which he'd been reading in the cellar. She read out the numbers: '23, 29, 38, 42, 44 and 46.'

'So?' said Manny. 'That wasn't one of our lines.' He looked up at Jim, who gave a shrug and a vague nod of agreement. Delia pressed on.

'Correct me if I'm wrong, Mr Green. Each of you picked a regular line – six lines in all and put five pounds in the kitty every five weeks. Alistair Waring would buy the tickets. And if one of the

372

lines came up you would all share the winnings, irrespective of whose line it was?'

'Something like that.'

'Precisely like that, Mr Green. In fact, I believe Mr Waring had a legal document drawn up to that effect.' Delia took a sheet of paper from her file and handed it to the clerk for him to give to the judge.

Figgis got wearily to his feet. 'My Lord, we appear to be discussing a winning Lottery ticket that has nothing to do with the so-called Syndicate as the winning line wasn't one of theirs and even if it was I can't see a connection with this case.'

'I must confess, Mr Figgis, I'm losing the thread of this whole line of questioning. Would you come quickly to your point, Mrs Knowles.'

Delia smiled, apologetically. 'M'Lord, this is one of the pieces of new evidence which I was given only this morning by the wife of the accused. It's Mr Ormerod's copy of the Lottery agreement, which has a great deal of bearing in this case.'

'A great deal, Mrs Knowles?'

'Yes, m'Lord.'

'Very well.'

Delia continued. 'You will see, m'Lord, in clause five of the document it states quite clearly that should any syndicate member fail to pay his subscription then his numbers won't be entered and he will not be due a share.'

The judge took the agreement and scrutinised it, then passed it back to the clerk who gave it to Figgis, who passed it back to Delia without looking at it. It was his way of telling the jury that the document was of no significance. Delia looked at Manny.

'Did you ever win much, Mr Green?'

Manny shrugged. 'We once got four numbers and won about seventy quid – and we've won a few tenners. Nothing to write home about.'

'Right – m'Lord, might I now refer to the next piece of newly allowed evidence – Mr Waring's journal.'

'You may.'

Delia looked at Manny, then down at the journal. 'Mr Green, according to Mr Waring's journal, four weeks before he died, the Lottery subscriptions were due and you didn't pay up, so Mr Waring invoked the clause excluding you from your share and only five lines were bought. I assume he informed you of this.'

Manny hesitated; Delia pressed him. 'Mr Green, there are two surviving members of the syndicate who will confirm this.' She inclined her head towards Jim, who was listening with intense interest. 'One of them is standing over there in the dock.'

Figgis got to his feet again. 'My Lord, I believe one of these witnesses is the accused, the other is in custody on a major theft charge and I'm still not spotting any relevance.'

'M'Lord,' countered Delia, 'their reputations make this document no less legal, and I'm coming to the relevance.'

'Oh, I do hope so, Mrs Knowles.'

Delia now looked sternly at Manny. 'Mr Green, were you or were you not behind with your payments to the Lottery syndicate?'

Manny didn't know whether to lie and bluff it

out, but he suspected she had something up her sleeve that might catch him out if he lied. 'Maybe I did get a fiver behind,' he said. 'It was only the odd fiver. Who's going to make a fuss over the odd fiver?'

'Well, Alistair Waring for one. He was a very fussy man, so I'm told,' said Delia.

'You could say that.'

'A stickler for details – probably got on people's nerves because of it?'

Manny grinned, nervously. 'He was, actually.'

'In fact Mr Waring's own line consisted of the ages of all the members, did you know that, Mr Green?'

Manny noticeably stiffened. His hands gripped the rail of the witness box. Knuckles white. 'I'm not sure how he worked his numbers out. We all did them differently.'

'Well, that's what he did,' Delia told him, 'and when you each had a birthday he altered his numbers to suit.'

'Did he?' said Manny.

Jim was now paying close attention, shaking his head slightly.

'Yes, he did,' said Delia. 'The trouble was he didn't mention this to anyone, so when his line won the jackpot, no one else but him knew. The rest of you thought you'd only got two numbers on that line. But in fact four of you had got older, so four of the numbers were different.'

Jim was gaping, open-mouthed. Tracey was beginning to smile. Manny was sweating. 'Well, he told me nothing about it.'

'Actually, I think he did, Mr Green. I also think

he told you that the syndicate had won the jackpot and that you weren't entitled to a share. He'd rung all the other members that morning to invite them to his house so that he could tell them of their good fortune, but first he called you round to tell you of your bad fortune.'

'How do you know this, Mrs Knowles?' asked the judge.

'Well, I have to admit to it being an educated guess, m'Lord.'

'I see – would you care to educate me, Mrs Knowles?'

'Gladly, m'Lord. You see, Mr Waring very helpfully made a note of his, erm, his daily doings in his journal. M'Lord, perhaps you would like to look at it? I've stuck a couple of *Post It* notes to mark two pages of interest. At the beginning of the journal is a page where Mr Waring has written down the Lottery numbers, with alterations to one of the lines which coincides with the advancing ages of the group. This line matches the winning Lottery numbers. The other page is in the calendar section, dated Sunday July 17th.'

She picked up Alistair's journal and handed it to the clerk, who handed it to the judge.

'M'Lord, in his journal, on Sunday July 17th, the day after the winning Lottery ticket was drawn, Mr Waring has written, and I quote, *"Get Skinny Bollocks round and tell him his bad news first. Show the rest of them I was right to have it all made legal. I just want to see the look on his face, hah ha. Teach him to pay his subs".'*

The court looked on in silence as the judge scrutinised the appropriate pages, made a few

376

notes, then handed it back to the clerk, who showed it to an outwardly disinterested Figgis before it was handed back to Delia. She looked up at Manny. '*Skinny Bollocks.* I don't wish to appear rude, Mr Green, but I'm given to understand that's a name your friends sometimes call you.'

There was sniggering from some sections of the court which earned a glare of disapproval from the judge.

'That's right,' Jim shouted. 'Short arms, deep pockets. Never buys a round if he can help it – and he definitely didn't pay his Lottery subs for that last month. We all could've told yer that.'

The judge turned his glare on Jim but let it go. Manny said nothing. Delia pressed on.

'I imagine you thought that him telling you like that was a really nasty thing to do to you. He could simply have said nothing and let you find out in your own good time. Rubbing it in like that might well make a man react violently. I don't think I'd have been too pleased, had he done it to me.'

Manny rubbed his neck, vigorously. 'What are you getting at?'

'Mr Green,' Delia spread out her hands, palms upwards, encouraging him to admit to what was undeniable, 'surely you're not denying this happened?'

'Course I'm bloody denying it. You're making it up as you go along.'

She brought her hands together and rubbed them thoughtfully, then asked, 'Tell me, Mr Green, have you ever over-reacted to a situation?'

'I don't know what you mean.'

'I mean have you ever over-reacted enough to,

say, kill an innocent man?'

Figgis sprang to his feet, his face flushed with annoyance. 'My Lord, this is getting beyond a joke. First the Lottery, then this. Does my learned friend know the meaning of the word relevance?'

'M'Lord,' said Delia. 'Mr Green is the main witness for the Crown against the accused. His general character is therefore relevant, which is why we did some background checks on him.'

'You may continue, Mrs Knowles, provided you do not lose us all completely in the maze of your questioning.'

'Thank you, m'Lord. Correct me if I'm wrong, Mr Green. Your childhood was not ideal.' Manny chose not to correct her, so she continued: 'Fostered at the age of three, then sent into the first of many care homes when you were seven.' She looked up at Manny with an expression he mistook for compassion. 'Then, when you were seventeen you joined the army, did you not?'

'I did.'

'In August 1987, whilst in the army, you shot dead an unarmed, albeit drunken youth in Londonderry. There were those who accused you of overreacting.' She glanced at Figgis. 'I trust my learned friend now appreciates the relevance of my questioning?'

Figgis said nothing. The judge gave her an appreciative nod.

'I were never charged with anything,' protested Manny.

'True,' conceded Delia, 'that is confirmed in your army records. I understand you had a nick-name in the army as well – Shooey, wasn't it?'

Manny looked at her with something bordering on hatred in his eyes. He didn't answer.

'Given to you because you enjoyed shining your army boots. In fact you used to polish the boots of your army comrades, so they called you The Shoe Shine Boy – or Shooey for short.'

Sam knew the jury would be impressed at her producing such an obscure fact. It seemed to have no relevance other than to show the court she'd done her homework on this man.

'Something like that,' said Manny.

'And in November 1987, three months after the shooting of the youth, you were given a medical discharge on psychological grounds, were you not?'

'Something like that.'

Delia allowed the jury a few moments to digest what they had heard so far, before she continued.

'Mr Green, exactly how did you react when Mr Waring denied you your share of over five million pounds? Your share would have been in the region of eight hundred and ninety thousand.'

The blood had drained from Manny's face. Figgis was scowling at him, as if the Crown losing this case was a far bigger tragedy than his star witness losing his freedom; a smile was gradually appearing on Jim's face; Sally was gripping Sam's arm and Tracey was wondering where the money was.

'This is rubbish!' shouted Manny. 'I'm not on trial. I'm here as a witness, you can't do this to me.' He folded his arms, petulantly. 'I'm not answering any more questions.'

'Mr Green,' said the judge, 'as you say, you are

379

not on trial in this court, nor are you obliged to answer any questions that might incriminate you in the event of any future legal proceedings taken against you.' He then looked at Delia. 'This is a most odd turn of events, Mrs Knowles. Apart from the journal, do you have any other evidence to support this theory?'

'I know that the Lottery ticket hasn't yet been claimed, m'Lord. So if Mr Green has it, it begs the question, where does he keep it?'

'Where indeed?' mused the judge, sagely. 'Now there's a puzzle one doesn't come across every day. Where would a person keep a scrap of paper worth five million pounds? Do you have any suggestions, Mrs Knowles?'

'I do have one suggestion, m'Lord. A desperate thief with a winning five million pound Lottery ticket wouldn't want it to be too far away from his person – in fact it's my feeling that our desperate thief might well have it on him right now.' Delia quickly returned her attention to Manny and asked him sharply, 'Mr Green, did you kill Alistair Waring and steal the Lottery ticket from him?'

'Oh, for goodness sake, Mrs Knowles!' said the judge. 'You don't have to answer that question, Mr Green.'

Manny said nothing. The members of the jury were leaning forward in their seats, wishing that Manny *did* have to answer that question. Delia was aware of this and proceeded as though Manny had admitted his guilt. 'Mr Green, I'm at a loss to know why you didn't claim the money from the ticket which, I'm guessing, you still have on your person, or why you saw fit to commit two more murders, but I'm sure another court will get to the bottom of these mysteries.'

'I haven't got no winnin' bloody Lottery ticket,' whined Manny.

'In that case you won't object to the police escorting you to a place where they can do a body search on you.' Delia smiled down at Figgis. 'If I'm wrong about this I will apologise profusely.'

She had arrived at a moment which, if Manny didn't react as she hoped, could go horribly wrong. Sam and Sally also knew this. Sally's fingernails bit into Sam's arm.

'M'Lord,' said Delia, 'it might save time and inconvenience if Mr Green simply handed over his wallet for examination. It's where I would expect such an item to be.'

'Is it really?' said the judge. 'Well, Mrs Knowles, an apology from you is something I would dearly love to hear.' He turned to Manny. 'Mr Green, even I cannot see how the counsel for the defence can possibly have any knowledge of what you have in your wallet, but I would ask you to indulge this court. You may object if you like, with no reprimand from me, but to comply will move this case swiftly along and in any case I suspect that Mrs Knowles has notified the police of her suspicions and you will be thoroughly searched anyway.'

'I have indeed done just that, m'Lord,' confirmed Delia. She looked at Manny. 'Just the wallet will do, Mr Green. If you give it to the usher, I would be obliged.'

Just the wallet? The judge was looking at her, planning on asking her, if she did think he had it on him, how on earth she could be so sure it was

381

in his wallet and not simply in one of his pockets or stuck down his sock or something. Then he glanced at Sam in the public gallery and suspected a bit of trickery was afoot. If the ticket *was* in Manny's wallet no doubt Figgis would spring to his feet and call foul play. One way that Delia could have known for certain the ticket was in Manny's wallet was if it had been planted there without his knowledge and she somehow knew about it. After which, much shit would hit the fan. Awkward questions would be asked of Delia and the trial might well collapse. Even if Manny was guilty he might well get away with it on procedural grounds. On the other hand there wasn't a person in the courtroom who wasn't dying to see what was in Manny's wallet – and that included the judge. Delia, Sam and Sally were looking at Manny, hoping he'd crack before he got his wallet out.

Manny felt his legs weaken. He gripped the rail of the witness box. His eyes swivelled, wildly, around the court, which was full of people who were staring at him as if he were a piece of dogshit, just like they had Private Shooey. In his wallet was a piece of paper worth over five million pounds and these bastards were going to take it from him. There was no way out of that. He was wishing he'd cashed it in earlier; taken the money and run, and to hell with all their suspicions. It was his money. He'd gone through a lot to get this money.

'It's not yours!' he screamed. 'It's my money!' His hands were shaking as he gripped the rail.

Sam and Sally let out their pent-up breath. It was now too late for Manny to claim the ticket had been planted there without his knowledge. Delia felt a surge of triumph, which she held in check. 'It's money you murdered people for,' she said, calmly.

'I don't fucking care. It's my money!'

Don't fucking care? The judge's ears pricked up. *In that case I'll teach you to fucking care, mister!* Figgis got to his feet and was immediately waved back down by the judge, who said, 'Please continue, Mrs Knowles.'

'I'm obliged, m'Lord. Mr Green, you killed three men for that money, three of your friends. Don't you have any remorse?'

Manny closed his eyes and went quiet as he seemed to ponder her words. The whole court looked, expectantly, at the man in the witness box, who had gone there as a witness for the prosecution, and who now was in deep trouble. The only sound was that of the court artist's pastel crayons scraping across paper as he captured this moment for posterity and the highest bidder. The court reporters scribbled furiously. This was a great story and how they loved Manny Green for providing it. Manny's eyes opened and his demeanour suddenly changed. It was as though he'd accepted the inevitable; like a man who had just woken up to the truth.

'All right, I shouldn't have shot Dave – he were a good bloke were Dave.'

'What about Alistair Waring and Rudolph Mace?' Delia's manner had no censure in it. She just sounded curious.

'Never got on with 'em.'

'So, you've got no remorse about killing Alistair

383

and Rudolph?'

Manny shook his head and said, 'Not really.' He looked over at Sam and called out, 'Nearly got you as well, Carew.'

He said it so matter-of-factly that a shiver shot up Sam's spine. It was shock at the thought that so many people could want to kill him.

'Mr Carew is well aware of that,' said Delia. 'I believe that is what led him to suspect you for the murders. You might have been wise not to have involved Mr Carew.'

This took Manny aback for a few seconds as he realised his folly in trying to get Sam killed. But it had been folly to kill anyone. He'd no need to be in this predicament. He returned his attention to Delia. 'I'm sorry for dropping Jim in all this shit, though. I should never have done that.' He looked at Jim, took out his wallet and removed the Lottery ticket. 'I never cashed it, Jim.'

The usher took it from him and passed it to the judge who scrutinised it. Such an innocuous scrap of paper, yet the cause of so much trouble. He then passed it back with the words, 'I suggest this be kept somewhere very safe until its rightful owners can be ascertained.'

'M'Lord,' said Delia, 'I suggest that the rightful owners of the ticket are the five Syndicate members, or their heirs.'

'Indeed, well, I won't ask you how you were so certain it was in his wallet,' said the judge. 'That moment has passed – luckily for you.' He added the last three words with a meaningful nod in her direction.

Delia flashed him an innocent smile. 'I was

384

relying on an educated hunch passed on to me by one of my team, m'Lord.'

The judge looked at Sam, trying to work out how he could have been so certain without having looked inside Green's wallet himself – possibly that very morning. He dismissed such a thought from his mind. Surely not even Carew would dare do such a thing inside the law courts. Sam was thinking that the five hundred quid of Tracey's money that Freddie Lightfoot had charged was money well spent. Freddie was a reformed pickpocket who had now refined his act to become a table magician, much sought after at Rotary dinners and the like. It had given Sam a chance to check the contents of Manny's wallet. He had suspected Manny wouldn't like to be far away from his five million pound ticket at any one time, and a quick glance inside his wallet had proved him correct. Freddie had replaced the wallet as Manny was coming out of the Gents. It had quite surprised Sam when Jimmy O'Connor had come up with the name Green. Sam was expecting Jimmy to come up with a name he'd never heard of.

The judge held up a hand to postpone another question from Delia. 'Mr Green, just so this court is absolutely clear, are you admitting to the murders of Alistair Waring, Rudolph Mace and David McLeish?'

There was an expectant hush in the court. Manny frowned at the question and said, 'Well, yeah, I thought I just had – I'm very sorry, if that's any help.'

The hush became a loud murmur of amazement. Jim punched the air and gave a shout of triumph. Tracey beamed, as did Sam and Sally.

'M'Lord,' Delia was saying, 'in view of the fact that the key prosecution witness has just admitted committing the murder himself, might I apply to the court for this case to be dismissed?'

'You may, Mrs Knowles – I hardly think we need waste any further time or public money. Is the Crown prepared to drop charges, Mr Figgis?'

'We don't appear to have much option, my Lord,' muttered Figgis.

'Case dismissed. Mr Ormerod you are free to go, and you go with the court's apology.'

CHAPTER SEVENTY

Manny was already being led away by two policemen. Jim was out of the dock and hugging Delia. 'It's probably Sam you need to thank,' she said. 'He came up with all this Lottery stuff.'

Over Delia's shoulder Jim gave Sam a nod of reserved gratitude – the gratitude of a man who suspected that his savour might well have been screwing his wife. Sally was wondering why Jim wasn't showing more appreciation and Sam was wondering what the hell Tracey had been telling her husband.

'He's suspicious of every man who's been near me,' murmured Tracey into Sam's ear as she walked past him. 'I'll make sure you get the balance of the twenty grand fee for services magnificently rendered, plus a nice fat bonus when we get our share of the five mil.'

'What did she say?' asked Sally.

'She says Jim's suspicious of every man who comes near her and she'll make sure I'll get my full fee.'

'And *does* he have grounds for suspicion?'

'What business is that of yours, Miss Grover? The last I heard you were betrothed to a gentleman from Bath called Robert.'

'I'm not betrothed yet.'

Sam was encouraged. 'Has he asked you?'

'Yes, he asked me before I came away. If I say "yes" he has big plans.' She looked at Sam with an unspoken apology on her face. 'He's a lovely, gentle man, Sam. I'll have a really happy life with him.'

'You deserve it, Sal. By the sound of it you're going to say "yes".'

She looked down, then away from him, as if she couldn't say this to his face. 'I am, Sam. I'm going to marry him.'

Sam's heart sank to his boots. There had been a time when he'd once pushed her into the background and gone off with the love of his life, Kathy Sturridge. He'd persistently avoided commitment to Sally, despite their long standing on/off engagement. He had no right to try and persuade her to stay with him.

'Right – er, when do you go back?'

'Tonight – I've done everything I came here to do.'

He kissed her on her cheek and forced himself to say, 'I wish you all the luck in the world, Sal – and thanks for everything.'

EPILOGUE

It was three weeks since Sally had left Unsworth for good, to live with her new fiancé. Sam was feeling quite down – not the same as when his lovely Kathy died. Death's a bit more final than simply running off with another man, but it was pretty bad. It left him feeling bloody-minded, which was why he'd spent time tracking down Eli John to arrange a meeting which, Sam said, was to be 'mutually beneficial'.

It came as no surprise to him when Eli actually showed up. Over the phone the travellers' leader had sounded confident that, apart from a brief, inconclusive video of him and Eli leaving his office, Sam had no way of proving that Eli had stolen his money or tried to kill him – and Sam had to admit that he had a point. It was almost a month since the kidnapping and the money had practically disappeared into the ether. Any forensic evidence linking Eli or his men to Sam's attempted murder was lost in the ashes – including the life-saving mobile phone. It was his word against Eli's, not enough for a conviction, especially if Eli had a solid alibi which, apparently, he had.

Still, Sam had to admire the nerve of this otherwise detestable little man, turning up like this – alone, facing a much younger and bigger man whom he had robbed and tried to murder; a man who could knock seven bells out of him without much effort. Maybe Eli knew something about Sam that Sam didn't know about himself. He leant against his Jag as Eli stepped out of his Mercedes. Normally, Sam didn't believe in status symbols, but his car took away any edge that Eli might have felt he had. They met in the travellers' field on Cenotaph Hill.

'I'm surprised the council haven't made you clean this place up,' commented Sam, looking around at the burnt out wrecks surrounding them.

'The council tends not to keep in touch wid me,' said Eli. 'Anyway, this is a memorial to the harm done to us.'

'The man who did this,' said Sam, 'did it as an act of misguided gratitude towards me. I never planned it.'

'Jimmy O'Connor has plenty to answer for,' snarled Eli.

'I've paid for what he did to you.'

'Ye paid barely half.'

'Really? I assume you divided my money out fairly amongst your beloved people?'

Sam already knew it was a stupid question. The look in Eli's eyes confirmed this. 'I thought not. What will your people think when they find out?'

'They'll get their shares.'

'The ones I spoke to are wondering when.'

Eli gave an uncertain sneer. 'Yer lyin' – no way do ye know my people!'

'I know enough of them to track you down. The ones I spoke to now know about the money and they'll be pleased to collect once they catch up with you. Mind you, knowing their morals I

389

reckon they'll take more than their fair shares as payment for their silence.'

He fixed Eli with a hard, slightly unbalanced stare. 'But there's one person you haven't bought. One very loose cannon who right now is really, really mad at you – madder than he was before he burnt your camp down. He knows what you did to me and what you stole from me. I don't need to go to a court of law to prove it to him. My word is good enough for Jimmy. He's got a fixation about me – it's all a bit weird, really.'

Sam was making it up as he went along but Eli wasn't to know that. The evidence of Jimmy's supposed madness was all around them. It was why Sam had chosen this meeting place. The travellers' leader now looked uncomfortable. 'What are yer tellin' me?'

'I'm telling you that Jimmy doesn't think his job is finished. If I'd died in that fire he'd have devoted his life to tracking you down. As it is, he feels honour bound to seek retribution on my behalf whether I ask him or not. So far I haven't told him any different. He knows people who know you and he wouldn't have any trouble finding you. Let's face it – I didn't. I just asked a few questions, laid out a few quid and bang – I'm given your phone number. A few more quid and I'd have been given your whereabouts. Your community is very easily bought.'

Eli looked around, nervously. 'Where is he now?'

Sam laughed. 'Hey, I don't blame you for being scared – he could be anywhere. It'll take a phone call from me to tell him to back off.'

'If ye wantin' yer money back ye can fuck off!'

growled Eli.

'I've told you what I want.'

'OK – I want proper payment,' said Eli. 'Twenty grand cash is what you agreed.'

'It's a figure I mentioned – I never agreed to pay it,' said Sam. 'I mentioned it to get you here. Obviously I'd no intention of paying it.'

'In that case the deal's off.'

'Fair enough. In that case I don't make the phone call to Jimmy – that's the only price I'm paying. You give me the land, I give you your life. It's a once-only offer.'

Eli scowled and cursed and slouched back to his car. His body language told Sam that this man didn't want to leave with the threat of Jimmy's vengeance hanging over him. Sam got into the Jag and turned it around, pointing towards the exit gate, but allowing Eli to get there first. As Sam suspected, Eli stopped. Sam remained in his car. Eli sat behind his wheel without making a move; he rolled himself a cigarette as he thought about Sam's offer. Sam lit up a Marlboro as he waited. He'd cut down to ten a day; Sally would have been impressed. Eli was surrounded by frightening evidence of Jimmy's work on behalf of Carew. A cold wind blew across the field, rattling through the burnt out shells of what once had been the travellers' homes. If he drove away the man who did this would be forever hovering around him like a dark and unstoppable hobgoblin of death, waiting to pounce. Sam smiled as he read Eli's thoughts. After five minutes the traveller got out and walked back to Sam.

'OK, call the fuckin' madman off.'

'Have you got the deeds?' Sam asked him.

'How do I know I can trust ye after yer reneged on the money?'

'I didn't renege on the money, I just lied to a thief – there's a difference. You can trust me because you know my reputation. Give me the deeds, I make the call.'

Eli stared, long and hard at Sam, then he took a large envelope from inside his coat and handed it over. Sam checked the contents and made sure the transfer documents were duly signed, sealed and witnessed. He then picked up his phone. It rang three times.

'Jimmy, it's Sam. I'm ringing to tell you that things are cool between me and Eli John – we've sorted things. There shouldn't be any more trouble between us... What?... Come on Jimmy, I've given him my word... OK, OK – don't tell me, tell him.' He held the phone out to Eli. 'Jimmy wants a word – he's not happy.'

Eli took it and muttered, 'Hello?'

The growling, Irish voice on the other end sent a chill down Eli's spine. 'Ye give Sam Carew any more trouble an' I'll show ye just what trouble is. Do I make myself clear, ye little pikey gobshite? Ye've only had a taste of what I can do.'

The phone went back to dial tone. Eli handed it back to Sam, who put it to his ear, then into his pocket. He looked up at Eli and said, 'I assume you got the message. I won't shake hands; just go, and be thankful I've saved your miserable life.'

Eli said nothing. He didn't normally respond to threats, but this madman Carew and his madman friend were the real deal. He walked back to his car and drove away. Sam dialled another number.

'Alec, I've been doing a bit of business. We've just acquired two acres of building land – my contribution to the cause... The travellers' site at the bottom of Cenotaph Hill. It's due to go before the planning committee on Thursday... No, it's a guaranteed rubber stamp job – the Planning Department's already approved it. I mentioned to them that the only way to keep travellers off the site is for me to buy it off them and build on it. I've never known the council move so quick... No, Eli didn't know a thing about it – anyway he's a travelling man, what would he want with a site for umpteen luxury dwellings?... What?... Yeah, we should sell it straight on. As it happens I've already got a buyer for it. He wants a quick completion. It'll cover what was stolen from us many times over.' Sam was going to add, *'And pay for my car,'* but he thought Alec might not appreciate that.

He then rang Mick, one of Carew and Son's Irish groundworkers. 'Well done, Mick, whatever you said to Eli scared the hell out of the silly sod. There'll be a nice drink in your pay packet this week.'

When he got back to the office the door was unlocked and he could have sworn he had locked it. Apprehensively, he pushed it open. The reception area had been tidied, easing his trepidation a little. There were fresh flowers on the window ledge, which ruled out Alec, as did the whiff of familiar perfume. He walked through to the back office. Sally was just putting the phone down.

This surprised and pleased him more than somewhat. He hadn't seen her for a month. She should have been two hundred and fifty miles away.

'Sally…?'

'Sam.'

He looked at her, waiting for a more comprehensive explanation regarding her presence here. None was forthcoming. She just sat there, looking great. There was a smile playing on her lips and she looked pleased to see him. He was at a loss what to say.

'Shouldn't you be er, having fittings for your wedding dress or something, round about now?'

She got to her feet, walked around the desk and stood in front of him. Sam couldn't help but notice her slight limp. It always made him feel guilty. His heart started pounding, uncontrollably. Her Chanel perfume, the flashes she'd had put in her dark hair, the abundant cleavage pressing against her silk top all conspired to take his breath way. Bad people had tried to take his breath away in the past, but Sally wasn't bad. Sally wasn't bad at all.

'We've got a job to do in Amsterdam,' she said, 'or had you forgotten? I've just rung Stuke White and told him I'll be tagging along. I've booked the Amstel Hotel again.'

'Stuke White.'

'Yes, he said it was OK – in fact he said it would be a pleasure to have me along.'

Sam stood there for a few silent seconds, wondering what was happening. 'Right,' he said, eventually, 'what about the, er, the wedding? Did you er, did you actually get engaged to Robert?'

394

He tried to disguise the hope in his voice.

'As a matter of fact that's what I've come to tell you. Sam, I've been putting it off for so long and yesterday Robert decided to force the issue. He turned up with a diamond solitaire as big as a peanut. God knows what it cost – and all these wonderful plans for after we get married...'

After we get married was all Sam heard. So, she was marrying him – and so soon! She held her left hand up in front of his face. He looked away, choosing not to admire her peanut-size solitaire.

'Congratulations.'

He forced the words out.

'Look,' she said.

He looked. Her fingers were ringless.

'I said no.'

'I see.'

His spirits rose again. She put her ringless hand on his shoulder. 'I feel really rotten about it – and it's all your fault.'

He was still trying to catch his breath. This was turning out to be a hell of a lucky day. 'Oh, sorry – erm, remind me, why is it my fault?'

Her face was flushed and he couldn't tell if it was anger or something else. Whatever it was she looked stunning. 'Because I knew if I ever came back here I'd get hooked on you again! It's that barrister's fault as well. She said you were besotted with me. Are you besotted with me, Carew? I'll be really bloody annoyed if you're not besotted with me!'

'Besotted? Yes, I am, Sal. I am most definitely besotted with you.'

'I hate you, you know that, don't you?'

'What? How do you mean you hate me? I always thought you quite liked me.'

'No, I've always hated you, Carew. Correction – I hate what you do to me.'

'Sal, I don't do anything to you. I've always held you in the highest regard.'

'Highest regard? I don't want to be held in the highest regard. I want you to be besotted with me.'

'I am besotted with you. I was really miserable when you told me you were going to marry Robert – you ask Owen.'

She placed her other hand on his other shoulder and fixed him with a dreamy stare. 'You should have heard his plans, Sam. White wedding in a really pretty church in the Cotswolds; three week honeymoon in the Seychelles; beautiful house; devoted husband with well paid nine to five job...'

It sounded to Sam as if she was comparing life with him to life with Robert – and he wasn't coming out of it very well. Was she talking herself into going back to her erstwhile fiancé?

'Sal, look, I really can't compete with all that stuff.'

'Sam, do you think I don't know that?'

She pulled him to her, kissed him, fiercely.

'Carew, you're ruining my bloody life!'

Acknowledgments

To Stephen Oldroyd for his guidance on court procedures; to Ian Harrison who keeps me up to date with police procedures; and to my wife, Valerie, whose firm belief in my writing keeps me battling on. Thanks also to Adam Williams for designing my new website:

www.kenmccoy.co.uk

The publishers hope that this book has given you enjoyable reading. Large Print Books are especially designed to be as easy to see and hold as possible. If you wish a complete list of our books please ask at your local library or write directly to:

Magna Large Print Books
Magna House, Long Preston,
Skipton, North Yorkshire.
BD23 4ND

This Large Print Book for the partially sighted, who cannot read normal print, is published under the auspices of

THE ULVERSCROFT FOUNDATION